Heart Choice

Robin D. Owens

BERKLEY SENSATION, NEW YORK

THE BERKLEY PUBLISHING GROUP
Published by the Penguin Group
Penguin Group (USA) Inc.
375 Hudson Street, New York, New York 10014, USA
Penguin Group (Canada), 90 Eglinton Avenue East, Suite 700, Toronto, Ontario M4P 2Y3, Canada
(a division of Pearson Penguin Canada Inc.)
Penguin Books Ltd., 80 Strand, London WC2R 0RL, England
Penguin Group Ireland, 25 St. Stephen's Green, Dublin 2, Ireland (a division of Penguin Books Ltd.)
Penguin Group (Australia), 250 Camberwell Road, Camberwell, Victoria 3124, Australia
(a division of Pearson Australia Group Pty. Ltd.)
Penguin Books India Pvt. Ltd., 11 Community Centre, Panchsheel Park, New Delhi—110 017, India
Penguin Group (NZ), Cnr. Airborne and Rosedale Roads, Albany, Auckland 1310, New Zealand
(a division of Pearson New Zealand Ltd.)
Penguin Books (South Africa) (Pty.) Ltd., 24 Sturdee Avenue, Rosebank, Johannesburg 2196,
South Africa

Penguin Books Ltd., Registered Offices: 80 Strand, London WC2R 0RL, England

This is a work of fiction. Names, characters, places, and incidents either are the product of the author's imagination or are used fictitiously, and any resemblance to actual persons, living or dead, business establishments, events, or locales is entirely coincidental.

HEART CHOICE

A Berkley Sensation Book / published by arrangement with the author

PRINTING HISTORY
Berkley Sensation edition / July 2005

Copyright © 2005 by Robin D. Owens.
Excerpt from *Heart Quest* copyright © 2005 by Robin D. Owens.
Cover art by Tim Barrall.
Cover design by George Long.
Interior text design by Kristin del Rosario.

ISBN: 0-425-20396-4

BERKLEY® SENSATION
Berkley Sensation Books are published by The Berkley Publishing Group,
a division of Penguin Group (USA) Inc.,
375 Hudson Street, New York, New York 10014.
BERKLEY SENSATION and the "B" design are trademarks belonging to Penguin Group (USA) Inc.

PRINTED IN THE UNITED STATES OF AMERICA

10 9 8 7 6 5 4 3 2

Praise for the futuristic fantasy of Robin D. Owens

Heart Duel

"[A] sexy story . . . Readers will enjoy revisiting this fantasy-like world filled with paranormal talents."

—*Booklist*

"An exhilarating love story . . . The delightful story line is cleverly executed . . . Owens proves once again that she is among the top rung of fantasy romance authors with this fantastic tale."

—Harriet Klausner

"With engaging characters, Robin D. Owens takes readers back to the magical world of Celta . . . The characters are engaging, drawing the reader into the story and into their lives. They are multilayered and complex and grow into exceptional people."

—*Romance Reviews Today*

Heart Thief

"I loved *Heart Thief*! This is what futuristic romance is all about. Robin D. Owens writes the kind of futuristic romance we've all been waiting to read; certainly the kind that I've been waiting for. She provides a wonderful, gripping mix of passion, exotic futuristic settings, and edgy suspense. If you've been waiting for someone to do futuristic romance right, you're in luck; Robin D. Owens is the author for you."

—Jayne Castle

continued . . .

Titles by Robin D. Owens

HEARTMATE
HEART THIEF
HEART DUEL
HEART CHOICE
HEART QUEST

Anthologies

WHAT DREAMS MAY COME
(with Sherrilyn Kenyon and Rebecca York)

*To Morgan
and Diva*

241 RANGE

GREAT WASHINGTON
BOGHOLE

DRUIDA

HARD ROCK MTNS

GAEL CITY

GREAT
PLATTE
OCEAN

DEEP
BLUE SEA

BRITTANY

CELTA

One

Get Me down! GET ME DOWN! The telepathic de- mand was imperious.

Straif Blackthorn had just descended the stairs of the door of the Green Knight Fencing and Fighting Salon, after his daily bout with his cuz Tinne Holly, when he heard the command.

Get Me down!

The mental cry, attached to a screech that could only come from a Siamese cat, speared through his head.

He wanted to put his hands over his ears as the pitch built and the torment continued, drowning out the swish of pouring rain. But a hunter always kept his hands free.

Straif glanced around the sidewalk and street. The smallest shiver of movement caught his attention. There, atop a gray stone wall, crouched under the small overhang of a second-story windowsill, was a damp cat. A Fam—Familiar—an intelligent animal with psi powers that could mentally communicate with people.

She glared at him with bright blue eyes. White with a dark mask of brown, she didn't look purebred Siamese, but when she shrieked again, he knew he couldn't deny that piercing note in her yowl. *Get Me down. I do not belong in this filthy rain.*

The rain of Celta smelled fresh and clean, even here in Druida City. The city added its own aromas, that of evening dinners, the scent of glider, stridebeast, horse.

And wet cat.

You, Straif Blackthorn, you come here and get Me down, the cat meowed.

He scowled. Small, dainty, half-Siamese, and telepathic. It could only be a female. And it could only come from the GreatHouse T'Ash.

Warily he moved under the window and reached up.

She jumped down instead. "Umph!" he grunted, as she landed on his shoulder and dug in her claws. "Stop it, or you're ending up in the gutter, cat."

Balancing, she retracted her claws until they just hooked into his clothing. *I am a Fam, daughter of the Cat Zanth who is Familiar to T'Ash.*

"I can tell."

I am YOUR Fam.

Straif stiffened, turned his head to stare into her blue eyes. He noticed her pink nose, her elegance.

I will be good for you, a close companion.

He wondered if that would be true. "Let's consider a temporary alliance, for, say, six eightdays."

She sniffed, then rubbed her head against his cheek. He lifted a hand larger than her head and stroked her jaw. She purred. Her fur felt incredibly soft under his fingers. Her purring and the feel of her softness, her daintiness after his years on a hard trail through much of untamed Celta, sparked a warmth of tenderness inside him. She could speak to him by mind, using Flair—psi powers. Perhaps she could be a companion.

"Six eightdays," he repeated.

One last rub, then she sat up straight, replying, *Unnecessary. You will adore Me. Everyone adores Me.*

Straif sighed. It was inevitable that with his new life, he'd take on new burdens, as well as shouldering all the old ones, the old responsibilities that meant old griefs.

I heard this morning that you are staying in Druida and opening up T'Blackthorn Residence.

News traveled fast. Just that morning he'd made the decision to finally move from a guest suite at his uncle T'Holly's. He could no longer bear the underlying sadness of the household.

So he'd decided to open his own home. He hadn't visited T'Blackthorn Residence in some time, and he dreaded going to it now, so his steps lagged.

I will help. I am a Cat of great taste. Surely you have noticed My beauty.

"Right." He walked back out onto the sidewalk.

Most people call me stunning. She shifted on him. *If we walk in the rain, I want a weathershield.*

He sighed out a Word, curving a shieldspell around her.

She delicately hummed a small purr. *Very nice. I knew I made no mistake in taking you as My FamMan.*

"Right."

Where do we go?

He wanted to hunch his shoulders, more against the thoughts that threatened to inundate him than against the rain.

"T'Blackthorn Residence," he said. Since he was Grand-Lord T'Blackthorn, it was appropriate that he live in his ancestral home, on his ancestral estates. Even though he was the sole Blackthorn. The last Blackthorn. The one Blackthorn who'd survived the Celtan Angh virus that had swept through the weak Family genes and killed his uncle and aunts and cousins. The remaining Blackthorn who still grieved for his sister and parents.

I approve. I was born for a FirstFamily Residence. I always knew it. The cat nodded, and her whiskers tickled his cheek, bringing him from thoughts as gloomy as the day.

"Right. Well, Stunning—"

A small paw prodded his face. *I am stunning. That is My beauty. My name is Drina.*

"Drina, huh?"

Drina. It is a Blackthorn name.

He sighed again. She was going to drag his emotions back from the frigid storage where he'd placed them when his Family had died fifteen years ago when he was seventeen. Since then he'd tried to keep his feelings completely superficial—except his fierce resolve to find a fix for his Family's genes and so ensure the survival of his line.

They'd passed through middle-class Druida and into Noble Country, huge, old estates claimed by the first settlers of the three colonial ships. Straif's steps slowed.

A couple of years ago he'd been summoned by his maternal uncle, T'Holly, to track and find his cuzes Holm and Tinne Holly. After their reappearance, Straif had come and gone in Druida, but hadn't ever returned to his estate.

When Straif entered the greeniron gates, he understood why. T'Blackthorn Residence had once been a showplace, one of the most beautiful buildings in Druida.

Now the many arched windows looked blind and dirty. His gut tightened as he saw some gray, scaly Celtan lichen had crept up the mellow blond bricks of the house, destroying it as surely as the virus had destroyed his Family. He groaned.

Drina leaned her small body against him; the gentle resonance of her reassuring purr vibrated from her side to his face. Straif drew in a deep breath.

This was his fault. He couldn't bear to be reminded of his past, so he'd let the upkeep of the Residence slip. Now he would pay.

This will take many great spells. Much of your Flair and strength and energy and knowledge. Much gilt.

"Right."

She sniffed, then slightly opened her mouth and curled her tongue in that sixth cat sense of smell-taste. *You have great Flair—great psi power. I have chosen well. I will help you.*

"Thanks." Wanting to get the worst over with, and not able to endure looking at the sad outside of his Residence, Straif teleported them into the den. It was the office of the Grand-Lord, where all Family discussions took place and all decisions were made.

Miller moths circled around them in a cloud. Drina hopped down to chase them.

Straif ignored her and glanced around the room. The warm Earthmaple paneling comforted him, as did the dusty folds of purple velvet drapes and the ancient desk topped with a furrabeast leather blotter. He could almost see his father sitting behind the desk, looking at him, fingers steepled in his habitual gesture. Grief stormed through Straif like a caustic whirlwind, swirling memories of his Family—his mother, who matched his father in quiet, gentle, steady nature. Then images came of his irresistible scamp of a sister, Fasha, the only extrovert of the Family, more Holly than Blackthorn. How he missed Fasha, her optimism and determined cheerfulness. How he wanted that in his life.

Never to see them again. No wonder he had fled his life here, searched throughout Celta for some oracle, some native herb or bacteria that might provide an immunization for the awful virus. The Angh virus that was fatal only to Blackthorns.

"Welcome home, T'Blackthorn," a deep voice soughed. Straif shuddered. It was the voice of the Residence, the voice of a long-dead GrandLord T'Blackthorn.

"Thank you, Residence."

"There is much to be done."

"It will be done," Straif vowed.

"I have maintained the elements of the central House-Heart. The hearth fire crackles, the fountain bubbles, the wind tinkles chimes, the scent of rich earth rises from the floor."

Straif cleared his throat. "Thank you."

"It is good that you return. Please activate the standard arrival, general habitation, and housekeeping spells."

So Straif chanted the litany that would bring the Residence back to life—ignite fires and provide light, air rooms and clean them. The husks of dried moths in the ResidenceDen disappeared. Drina leapt back up to his shoulder.

When all was as tidy as possible, he said, "I would like a tally of the food available in no-time storage."

A holosphere appeared with images of great haunches of meat, bins of fruits and vegetables, barrels of beer and wine, cartons of grain.

"The storage no-time," said the Residence. "Would you like to see a list of the prepared meals?"

"Yes."

I only eat shredded furrabeast steak of the highest quality, said Drina.

Straif repeated her words aloud.

"Of course," said the Residence. "Welcome, T'Blackthorn Fam."

Drina preened. *I also eat cocoamousse.*

Straif sighed but told the house.

"T'Blackthorn will need to hire a cook," said the Residence.

"Right," said Straif. He'd have to hire several people of the highest integrity. Most Residences were staffed by Family members, proud to be of service to the Head of the Household. They had all died.

A nip on his ear made him jump.

Drina landed on her feet and hissed at him. *You forgot Me. I am your Fam. No more of this gloom. We do not allow gloom anymore at T'Ash Residence. D'Ash says so. It is a good rule.*

Straif bared his teeth at the cat.

She sat and stared haughtily back at him.

"T'Ash—"

All T'Ash's Family died, too, but he stayed. He did not run away.

"I was looking for a cure!"

She flicked her tail back and forth. *Did you find one?*

"No."

Drina swiveled her head slowly, taking in the state of the once richly elegant room. She sniffed. *This place is not acceptable to a Cat of My High Degree. There is not even one pillow adequate for Me to sit on! We must do something about it immediately. Teleport us to Lavender Square, to The Four Leaf Clover, Mitchella's shop.*

"I thought I'd go to T'Apple for advice in a day or two." After he'd surveyed what needed to be done and gotten over his shock at the state of his home, when he began to plan.

Now Drina curled back her muzzle, showing tiny pointed teeth. *The Four Leaf Clover, now. Trust Me.*

He narrowed his eyes. "Trust you?"

Her tail whipped back and forth.

Trust Me and follow Me.

"You want to go out in the rain again?"

It will be worth it. You will make Me a weathershield.

Straif looked around the room. He certainly couldn't bear to stay here.

The Residence spoke once more, the tones the only voice

of his childhood remaining. "I have drawn off much of your excess energy for the initiated spells."

Straif noticed, he felt weaker by the moment. "Right. We need something more than just a private Ritual by me to give strength to the generational spells. I'll set up a special Ritual of several FirstFamily Heads of Household."

Time to shop. Drina tapped a paw on his boot.

Straif stared back at her.

A female. He had a female Fam.

He blinked, then looked around the room that was now lit by firelight. Everything appeared dingy and old and worn.

And hopeless.

Time to shop.

He stared down at her again. A female Fam. He was going to hear those words a lot.

*H*e took the image of *Lavender Square* and the storefront from Drina's mind and teleported them both. One glance at the shop had him sucking in his breath at the artfully arranged and rich sensuality of furnishings in the display window.

Drina mewed in displeasure. *It is closed.*

Straif tore his gaze from a pair of lady's golden dancing slippers seemingly kicked off. They angled against a fall of burgundy velvet that was draped across the gleaming wooden arm of a boudoir chair.

Drina sniffed. *You are T'Blackthorn with tracking Flair. Track Mitchella.*

He slanted her a sour look, wanting to spend more time viewing the luxuries of the window, appreciating the woman's taste, judging—

Drina's mew shrilled.

"Right." Automatically he shifted the focus of his eyes so he saw the distinctive colored aura-heat trails unique to every person. He narrowed his gaze. The doorway held a tangle of colored paths, but a small pool of bright yellow orange sparkling with gold flecks was obviously Mitchella Clover. He blinked. He hadn't ever seen a color quite like that. Simply the most beautiful trail he'd ever seen.

Let's get going! Drina yowled.

Straif sighed. She continually urged him on when he wanted to indulge his natural curiosity—his investigative bent.

He stared down at her. *Why are you in such a hurry?*

She flattened her ears and glared at him. *It is misting. Big FamMan. I am getting wet! And I want a GOOD pillow to sleep on tonight.*

With a small whoosh of displaced air that made her jump, he formed a weathershield around her. *I could 'port your old pillow from T'Ash's,* he offered.

Her paw streaked out to bat his boot, and he took the hint to track the elusive GentleLady Clover. He kept one eye on the pulsing aura-trail and one on his new Fam, awaiting her answer.

Drina lifted her pink nose. *They never treated Me as I deserved.*

"Hmm," Straif said. "Did you have a pillow at all?"

Drina sniffed in disdain, and Straif hid his grin. Apparently not. Obviously she thought to train him to her requirements. Still the humor she induced might make it worth while to be wrapped around a dainty paw.

*In a booth at The Woad Garden, a private club she belonged to, Mitchella stared into her wine and wondered how much longer she could keep The Four Leaf Clover open without asking for a loan from her family. She winced. She'd probably get the loan, but she'd get meddling partners, too, and that wasn't what she wanted.

Her mouth turned down. She was already lacking because she was sterile. In the huge family of Clovers who prided themselves on being the most fertile family on Celta, Mitchella was the only one in her generation unmarried and without a brood of children. Macha's disease when she was a girl had taken that from her. Sometimes the ache was so soul-deep that she could hardly bear it, even though she loved her ward, Antenn Moss, as if he were her own son. But Antenn was growing quickly and would leave her house for journeyman education soon. Another depressing thought.

So she set her mind back on her interior design shop. To have to admit to her family that her business was still struggling after four years, when she'd been sure it would be solid and successful by now, was another mark of deficiency.

She took a sip of her wine and grimaced. The Woad Garden catered to the upper middle class and lower nobility, but Mitchella's palate had become educated with the fine wines served at T'Ash Residence during her frequent dinners with her friend Danith. Thank the Lady and Lord for Danith D'Ash! Because of Danith and the complete starkness of T'Ash's new Residence, Mitchella had stayed in business this long. She'd even managed an uneasy truce with the GreatLord himself after their rocky meeting a few years ago.

She sighed and settled deeper into the smooth furrabeast leather bench. No one else was in the room, hardly anyone was in the club. Everyone was home with their families, their HeartMates, their children this rainy spring night. Only Mitchella was alone. She rolled her eyes at the self-pity, a sure sign she was tired. Usually she had too much energy to indulge in such stupidity. Well, she was human—that meant she had moments of foolishness.

Mitchella pushed her glass aside and leaned back on the firm-but-giving bench back. She nodded. She'd done a good job with The Woad Garden. A smile hovered on her lips. This chamber was a dark hunter green with gleaming oak trim and shutters. With the brown leather benches in the booths and a touch of brass in the accessories, it was supposed to appeal more to the masculine patrons, but she'd ensured that a woman would feel comfortable, too.

A bit of pleasure warmed her. She'd done a good job here, and *every place* she'd consulted. Why was it so difficult getting commissions? She tapped her fingers on the table and noticed her nail tint had faded. Feeling like she wanted something a little more elegant than the jade that matched her onesuit, she concentrated. After a moment her nails became a delicate, shimmering pink.

She was still admiring her hands when Weat, the owner's younger son, poked his head into the room. When he saw her, he grinned. It was so good to see someone brighten at the sight of her that Mitchella relaxed and sent him a genuine smile. His stare fixed on her breasts, as often happened with boys that age, and his glance glazed a bit, then he hurried to her. "There's a man here to see you about business." Weat darted a glance around the room. "You can use this room for a while, if you'd like." He grimaced. "We aren't busy tonight."

Mitchella rose and shook off her gloom. A little humming in her bones let her know her future called. She *knew* it was only a matter of time before The Four Leaf Clover exploded into success. Perhaps this was the moment!

She beamed at Weat. "Thank you very much, GentleSir."

Weat flushed. "I'll send him back."

A moment later a man's large outline filled the shadowy doorway.

As he walked into the mellow light, her insides tensed. He should have looked out of place in the elegant club, but he didn't.

She studied him, aware of contradictions. He moved with supple grace and carried himself with inherent arrogance—an arrogance that shouted "nobleman." Yet he displayed more than a few rough edges.

His clothes, though of good quality, looked frayed at the shirt cuffs. And the shirt cuffs showed no embroidery denoting a noble name. She relaxed. Though she cultivated a good, professional manner for Nobles and interacted well with NobleLadies, she didn't like NobleLords.

But this man wore working trous with narrow legs instead of excess, costly fabric caught and cuffed at the ankles. Scuffed and scratched celtaroon boots—and it took heavy duty to scar celtaroon—molded his narrow feet and muscular calves. The celtaroon itself had faded from its original orange and blue pattern to beige and gray, a process that took years.

His jaw showed dark stubble, and his body looked far harder than anyone would expect a pampered nobleman's to be. She could only figure that the aura of complete power was due to his competence in the untamed wilds of Celta.

He sizzled her nerve endings. She was a tall woman, built on voluptuous lines, but he was taller still, with shoulders that could block her view. Dark and dangerous, with only a hint of refinement and an undercurrent of sensuality. Her senses thrummed to life in pulses that sent a flush under her skin and stirred her. She smiled, pleased at the hum of attraction; it had been a while since she'd had a lover.

She glanced at his wrists again. He didn't wear marriage cuffs.

Mitchella swept a wisp of tumbled hair behind her ear, glad she was wearing the jade silkeen onesuit that contrasted well with her flame-colored hair. She shifted her shoulders a bit so more tendrils fell over the curves of her breasts, and she smiled, adding a bit of her Flair—charisma—to enhance herself.

Two

❤

The intriguingly sexy man raised his brows as she stepped from behind a wing-backed chair. His eyes widened as they lingered on her body.

Her onesuit was cut less full than fashion demanded, shaping her breasts, waist, and hips. She'd paid an outrageous sum for it, but now it was all worthwhile.

"Can I help you?" She didn't have to lower her voice to huskiness, her attraction to him made it come out that way.

"I'm afraid so." His voice was deeper than she'd imagined, richer, with cultivated tones. "I need some good decorating skill and many new furnishings."

She liked the way he said "I need." She could imagine him saying it in more intimate circumstances with the rich, mellow note in his voice turning rough and demanding, and she felt a quiver.

Then her mind took over. Good skill and many furnishings: sounded like a nice, expensive job. She refrained from rubbing her hands together, but her smile expanded.

He turned and cocked his head, then again met her eyes. "I'm told you're the best." It rumbled out of him, quietly, and all Mitchella could think of was tangled bedsheets.

She wet her lips. His cobalt gaze fastened on her mouth.

She hadn't meant to tease him, her throat felt uncomfortably dry, and the effect he was having on her body began to unnerve her. She had to take care, she couldn't afford to lose a lucrative commission.

"I'm grateful for the praise." She struggled to sound calm. His virility kept her off balance. "May I ask who recommended me?"

He smiled, a curve of well-shaped lips in a strong jaw. Her heart pounded harder. "You may." He took a step forward.

Now she could smell him, and the scent of tough masculinity was highlighted by the clean fragrance of sage. Sage conjured up a traveling man, an explorer. And she knew it was true of this man with every beat of her heart. She inhaled and exhaled audibly.

He leaned closer.

"Rrrrowww!" demanded a dainty cat, gliding into view.

"My Fam." He shook his head in amazed amusement.

Everything in Mitchella tightened in wariness. She recognized Drina. Only powerful noblemen had Fams, and she didn't care for noblemen. Her friend Danith's husband, T'Ash, had once teleported her across the city with an angry thought. Mitchella had never forgotten the sheer terror of the experience. She and T'Ash still treated each other guardedly, though he'd apologized and she'd accepted it.

A Fam, a cat raised by GreatLady Danith D'Ash, and Drina's own sense of complete superiority added up to only one thing: This man was a noble of the highest class. Mitchella's smile turned merely courteous as she moved behind a large wooden antique buffet partitioning the room, putting a barrier between them.

"Drina," Mitchella said flatly. She inclined her head to the cat. "Greetyou."

Drina sat like a small, elegant white and beige accessory to the room. Her tail curled over dark brown paws. "Prrrp," she mewed politely.

The NobleLord glanced down at Drina. "She made an unexpected stop, otherwise she would have arrived with me."

Drina stood, stretched, and with waving tail, began to explore the room.

Mitchella bit her lip. His gaze heated, and he strode forward, with masculine grace that almost equaled the Fam's. But now Mitchella's mind was firmly in control of her body. She slammed a door on her desires. Being sterile, there could never be anything more than a brief liaison between her and a nobleman. He would want to continue the Family line.

She cut the small aura of charisma and let her eyes cool.

"And you are?" she asked.

His eyes narrowed, and he eyed the buffet between them. His nostrils flared, and he smiled, still attracted.

Too bad.

"Blackthorn," he said in a husky voice. "Straif Blackthorn."

Worse than she'd thought. A FirstFamily GrandLord. Nothing could ever come of a relationship with this man. Never ever.

"I'd heard you were back." All she knew was he'd come and gone from Druida several times in the past years. She didn't pay much attention to noble activities.

She recalled his GrandHouse Residence. Her eyes widened. Oh, how she'd love to get her hands on that house. Passion for her craft surged within her. "Are you going to restore T'Blackthorn Residence?"

The Italianate house of many arches made her fingers itch to return it to its former beauty. She must have the general plans and history of the Residence in her files.

He lifted a brow at her, perhaps from the change of attitude from the sensual to the practical, then moved up to the buffet and leaned against it—into her personal space. He didn't stop his own provocative signals of male interest and intent.

Damn! She hoped she hadn't issued a challenge. Straif Blackthorn—she stiffened, remembering old school lessons, the Blackthorns were trackers, explorers, and hunters.

He sent her a heated glance from half-closed eyes, and she felt the tingle from her toes to her head that sparked small shocks throughout her middle. She refused to react and kept a pleasant smile on her face.

He blinked, and the sexual look was gone, replaced by one of measuring consideration.

She could only hope that he'd hire her as a decorator and leave the rest alone, so she kept her expression professional as she reached into a pocket for her business cards that showed room models. Not taking her eyes from him, she withdrew a card and handed it to him.

It was pink. Far too feminine for him. "Wait," she said, "I gave you the wrong card."

He ignored her and let it sit on his palm. Mitchella suppressed another quiver at the contrast between the pink "marbled" card and his calloused, tanned palm.

He stared at the card, then back at her, a slow smile moving over his face. "It takes a certain kind of woman to carry off pink." His glance flicked down her again, "and a green silkeen onesuit. I think you're just what I'm looking for."

She tired of playing games. "I'm only interested in restoring your home, GrandLord."

Now he raised sandy brows. "Is that so?"

"Yes."

He watched the rise and fall of her bosom with appreciation. "Drina recommends you," he said.

Drina hummed in her throat. The cat stood at an open shutter, admiring her reflection in the window.

T'Blackthorn looked over his shoulder at his Familiar and smiled with sincere amusement that made Mitchella catch her breath. "Drina says she is a Cat with excellent taste."

Mitchella managed a smile. "She certainly thinks so."

His thumb rubbed the indentation on the card, triggering the projection of a model room holo about one and a half by two meters. The pink marble walls contained darker streaks for visual interest, and all the furniture was a glossy deep burgundwood. The bedsponge lay on a stand, with diaphanous curtains layered around it and attached to the ceiling. The curtains swirled with the slightest hints of sparkling rainbow-pastel glitter, as if a fairy galaxy had been caught in their folds.

As he gazed at the room model, the sensual tension spinning between them quieted to something deeper and more serious.

T'Blackthorn touched the image, and it disappeared. He curled his fingers over the business card, his face taut and his eyes yearning. "I've spent years in the wilds. I've missed the furbelows of very female women, of Ladies, and forgotten how—soft—your sex can be."

"You've stayed with the Hollys." She'd heard that much.

He raised an eyebrow. "My uncle and cuzes, and other relatives, a Household mostly of men. My aunt, D'Holly, is a very dynamic woman."

"And feminine." Mitchella had met D'Holly once.

"T'Holly Residence is decorated with weapons in patterns on the walls—circles and diamonds of knives, spears, swords. All within easy reach. There are paintings of battle, tapestries of hunts," he gestured with the hand holding her pink card, "male stuff." He moved his shoulders impatiently. "I'll take it," he murmured.

"Take what?"

"The room. I want one just like it in my Residence. You have the job."

Glee blossomed inside her. She could barely keep from dancing around the room. This would make her reputation!

He smiled, and she knew she shouldn't be near this man. She should run as fast and as far as she could away from him. But an opportunity to design the interior of one of the only twenty-five FirstFamily Residences would never come again. And T'Blackthorn's! It had been a showplace once, one of the most beautiful houses in Druida. She could make it so, again.

She looked into his dark blue eyes.

"I want it." He flicked his thumbnail on the card and the model room spun once again into life. "I'll take it. No expense spared."

Mitchella had always dreamed of hearing those words. Now they tempted her beyond all bounds.

He collapsed the holo and tucked the card in a hidden shirtslit pocket. Then he put an arm on the buffet and leaned forward. "You have more?"

Mitchella backed up. "More?"

"More cards—room models."

She pulled out her cards and offered him the one of mock-furrabeast leather grain. He activated it. A meter-sized image of a masculinely furnished den materialized. T'Blackthorn tilted his head. "Nice. A little conservative for my taste." He shot her a look. "You'll remember that."

"That's my business. Of course."

He nodded.

"We'll meet tomorrow at Midmorning bell, then. I want to

start work on the pink room immediately, in the MistrysSuite."

Mitchella stiffened her backbone. "Absolutely not."

T'Blackthorn raised his eyebrows.

She lifted her chin before answering. "Your wife must decorate the suite."

He scowled. "I'm not married." He rubbed the stubble on his jaw. "I think I have a HeartMate. I touched her during my last Passage when I learned to control my Flair."

Mitchella should have been relieved. Of course he'd have a HeartMate, someone he'd bond with body, heart, mind, and soul. Most FirstFamily Nobles were that lucky. It came of having great psi powers and breeding for Flair. Bonded HeartMate couples led to more stable Families and increasingly Flaired children.

Instead she flinched inwardly. He had a HeartMate. It would be complete folly to have an affair with him.

As if he'd read her mind, he said, "I'm not ready to find or bond with my HeartMate. Everything must be perfect before I do that. T'Blackthorn Residence must be restored and sparkling. Other—problems—must be solved."

So he'd be happy to have an interim affair with a commoner before he sought his HeartMate. Typical man. Typical Noble. The thought bolstered Mitchella's resistance to the electricity between them.

"I'll be glad to make T'Blackthorn Residence as perfect as possible, GrandLord," she said coolly, professionally.

Drina jumped up on the buffet and swiped a paw at one of the pink cards Mitchella still held. The cat impaled it on her claw. She tapped the indentation and the pink model room appeared. Staring at T'Blackthorn, she mewed.

His lips quirked in amusement, and he slid a sidelong gaze to Mitchella. "She wants the pink room." Narrowing his eyes, he studied Drina, then glanced back to the model bedroom. Now a small Drina image sat regally on the bed.

T'Blackthorn shook his head. "She said the room would complement Her, make Her look beautiful. She's right."

They were both right, Mitchella realized. The cat looked perfect in the room.

He gazed at Drina, and when he spoke, his tones were quelling. "Your room is the small dressing room between the

MasterSuite and MistrysSuite," he informed the cat. "I'm sure GentleLady Clover can decorate it to your undeniably good taste."

Drina pressed the holo control on the business card again and again, until the pink room, magnified and distorted, overwhelmed the real room they stood in.

"Very well," T'Blackthorn sighed. "I'll indulge you this once. The Heir'sSuite has a playroom that shares a wall with the GrandLord's MasterSuite. I'll convert that room into your bedroom and have a connecting door cut."

Mitchella barely kept herself from goggling at T'Blackthorn's casual wave of a hand as he outlined the reconstruction.

Drina flexed her paw, and the model room vanished as the card spun to the carpet. It was just a business card again. With a claw-hole in it.

He looked at Mitchella, his gaze lingering on the tumble of her hair, her face, her lips. "I think we will do very well together."

"That's my job."

He offered a hand. Reluctantly, Mitchella gave him her own. Instead of shaking it, he lifted it to his mouth. The soft pressure of his warm lips went directly to her center. She pulled away, pasting on another professional smile.

"Tomorrow at Midmorning bell, then," he said.

"Yes." She'd be up all night studying all the information she could on T'Blackthorn Residence. She was sure she recalled it being featured several times in various publications on architecture, furnishings, how the FirstFamilies lived. She needed plans and dimensions. Old holos of how the rooms looked. Perhaps she could even get some sort of idea of the previous owners' tastes.

Then realization struck.

The Blackthorn curse.

She stared at him.

He, just like T'Ash, had lost his entire Family.

But not to a rival nobleman—to some disease. Her stomach clenched. This man and she had another thing in common. Loss. He had lost all he loved in the past. She had lost the hope of children to love in the future.

T'Blackthorn stilled as if understanding she'd finally

remembered the history of his line. She wondered if he read her own heartache.

They shared a moment of silence throbbing with untold griefs. Then, T'Blackthorn inclined his head. "Merry meet."

"And merry part," Mitchella replied through dry lips.

"And merry meet again," he said. "Come, Drina."

Drina brushed against Mitchella, purring loudly, leaving little white hairs clinging to her onesuit, then jumped to T'Blackthorn's shoulder.

"Right," Straif said to his Fam, then looked again at Mitchella. "Drina thanks you for the pink chamber. We'll start with that." Cat attached to his broad shoulder, he strode from the room.

Mitchella let out a breath she hadn't realized she'd been holding. She'd hurry home to research T'Blackthorn Residence. At least doing the first room would be easy.

It was, after all, her own bedroom.

Since T'Blackthorn Residence had siphoned off much of his energy, Straif decided to walk back home. Even the thought of facing his decrepit home didn't lower his spirits—much. He'd already taken steps to make it beautiful again, as lovely as it had been in his childhood. A place of warmth and comfort. Just one glance at Mitchella Clover and he knew she could fulfill his dreams for his home. And maybe for himself—for a while, too.

Mitchella Clover is not too ugly for a human, Drina said.

Straif laughed. He supposed that was a compliment. His spirits lifted. Mitchella Clover was fascinating and beautiful, and he enjoyed the sizzling punch of sexual attraction between them. He felt more himself and alive than he had for a long time.

"What about me?" he teased the little cat sitting on his shoulder. He had plenty of years in the wilds of untamed Celta—since he'd just turned seventeen—and showed the wear of them on his body.

You are beautiful, Drina said.

Straif stopped in his tracks. He turned his head and came nose-to-nose with the cat. "I am?"

I am stunningly beautiful, and you are my FamMan. That makes you beautiful, too.

He blinked at the cat-logic. He'd never heard of beauty-by-association before.

You are beautiful inside.

That was stunning, all right. Since he didn't know what to say, he kept walking, taking the turn onto Bountry Boulevard, moving from middle-class Druida to Noble Country. The tree-lined street was one of the oldest in Druida and ran along the edges of many of the FirstFamilies estates. Full dark had fallen, and arrhythmic patters of raindrops splashed from the trees. Drina hissed. Straif strengthened the weathershield around her until she was safe from any drips.

He cleared his throat. "I disagree about Mitchella Clover; she is very beautiful."

Drina tensed, her claws biting into his shoulder.

"Ah, her coloring complements yours." That was certainly true, and both females projected femininity. He couldn't see sharing a rough campsite with either of them. A wisp of memory brought back the last time he'd seen a woman's face in the flames of a campfire—and his last lover.

He'd had a simply-sex affair with a lady on the southern continent of Brittany until he'd gotten word that the Holly-Hawthorn feud was heating up and his uncle, T'Holly, needed him. Once he'd arrived in Druida, like everyone else in the Holly Household, he'd been preoccupied with the feud and its aftermath.

He hadn't even gone to see his occasional lover here in Druida, GraceLady Kalmi Lobelia. But then the last time he'd seen Kalmi she'd raged at him for leaving her. He'd figured she never wanted to see him again. A pity because she'd been a good prophetess and there was always the chance she might see the way to repair the defect in his Family heritage.

He stretched his legs in a stride, feeling the smooth working of his muscles. He'd been without a lover for over three months. Now the thought of Mitchella Clover raised his spirits. He'd been honest in telling her he had a HeartMate, but had also informed the exquisite lady that it would be a long time before he went in search of the woman to claim her as his wife—years perhaps. He wasn't even sure where he'd stashed the HeartGift he'd made during his last Passage—the mental trial that freed his psi power, his Flair.

Finding his HeartMate was another goal that could sink him in gloom. Refurbishing his home might take months, but he was still no closer to a fix for his flawed gene than he had been at seventeen. It could still take a long time, but that was for the future.

Right now he anticipated a few months with the delectable Mitchella. Though she was a commoner, she had a nice bit of Flair, and he sensed she knew how to play the sex game. He wouldn't push—much. All he had to do was to depend on the heated attraction between them. Sooner or later they would wind up in bed.

Drina yowled in his ear, and he tensed. He'd been ignoring her, and her mews had escalated.

"Yes?" he said.

A pillow for Me.

"Right." He noticed she'd made the request as they were passing T'Holly Residence where he'd stayed until that morning. He smiled. She was one smart feline. He stopped by the greeniron gates and rang a small bell. Through Flair-technology the sound would echo within the castle. Straif faced the crystal scrystone.

Three

♥

O*nly a few seconds passed before the T'Holly butler's* face appeared in the gate scrystone. He inclined his head at Straif. "How may I help you, T'Blackthorn?"

The man's face appeared strained, reflecting the tension of living in a Residence where the Lord and Lady were deteriorating under the weight of broken Oaths of Honor at disowning their son, Holm Holly, when he wed his HeartMate against their wishes. Yes, Straif had been right to leave this place. Better the ghosts of his own dead than the ghosts of the living Hollys.

Straif shifted until Drina, riding his shoulder, showed into the scry. "Might I borrow a plump pillow for my new Fam? Perhaps the one in the guest room I've been using?"

The butler smiled, and his eyes twinkled. "I'll send it to the coordinates of T'Blackthorn ResidenceDen, as I did your traveling bedroll and other possessions."

"Right. Many thanks."

The butler cleared his throat. "Perhaps blue velvet would be acceptable?" His lips twitched as he studied the regal Drina.

To match My eyes. Yesssssss. I want gold tassels, too.

Straif winced. "I have a request for . . ." He didn't know if he could spit it out. What possessed him to accept a Queen-of-the-Universe FamCat?

Drina brushed the side of his face with soft, soft fur and purred, sending approving and affectionate thoughts.

"I have a request for a blue velvet pillow with golden tassels," Straif said.

A cough came from the butler. "Quite so," he choked out.

"Thanks. Merry meet," said Straif.

The butler's face fell into serious folds, "And merry part."

"And merry meet again," Straif ended. They both knew it was a lie. There was no merriment in the Holly Family, but they themselves had to learn how to deal with their changed circumstances. Straif could no longer help.

Straif nodded, cut the call, and walked away from T'Holly Residence. It was a couple of miles to his home.

Drina revved up her purr. *Mitchella Clover likes you. I saw.*

Now that was a cheerful topic. "I like the looks of her, too."

She will do well by T'Blackthorn Residence.

"I agree."

She is a good friend of Danith D'Ash. I know much about her.

"Of D'Ash?"

Drina gave a delicate snort. *Of Mitchella Clover.*

Straif knew exactly what the cat was doing. She was repaying him for the pillow. Cats tended to take favors seriously. He was surprised to hear himself say, "I think I'd like to find out about her all on my own." The Blackthorns were hunters and trackers, puzzles appealed. And a woman they had to track and find and unravel was a challenging prize.

The little cat settled more comfortably—for them both—on his shoulder.

Very well. She continued to purr all the way home.

Mitchella *was in the tiny space that served as her den,* surrounded by papyrus, when the door to her small house slammed and her twelve year old ward, Antenn, banged in.

"There's a hot furrabeast sandwich for you and crunchies for Pinky in the no-time," she called. After grove-study with all the other Clover boys, he'd stayed to play sports in the courtyard of the sprawling Clover homestead. Mitchella heard the faint hiss of the no-time shield falling, the clatter of a plate, and her ward's tromping.

"You're in the den," he mumbled around a mouthful of sandwich. He shoved a bunch of books aside and plopped his damp and slightly muddy self down on the twoseat. Mitchella didn't even wince anymore. Her furnishings had taken a battering when she'd accepted Antenn as a ward three and a half years ago, but after just a month she'd realized the boy gave back in companionship much more than the value of any inanimate object.

He swallowed, slurped at a cylinder of cinnamontea, then grinned. "You look happy. We have a job?"

Mitchella set aside the drawstick, rolled her shoulders, and smiled back at him. "The best, the *very* best."

"Guess I'll be able to stop ducking the Clover boys' questions, then, huh?"

Mitchella stiffened. "Have they been . . . pestering you?"

Antenn waggled his eyebrows. "All the Clovers gossip a lot, and since we don't live in the compound, they like to talk about us. I can handle the boys, and everyone else, too." He threw out his skinny chest. "It isn't as if the Clovers are Downwind Triad gangs."

That he could speak so casually of the past pleased Mitchella, and she relaxed, then picked up the drawstick and fiddled with it. Naturally the other Clovers would gossip about her. She had her own business instead of working at the family furniture concern. She rented a house instead of living in the large jumble of Clover homes on Fabacay Square. She was sterile.

Antenn angled on the sofa, putting his feet, sans boots, she was glad to see, on the cushions, knocking off more papyrus. Pinky, his small cream-colored tomcat, trotted in and hopped up on Antenn's lap. "Tell me more about the job," Antenn said.

Mitchella passed over a holostone on which she'd copied various views of T'Blackthorn Residence, inside and out. The egglike stone also held images of the furnished rooms and floor plans. Antenn stuck his thumb in the indentation and flicked through the holos.

"Beautiful house. Must be a Noble's—wait, this is T'Blackthorn Residence!" His expression clouded, and his voice held a note she hadn't heard in a long time. Sadness, despair. Trouble.

All Mitchella's maternal instincts rose as she studied Antenn. She wanted to pull the boy to her, but he'd sneered a few months ago that he was too big for that anymore. "You know T'Blackthorn Residence?"

His lips compressed—old gang secrecy? Then he shook his head, stopped the holostone, and tossed it to a mat on her desk. "We ran there. The Triad," he spoke jerkily. "Got a girl. Turned out to be T'Ash's girl." He smiled humorlessly and looked far older than his twelve years. "T'Ash got her back. We all ended up at T'Blackthorn's. Guess that's where T'Ash hid when he was a kid on the streets. There were a couple of fights."

Mitchella knew the story now. How could she have forgotten? She was Danith's best friend, and though it had been a long time, the events would always live in everyone's memory.

She raised a hand for him to stop, but Antenn was staring at a painting ahead of him on the wall, chin quivering. She knew he didn't see the art, but the past. His fingers trembled as he petted Pinky. Pinky rumbled a purr, turned over onto his back to have his stomach rubbed, paws curled. That brought a faint smile to Antenn's lips, and Mitchella was glad. Neither Antenn nor she needed to recall the deaths of the Triad, one of whom was Antenn's brother.

Gritting her teeth she added another reason other than Straif Blackthorn that this job would be trouble. But she had no choice. And the Residence was so beautiful. Running a hand through her own hair, she chose her words carefully. "If I could, I'd reconsider the commission, but I need the job. A FirstFamilies GrandLord's Residence."

Antenn turned his head and smiled sweetly at her, and her heart contracted. She loved the boy, he was closer than any of her nephews, like her own son. She swallowed, then smiled back. Someday that sweet smile of his would win a woman.

Carefully, he lifted Pinky, stood, and placed the cat on the worn blue velvet nap of the twoseat. Antenn took the two steps to her desk and looked down at a two-dimensional drawing of T'Blackthorn Residence. With his forefinger he traced the lovely lines of the house. "Nice place. It will make your reputation." He grinned, but it wasn't as carefree as the one he'd walked in with. "It doesn't look anything like that now, or didn't a couple of years ago, and it could only have gotten worse. You're gonna work your tail off."

She wished he hadn't said that. Before she could respond, he patted her on the shoulder. "I have some grove-study to do."

That was a first.

He whistled to Pinky. The cat grunted, rolled off the sofa to land lightly on his paws, and agreed to follow him.

They both left the den, and it was a lot lonelier. Antenn didn't pound up the narrow stairs, and that was worse.

She rubbed her temples, glanced at a holo of T'Blackthorn Residence, and recalled the hip-shot stance of the very virile Straif Blackthorn. Oh, yes, this job was going to be *trouble*.

In the low light, *Straif trod to the far end of the corridor in* the east wing to a small parlor, too dim in both light and his own recollection to harbor memories. He banished the dust from the carpet and furnishings with a tiny spell that used the last of his energy, then he set up his bedroll and Drina's pillow on a divan. He undressed, carefully set his whittling tools on a table. He hadn't wanted anything from the house when he'd left except his travel pack, but the set of tools a G'Uncle had given him had been in the pack. It had taken him a couple of years, though, before he could use them.

Straif still didn't want anything from before. He crawled into the travel-bedsponge he'd used so long. With a small, demanding mew, Drina clawed at the top of the cover. Grunting, he lifted it up for her. She slid her cold, damp nose against his cheek and cuddled up near him.

"Why aren't you on your pillow?" he asked groggily.

You are warmer. You are a hard pillow, but you will do.

She might do as a Fam, too. But his last thought was of the brilliant Mitchella Clover. She would *definitely* do as a lover.

He'd be sure to convince her of that, whatever it took. Even restoring the Residence wasn't as important as getting her in his bed. Why, he didn't know, and supposed the idea should concern him. But he was expert at banishing the demons of the past.

That night Mitchella slept deep and dreamt of a lover. Even in the dream she told herself she did not know his face and form, but his hands were calloused, and he smelled of sage. His voice was rich, deep, and said things that excited her as his fingers explored her body. She panted and moaned and yearned with the deepest hunger to have him enter her, cover her.

A scream ripped her from sleep, and she rolled off the bed and grabbed a robe in one motion. Antenn. Another nightmare. Sometimes he spoke of them, sometimes not. Mitchella sensed that in all the time she'd been his guardian there were bad experiences he'd hidden from her.

When she reached the door of his room, he was sitting bolt upright and shaking, but gave her a wan smile. Pinky crouched at the bottom of the bed, lashing his tail, as if he could find the dream and pounce on it.

Mitchella sat on his bed, ran her fingers through the tousled boy-brown hair. She sighed. "You had nightmares about the gang again. Those holos of T'Blackthorn Residence probably set them off." Risking rebuff, she leaned in and gave him a squeeze. To her surprise, he buried his head in her shoulder.

"Do you want to talk about the dreams?"

"No."

"I'll give up the job." It was a pang, not having the once-in-a-lifetime experience, knowing to the tips of her fingers that she could handle the project and she would never lack work again. But nothing was worth hearing the child's screams in the night.

Now he pulled away, grabbed a softleaf from his night table, and blew his nose. "No. T'Blackthorn Residence is *big*, and it's a real mess. This could make us a mountain of gilt."

If the boy was thinking of money, he was back in the real world, and all right. She tilted her head. "True."

"We could buy our own house. Better, we could *build* our own house."

Her heart clutched. Through T'Ash's Testing Stones it had been determined that Antenn had a Flair for architecture. Just a moment before she'd been thinking of him as a child, now he was considering the future like a boy growing into a man.

She was sure some of the experiences he'd had as a young child following the Downwind Triad gang had been incomprehensible to him at the time, but as he matured, he understood them better and grew even more adult because of that.

"Besides"—his hazel eyes met hers steadily—"you've always said we should face our fears and problems. You've faced that you're sterile."

Hearing it said aloud and baldly still hurt, and as she thought of *her* dreams she knew that though her mind and heart had accepted the idea, her body still wanted to make babies. And she'd been dreaming of Straif Blackthorn for goodness sake! But still she managed a crooked smile for Antenn. "It's something I deal with on a daily basis."

"But you do so." His chin jutted. "I can face my fears, too. Since you'll be working at T'Blackthorn's, I'll have to go there now and then, like with some of your other jobs, right?"

"Yes."

He turned and pummeled his pillow into an acceptable shape. Pinky trotted up from the end of the bed to lie on his own pillow, beside Antenn's. It was unsanitary, had always been unsanitary, but how did you explain that to a boy who'd lived in the slums? And companionship was so much more important.

"So I'll deal with my fears and my past," he said.

Mitchella's smile widened. He'd said that as if he'd had twenty years of criminal activity behind him. She smacked a kiss on his brow. He turned red and wriggled. "Good night."

"Good night." She rose and went to the door. "Nightlight!" she ordered, and a small glowing ball of light hovered in the far corner of the bedroom.

"Mitchella?" asked Antenn as he scooted back under his covers.

"Yes?"

"T'Blackthorn Residence isn't really cursed, is it?"

"Absolutely not."

"Good," he said.

She closed the door softly behind herself and walked down the short hallway to her own bedroom. The Residence wasn't cursed, the Blackthorns had never had bitter enough enemies to do that. No, if anything was cursed, it was the Family, poor souls.

As she slid into her own bed she thought of her own abundant family. They could be unbearable at times, but she loved them. How hideous to know that every few generations a common Celtan virus could sweep through your Family and kill you all. Just because the gene that had mutated in most Celtans to protect them from the illness was faulty in you and your Family.

She shivered. Life on Celta continued to be hard. She'd suffered Macha's disease as a child, and it had left her sterile. Though life spans were longer, people didn't flourish on Celta like they had on Earth—except the Clovers.

But it wouldn't do to pity T'Blackthorn. Not only would he loathe such a feeling from her, but it could lead her into softer emotions that he could exploit. He was not a man to be pitied. He was a FirstFamily GrandLord with a HeartMate, and she shouldn't forget that. She could envy him the power, wealth, and love that he'd have in his life.

S _traif's nose itched. He rubbed it. The tickling came_ again. He shook his head, but couldn't escape the sensation. Finally, he opened his eyes—to a looming cat brushing her whiskers under his nose. A surprised cry caught in his throat. "Aarrrgh," he croaked.

Drina smiled beatifically. _Time to eat. Minced clucker for breakfast would be good._

Straif would prefer eggs, but he'd have to find the kitchen, first. He wondered if there were any prepared breakfasts in the no-time food storage. Grimacing at the thought of scavenging on his own in his decaying home, he decided that he might have been hasty in leaving the Hollys. He did like his breakfast.

He sat up and stretched as he looked around the room. The

walls of the small parlor were covered in deep purple fabric with traces of curlicued gold. Straif winced. If those lines still gleamed after all this time, it must be real gold, and he'd neglected it. Getting the value out of that wallpaper would probably be futile. Cleaning it would probably cost more than it was worth. He grit his teeth. More evidence of his lack of care and attention for his home.

Drina set her forepaws in his thighs and extended her claws to prick through his travel blanket. *Food!*

Well, the cat had her priorities straight.

"Right," he said. He cleared his throat. "Residence?"

"Yes," it answered immediately, and Straif sensed it had only been waiting to be addressed.

"Are there any breakfast meals in the no-time?"

"No."

Straif frowned. He'd need a cook, but how could he ask anyone else to live and work in such a shambles? He stood, picked up his traveling blanket and snapped the dust from it, folded it, and pulled on his trous.

Drina sat regally, lifted her little pink nose, and mewed.

"How about minced clucker, do we have any of that?"

"Indeed," said the Residence.

Pulling on his shirt, Straif crossed to the door, opened it, and entered the wide corridor, which was much lighter than the room. He glanced over his shoulder. The dark purple room might have been beautiful at one time, but he didn't want to keep the color. He'd change the entire room. Meanwhile, since it resonated with no memories, it would be a good office.

He set his shoulders. The kitchen was to the left. He recollected that there were rooms for the cook off the chamber. That might be a good place to stay. Rubbing his jaw and feeling the prickle of rough beard, he cheered at the thought of a bathroom. He lengthened his stride until Drina mewed a protest.

"Huh," he said, looking down at her. "Keep up."

She sniffed.

He'd been around enough cats to know that it was an exclamation of disdain.

They reached the door at the end of the hallway that led to the kitchen. It swung easily on the hinges, squeaking a little.

He entered the kitchen and eyed it, scowling. He wasn't

sure what a prime kitchen should look like, what tools it should have, but the appliances seemed big and clunky. Just as with everything else, time had passed in the kitchen with no modernization. Flair technology continued to be refined, so less and less psi power was needed to work common spells. Flair itself was growing stronger and more common in the populace. Straif had experienced that in his travels.

One wall showed doors to the no-time compartments—storage areas for uncooked foods and full meals. He stared at them, hands on hips. "Residence, which one holds the minced clucker?"

An indicator lit up on a small cabinet. "The Fam meals," the Residence said.

"I thought we didn't have Fams for a long time?" Straif opened the storage area to see a lustrous purple pottery bowl filled with steaming clucker. He sniffed. It smelled good. Too bad he was set on eggs.

He took out the bowl, warm from the meat inside, and placed the meal on the floor. Drina glided up, sniffed, made a sound of approval, and started to demolish the meal in quick, dainty bites.

Straif looked around. There was no place for an open fire—the only way he knew how to cook. He frowned, searching his memory. "Don't we have a fire pit, somewhere?" He could cook over a campfire.

"There was a fire pit at the west end of the wall below the terrace. It was destroyed in one of the gang fights," the Residence said.

Anger surged through Straif that his estate had been so abused. His own fault, but another task—to shieldspell the grounds. That would take a lot of Flair, and it was something that he wouldn't want anyone else to initiate.

"Ahem," the Residence said.

"Yes?"

"T'Ash furnished a GardenShed. It might have breakfast meals in a small no-time."

Straif blinked. "Really?" The morning was looking up.

Drina burped.

Straif picked up her empty bowl and put it in the wash cabinet.

I know which GardenShed that is. I can take you.

"Right, we'll go out to the GardenShed."

"There is much we must discuss, GrandLord Straif T'Blackthorn," the Residence rumbled. Straif figured it used his name to emphasize the point.

"And we will discuss that as soon as I return. In the meantime, please divert some housekeeping energy to clean the kitchen apartment. My Fam and I will live there for a time."

"You are the GrandLord. You should occupy the Master-Suite."

His gut tensed. "Not yet." His stomach rumbled. "Breakfast, first. You are still draining much of my energy, and to keep up my strength I will need to eat."

The atmosphere of the Residence shivered as if with thunder. All of the fine hair on his body rose.

"I insist that you—" The Residence's voice thickened.

"Later!" Straif strode down the short hallway from the kitchen to the outside door of the west wing, ignoring the cook's apartments. He wouldn't let the Residence make him feel more guilty than he already did. He'd been on his own a long time now, had responded to and fulfilled his Uncle T'Holly's requests, had exchanged favor for favor to other Ladies and Lords of the FirstFamilies as necessary. He was a man now, not a scared and grieving seventeen-year-old boy.

He circled back to descend the steps from the terrace to the grounds in the rear of the house.

Drina joined him, nearly running. He was learning to read her already. The stiffness in her tail indicated she wasn't too pleased with him.

Four

♥

The terrace steps weren't in too bad a shape; a simple fix-it spell should take care of them.

At the bottom of the staircase, a huge lawn stretched to the edge of the hillside the Residence was built on, and another set of steps went down to the Pendef River and his personal dock. He didn't look at the grounds, but followed Drina as she put on a spurt of speed and angled to a GardenShed. Even from this distance it looked in good shape, solid, sturdy, cared-for. Frowning, he vaguely remembered snatches of conversation from his childhood, his father giving orders that the GardenShed be provisioned with a no-time, a bedsponge. Unusual now that he thought of it, but something that had just drifted past him at the time. And did he, himself, dimly remember the dark form of a large, rough boy lurking in the grounds? Once watching a ball? That would have been the orphaned T'Ash.

Drina yowled, attracting his attention. She held her nose in the air. *The Fountain of the Dark Goddess doesn't work.*

Straif grunted. Nothing was in acceptable shape.

The fountain has holes where my sire, Zanth, gouged out the lambenthyst stones. Bad Cat.

That stopped Straif in his tracks. "Say again." He tried to

keep his tone even, but anger churned in his gut, ready to flash into rage.

Smiling as she snitched on her sire, Drina said, *Zanth took the lambenthyst stones from the fountain and gave them to T'Ash. T'Ash took them somewhere.*

An incoherent sound of fury spewed from Straif, and he turned back to shoot across the width of the grounds and into the T'Blackthorn sacred grove to the Fountain of the Dark Goddess. Sure enough, two of the tiers showed gaping holes where once shining purple stones glowed. His fingers curled into tight fists. "I'll fight T'Ash for this."

Drina joined him, panting. *You go too fast. Run, run, run. All we've done today. It will demand much nap time later.*

He sent her an angry look. She ignored him and sat, raising a delicate paw to remove specks of dirt. *You sound like a Holly.*

"My mother was a Holly."

You should talk to T'Ash first. From the GardenShed. There is a scrystone there that he made. He had a reason to take the stones. The curse.

Everything stilled in Straif, even his sweat. The curse of the Blackthorns was their flawed gene that made them fatally susceptible to a common Celtan disease. T'Ash had taken the stones because of the curse? Could it be that T'Ash had found a cure for T'Blackthorn's ailment while Straif was searching Celta? Why wouldn't the man have told him? Straif found himself gritting his teeth and loosened his jaw. "You can be sure I'll discuss this with T'Ash." He whirled and started back to the GardenShed.

Wait! Pick me up. I must have energy to help you and Mitchella Clover in the Residence this morning. And to shop this afternoon.

Straif flinched. Reining in his impatience, he scooped up the small cat, lifted her and set her on his shoulder, and took off at a rapid pace. She dug her claws into his shoulder, and he hissed at the pain. He'd have to make sure the medical cabinets were stocked. If this continued to be her favorite perch, he'd ensure his shirts were augmented with shoulder pads. He scowled. Now that he was back in Druida, he'd need more clothing, better clothing, tailored clothing, which meant he'd have to visit GrandLady Pyra and have her take his measurements.

When they reached the GardenShed, Straif walked around it. It was the best-kept structure on the estate, better than the walls and the greeniron gates. He squinted and saw the aura of strong shieldspells. He opened the door and found a large, comfortable room with bedsponge, medical cabinet, no-time, and sink. A sheet of papyrus lay on a table. He picked it up and writing appeared.

"To T'Blackthorn, Greetyou.
With the help of your Residence, I have
bespelled this papyrus to interact with only
your skin perspiration. Please note the
following Flair commands that will initiate
various spells."

Straif scanned the rest of the sheet, tucked it in his pocket. Crossing to the no-time, he touched it and said, "Breakfast."

A list of ten hearty meals was recited in T'Ash's rumbling voice.

"The three eggs and crispy porcine strips," he said.

I would like a crème brûlée for dessert, Drina said.

Straif snorted but got the food for both of them and they ate.

Belly full of food, he decided he wouldn't skewer T'Ash after all. Maybe he'd only beat him up a little. A smile hovered on Straif's lips. They were evenly matched. T'Ash was larger and had the muscles of a blacksmith, but Straif was tough from wandering Celta—and sometimes hiring out as a guard for merchant journeys.

Drina's small, pink tongue swept her muzzle and whiskers. *You must find someone who cooks well for us.*

Straif's face froze. Not one of the Family, for there was no Family. This was hard. He should have cared for the estate all along, visited it, watched over it, then it wouldn't have been this hard to face it and restore it. He swallowed.

Tapping the scrystone set in the wall, he said, "T'Ash."

Drina jumped up on his shoulder.

The facets in the crystal sharpened, coalesced into a man's face. "T'Ash here," the GreatLord said.

Something in the man's narrowed eyes made Straif approach the topic of the missing stones obliquely. He'd state a need first, as if showing a vulnerability. "I would like to hold a RitualCircle of several FirstFamily Heads of Household here on full twinmoons, to power up T'Blackthorn Residence."

T'Ash's black brows arched over his skycrystal blue eyes. "Agreed." He hesitated a moment. "A good idea." A fleeting smile crossed his olive-toned visage. "I had not thought to do such a thing when I rebuilt my own Residence. T'Ash Residence, too, could use a celebration, and T'Ash Family. My wife is with child, our first."

"Congratulations." Straif felt a warmth as well as envy at T'Ash's news.

"The T'Ash Family line continues." T'Ash closed his eyes a moment. "I had thought, for a while, that I would be the last."

Those words were enough for Straif to understand T'Ash's sympathy for the sole member of the Blackthorn line—Straif himself. T'Ash knew, none better, that Straif must ensure the Blackthorn line continued.

Like all FirstFamilies, the survival of the Family was Straif's primary goal. That was why he had to find the cure for his vulnerability to the Angh virus. Simply so flesh of his flesh, blood of his blood would descend in an unbroken lineage from the past and the visionaries who had funded the Colonization and made the long journey to Celta, to the future where Straif's descendants would finally tame and claim Celta for their own.

Celtans still struggled to populate their planet. Though their life spans were far longer than those of the people of old Earth, a twisted genetic code such as his, sterility, and low birthrate made the Colonization slow. Even now, after four centuries, humans only had a toehold on Celta and could very well die out.

Straif had to find a remedy to correct the faulty gene.

He also had to find a wife.

T'Ash's voice pulled Straif from his thoughts. "Spring equinox is an eightday after the full twinmoons. Will you participate in a small RitualCircle to dedicate T'Ash Residence the eve of the equinox?"

"A fair trade," Straif said.

"Done."

Straif said, "There seems to be an outstanding matter of some stones . . ."

T'Ash grimaced. He looked to his left. "I told you one day T'Blackthorn would want those stones," he muttered to someone outside the viz image.

A loud feline yawn was his only answer.

T'Ash turned back to level a gaze at Straif. "I don't know if the reason your Family became defenseless against the Angh virus—the Blackthorn Curse—was linked in any way to the stones or not. But, know this, T'Blackthorn, those stones were ripped living from the heart of a mountain and split from one great crystal. A disgraceful action on the part of your Family."

Straif blinked and caught a harsh breath. He'd never heard of such a thing. But could something that destroyed the Blackthorns' immunity to the sickness have come from a mine? "The lambenthysts?" he croaked, wondering if this new idea might be true, might be the key to finding a cure or an immunization against the Angh virus for him.

"Your Family no longer held the mine. I purchased it and returned the stones. I, my wife, Danith, and my Fam, Zanth, all visited a Healer after the trip. No trace of the virus was in our bodies before or after the trip. We all had a genetic scan also, and the gene that grants the immunity to the virus had not changed, as it has in your Family."

"You don't have the weak gene of the Blackthorns."

"No," T'Ash replied softly.

Straif forced his teeth apart to say, "Right."

T'Ash studied Straif in silence for a moment. "I would suggest," he said carefully, "that you send a Healer knowledgeable about your disease to Old Grandfather Mountain to check on any bacteria living in the mine. I believe that it would be too dangerous for you to go."

"Right. Something could flaw my genetic heritage even further." As he said the words, he became aware of a nasty taste in his mouth.

Drina leaned close to his head and revved up her purr. The sound pulsated through his bones.

"Ah!" T'Ash smiled. "Drina is with you. She was most insistent that she belonged to you and would become FirstFam of T'Blackthorn."

Drina placed a paw on the scrystone to communicate. *He belongs to Me,* Drina corrected with a sniff.

Her small, cat tones were overwhelmed with loud, rude, male cat rumbles. *Cat is vain, vain, vain. Glad she's gone. She doesn't share.*

"Vain, huh, Zanth?" T'Ash said, once again looking to the left. "This is from a cat who wears a fortune in emeralds as a collar."

Mine. Mine. Mine. Mine. Mine. Mine, Zanth roared, a black and white paw stretched into the viz, claws extended.

Drina sat up straight. *I need a collar. Sapphires. Or perhaps skycrystals, to match My eyes.*

T'Ash's strong, white teeth flashed. "T'Blackthorn might need all the gilt he can lay his hands on to restore his Residence. This isn't time to think of expensive collars for his Fam."

Drina hissed. Tiny droplets of spit reached Straif's ear.

"Checked on your finances yet, T'Blackthorn?" T'Ash asked.

"No." In the months he'd been back and forth to Druida, he'd lived with the Hollys in their fortress, drawn his monthly noblegilt from the Council, banked what he didn't need in a simple account, and lived on payment for various hunting jobs.

When he'd left, fifteen years ago, he'd placed the T'Blackthorn fortune in the hands of canny T'Reed to invest, with T'Rowan as watchdog. He didn't recall the original amount. The thought depressed him. He'd be spending time on accounts. As a man of action, he loathed time at a desk, puzzling over figures on papyrus. Still, unlike the T'Ash holdings, the centuries-old T'Blackthorn fortune had not been stolen, or the lands and estates dispersed to other Houses.

He must be an extremely wealthy man.

Straif ran his hand down Drina's soft, fine fur and garnered comfort. She continued to sit rigidly and growl lowly at her sire, Zanth. "Drina, I think our House can afford a pretty collar for my Fam."

She arched under his hand, her purr became triumphant.

Vain, vain, vain, said Zanth.

Straif met T'Ash's gaze as he continued to pet his cat. "You remember the color of Drina's eyes, T'Ash?"

T'Ash nodded. "Well enough."

"Make me a collar for her, will you?"

"Yes. But much as I often wanted to wring her neck, I never did, and we'll have to measure her for the collar."

Raising his brows in mock surprise, Straif said, "Drina assured me that everyone adored her."

A belly laugh rolled from T'Ash. Zanth snorted.

Drina said, *Everyone who is Anyone adores Me. I want a pendant on my collar, too. A blue diamond, I think.* "Yessss," Drina actually vocalized. *I want blue diamonds. Like my eyes.*

"Blue diamonds are more costly than emeralds," T'Ash said. Zanth yowled.

T'Ash winced. "You've wanted an ear stud, Zanth. I'll make you one." He switched his gaze back to Straif and nodded. "I'll see you later. Come to dinner tonight, and we'll measure Drina in my Residence workshop and talk about the living stones."

"Right. Merry meet."

"And merry part," T'Ash responded.

"And merry meet again. Until this evening," Straif said.

"We'll see you then. Both of you. Blessed be."

"Blessed be," Straif said, cutting the connection. He sat, propping his arms on his knees and leaning his head in his hands, then rubbed his face. It had begun. He had donned the mantle of his title. And his duties.

He was no longer a wanderer, a hunter living from job to job, searching for an answer.

He was GrandLord T'Blackthorn, with a life of duty and obligations.

No more than a moment later, Drina said, *Mitchella comes.*

The comment energized Straif. He shoved back the chair and exited the GardenShed, Drina trotting at his heels. Though his spirits lifted at the idea of seeing Mitchella again—and in bright sunlight—he wondered if he'd still feel the punch of sexual attraction. Unusually *great* attraction. He had the lowering thought that he'd dreamed of her last night.

He hurried up the terrace stairs and around the house. Drina kept up, but she snarled mentally. Maybe she'd need more than one pendant of diamonds. Then he saw Mitchella studying the Fountain of Three Goddesses, looking so much better than the exquisite stone women, and his heart lurched in his chest.

$\mathcal{M}$itchella was grateful for the lip of the strong stone of the basin she leaned against. For a FirstFamilies Residence, the security had been pitiful. She'd been asked her name at the greeniron gates and walked in. The Residence itself would be protected better, but she was still shocked that it was so easy to gain access to the estate.

The grounds were a mess of tangled plants. She hadn't seen anything like it since the Clovers had traveled en masse to the countryside to view land they wanted to purchase for a family summerhouse. She'd been a teenager at the time. She shuddered, recalling the long hours of aching muscular labor to bring the land and house up to respectable standards. Though now she thought of it, buying that place and helping furnish it was the start of her interest in interior design. Further, the home had gone through several styles, and the last few had been completely created by herself. Another thing to be proud of, yet her family took her efforts for granted.

At first glance, the exterior of T'Blackthorn Residence was in a dreadful state. A Celtan lichen grew up the underlying creamy yellow stone. With a professional eye, she gauged that they'd be just in time to prevent damage . . . another few months and the integrity of the outside stone would have been compromised.

Ensuring the Residence was whole and strong must be her priority before redecorating. She wondered how best to determine the extent of any structural damage and how best to restore it. She'd never worked on a Residence so large or so old.

Taking a note flexistrip from her pursenal, she recorded her thoughts. She was about to walk up the gliderway to the front entrance when T'Blackthorn himself strode around the west wing. Once again she was glad of the fountain's support, as her pulse quickened just at the sight of his lean, tough body prowling toward her. A warmth flushed her as a few images from her erotic dreams last night flickered in her mind's eye.

She straightened. She'd dressed carefully in dark blue trous and a short tunic that came to mid-thigh, both of sturdy material, since she hadn't been sure of the state of the Residence and whether she'd be doing any physical climbing or crawling to check out windows and floors.

Then T'Blackthorn was in front of her, and she caught his scent and wanted to jump into his arms. She was definitely making a mistake in taking the job.

Though his stance seemed easy, his expression was closed, and Mitchella wondered at it. Then he glanced back at the Residence and guilt, even vulnerability, flickered over his features. Ah. This was something she was used to, but more from social-climbing midclassers than from a FirstFamily Grand-Lord. Always thinking their homes weren't quite in the shape that they wanted her to see, as if she'd judge them by their surroundings.

There'd been T'Ash, wary of any comment on his Down-wind slum background, baffled about furnishing his beautiful Residence. He'd also been resentful that his HeartMate consulted with Mitchella to help with the furnishings. As if Danith D'Ash would have the time to design a huge Residence with everything else she was doing.

And that was the key to the matter. Some people wanted a statement of the class they wished to become and didn't know how to make that statement, and hired her. Some doubted their taste. Some needed guidance in determining their own personal style.

But more often than not, some people were simply too busy to devote time to their homes. They needed help. And Mitchella was here to help.

She smiled, quite professionally.

Straif scowled.

So she lifted her brows. "GrandLord T'Blackthorn, shall we proceed?"

"Call me Straif." Smoothly he took her arm and started walking toward the front of the Residence. He still frowned.

"GrandLord—"

"I've been in the wilds since I was seventeen, most of Celta isn't so formal as Druida."

"You're from the highest noble class," she said.

He grunted, then slanted a look at her. "May I call you Mitchella?"

His low voice saying her name ruffled her nerve endings in a too-sensual manner. "Of course," she said coolly.

"Good."

They were very close to the front of the house now, nearly within the semicircular wings arching toward them.

"The back of the Residence is the famous view," Mitchella murmured. "Though the front is equally graceful and lovely."

"You can see the back from the river, and the lawn and gardens are so large there that it is easy to image for holos."

He hesitated, and she sensed that he dreaded touring the Residence.

"I have the plans of T'Blackthorn Residence. Would you like me to do a preliminary survey on my own?" she asked gently.

His gaze burned—with anger, with pain. All directed at himself, she thought.

"No," he gritted out. His shoulders shifted, straightened as if taking on a burden. Broad shoulders.

His calloused hand cradled her elbow as they mounted the two stairs to the large front porch and the double door. As they reached the doors they swung inward with a little creak.

In the large front hall, checkerboarded in black and white marble, Drina sat on a black marble square, looking perfect. She was obviously posing, and Mitchella's gaze sharpened at the cat's smile. Drina could have definite ideas about the Residence, ideas that might be contrary to Mitchella's.

Five

❦

"Greetyou, Drina," Mitchella said to the small cat posing in the center of the grand hall.

The cat mewed politely, but didn't move.

Mitchella glanced around the well-lit chamber. Beautifully proportioned, a marble staircase curved upward to the second story. The walls and the ceiling moldings had once been white but were now gray. That seemed to be the total damage.

"The interior is in good shape," she said. There must have been surprise in her voice, because Straif dropped his hand and walked over to Drina, picked her up, and set her on his shoulder.

"Yes, no damp or mold or rot. We Blackthorns build to last." There was a note of pain at being the sole remaining Blackthorn. "The furnishings, especially all the fabric, are bad. The Residence had enough energy to keep itself safe and sound. As for dust," he turned back to face her, and his smile was twisted, "the Residence has been draining my energy at intervals since last night for housekeeping spells."

She stared at him, knowing her eyes rounded. Of course she'd heard about the great spells practiced by the nobles, but somehow this sounded—not nice. Frowning, she scrutinized him. "You look in fine shape, too." The words came from her mouth without thought.

His grin was swift and dangerous. "My thanks." He shrugged, then swept his glance around the chamber. "The Residence informed me of all the basic problems. The worst is that parasite growing on the outside."

"If that's the case, our job will be easier. We're in time to prevent any permanent damage."

One hand petting Drina, Straif tilted his head at Mitchella. "You can tell that?"

"Of course. I should have options for its removal for you by tomorrow—"

"We'll do a FirstFamilies Ritual at next full twinmoons," Straif said.

Mitchella goggled. She hadn't even thought of that. He appeared casual, even rough, but she'd better not forget that despite appearances, this man was very powerful. She swallowed. "Yes, that should take care of any minor problems in the Residence." *Or any major ones.*

Mitchella said, "Everything I could do by muscle and labor, you could do by paying great Nobles or trading them favors. Why don't you?"

Straif raised an eyebrow and said drily, "Because in my case, I think they'd overcharge—or insist on equally great alliances or favors. It's not wise to be too deeply indebted to FirstFamilies Lords and Ladies."

Nodding, Mitchella said, "I see." T'Ash had said the same.

"That leaves us with your specialty, interior design," Straif said.

"I have drawings and holos of the Residence in the past . . ."

His face tightened. "I'm sure I do, too. Residence-Library," he addressed the archives of the Residence, "where are the plans, drawings, holos of the previous styles of the Residence?"

"Older records are in the ResidenceDen, the last Grand-Lady D'Blackthorn, your mother, redecorated just before you were born—"

"Stop," Straif commanded.

Now he appeared pale. The man was going to have to face

some deep problems that he'd avoided for years. She wet her lips, crossed over to him, and put a hand on his arm. He looked down from the few centimeters that separated their heights, eyes stark.

"Perhaps you might consider a whole new style," Mitchella said.

He jerked a nod.

Feeling more in control of the project, Mitchella continued. "Let's take a look around, and you can tell me of your color preferences and what you like and dislike about each room."

He narrowed his eyes and studied her, as if examining her for evidence of pity. She kept her bland professional expression.

He shrugged, and Drina protested with a mew.

"Right," Straif said, and wheeled to the left. "We can view the west end first."

Drina meowed loudly, and he set her down.

As they traversed the hallways once beautiful with paint and other wallcoverings, Straif's manner subtly altered. His gliding walk showed breaks in the smooth rhythm, his voice was strained, his expression impassive.

Mitchella recorded his comments and her own on the flexistrip, noting his tastes as well as his decisions on what furnishings to keep. Drina made cat noises that Mitchella ignored.

The Residence itself was beautiful, with paneling that had resisted deterioration; fine moldings and discreet carvings emphasized the architecture. How Antenn would love to study this building.

She soon realized Straif wouldn't enter many of the rooms, an added difficulty. He'd waved her into the ResidenceDen with a curt order of "change it all," and she merely scanned it. It incorporated so many of his preferences that she was surprised that he hated it. But with a fast look around, she realized it showed the stamp of his father, perhaps his FatherSire, too, who had formed Straif's own tastes.

This room would hold too many memories for him. She didn't linger, but thought it would be a challenge to make Straif comfortable in the room. The natural focus of the chamber was the windows. The best way to give Straif a room that he'd enjoy was to relandscape the grounds outside the windows. She recorded everything with an image sphere.

Returning to the hall, she saw Straif studiously avoiding a large closed door opposite them. She nodded at the door. He pretended to look, but his glance slid by. He shoved his hands in his pockets and turned to walk to where the main building curved into the attached wing and the stairs leading upward.

Mitchella frowned as she thought of the floor plan she studied. "The room we didn't enter was the ballroom?"

The chamber took up a great deal of that half of the floor. Why would he dislike the ballroom?

"Yes. I won't be going in there. Ever."

That was clear enough.

"I'd like to demolish it." He marched up the stairs at a quick pace and couldn't have heard Mitchella's smothered protest. She remembered the magnificent room now. As she watched him move swiftly up the stairs, she noted his smooth stride. With a Holly mother, no wonder the man was so graceful. From her studies she knew the Blackthorns had always been good dancers, had enjoyed giving balls. Why would he break with generations of tradition?

A hideous yowl came from Drina. Back arched and hair on end, she backed away from the ballroom door. The small cat whirled and sped past Mitchella up the stairs, ears flattened.

Nibbling her lower lip, Mitchella realized she needed more information about her client—from whom, she didn't know. Maybe when she had dinner with Danith D'Ash tonight, they could decide whom to approach and how.

Straif waited for her at the top of the steps, face closed, and she knew that the family rooms would be worse for them all. The first few bedrooms on the second level were easily entered and discussed, they'd been guest rooms and a guest suite.

Then, in at the third room on the left, Straif stopped to stare at a door. "The Heir'sSuite," he said tonelessly.

"You are no longer the Heir," Mitchella soothed. She was *not* going to ask if there was anything in the rooms that he wanted. Growing up with brothers and as a mother to Antenn, she could spot important treasures. Perhaps later, as he grew accustomed to the project and she knew him better, she could give him old items he might still like. "We can decorate the room in a manner that would welcome either a boy or a girl."

He blinked and an odd expression crossed his face, as if it was the first time he'd thought of his progeny as real children. Mitchella ignored a twinge of pain at the thought of her own sterility.

"That's a good idea."

Drina sniffed at the bottom of the door and wrinkled her nose, then made a little sound in her throat.

Straif actually smiled. "Drina says it smells like boy—sounds like she doesn't much like boys."

Mitchella chuckled. "She's a prissy cat, I don't imagine she does." Since it didn't seem like they were going to open the door, she urged Straif on with a little tap against his back.

But his steps lagged. Tension rose from him as they drew even with the next door on the left, the one in the middle of the corridor. Straif flicked his fingers at the intricately carved lintel, the heavy door. "The MasterSuite," he said.

Drina hummed in approval, walked around the door, stretched up on the door flexing her claws to give it her scent. The door swung wide on a dark-paneled room, and Straif turned abruptly away. A muscle twitched in his jaw as if even the small glimpse was too much for him to bear.

He whispered. She looked at him. "What did you say?"

"I didn't say anything." When he met her eyes, his gaze fixed on her face, ignoring the open door behind her.

Mitchella rubbed her temples. "I could have sworn you said something." She frowned in concentration. "Something about finishing the MasterSuite first so you can take your proper place in the Residence."

Straif looked startled, then arched a sandy eyebrow. "The Residence was talking to me on a private channel that takes less energy than general audio. Interesting that you can hear it. Probably because you have an affinity with homes due to your profession."

Her pulse picked up pace. Another strange and unusual thing, mental connection with a sentient house. How did she handle this? With a professional smile she said, "My Flair isn't great, and T'Ash Residence hasn't deigned to speak with me, but if T'Blackthorn Residence wishes to I'll make every effort to be receptive on all levels." This job was becoming a lot of work.

She glanced inside the MasterSuite, and her chest tightened. The furnishings were in good condition; obviously the Residence had tried to keep this suite in the best condition possible with its limited technology-spells.

Everything was in place as if Straif's father had just left and might return. Mitchella swallowed hard and shut the door.

Drina was having a conversation with Straif that included whining and tail-lashing from her and firm statements from him. He stood with hands on hips, and Mitchella had no doubt they communicated mentally, too.

"Yes, I said I'd convert the Heir'sSuite playroom for you, and it would be the first one redone, but I've reconsidered."

Drina huddled into herself, looking small and pitiful, then raised huge blue eyes to Straif.

His face hardened. "I won't be staying in the MasterSuite. You'll be up here all alone."

Mitchella saw the flash of calculation in the cat's eyes and wondered if Straif had, too. Drina rose and flowed to Straif and rubbed against his boots, purring loudly. Or Mitchella guessed it was loud for Drina. Pinky purred much better.

Along with Drina's blandishments, Mitchella felt an odd tickling in her ears and mind that corresponded with a faint thickening in the atmosphere around her. She strained all her senses and caught the whisper of the Residence.

"—you are T'Blackthorn, it is best that you live in the MasterSuite."

"I'll consider it." Straif strode down the hall. With a little smile, Drina hurried to catch up with him. Mitchella was determined to draw up a redecorating scheme immediately for the MasterSuite. The cat and house would convince Straif to live in the rooms.

Several meters along the corridor, he indicated another door. "The MistrysSuite." His tone was expressionless, but dread radiated from him. She took his arm companionably, ready to move him away from pain. "We agreed the Mistrys-Suite should be decorated by your HeartMate."

He didn't budge, but stared at the heavy door, intricately carved with symbols of the Blackthorns: The Blackthorn tree was in the center and in each corner was a carved image of a wolf.

Inhaling deeply, he met Mitchella's eyes, his own darkening with emotion. "My mother's rooms. The suite will need to be cleaned. The . . . the furnishings inventoried. Stored." His body vibrated under her hand. "I haven't been in there since my mother died. Since everyone else died."

That shocked her. Definitely time to calm the client, get him moving away.

His eyes went a little wild as he looked down the hallway. "My sister's suite is next."

Time to get him downstairs where the rooms weren't quite as personal. Maybe. Everything indicated that he'd walked away from the house—the *Residence*—as a very young man. Everything was just as the last living occupants had left it. It was a privileged person who could just leave things behind for years.

To her right was the staircase down to the grand hall. Mitchella prodded Straif and finally got him turned away from the closed doors and moving down the stairs. Drina helped by keeping pace and purring.

Nevertheless, Mitchella wanted her guess confirmed, wanted to know what to expect when she entered the rooms she hadn't seen. "Did you have anyone—ah—go through the house, ready it for your long absence?"

"Does it look as if I did? No. I let the Residence take care of itself. I don't know if T'Holly or D'Holly, my maternal relatives, came here at all after—afterward."

"I'll check with them." Somehow she'd find the nerve to talk to the leaders of the FirstFamilies. Perhaps she could learn of past events from them, too.

If the place wasn't a FirstFamilies estate, she'd have gently advised him to move. No chance of that. So the best thing to do was to completely redecorate. She discarded her first plan of bringing the Residence exactly back to the recorded holos. That wouldn't be a blessing for Straif. It wouldn't make him comfortable.

She couldn't imagine living in a home that wasn't comfortable. The energy vibrations would warp the individual and perhaps the Residence itself. Even Drina was affected by the tour. Her step had been nearly prancing as she started; now she lifted and put her paws down as if they hurt.

Once on the first floor, Straif looked around and grimaced. "I thought to use the cook's apartment as a living space for now. It's at the far end of the west wing." He shrugged.

Drina sat on the toe of one of his boots, lifted her small head, and mewed.

Straif scowled. His lips thinned. Finally, he sighed. "The Residence can clean the Heir's Suite playroom for you."

The faintest voice sounded in Mitchella's head. "There was once a Famdoor from the hall to the playroom. I will dissolve the barrier and open it again," said the Residence.

Both Drina and Straif nodded. They obviously heard the Residence, too, and much better than Mitchella. Ah, well, they were both more Flaired than she.

Drina rose to her feet, angled her body in a long stretch, and trotted back up the staircase.

Mitchella chuckled. "So, as long as the scent of boy is removed from the playroom she will be happy to live there."

Straif grimaced. "I haven't had Drina as a Fam for very long, but I think she expects perfection." He shrugged again, but his voice sounded lighter. "She'll no doubt supervise the cleaning." He gestured to the left. "I've found a sitting room that can serve as a base of operations. Our contract is there, with the terms we discussed."

His hand slid down to clasp her fingers, and she realized with a flush of heat that she'd been touching him far too much, too casually, as if he were more of a friend than a client. Her nerves shivered as she became intensely aware of the strength and warmth of his fingers around hers, the callouses on his hand, the tingle of *Flair* he transmitted to her skin.

Her breath came shorter, and she steadied it. They walked to the room in silence, but now that she experienced the attraction to him again, she could only think of his body, how their steps matched. How they might match in bed.

He stopped at a door midway down the corridor and opened it to a dark purple room. Mitchella flinched at the sight of heavy velvet curtains coated with grime and frayed upholstery. At her reaction, Straif dropped her hand. Her lips thinned in irritation at herself. Nothing to do but act grandly.

Mitchella swept into the purple parlor before him. It was far too dim for Straif's need to appreciate her. Just the simple walk down the corridor with her, the sensual heat and movement of her body beside his, had distracted him from painful memories and set his mind on the future.

With a wave of his hand and a murmured Word he sent the drapes opening, and watched with a wince as several dropped to the floor in heaps. The windows were filthy, as if they were covered with some sort of scum. Racking his brain, he couldn't think of the proper spell to clean them.

She stood in the middle of the room, hands on hips, surveying it. "Are the standard housekeeping spells in effect?"

Before he could answer, the Residence replied with surprising eagerness. "Yes, Gentlelady Clover."

Mitchella hesitated, cleared her throat. "Is that you, Grand-House T'Blackthorn Residence?"

"Yes, Gentlelady Clover. I have communicated with T'Ash Residence. It is most pleased with the results of your skills. It has shown me your work." The Residence sighed. "It brags. It is still a very young Residence, no more than two decades old."

Straif enjoyed the blush that enhanced Mitchella's beauty. "My thanks for your kind words, Residence." Her smile made Straif forget the state of the room, drew him to her.

"Clear windows," Mitchella said. The room darkened into blackness for an instant, there was a swish, and a moment later the glass of the windows sparkled. Light seemed to dance into the room, and Straif felt a corresponding lift in his spirits.

Striding over to a small desk, Mitchella scanned the contract and nodded, but didn't sign it.

Mitchella turned the desk from facing the windows to facing the inside of the chamber. Then she sat, set the contract aside, and pulled out a writing tablet and drawstick. She glanced at him, that professional smile on her lips.

Straif vowed to turn that smile into something more sultry before she left the room. He wondered if she was trying to make him feel awkward. It wasn't working. He prowled to the twoseat at right angles to the desk, sat, and stretched out his legs. He found himself steepling his fingers as his father had been wont to do in his ResidenceDen. The image brought less pain than it had the night before.

Mitchella leaned forward, her full breasts shifted and caught his focus. She huffed a breath. "GrandLord T'Blackthorn, may I have your attention?"

"Oh, you do. You certainly do." He didn't bother to mask the huskiness in his voice, the attraction in his gaze. He smiled slowly. "Call me Straif."

She nibbled her full bottom lip. Another immediate goal entered his mind. He'd taste those lips before she left. "Straif, then. I need to ask you a very important question."

Six

Straif met Mitchella's gaze. "Yes, what is your very im-
portant question?" He wished it would have something to do
with them and sex, but figured she'd stay on the painful topic
of his Residence.

"You're very sure that you don't want to restore the
rooms of the Residence as they were. You wish everything to
be different—to follow your own taste?"

Just as he'd thought, nothing about exploring each other
intimately. Her question *was* tough. He should think about it,
but he didn't want to. He never wanted to see some rooms as
they once were.

"I want it changed." His voice was even rougher. "Especially the ResidenceDen, my sister's rooms. I never want to
see the ballroom as it is or was again."

Mitchella exuded sympathy, as if she'd thrown a soft,
warm cloak around him. He liked the feeling. Concentrate on
her instead of his raw memories. Think of the last septhour,
how they'd walked the Residence together and it hadn't been
as bad as he'd dreaded.

Yes, they'd collaborate well—and be fiery in bed.

"Then I won't consult the ResidenceDen records," she said.
"We can start from the ground up, literally."

She made a note on the papyrus tablet. "Most of the furniture needs only to be cleaned or have minor repairs, then you can choose which to use and which to store."

That sounded like another in-depth tour. It wasn't something he'd subject himself to. He sat up straight. "I don't want the ResidenceDen, the Master- or MistrysSuite, my sister's rooms or my old Heir'sSuite to remain the same in any way. As for the ballroom—" he sucked in a deep breath "—I will not step into that room. I'm not sure I want it to remain one room." He waved a hand. "Consider alternatives."

Mitchella decided to find out what had happened in the ballroom as soon as possible. She tapped the drawstick on the papyrus. "GrandLord—Straif, why don't we work this way, I'll oversee the cleaning and refurbishing of your Family's possessions in those chambers, make an inventory, and arrange the items to be stored. Then I'll work up a proposal for each room for us to discuss and present you with holo-models. Does this sound acceptable to you?"

Straif thought a moment. "Yes."

She nodded. "Very well."

"Ahem," said the Residence, in general audio mode.

Mitchella jerked a little.

Straif thought it was good that the Residence went audio. Mitchella was someone else for it to talk to. He was feeling surly to his home, and Lady and Lord knew that Drina was only interested in topics that related directly to her.

Shaking her head, Mitchella laughed a little. "I'm not used to being addressed by Residences. Please feel free to advise me—"

"Wait." Straif lifted a hand. "The Residence can advise, but I don't want you making any changes based solely on its notions. All the final decisions are mine."

Her manner cooled before his eyes. "Of course. As you wish," she said.

"Residence?" Straif asked.

"I need more energy from you."

"I hear you. We'll discuss this later."

"Fam Drina is now in the Heir'sSuite playroom, demanding a better cleaning. I will need Flair to institute a complete molecular cleaning of that room and the MasterSuite," said the Residence.

"I don't want the MasterSuite—"

"Straif," Mitchella said softly, rising and crossing the room to stand in front of him. He took her hand, keeping his fingers entwined with hers, and looked up into her deep green eyes. "Yes, Mitchella?"

She inhaled, and her magnificent breasts rose. A beam of sunlight lit her hair and highlighted the red of her lips. He felt better already.

"Everyone with any sensitivity knows that this will be difficult for you—physically, mentally, and emotionally. Not to mention what it will cost you in energy and Flair. I'll do everything possible to make your Residence a home for you."

Her words comforted him. More, her concerned expression, the way her body leaned forward in sympathy. Her very presence soothed him—the soft, beautiful curves of a civilized woman, her pale skin and big green eyes.

As the silence grew he found that though being with her calmed his raw feelings, it aroused in him something else. *Attraction, lust* weren't the right words. Something about her stirred his deepest self.

Using the skill of a hunter on the track of a wary animal, he stood slowly, so he was a hand's breadth from her. One large breath of hers would brush her magnificent breasts against his chest. Sparks of passion sizzled through his blood, concentrated below his belt.

She didn't back away, but her eyes narrowed.

He curved his hands around her face, and the softness of her skin against his calloused palms was so sweet it closed his throat. He bent his head, not much, for she was a tall woman, a woman who'd match him.

His lips brushed hers, and they, too, were soft. Pliant, rich, tempting beyond measure. A groan of appreciation tore from him. He needed more. He needed all. But she was a woman who deserved the best he could give—tenderness, respect, not rough and wild passion.

Not yet.

His fingers plunged into the lushness of her hair, the silken glide of it over his hands was rich beyond belief. It glinted a hundred shades of red in the sun, and he was nearly dazzled enough to forget his intention to kiss her. Nearly.

His lips slid across hers once more, and the scent of her, floral and earthy—and womanly—spun in his head until he had to taste her or die. Gently, gently, he swept his tongue across her lips, and the unique flavor of her flashed through him until he shuddered.

She wasn't responding. She stayed still under his hands, his mouth, but did not yield. Did not participate. He groaned again, in despair. This woman was everything he'd missed for so long in his self-imposed banishment. Yet he dared not touch her roughly. He dared not lose her.

He could only court her, ignore the wild clamoring of his blood to take and ravish and forget everything of himself in her. He *would not* be rough. He nibbled at the corner of her mouth, once again tasted her.

And her breasts touched his chest, withdrew, brushed him again. Her mouth opened, panting.

Yes!

He wanted to yank her to him, feel all of her against him. Instead he thrust his tongue into the dark, damp hollow of her mouth, learned her taste that sank deep into the core of him.

Her tongue slid against his, then she was against him, her arms wrapped tight around him, so he felt enveloped by sheer femininity. Her body pressed against his, her hands set against his head for a kiss—a kiss so deep he thought he'd perish.

All thought fled. All control. His hands went to her lush bottom and squeezed, hauled her close so he could feel the soft warmth of her stomach against his erection.

Her long leg slid up along his, and he shuddered with desire. She hooked her thigh over his hip and pressed herself against him, and the hot, damp softness between her thighs was rubbing his arousal, and his head exploded with pleasure, and he took her mouth, plunging his tongue in and out, and he kneaded her bottom, and she slid her breasts against his chest, and they toppled and fell onto something soft and dusty, and her fingernails dug into his back, adding a sweet tang of pain to the pleasure, and his hands pushed up her tunic, and his fingers curled over the top of her trous, and he felt the pliant flesh of her stomach and—

What are you doing to My pillow! Drina screeched. *It is time for lunch, too.*

Mitchella shot off him. He didn't know how she untangled herself so quickly. He reached, but she was beyond his grasp.

She stared down at him. Her tunic fell over her trous, and she looked well-clothed, but her fiery hair tumbled around her shoulders, bright in the sun. Her bosom rose and fell. Her face was flushed, her eyes luminous—with shock and anger.

Straif opened his mouth, but his mind wasn't working and he had nothing to say. He was wrecked, angled half off the twoseat, only conscious of the throbbing of his body. The agonizing cold of being alone. The sunbeam didn't reach where he lay.

Drina hopped up to the arm of the twoseat and stared down at him. She looked upside down.

You are squashing My pillow. It may never be the same.

Straif was sure he'd never be the same.

Mitchella stalked over to the desk. He could only glimpse the movement of her bottom beneath her clothes. His senses clouded.

Drina jumped onto his chest. His breath whooshed out. He sat up, and she fell to land four-footed on the floor. She glared at him.

Papyrus rustled as Mitchella stacked them together, inserted them into her carrycase along with an audio note flexistrip. With deliberate movements, she set imaging spheres inside, too. Then she walked over to the twoseat, still keeping her distance from him, and whisked Drina's pillow off the couch. With a small shake and a Word from Mitchella, the pillow plumped, the golden tassels smoothed. The pillow looked better than it had when he'd gotten it from the Hollys.

She dropped it on his lap. "Send it to Drina's room."

Since she was in a dangerous mood, and he sensed she might just walk out on him and the job, something he didn't think he could bear at the moment, he did so.

Looking down at the little cat, Mitchella said, "Residence, how clean is Drina's room?"

"A deep housekeeping spell has finished. Molecular cleaning—"

Mitchella said, "That can wait until later. Drina, why don't you inspect your room and see if you want any of the current furniture?"

Did that mean Mitchella would stay on the job despite his lack of control? Straif sucked in his breath and shifted on the seat.

Drina sniffed, but glided to the door. She threw a glance over her shoulder as if she expected Straif to open it for her. He grunted, but didn't move. With a flick of her tail, she teleported away.

When he looked for Mitchella, he saw her behind the desk again, her carrycase tucked under her arm. Her face was still flushed from passion, but now her gaze was cold.

He didn't like the look in her eyes, but he kept his mouth shut.

"I don't want you to kiss me again. I want no more incidents like the one on the twoseat, you understand?"

Straif stood. It was difficult to saunter with an erection, but he managed. Her gaze didn't drop below his face. He admired the professionalism of that, even though he wished she'd show she wanted him.

When he reached the desk, he stopped. "I understand, but I don't agree."

"If you don't agree, then I must resign from this project. You have a HeartMate and a duty to your Family. I will not be a simple fling for a bored noble."

Anger shot through him, and he clenched his fists but kept his voice quiet. "Nothing about you is simple. An *affair* with you would not be simple, but deep and passionate. I promise to cherish you as long as we are together." He needed her.

She bit her lip. Her gaze scanned the room. He felt her Flair probing the Residence. When she met his eyes again, a hint of vulnerability showed in them, and his gut tightened with the need to protect her.

She took a deep breath, and he struggled to keep his gaze on her face. A lovely face, mouth swollen from the wild kisses they'd shared.

"I need this job," she said.

He didn't like that she thought of it as a job.

His face must have changed, or she read him better than most, because she lifted her chin.

"More, I believe the Residence needs me. I think I'm the best person to restore it." She touched fingers above her left breast and Straif couldn't help it. His glance fell to watch her gesture, and he stared at those large, full breasts that he hadn't really gotten his hands on yet, let alone his mouth. At the thought of suckling her breasts, saliva pooled. His body, which had begun to ease, tightened again.

Her nipples peaked under her tunic at his stare, and he suppressed a groan.

"No more passionate interludes." Her tone was a little unsteady, but the resolve behind it firm.

He met her gaze. "I can't promise that." His hands itched to touch her, so he hooked his thumbs in his belt. "I want you." He needed her—everything she was. "There's desire between us; has been since we first laid eyes on one another."

She dropped the carrycase on the desk and started unloading all her work. "I'll leave you my notes and bill you for the time I spent on them."

He set his teeth. "I can promise not to put my hands on you." He could last until she broke, he hoped. "Not to put my mouth on you." This wasn't helping him keep cool. "But if *you* put your hands on me, I won't stop. We'll be lovers, and not one-night lovers."

"That could jeopardize this project."

It wasn't life or death. What could happen, the place could look tasteless, bad? No worse than now. Another reason he needed her. But she took her work seriously, so he just nodded. "I accept that." He wanted her more for a lover than for her skills, now.

Her lips thinned. What a shame, flattening a mouth like hers. She should never do that, but he wasn't about to tell her. Hesitation flickered in her eyes.

"It will be your decision, Mitchella. It is always a lady's decision." Nothing wrong with trying to tempt her, though. Her passion was hot. He wondered what experience she had with resisting temptation. Not much, he fervently hoped.

He held out his hand with a charming smile he'd learned from his mother, a Holly. "You're a professional. I respect that. We can deal with each other professionally. Sign the contract."

She stared at his hand. "No fraternizing outside the project."

He could work around that. He lifted his brows. "I think restoring my Residence to its former beauty will take up most of our time. We'll be working closely together. I repeat my promise, I'll keep my hands to myself."

Mitchella's stare fixed on his mouth.

"And my mouth." He wiggled the fingers of his out-stretched hand. "You'll be the one to make the first move. Everything will be in your hands."

She grabbed his hand and shook it, once, stuffed the papyrus and holostones back into her carrycase. With a scowl, she looked him up and down. "You don't think I can resist you?"

He was praying she couldn't.

"The Residence needs both our best efforts," he soothed.

Looking around again, she sighed. "Yes." She signed the contract, glanced at a timer that wasn't working, then at the one on her wrist. "I'll purchase everything for Drina's room this afternoon and have it delivered. Drina can supervise the placement of the furniture." Mitchella's lips curved. "The bedroom in the model used the top line of furniture from my family's factory, from Clovers. If you object to giving them business, let me know. I assure you everything will be completely honest—no inflated prices."

For the first time since their kiss, she met his gaze, her own earnest.

"And I trust you completely," he said, wanting to bend the short distance to put his lips back on hers. He already missed her taste.

She pinkened at his compliment and smiled fully, openly. It caught at his heart.

"We'll do right by you," she said with a middle-class sincerity that charmed him.

"Of course."

"I'll be back in the morning with an excellent Flaired wall tinter. We should be done with Drina's room in a couple of hours." Then she turned and opened a door in the full-length, multipaned glass windows that he hadn't even known was there. Spine stiff, and her fine bottom moving nicely beneath her clothes, she left.

She needed the job. Nice of her to tell him. He wondered why, but he'd find out. He could certainly use the information.

Straif inhaled, drew her scent deep within himself. With unfocused eyes, he studied interweaving aura-trails—Mitchella's, his deep silver-blue-green, Drina's dainty light blue mincings. Near the twoseat, and on it, were huge streaks of red so hot it nearly seared his eyes. He grinned. He'd used his tracking Flair all his life and never seen anything like that red.

Who could resist passion like that?

*B*riskly, *Mitchella walked down the long gliderway, a* thousand plans for the Residence flitting through her head. It was always this way with a new job. And what a project this was! It would definitely bring her fame and fortune. There was nothing she couldn't do with a "no-expense-spared" budget.

Looking around, she saw she was out of sight of any scrystones, and no one was around. She did a whirl and a dance and sang. No one in the world ever wanted to hear her sing, so it was always a solitary pleasure. She pirouetted up the path, enjoying this moment of sheer triumph. Later would come the hard work and sober thoughts. This was a time of happiness.

But the joy faded incrementally as a shadow fell over her mood, an itching started between her shoulder blades. Again, she stopped and looked around, and again she saw no one in the lush tangle of greenery, though she *sensed* someone. Her Flair wasn't great, and mostly involved charisma—a salesperson's Flair—but still . . . She slowed and kept her gaze sharp. Nothing but a steady feeling of oppression.

She reached the greeniron gates and let herself out, hurrying away from the estate and along the avenues of Noble Country, but the tension didn't diminish until she joined others at the public carrier glider plinth. Holding her bag tight, she studied the people at the stop, then relaxed as she eased into conversation with them. No one odd.

As the huge glider pulled up and she boarded, she realized that was why she was spooked. Not only did she think someone was watching her, but she thought that someone wasn't quite right.

She shook off the feeling. No one had been on the estate today, but in the past a mind-linked Triad gang—Antenn's brother's gang—had fought there; perhaps their madness lingered. There was no curse on the estate, on the Residence. She'd have felt that easily enough. She wouldn't let such an idea enter her mind. This project was going to make her career, and she wouldn't let anything stop her from doing it right.

Not even her most unprofessional desire for Straif T'Blackthorn.

*To ease his hot blood and tight body, Straif walked his es-*tate. Let Mitchella restore the inside, he'd take care of the grounds. Outside there would be no horrible memories of sickness and death. Instead of remembering his mother and father wasted with hollow cheeks and dull eyes, he'd see them as they stood strong and proud officiating as the Lord and Lady during Family Rituals. Instead of the sharp image of his sister's curled husk of a body, he'd remember her vibrant laughter as she played hide-and-seek with him.

Long grass, bushes, and trees grew dense in the gardens; the walls were solid except for a small broken door. There he sensed old fear and rage and evil. The gangs had used that door, particularly the Triad that had challenged T'Ash. His jaw set in anger that his estate had been invaded, used as a battleground. Following the years-old trail, he found where every Downwinder gang member had died, noted the traces of his cuz Tinne Holly and T'Ash. Hands on hips, Straif decided he'd need a priest and priestess to cleanse the ground, in addition to his own ceremonies. He strode up to an odd circular area and into the center before he realized it was clear due to strong sex magic.

Seven

As soon as Straif stepped into the cleared circle he was hard again. More than sex magic—*loving* Flair, and it was so strong because it was tied to Passage magic.

Passage—the times when a highly Flaired person's psi overcame them and the power was mastered or the person shattered. The strength of the energy was doubled—someone had experienced two Passages at once. A female.

Wild emotions rushed through him—lust, loving, fear of loss. Traces of the other emotions that came with Passage were blessedly little more than echoes. But still vivid images came to his mind, framed by what *he* wanted instead of the actual past. He saw Mitchella's body in moonlight, curved and waiting for him, passion on her features, beautiful arms reaching for him. He was naked and aroused and ready. He groaned and pulled away from the vision, walked away from the circle of influence, knowing his nights would be restless until he had Mitchella.

Waiting on the verge was Drina, her tail curled around her paws and pink nose lifted. She curled her tongue in the additional cat sense and said, *T'Ash and D'Ash mated here.*

That answered the who. Now free from the sizzling desire, he could see T'Ash's Flair trail.

"Right," Straif said. "I'm going back to the broken door in the wall and setting a sealing spell on the wall section."

Much violence and pain.

"Yes. More than I want." Didn't he have enough pain associated with his estate—the death of his Family—without coping with the destruction that others had brought to his land? That tasted bitter.

Drina trotted beside him. *Much sign of kin-to-you in fight, and a hunting cat.*

The tension in Straif eased a little, he sharpened his Flairsight. "Tinne Holly, and Passage Flair from him, too." Straif sighed. "No doubt that triggered many of the events that transpired, but I wish the whole thing had taken place somewhere else."

You can ask T'Ash for the whole story tonight. Drina sniffed, placed a paw on a curvy line that shone emerald to Straif. *Sign of My sire, Zanth. He still hunts here.* She glanced up at Straif. *Maybe you should forbid him.*

"Huh." Like forbidding a cat would be anything but futile.

They reached the wall, and Straif summoned as much energy as he could to say the spell to seal the wall. When he was finished, a fine slick of sweat covered his body, but as he looked at the tall brick wall, there was no door. He managed a crooked smile. This was a small thing, but vital. His estate would never be breached again from that door. It was also the first new spell he'd done to restore his home. It felt good.

He was still cheerful when he strode up the outside terrace steps and into the west wing.

"Welcome, T'Blackthorn," said the Residence. It sounded conciliatory. "Your shieldspell is potent. Well done."

"Thank you, Residence."

"A snack of furrabeast bites awaits the Fam. A mixture of fruit and nuts your mother made for you when you were a child is in the no-time."

Aching pain speared Straif at the memory, then faded—quicker than any had before, and he was grateful. "Thank you, Residence." His voice was steady and that was good, too.

"GrandLady Kalmi Lobelia vized and left a message in the holocache," said the Residence.

Straif grunted and followed Drina into the kitchen.

How do I access the no-time? she demanded of Straif, not contacting the Residence itself.

Straif snorted but relayed the question. The house indicated a small ident stone on the floor near the Fam no-time. Drina set her paw on the stone, and an instant later the bottom of the Fam no-time slid up, showing a plate of food. The cat dug in. Straif tapped the large no-time and a bowl of his fruit-nut mix appeared. He popped a handful into his mouth and crunched. It was as fresh as if his mother had made it a moment before. It was her recipe, something he'd never duplicated. With the taste, memories came of her making it with her own hands, of his sister throwing bits of it at him throughout his childhood.

He chomped down on the mix a little too hard and bit his tongue. He swore. To distract himself, he went over to the scry-bowl set on its own table and flicked the rim with a fingernail. "Holocache."

"One message," reported the bowl.

"Play it."

A holo formed above the bowl, but it was wavery, dim, and gray with gloom. He narrowed his eyes, but the figure remained indistinct and he realized it was an accurate projection of his old lover, Kalmi, in her ResidenceDen.

"Greetyou, Straif." Her voice was strong and mellifluous with natural Flair, a beautiful voice. The voice of an Oracle. "I hear you are remaining in Druida, and I know that T'Blackthorn Residence is a wreck." Straif winced. "Please feel free to stay with me. Farewell." Her voice was bored, as if scrying from duty, or maybe because he was a FirstFamily GrandLord again.

Straif paused the holo before it faded and looked at Kalmi. He couldn't see her face beneath the cowl-scarf Oracles wore as a sign of their profession, nor were her surroundings clear. Now that he thought of it, they'd always made love in the dark, and he remembered her Residence being dim. Of course, her ResidenceDen, where she did her prophetic work, would be shaded so she could use her Flair for prophecy better, but he recalled the house as one of gray shadows.

"Scry dismissed," he said, and the holo vanished. He crunched another mouthful of his snack and wondered if

Kalmi was so weary with ennui that he'd be a welcome relief. She was a woman who needed constant stimulation—liked it to heighten her Flair.

But at their last parting, she'd thrown things at him in a fury that he was leaving to follow the lead on an herb that would bolster Blackthorn immunity to the Angh virus. She'd predicted the search would be futile. She'd been right.

Over the years he'd spent a lot of time with Kalmi. She was secondary in prophecy to the GreatHouse Vine.

One of the few things he'd done before he'd left Druida the first time at seventeen was to consult the ancient GreatLady D'Vine about his quest for a cure for his faulty gene. He'd ached for his Family, wanted to found another, but he *never* wanted to be the surviving Blackthorn a second time. D'Vine had stared at him with her penetrating gaze, and though he thought she'd seen his future, she'd refused his gilt and refused to tell him anything. Which had shivered his nerves for years. So he'd never dared face the old woman again. Instead, he'd gone to Kalmi.

He thought of her, of how he'd slaked his pain and need in her body. How he'd touched her with tenderness. But somehow, even before that last scene, their affair had soured. He couldn't pinpoint the time, or how, but now he knew any feelings he had for her were gone, never to return.

He erased the holo.

*T*hat evening, Mitchella dressed for her usual dinner with T'Ash and D'Ash in a mood of cheer. She had work! Excellent work, independent of any referral by her good friend Danith. Life's wheel of fortune was finally turning for her, and soon she'd be on top! Of course, indirectly, Danith had referred Drina to her, and Drina T'Blackthorn, but if Mitchella knew anything at all, it was that cats didn't do anything they didn't want to. Drina was a snob and a snot, but the little Fam had good taste.

So Mitchella would celebrate with D'Ash and her Heart-Mate, and wouldn't let the drawbacks of the job enter her mind or pass her lips. With a little time since the kiss and an upsurge of optimism, Mitchella had determined that she was capable of being completely involved in the project and completely uninvolved with the GrandLord. He was a gentleman. He'd take "no" for an answer. She would *not* let her body rule her head because it would doom her career.

She wore an expensive, long emerald tunic embroidered with gold-looking thread, a garment that she'd scolded herself for purchasing when her income was so low. She'd hidden it in the closet to forget the expense. She fluffed her hair with a small spell and donned the glisten earrings and necklace Danith had given to her as a nameday gift. T'Ash had made the set, and if she wore it, he might even speak to her civilly.

It was time they put that little incident between them in the past, not to be remembered. After all, she'd been the one thrown across the city, all he had experienced was a bit of anger at her falsehood that Danith was sterile. Yes, this was an evening for new beginnings, new plans.

Impulsively, she reached for her new crystal oracle ball for a quick daily divination, but before she picked it up, Antenn's lagging footsteps clumped to her door and he pounded on it.

She opened her door, bent down, and smooched his forehead.

He sniffed. "You're wearing perfume, why's that if you're just going to the T'Ashes?"

Reaching out, she ruffled his hair and patted his cheek. "Women don't use perfume just for men, you know. I like the smell, it makes me feel exotic." She whirled. "Danith likes this scent, too." Mitchella opened her mouth.

"Don't sing!" Antenn clutched his chest. "Zow. You look great, you smell great. You'll have a great time. I'm glad you feel great—just don't sing."

Mitchella turned the first notes of a tune into a laugh. "Are you sure you want to stay here alone instead of visiting the Clover Compound?"

With a weary sigh, Antenn propped himself against her doorjamb. "I'm tired of the Clovers."

Hearing the incipient whine in his voice, Mitchella kissed his cheek. "You've been very good, so I'll grant this strange need for solitude."

He grunted. "You Clovers think being with people is the best thing in life. We aren't all like you, you know."

Mitchella just raised her eyebrows.

The scrybowl trilled from downstairs. She flitted from the room and down the stairs. Running a finger around the top of the bowl, she answered, "Here."

"*You know,*" Straif said to Drina as he strode to T'Ash's, "though we talked about your jewelry this morning, we are still in the probationary phase of this relationship."

Drina was walking instead of riding on his shoulder, and she stopped in midstep and looked up at him with cold, blue eyes. She hissed. She snarled.

Straif suppressed a grin. "Not to mention the gilt I'm spending on a room especially decorated just for you."

She sat. Her whiskers twitched. She lifted her nose in the air. *I am helping Mitchella Clover restore the Residence for Our status and comfort.*

He noticed comfort came secondary to the cat. He thought Mitchella already knew it was his first priority. Straif rocked back on his heels.

"All you did today was bully me into giving you a room and bully the Residence into cleaning it."

Drina hissed again. *I accompanied you and Mitchella on the tour. I examined the rooms by Scent and know which ones are Not Good for Us.*

Straif scowled. "Do you?"

You smelled different at different doors, she ended with excruciating honesty.

He shifted his shoulders. "I see."

Straif said, "You also raucously interrupted a private moment between Mitchella and me. If you want your jeweled collar and your pretty room, you'll be more discreet and better behaved."

Mating. Boring, Drina huffed, rising and turning onto the street to T'Ash Residence.

Straif caught up with her easily. "Your word that you won't deliberately disturb me when I am—taking pleasure—with Mitchella Clover again. Or you'll have a plain collar."

Drina stopped, flattened her ears, glared at him from the corner of her eyes. Her tail lashed. Straif kept quiet.

With a final hissed breath, Drina turned and trotted to T'Ash's greeniron gates. *I agree.*

Straif positioned himself in front of the scrystone set in the wall next to the gate and flicked a fingernail against it to activate the viz.

"Name?" asked a smooth, rich voice. The man looking out from the stone was older and distinguished with features far different than T'Ash's own. A hired man, just as Straif would have to hire someone who would have no blood in common with his Family.

"T'Blackthorn," Straif replied. He stooped to lift Drina to his shoulder. "With my Fam, Drina."

The man flushed slightly, then said in dour tones, "Drina."

"Another admirer?" asked Straif.

Drina sniffed, lifted a paw, and licked it. Nice trick since she was balanced on his shoulder. *He is nobody. Everyone who is Anyone adores Me.*

"The shieldspell on the gates is now modified to admit you two," the butler said.

"Right," Straif said. No one seemed to like Drina. Fancy that. For a small cat, she sure had made her presence felt.

One-half of the gate swung open.

Drina rubbed her head against his cheek and purred.

Well, maybe he liked her. Most of the time.

It is Midweek evening, she sent mentally.

"That's right." Straif stopped and watched the gate close securely behind him, then started up the long drive to T'Ash's modern Residence made of security armourcrete.

Mitchella Clover eats with Danith on Midweek evening.

Straif paused, stroked Drina's head. She butted against his palm. He grinned. So much for Mitchella's "nonfraternization" policy, and he was completely innocent of ulterior motives. Up to this point. His pulse quickened.

I can provide information, Drina said delicately.

"Hmm," Straif said.

I can also help you be private with her.

"Oh?" He wouldn't need Drina's help in any way, but it might be interesting to see the cat's maneuvers.

I am a wonderful FamCat for You. She licked his cheek.

He jerked away. "You don't need to do that." He'd much rather have Mitchella nibble on him.

Drina sniffed, then purred. *Do I get My collar?*

They'd reached the huge, rounded-topped doors of the main entrance to T'Ash's Residence. It was a beautiful house, but it had no history, though Straif had heard T'Ash had managed to save the HouseHeart from discovery and burning.

He stood for a moment and realized the burden of his grief had lessened a little. He still had his Family home, Family possessions. An image of his mother smiling at him as she sat near her elegant, old Lady'sDesk came to Straif. That was a picture he liked in his head. Both his mother and the desk had been beautiful, had suited. And though he didn't want to see the desk again, not now, not soon, there was comfort in the fact that it still existed—a part of his Family's generational history, his mother's history, his own.

He had a Residence, a home. He was blessed.

Do I get My collar? Drina's tone sharpened.

Straif shrugged. Drina hung on. He lifted his hand to the door knocker, thought of watching Mitchella across the dining room table, Mitchella taking other meals with him at T'Blackthorn Residence, Mitchella eventually in his bed.

"Your collar, Drina? Why not?" He grinned and banged the knocker. "I'm going to get what I want."

Mitchella's cuz, Trif Clover, looked out from the smooth surface of the water in the scrybowl. She pouted. "I'm bored and tired of being here alone in MidClass Lodge and don't want to go to Clover Compound. Can I come over?" Then her glance sharpened. "Nice tunic, do you have a new gallant?"

"No. Just wanted to dress up a little for my Midweek dinner with the Ashes." Mitchella studied Trif. She looked a little pale. Everyone in the Family knew that she had the greatest Flair, and the storms of her Passage to master her Flair starting at seventeen had lingered for nearly two years. They all worried.

"I can cancel, or you can come along." She should talk to the family about having T'Ash Test Trif's Flair. Another Test couldn't hurt, and it might ease everyone's minds. T'Ash liked all the Clovers except Mitchella and her brother Claif, and

T'Ash loved showing off his Testing Stones, so Mitchella was sure he'd go along with another Test.

Trif wrinkled her nose, shifted her shoulders.

"I don't want to play with the nobility tonight. I'd have to mind my manners, and I don't want to."

"Danith wouldn't care."

"No, but who knows who else might be at T'Ash's?"

"Just the three of us. And the animal menagerie," Mitchella said. T'Ash was always as antisocial as Antenn felt tonight.

But Danith wasn't.

Trif's bottom lip stuck out.

"I don't want to work at heavy conversation or being nice." She held up a small package. "Uncle Mel anticipated my nameday, and I have a new holoconstruct of Ancient Earth that I want to put together and morph."

Antenn, with Pinky draped over one skinny shoulder, nudged Mitchella to one side of the scrybowl and looked in. "Where'd Mel get that?"

"He took me to the Ship, *Nuada's Sword*."

"Zow! You went to the Ship? Did the construct cost much?"

Trif dimpled, wiggled her brows at them both. "Invite me over, and I will tell all."

Mitchella laughed. "I foresee an end to both of your evening doldrums. Trif, I have a new project." Mitchella straightened to her full height. "I'm renovating T'Blackthorn Residence."

Trif's eyes widened, and her mouth hung open for an instant. "Blessings! What a coup." Her glance went to Antenn. "Antenn can tell me all about it."

"Yes." He smiled into the scrybowl.

"I'll catch the public carrier and be there shortly," Trif ended the call.

Mitchella squeezed Antenn's shoulder. "Happier now?"

Grinning, Antenn rubbed his hands. "The Ancient Earth contstruct and Trif are welcome here tonight."

Mitchella only waited long enough to let Trif in and get her settled before donning her raincloak and strolling off to the public carrier and the Ashes.

Eight

The public carrier glider system was fast and efficient, and Mitchella reached the Ashes' a few moments before dinner would be announced.

Danith opened the door herself and hugged Mitchella. "Where's Antenn?" she asked. Ever since she'd discovered herself pregnant, Danith had "practiced mothering" on various Clover children. Since she'd been the one to suggest Mitchella as a guardian for Antenn, she kept a sharp eye on their relationship.

"Antenn declined the invitation, he's at home, with Trif supervising." Mitchella said as she handed the T'Ash butler her wrap. She turned and looked directly into Straif Blackthorn's eyes.

He grinned. "What a coincidence. Mitchella has agreed to redesign my Residence. A very talented lady."

Mitchella darted a glance at Danith. She looked surprised, Mitchella was sure her best friend hadn't known of Mitchella's job with Straif, hadn't invited him to play matchmaker or anything. Of course she wouldn't. No one knew better than Danith that a FirstFamily Lord wanted children, a strong bloodline.

Now Danith was frowning at her. "You didn't tell me."

"We just had our first consultation this morning. I was saving the news for tonight."

Danith raised her eyebrows.

"I didn't know if GrandLord T'Blackthorn and I could work together," Mitchella said primly.

The man in question glided forward. "Oh, yes. We can." He offered his hand and studied her from under lazy eyelids.

Mitchella grasped his fingers to shake, and he lifted her hand to his mouth, turned it over and kissed the hollow of her palm, sending tingles of heat straight to her center. She slipped her hand from his, refusing to curl her fingers like a young girl, to hold the kiss.

T'Ash walked into the entry hall from his ResidenceDen, followed by cats. Only three, so Mitchella knew the rest of Danith's menagerie was excluded from the formal rooms this evening. Pansy, Danith's cat—not a Fam—mewed sweetly, and Danith picked her up. Zanth, T'Ash's Fam, trotted into the room as if he owned everyone and everything. He still was the ugliest tomcat Mitchella had ever seen, scarred from a thousand fights. Drina, Straif's Fam, minced in, nose high. She wore a string around her neck and whined—imperiously.

The other three people turned to her. Danith smiled and said, "We're measuring Drina for her Fam collar."

Mitchella choked; jewels for a cat!

Scowling, T'Ash said, "Drina will cost you a bundle."

Straif shrugged. "T'Blackthorns have more than one fortune."

Drina mewed. T'Ash laughed shortly. "That cat's arrogance never ceases to amaze me." He stared down at the half-Siamese. "We are finished with the topic of your collar tonight. I will *not* design and craft it now. It's time for dinner." He wrapped a burly arm around Danith's still slim waist and hurried her into the dining room. "You need to eat more."

"I am eating just fine," Danith said.

Straif offered his arm to Mitchella. "Shall we?" He sniffed. "Something smells very good."

Zanth shot into the dining room, Pansy followed, and Drina, tail waving sinuously, padded after the other two cats.

Chuckling, Straif caught Mitchella's hand and tucked it into the crook of his elbow, striding toward the small dining room that Mitchella had convinced T'Ash was acceptable for family meals. The table seated eight.

Mitchella gazed at Straif from under her lashes. He seemed much more lighthearted here, away from his Residence and the memories it called forth. This was the third facet she'd seen of the man. The first, the sexy loner she'd met at The Woad Garden, then the troubled man this morning, now this charming GrandLord. Perhaps it was the fourth facet— she couldn't forget the passionate man who'd pressed against her with desire and need.

"Do you think of us together?" Straif whispered.

Wildly, she wondered if he could read her thoughts and hauled her composure around her. "Why do you think that?"

"You're flushed and had a certain look in your eye. I can only hope that it related to me."

"Just because we are thrown together tonight doesn't mean I intend to see you after hours."

He pulled out a chair for her. "So I must thank the Lady and Lord for tonight and do all my wooing at the Residence."

"You mistake your words." Her smile was bitter. "We both know you are merely interested in seduction." Lifting and dropping her shoulder dismissively had him focusing on her breasts again, but she didn't care. Let him see what he'd never touch. Her control was strong, and she didn't think he'd be loverlike in front of other members of his class.

He scowled.

Danith said, "T'Blackthorn, you can sit next to T'Ash and talk about that miserable trip he and I took to the mines."

Straif frowned at her, but Danith ignored it. He strode around the table and jerked back the heavy chair next to T'Ash.

"I don't have anything more to say about the trip," T'Ash grumbled. He glanced over to the tiled corner of the room where the cats ate. "Though Zanth and I are in your debt, Blackthorn, for the value of the stones, even though your ancestors should not have taken the lambenthysts from their cave."

Danith grinned. "That was before my time with you, so *I* am free and clear of being part of any debt."

T'Ash flushed a little. His eyes softened as they rested on

his HeartMate, and he took her hand. "We were courting you."

Turning over her hand, Danith linked fingers for a moment, and Straif said, "The mines are only important because they might lead me to the cause of the mutation of my Family's gene that leaves us susceptible to the Angh illness. Blackthorns didn't always lack immunity to that sickness. That's my greatest priority, finding a cure for my gene."

For Mitchella the Ashes' loving gestures emphasized the coolness of Straif's words. His search for a cure was more important than restoring his Residence. Just as bonding with a HeartMate would be more important than an affair with Mitchella. She wouldn't leave herself open to such hurt.

The doors swung open, and servers brought in food and wine. Danith turned the conversation to the renovation of the area once known as Downwind. After new housing had been built in the southwest sector of Druida, FirstFamily Lords and Ladies had leveled the old buildings. Slowly, each section of the slum had been cleared of old energy and reblessed by priests and priestesses. In a few months, new buildings would be constructed. Mitchella's ward, Antenn, was studying with one of the architectural firms that was drawing up plans. All the Councils would vote on how the new portion of Druida would look.

Talk was lively, since everyone had their own opinions as to style. They all anticipated the posting of holominiatures in the GuildHall.

When the dinner ended, they walked to a sitting room. Mitchella tingled from the feel of Straif's body next to hers as they walked the short distance with matching steps, her hand on his arm. Smiling wickedly, he covered her fingers with his own, igniting sparks of pleasure in her core. She tried to look unaffected.

She'd decorated the sitting room, and as they entered, she studied Straif to see if he liked the room. Their tour of T'Blackthorn Residence had been so limited that she needed input on his preferences. He studied the room, but remained impassive.

Danith held open the door for the cats.

Zanth trotted in and stared at Mitchella. She'd finally figured out that the best way to treat the cat was with studied impoliteness. It was the only attitude he accepted from her. She ignored him.

Me going hunting.

Pain at the noise of his words shot through her head. Since she'd spent time with Danith and T'Ash, her Flair had increased slightly, and the cat also tried to make sure she could hear him, much as she'd care to forgo the experience.

"So go," T'Ash said.

"No celtaroons or sewer rats, please, Zanth," Danith said.

The tom grinned, and it was scary. He slid a glance to Straif. "Plenty of big rats in T'Blackthorn Estate."

Mitchella grimaced. Was that what she'd felt this morning— gazes of a rat pack? She blinked. No, it had been more intense than mere rodents. She eyed one of the twoseats and decided to play it safe and pulled away from Straif to take a chair.

"I walled up the garden door today," Straif said. He drew a chair out of an arrangement and close to hers, lounging into it.

Zanth sniffed. "Other ways in—for Cats. Good skirls to hunt there, too."

Straif waved a hand. "Go to it."

Zanth shot from the room.

Drina watched him with disdain, then pranced over to Straif and leapt to his lap, curled up, and began to purr. He petted her but looked at Mitchella from under lowered lashes.

She'd been separated from him for less than a minute, and she missed his touch. His glance reminded her of the kiss they'd shared—something she was sure he intended. Heat spread through her lower body, but she refrained from shifting. Her mind, her will, denied him. Her body wanted more.

T'Ash walked past the lord's wingchair to sit beside his wife on a plush twoseat and asked for tea. Danith and T'Ash ordered tea, Straif and Mitchella ordered caff. A moment later a server entered, pushing a large hover-tray that contained two china pots and several cups. As she studied the design, Mitchella smiled. She'd done good work, there, helping T'Ash and Danith devise a pattern for the Family china. It was colorful with delicate touches, something that reflected and pleased them both. Good work.

Smiling, Danith said, "Mitchella chose the china, and planned the interiors of this room and the dining room."

Mitchella sipped her caff. It was hot and dark and bold. She looked at Straif. "Tomorrow morning I'll bring you holos of my other work, and you tell me what you find acceptable."

The deep bong of the door scry echoed through the room. An instant later the butler hurried into the room, bowed to T'Ash while looking at Straif.

"GreatLord T'Holly is here, wishing to converse with T'Blackthorn."

"Let him in," T'Ash said. He looked under heavy brows at Straif. "T'Holly and I have a three-generation alliance, but I'll be glad to loan you a private room to talk."

Straif's jaw had set, and his eyes darkened to deep blue. "Trouble." He studied Danith, T'Ash. "We've already spun a thread of honor between us. I needn't be private." He laughed shortly. "I certainly don't want to have such a meeting at T'Blackthorn Residence."

Mitchella stood. "I'll leave."

Before she even finished her sentence, Straif leaned forward and bracletted her wrist with his strong fingers, looked up at her. "Stay."

Heat rose to her face. Though he sat and she stood, power radiated from him. "You can't want me knowing your private affairs."

"If T'Holly has left his Residence at this time of night and tracked me down, I have a feeling that my private affairs will not be too very private by the morning."

Reluctantly, Mitchella returned to her chair, and when Straif slid his fingers down to hold her hand, she didn't have the heart to withdraw her own fingers. Instead she squeezed his hand and smiled briefly.

He returned her smile, but a worry line formed between his eyes.

T'Holly was ushered into the sitting room. Mitchella stiffened. Everyone in this room but her was powerful in status and Flair—even her best friend, Danith, who'd risen to GrandLady status before she'd married T'Ash. And T'Holly was the most powerful man of them all, captain of the First-Families Council.

His glance swept the room. He studied and judged her in seconds, an appreciative smile lightened his face as he bowed.

Danith gestured to Mitchella. "T'Holly, my friend Mitchella Clover."

Hesitantly, Mitchella put out her free hand. He took her fingers and Mitchella trembled at his touch. Great Flair, but more, weariness—a darkness hovered over him. This is what a curse would feel like. Everyone knew that he and his Heart-Mate had broken vows of honor to their son Holm. It showed—in his appearance, his voice, his Flair. Mitchella stopped a shiver. Straif's fingers tightened on her other hand.

T'Holly brushed his lips across her hand and let it go. "The Clovers are a byword on Celta." For their fertility. Though she knew he meant it as a compliment, her lips pressed together. "I've heard of your work." Now he scanned the room, examining the furnishings and design. His face set into deep lines, and sadness haunted his eyes. "A very pleasing chamber." His smile was lopsided. "Not much like T'Holly Residence."

Danith had told Mitchella that no one cared for the way T'Holly Residence was furnished except the GreatLord. It had caused dissension between himself and the rest of his Family.

He glanced to Straif and back to her. "Since you are working with Straif, this involves you, too."

Mitchella had always heard the FirstFamilies knew everything as soon as it happened, now she knew it. Or maybe it was just that the gossip ring in the FirstFamilies was as quick and accurate as that of the Clovers.

Everyone tensed. Mitchella didn't want to stay, but there was nothing to do but fade back into her chair and hope that she could go unnoticed.

His gaze pinned her to her chair. "What I'm telling you," he stared at each one of them in turn, "is in deepest confidence, not to go beyond this room."

Her mouth dried. She looked for the caff tray. It was out of easy reach.

Face tight, Danith poured Mitchella another cup of caff and tea for herself. T'Ash surged from his chair and went to the bottles of liquor on the sideboard.

Potent Flair swirled throughout the room, and Mitchella realized T'Holly's words had been a binding spell. From under her lashes, she studied the others. They all appeared highly offended at the rudeness, but no one said anything. They probably sensed something more in T'Holly's Flair.

He sat in the commanding, oversized lord's chair.

Clinking glass against glass drew her attention to T'Ash, and she wondered if she'd have to commission more crystal. Perhaps it was too delicate for this sort of use.

T'Ash poured brithe brandy for T'Holly and whiskey for himself and Straif, handed them the drinks, then sat with Danith. Unobtrusively, Mitchella cradled the cup warming her hands.

"What is it?" asked Straif.

T'Holly looked at T'Ash. "You're allies with T'Blackthorn?" he asked formally.

"Yes," T'Ash said.

Straif's surprise flowed to her. His face showed nothing. She offered her hand, and he took it, sharing his satisfaction.

Drina sat up straight and mewed. Mitchella could almost hear her telepathic words. Gloomily she reasoned that if she spent time with that cat, she'd be able to hear her someday. As if Drina's attitude and vocalizations weren't enough.

"Of course you're allies with T'Ash, too," T'Holly said to Drina. He gazed at Danith. "Any word on an available kitten or cat for my HeartMate, D'Holly?"

Danith's spine stiffened, she reached for T'Ash and twined her fingers in his as if for support, then met T'Holly's gaze. "I can't, in good conscience, place a Fam in a Household that is under the shadow of broken vows of honor."

T'Holly's face went completely expressionless. Mitchella shrank back into her chair. Straif rubbed his thumb in the palm of her hand. The comfort was incredible—for both of them.

"That is too bad," T'Holly said. He sipped the brandy. When he looked up, his penetrating gaze fixed on Straif.

"The FirstFamilies Council received a notice from AllClass Council that a claim has been filed by another Blackthorn for the T'Blackthorn estate and Residence. The claimant states you have ignored your duties to your ancestral lands, to the Councils, and to Celta itself in not participating in GreatRituals."

Mitchella caught her breath in sheer surprise. Straif's fingers nearly crushed hers. He opened his mouth, but nothing emerged. His eyes appeared unseeing. Finally he croaked, "There are no other Blackthorns."

T'Holly smiled humorlessly, sipped his brandy, then answered. "The claimant provided genetic testing from a FirstLevel Healer. Not T'Heather, or I would have had the name out of him. Not" —he hesitated—"the former Lark Collinson," the HeartMate of T'Holly's disowned son. "or I'm sure you would have heard from your cuz."

Danith said, "That leaves only T'Heather's heir."

Another ironic smile from T'Holly. "Yes, and she is a very upright woman. I hesitate to pressure her."

"She's a generation younger than you, sir; a generation older than us. I don't think she'd speak to us." Danith looked at T'Ash. "Do you know of her alliances?"

"No," T'Ash said.

"Another Blackthorn," Straif breathed. "Who? How did— he or she—" He shot a glance at T'Holly.

"There are some things I'm not willing to divulge," the older man said. "I am dancing along the edges of my own vow of silence." He grimaced. "I will not break another oath."

"Of course not," Mitchella felt compelled to say into the heavy silence. Everyone seemed as stunned as she. T'Holly flashed her a smile that made him look years younger.

Straif cleared his throat. "Another Blackthorn."

T'Holly looked at him from over his brandy snifter. "Not a legitimate Blackthorn. Not born of a HeartMate or in wedlock."

Blankness showed in Straif's expression.

"Straif, your father was married to my sister, HeartMates. Your FatherSire was also HeartBound—but later in life. Before he found his HeartMate he was a man of wild lust." T'Holly shrugged. "According to FirstFamily gossip, he sired children, but we thought they'd all died."

After a gulp of whiskey, Straif said, "Apparently not. I would have welcomed another Blackthorn into the Family."

"Too late for that. The challenge has been filed. The claimant wants everything. You're adversaries now," T'Holly said.

"We'll stand by you," T'Ash said.

Straif's smile was grim. He nodded. "My thanks." He leaned forward, resolution in every sinew, eyes burning. "Too late. But I'll fight this claimant to my last breath." His eyes narrowed. "I've let my Residence and estate deteriorate, but I wisely invested the T'Blackthorn fortune and it's tripled.

That's in my favor." His lip curled. "The only things the First-Families respect more than gilt is Flair. How powerful is this Blackthorn's Flair?"

"The Blackthorn was raised from Commoner to Grace-House Level," T'Holly said.

"Not as powerful as my own, then. Another point in my favor," Straif muttered. "What Flair does the Blackthorn have?"

"I won't answer that. The claimant wishes to remain unidentified. I can give you no clues," T'Holly said.

"Who will be the determining body in this matter?" asked Mitchella.

T'Holly said, "The judge of Straif's and the other Black-thorn's claims to determine the true T'Blackthorn will be All-Class Council."

"Including GraceHouses, GrandHouses and GreatHouses, the FirstFamilies," T'Ash said. Consideration lit everyone's eyes—tallying alliances, Mitchella thought. Politics. Interesting to watch, but her heart ached for Straif. He had enough problems.

Straif leaned back and snapped his glass onto a nearby table. "I can win this. I haven't participated in many FirstFamily Councils, it's true, but I might have made the minimum six in the last three years. As for GreatRituals," his smile grew sharp, "I was at D'Holly's HealingRitual last summer, and I *presided*—acted as priest and Lord—for the FirstFamilies Forgiveness Ceremony in the matter of Ruis Elder." Everyone except Mitchella winced. Like most of Celta, she'd watched the Forgiveness Ceremony on holoviz. And like most Commoners, she'd enjoyed seeing the FirstFamilies kneel. Danith had been solemn and graceful, T'Ash stoic, T'Holly stern.

"Presiding over such an unique GreatRitual as the Forgiveness Ceremony must count as participating in at least three GreatRituals. There was much preparation for that Ritual. It was long and very draining in energy and Flair."

T'Holly nodded, sipped his brandy, then, with gaze fixed on Straif, said, "There's something else you need to know. The other Blackthorn doesn't have the Family's flawed gene."

Nine

"*What?*" asked Straif, desperately hoping that he'd misheard his uncle T'Holly.

"The Blackthorn who is claiming your estate and fortune is definitely of the Blackthorn Family bloodline, but not the dominant blood. The claimant does not have the flawed gene."

The world shifted, his vision grayed. For a moment, Straif thought of giving everything up—the Residence, the estate, the fortune, all his past. His future with his HeartMate. Thought of letting the *bad* side of the Family, his side, die out naturally. He would cut all his ties with Druida, wander Celta as he had done before when searching for a cure.

Mitchella must have leaned toward him, because he felt the warmth from her body come closer, her fragrance drifted to him. "You have great Flair, greater than this other," she said. "*You* know all the ancient traditions and Rituals and history of your Family, not this stranger."

"Since I was seventeen, I've looked for a remedy for my situation. It's been my only goal," he whispered.

Drina whined a mew and rose to knead his legs. Small sharp claws digging into his thighs focused his mind. She didn't stop there, but nipped his thumb.

I will NOT give up MY Residence, she projected so loudly

that he thought Mitchella might have heard, since she drew back. The fine hair on top of Drina's head ruffled his nose, and he found that he'd hunched over, as if from a blow.

T'Blackthorn Residence is Mine!

"Oh, well, in that case . . ." Straif said drily, straightening. The others laughed.

Drina sat, every inch of her small body radiating determination, looking as Noble as any cat could.

Straif imagined losing everything, and it was very different than conceding everything to one who might be better for the Family line. His head raised in pride as blood pumped through him at the threat to *his* Family. The Family he'd known and loved, not this stranger, living outside the T'Blackthorn gates.

"I won't quit," he grated. "I must work harder at discovering a correction for the deformed gene I carry. If I can do that, the Councils will award T'Blackthorn to me."

Mitchella withdrew her hand. When he glanced at her, she turned her head and met his gaze. "What of your Residence?"

"A good question," T'Holly said. "You have chased your cure for years to the detriment of your estate. The Councils can see that—easily, just by viewing your Residence. I rather think that whether you stay in Druida and restore it, and how well you renovate it, will be the primary test of whether you remain T'Blackthorn."

"Go on," Straif said.

T'Holly set aside his snifter and leaned forward. His eyes nearly pinned Straif to his chair. "You are currently in control of the ancestral estate and the Residence. If you leave Druida again, your Residence as it is, I think most people would consider that forfeiting your heritage."

"I would," T'Ash said.

Heat from anger and shame and guilt crawled under his skin. T'Ash would be his harshest judge, for T'Ash had had his Family ripped away, had survived Downwind and rebuilt his Residence, bonded with his HeartMate to rebuild his line. Straif jerked a nod to T'Ash. "Refurbishing the Residence will be my first order of business, then. I haven't been examined by the Healers here in Druida lately, nor have I requested a formal reading from the Vines. There are avenues in Druida for me to explore in mending my disordered gene."

"It isn't going to be as easy to win as you think, Straif. Get your testimonials in order, your documents showing that you didn't totally neglect your duties." T'Holly glanced at Mitchella. "Restore the Residence as quickly as possible." He stood and stared down at Straif, expression stern. "I sought you out because I wanted to tell you of this in person. But I also wanted to warn you, the T'Blackthorn Family funds on deposit with T'Reed will be frozen tomorrow until the title of T'Blackthorn is awarded again to you—or to the new claimant."

Blood drained from his head, leaving him clammy with cold sweat. He'd been without gilt before, usually in the wilds of Celta where it didn't matter. But he'd always known that he only needed the nearest bank or NobleHouse to replenish his gilt. No more. What would he do?

Drina mewed. Mitchella's warm fingers draped over his closed fist. "I'm a middle-class woman. I can make the Residence a showplace on a small budget." Since his vision had narrowed, he turned his whole head to see her. Her smile curved in appreciation of a challenge. A kernel of relief budded. She could do it.

"You came last summer at my request to aid me in my feud with T'Hawthorn and stayed at T'Holly Residence, but I paid you no gilt," T'Holly said to Straif.

Anger spiked. "As if I would take gilt for supporting my Family."

One side of T'Holly's mouth quirked. "You are blood of my sister. Your FatherSire, father, and you are all formally allied with my Family. You also came when we needed you to track your cuzes who had disappeared. You took no payment for that, either."

"I don't want payment for that." Straif recalled the accounts he'd studied in the afternoon. "I've done many explorations for the Councils, sent reports, charts, and maps to the Councils for their use. I've earned my annual noblegilt." His glance fell on his hands, scarred in his travels. He told the truth. But any gilt he'd accumulated sat in the same account as the T'Blackthorn fortune. "I'll contact T'Reed tonight and separate my personal funds from my Family's."

Mitchella's and Drina's resolve infused him, but his own

feelings were far beyond that. This was war. "I think I should move up the GreatRitual to rehabilitate the Residence from the full twinmoons to the new twinmoons." He shot Mitchella a glance. "That's only three days away. I can take care of the Grove of the Dark Goddess and clean out the fountain, but can you help with—say the west terrace for refreshments?"

An instant of panic lit her eyes, then she blinked. "Yes."

Smiling at T'Holly, Straif said, "Please bring as many of T'Holly Household as you wish to the GreatRitual, next new twinmoons." Mitchella's fingers twitched, but the more he thought about it, the more he believed it to be good strategy. He could remind everyone of his great Flair, Flair enough to rebuild a home, to direct a GreatRitual.

T'Holly inclined his head, one Noble lord to another. "I have no doubt that you will remain T'Blackthorn. The Noble Council is investigating the claim of the other, the qualifications, the character." T'Holly hesitated, then spoke lowly. "You should know, the other is not only a Noble, but one who takes Noble duties quite seriously, a respected member of the Noble Council."

Straif grunted. He'd already accepted that he'd made a bad mistake in leaving Druida so long to search for something that would make his Family safe again. Now he knew that mistake might very well cost him more than he could afford.

*M*itchella steadied her breathing. *The evening had been* one surprise after another. The most astonishing of all was how emotionally involved she was already with Straif Blackthorn. As she watched him absorb blow after blow, she reacted herself, with tenderness, determination, ready to fight his battles with him. She'd never in her life thought of fighting anyone's battles but Antenn's and her own. Perhaps it was living with Antenn that made her more vulnerable to Straif. Just as with Antenn, there was something a little lost under outward toughness.

She shouldn't take on his fights. She was a Commoner, with average Flair. In every way, he'd outclass her, win any contest. Still, the image of him wielding a broom at a huge cobweb or two that she'd spotted in T'Blackthorn Residence was apt, and if the battlefield was renovating T'Blackthorn Residence, she was the expert and he the novice. She didn't know how much gilt he might have personally, probably what she considered a fortune. With that she could certainly rehabilitate the house. Even with a tiny budget, she could convince suppliers to donate furniture, especially the Clovers. She could wheedle loans, call in favors. But the man belonged to the highest circles of Celtan society, so he'd have powerful alliances of his own. She was sure that there were vast storerooms of out-of-fashion furnishings in T'Blackthorn Residence. She'd bet her salary that most of what she needed to make the Residence a showplace was available there.

While she mulled over the new circumstances, T'Holly rose and bowed to T'Ash and Straif, kissed Danith's fingers and crossed to Mitchella. He studied Straif's grip on her hand with a slight smile, then bowed deeply, as if she was a Noble Lady. He waved a hand at the chamber. "You have shown excellent style and understanding of your clients, here. I am sure you will be equally successful in redesigning T'Blackthorn Residence. With your help, Straif will keep his title, estate, and fortune."

Mitchella's stomach plummeted as she realized that the outcome of this high-stakes maneuvering could very well rest on her shoulders—or depend on her taste.

Straif kept hold of her fingers and cradled them in both of his hands. "I have no doubt that between the two of us—"

Drina yowled. He glanced at the small cat on his lap.

"—between the *three* of us, T'Blackthorn Residence will amaze the Councils with its beauty."

"Of course," Danith said.

Before Mitchella could find words to answer all these expectations, T'Holly had left, escorted by T'Ash. She consulted an antique timer on the wall and smiled brightly. "I must go." It was earlier than she usually left, but she began to feel trapped in a net of Noble schemes. If so much depended upon her, she wanted to return to work immediately.

She jerked her hand from Straif's and stood. Drina increased the level of her purr, and Mitchella understood the FamCat preferred Straif's attention focused on her. Once again she hoped that their tastes would not clash. She glanced at Straif and found him watching her. They, and the Residence, must learn to work together, though she was sure each of them was used to working alone. Each of them had definite ideas. Wonderful. This project was becoming more difficult by the moment.

"I must go. There's much to do, and I have a feeling that we have little time." She glanced at Danith. "Do you have any idea how long AllClass Council will give us to repair the property?"

Danith shook her head.

Hands on hips, Mitchella stared at Straif. "Do you?"

"No," he said. "I don't. Perhaps a season, probably not longer. Since spring equinox is upcoming, I'd say we should plan on a large open-house or party on summer solstice."

A wave of horror washed over her. "So soon?"

He raised his brows. "Plenty of time."

That's what he thought. She turned on her heel and marched to the door, but he was there ahead of her, holding it open for her and Danith, who had followed.

Danith glanced from Straif to Mitchella, looking anxious.

Mitchella sailed through the door and down the corridor to the great hall and front door, aware of Danith and Straif following. The butler and T'Ash were in the entryway. When the butler saw her, he opened a concealed closet door and withdrew her wrap.

T'Ash took her cloak and dismissed the butler. Thrusting her cape at her, T'Ash scowled at Straif. "You're sure about this GreatRitual on new twinmoons? It's in three days."

"We can do it," Straif said. Mitchella nearly snatched her wrap from T'Ash's grip. The sooner she was out of Noble Country, the better. She'd have time to consider the new circumstances regarding the project, and plan.

But Straif took the cloak from her and settled it around her, resting his hands on her shoulders. They were warm and strong and strangely comforting. *He* should be the nervous one, but apparently he'd already accepted the startling situation.

Straif narrowed his eyes. "I must choose who I invite carefully." He bowed to T'Ash. "Thank you for saying we are allied."

T'Ash stuck out his hand. Straif stepped from behind

Mitchella to grasp arms with T'Ash. "I affirm a formal alliance with T'Ash," Straif said.

"I affirm a formal alliance with T'Blackthorn," T'Ash said, squeezed Straif's arm, then dropped it.

"Good," said Danith. "A person can never have too many friends. We'll be at your Ritual. We'll bring some Fams, too, those whom I'm training and have good Flair."

Drina sniffed, making it echo throughout the great hall.

Straif's lips twitched. "A good idea, D'Ash." A considering look came to his eyes. "I trust the Ashes, and any Fams. But as for human participants in the Ritual—"

"Invite Holm and Lark," T'Ash said.

Straif's startled look matched her own spurt of surprise.

"Do you think that's wise?" he asked.

T'Ash said, "It's been eight months since T'Holly and D'Holly have seen their son. Their broken vows of honor wear on them. Time to start the resolution of this whole mess. No better place than the neutral ground of T'Blackthorn estate. No better occasion than a GreatRitual where natural bonds can mend. All the other Hollys will welcome Holm and Lark, will make it easier on everyone."

Mitchella stared at T'Ash. She hadn't thought the man had such sensitivity. Danith went to her husband, stood on tiptoe and kissed his lips. "A very good idea, HeartMate."

T'Ash flushed. Danith slipped an arm around his waist, tilted her head at Straif, then a distant, inward look came to her eyes. "Ask Captain'sLady Ailim SilverFir Elder, too. She's heavy with child, due to birth soon, and such energy will help your Ritual. You can ask her to officiate as the Lady to your Lord."

Straif caught Mitchella's hand and lifted it to his lips. "Mitchella will be the Lady of that Ritual."

Again Mitchella jerked her hand free. "Absolutely not. I will *never* act as Lady in a GreatRitual. I have not the Flair."

Scowling, Straif said, "You're the woman who is and will be responsible for restoring the Residence, thus you are integral to the Ritual."

Mitchella took two strides away from him, toward the door, hugging her cloak close. "No. I *will not*. You have a HeartMate, I won't *ever* act as your Lady in a capacity that should belong to her."

"Ask Ailim Elder," T'Ash said. "Since her husband nullifies Flair and can't participate, she will be a single woman in the Ritual. Best to invite pairs, or ensure there is an equal balance of male and female."

"I agree that I should take part in the Ritual," Mitchella said coolly, "but I can pair with G'Uncle Tab Holly. He's the only Holly I know well." She smiled as she thought of the old man, owner of a fencing salon.

"How do you know him?" demanded Straif.

"He has many treasures from his seafaring days and wanted advice on what to display and still keep his rooms comfortable," Mitchella said. "I've worked with him. He's charming."

"I'll consider it," Straif snapped. "Yes, I'll have to think on who to invite." His smile was grim. "I might offer alliances." His expression sharpened.

Mitchella took three more steps toward the door. His Flair throbbed from him, nearly visible. She was seeing a powerful GrandLord calculate strategy.

"Right," he continued, more to himself than to her. "If I'm in the debt of several, they might be more inclined to keep me as GrandLord instead of the new claimant. More advantage to them."

The thought of being in debt to the most powerful cadre on Celta made Mitchella's stomach twist. She laid her hand on the door latch. The evening had been exhausting. She remembered Straif's words when they first met and shook her head at the irony. Restoring a GreatHouse, making it a showplace, with gilt no object. She always knew such a job was too good to be true.

"Merry meet," she began her good-byes.

"And merry part," Danith and T'Ash replied in unison. Straif's brows lowered. Drina made a happy sound.

"And merry meet again," Mitchella said.

"I'll escort you home," Straif said.

"No. It's after working hours, GrandLord. Please allow me the choice of my own company." She smiled not too sweetly.

Danith frowned and T'Ash growled, "T'Blackthorn." There was no future for a FirstFamily GrandLord who needed to reestablish his Family bloodline and a sterile woman. Mitchella was surprised T'Ash was concerned for her, but he'd do anything to spare Danith worry, especially now she was pregnant, including protecting her friend. Mitchella dipped her head in thanks, and his gaze softened. Perhaps they'd come to a common understanding after all. They both loved Danith.

"I'll see you tomorrow morning, then, at Work bell," Straif said, looking thwarted.

"Yes," Mitchella said. She'd just opened the door when a mental shriek and stabbing pain flung her against the wall.

Fire!

Ten

❦

Fire! The word, the image of flame and smoke, panic, burst into Mitchella's head and sent her reeling back into the wall.

"Fire!" she cried, echoing Trif's mental shriek. "My home. Antenn, Trif!"

Straif was there, his hands gripping her shoulders. "Visualize so we can 'port."

Danith wrapped her arms around Mitchella as she swayed, a telepathic link snapped between them. Danith grasped Straif's wrist and sent images of Mitchella's rented house and street.

T'Ash connected with them through Danith, grim. *Fire,* he whispered mentally. Before Mitchella could stave off his memories, she saw his Residence burn. She screamed again.

"I've got the coordinates. We go on the count of three," Straif said. "One. Two. *Three.*"

An instant later the cold rush of spring night air wrapped around them as they materialized outside Mitchella's home. It burned, flames flickering behind shattered windows, reaching upward from the second story to the roof. Neighbors crowded the street. Smoke rasped her eyes and throat.

"Mitchella, we've scryed the AirMages!" A neighbor shouted, mixed horror and excitement in her voice.

T'Ash and Danith stepped away from Mitchella and Straif.

"Antenn, my Antenn, Trif!" she screamed, flinging herself forward. Straif's steely grip held her back.

"I can't lose them!" She struggled with all her might, but he held her fast.

"I'll 'port inside. Mitchella, *think,* give me coordinates," Straif panted.

Her mind gibbered so she concentrated on the strength in his fingers.

"Where would they be, Mitchella?" asked Danith.

"Can you link with your cuz Trif?" demanded T'Ash. "I Tested her. She has more than ordinary Flair."

Mitchella *reached* with all her senses. Inhaled smoke and coughed. "Mainspace. Far left corner. Trif around Antenn around Pinky." She knew that room intimately, had tinted every wall, refinished the floor and baseboards, furnished it. Knew the exact dimensions. She visualized a holo of the chamber with a measurement grid. Sent the image to Straif.

He jerked a nod. "T'Ash?" snapped Straif, holding out his hand.

T'Ash settled into himself. "Right." He grasped Straif's hand. "On three. One. Two. Three."

They were gone.

Mitchella cried out and lunged after them, but Danith held her back with slim fingers on her arm and a twist of heavy Flair. "Let the men get them. They're FirstFamily Lords, with great Flair. We can't match them in that. We'll handle the cleanup."

There would be no cleanup. Not of the house. It couldn't be saved. Mitchella prayed the child of her heart and cuz were safe. Tears welled and leaked from her eyes. Her breath came in ragged sobs of fear. Though the fire raged, the only warmth Mitchella felt was Danith's fingers.

"The men have them!" Danith's face shone with triumph. "They're all 'porting to Primary Healing Hall. Let's go. I must care for Pinky. Does anyone in this neighborhood have a glider?"

Mitchella stared. Her throat had closed with terror, and she tried twice before she could speak. "We're not so affluent."

At that moment the AirMages showed up, six of them, each partnered with a Persun who stored Flair. They ran to surround the house. With trained efficiency as they raised their arms, a net of white light wove between them, multiplying from six strands to a full shining cloth of energy.

"I've scanned inside, no one's there," the SecondLevel Air-Mage in charge said. She stood close to Mitchella and Danith. The AirMage's Persun, a huge man, circled her waist to link with her. Unable to look away, Mitchella watched her belongings burn.

"Let's bring it down and smother the fire!" the AirMage said.

Slowly, steadily, the energy-cloth descended through the house. The Persun sucked in a loud breath as the energy from the fire being snuffed pulsed through the AirMage to be stored by him and later released constructively, to Heal or mend buildings or farm. His skin glowed.

Finally, the fire was out and the AirMages carefully equalized the air pressure of the vacuum inside the house with the atmosphere outside.

Even so, the house collapsed upon itself.

Mitchella bit her lip and swallowed hard. "I always knew the house was poorly made, but it didn't matter."

Danith hugged her. "It had charm."

"Charm is not always the best priority in purchasing a house," the AirMage said, pulling out a note flexistrip. She stated the time of the "incident" and aimed the device at Mitchella. "I take it you are the owner of the property."

The AirMage's tough tone stiffened Mitchella's backbone. "I'm the renter. The owner is GraceLord Jalap, and the insurance company is Saffron and Hops."

The AirMage said, "You weren't in the house? Do you have any idea how the fire might have started? It burned too rapidly."

At that moment a glider-for-hire swept down the street, Aunt Pratty hanging out the window and screaming, "Mitchella, where's my Trif?"

In a trembling voice, Mitchella addressed the AirMage. "I was at dinner with friends. I don't know how the fire started. My ward and my cuz were in the house. They're at Primary

Healing Hall now. That's my aunt, I must speak with her."
Mitchella ran over to join Danith who was trying to calm Aunt
Pratty, who'd exited the glider and leaned against it.

"T'Ash told me that Trif and Antenn have already been
seen by the Healers and can be discharged." Danith hugged
the tear-streaked woman, stroked her hair.

"I heard Trif scream. In my *head*." Pratty snuffled.

Danith handed her a softleaf.

Pratty continued, "Well, she always was the strongest
Flaired of my bunch. Are you sure she's all right?"

Danith cocked her head as if communicating with her
HeartMate. "T'Ash says smoke inhalation only. She should
be completely fine in a couple of days. Hoarse until then. Why
don't we go to them and take them home?" Danith gently
pushed the woman back into the glider and climbed in. "Coming, Mitchella?"

Mitchella glanced at the AirMage who said, "Go. A
guardsman will contact you about the fire." She looked at the
building remnants and sighed. "I'm sorry for your loss."

Mitchella didn't want to think of her loss. The narrow two-
story house was gone. Along with all her possessions, most
particularly her sketch books—and Antenn's. Creative work
forever lost. A great ache threatened to engulf her. But Antenn and Trif were safe, and for that she felt pure relief and
thankfulness.

By the time they reached Primary Healing Hall, Aunt
Pratty had murmured a cosmetic refreshing spell that tidied
her clothes and hair and erased tear tracks. Danith paid the
glider driver, led them into Primary Healing Hall and to the
Noble Sitting Room.

At the sight of Antenn, washed and clean and healthy,
Mitchella let out a whooshing breath. She ran to him, just as
Pratty ran to Trif. He grabbed her and held her hard.

"Are you all right?" she patted him, ran her hands up and
down his skinny arms and back.

"I'm fine. I'm fine. Mitchella, you came."

"Of course, I came. I'll never leave you." Her heart thumped
in her tight chest. She loved this child, and she only wished
she could have spared him this experience. He had too many
bad memories as it was.

He choked and buried his head in her shoulder, and she pretended not to hear his suppressed sobs. Making soothing noises, she rocked him, holding him close. He smelled like boy and the best herbal soap, and she found herself crying, too.

"Here," Straif said, and she started. He moved so quietly! He handed some softleaves to her. She took several and gave a few to Antenn. Furtively he wiped his eyes and blew his nose.

Danith appeared, holding a limp Pinky. "Antenn, he's fine. I sent him into a deep sleep. He'll wake late tomorrow morning."

Antenn disengaged himself from Mitchella, blew into the softleaves one last time, then cradled his small cat. "We're all right," he whispered. "We're really all right." His body shuddered. Glancing at Mitchella from under eyelashes spiky with tears, he cleared his throat and asked, "The house?"

Mitchella gulped. "Gone."

"Where are we going to stay?" asked Antenn.

A very good question.

"With me!" said Danith.

T'Ash slipped his arm around her waist, and she leaned against his awesome strength. His eyes dark, he looked at Antenn and Mitchella and said softly, "You are welcome to stay at T'Ash Residence. There is plenty of room." One side of his mouth kicked up. "Nothing furnished for a boy, yet, but that can be changed. It could be good for the Residence."

Beside her, Antenn's body still held a fine trembling. Mitchella hesitated. T'Ash was genuine in his offer. This evening had brought them to a new understanding—it must have taken all his courage to 'port into a burning building, but he'd done it. And saved lives.

Danith and Straif had expected it of him, and he'd acted like the Noble he was, not the enraged man who'd thrown Mitchella across the city. She could trust him now.

Aunt Pratty wiped away renewed tears. "Of course you'll both move back into the Clover Compound, and Trif as well."

"No, I won't!" croaked Trif. "It wasn't my house that imploded. I have a perfectly fine apartment in MidClass Lodge."

"I need you with me, my dear," sniffled Pratty.

"Just for a couple of days," Trif said, squeezing her mother.

Antenn had gone still. Mitchella hated the idea of returning to the large block of sprawling Clover homes.

"With the huge complexity of Mitchella's current project in renovating my home, I think that she and Antenn should stay on site at T'Blackthorn Residence." Straif's eyes were very blue.

Which would be worse, living with her relatives or T'Blackthorn; being smothered with attention and nosiness or in danger of being seduced? Or living with Danith and T'Ash, Commoners in a cool Residence, guests and not Family. At least at T'Blackthorn's she'd be fulfilling a purpose. At least Straif knew that Antenn must be included in any invitation.

The idea made her a little dizzy. She stared. "Are you serious?"

He smiled. "Of course. To get a real feeling for the Residence, you need to be there, to open yourself to it so it will speak with you."

Pratty moaned a little. "FirstFamily Nobles. They are all so *strange,* and so intent on getting their own way." When she realized what she'd said, she flushed red, but looked at Straif and T'Ash defiantly.

"Antenn and I must discuss this privately," Mitchella said.

Danith gestured to a door Mitchella hadn't noticed. "There's a small scry cubby."

Holding Antenn's hand, Mitchella crossed the room, opened the door, and shut it behind them. Like everything designed for Nobles, the little room held only the best. It was a narrow rectangle with light slate blue tinted walls, an elegant reddwood scrytable and a large golden scrybowl. One deeply cushioned tapestry chair was angled near the table.

As if his knees gave way, Antenn collapsed onto the thick Chinju rug, carefully protecting his cat from jarring. He scooted back against the wall, tipped his head back, and closed his eyes, stroking Pinky.

He was pale, his face thin with approaching manhood, expression serious. With a clutch of her heart, Mitchella wondered if this night had banished the last bit of young boy.

She folded herself next to him, glad to have the wall at her back. For a moment she wanted a cat to pet, thought of Drina, and decided she wouldn't take a chance with a FamCat. "What do you want to do? I'd rather not go back to the family." She shifted her shoulders and released some tension, sagging against the wall.

A small smile curved Antenn's lips. "They're great to visit, but exhausting to live with."

Mitchella chuckled. "Ah, yes, my solitary boy." She brushed brown hair from his forehead.

He grimaced.

"Did I hurt you? What is it?"

"I ran with a gang once."

"You tagged along after your *brother*."

When he opened his eyes, his hazel gaze was intent. "Yeah, but my brother and his Triad-mates tried to take T'Ash's woman, tried to kill both of them."

"T'Ash doesn't hold that against you!"

"Oh, yeah?"

"He *doesn't*." She wouldn't have been sure earlier that evening, but knew, now. "This situation has reconciled things between T'Ash and me. I trust him now, even with you." She tugged gently on a lock of his hair.

"All right." He made a face. "Then I think he and Danith would want to practice on me, as a kid, as a boy. T'Ash is sure that he's going to have sons."

That was true.

"And there's that Zanth FamCat." Antenn lifted Pinky from his lap to his chest. "Zanth is six times Pinky's size. Pinky will always be a little cat. Zanth might tear him up."

Mitchella nearly shuddered at the thought of Zanth herself. "So you don't want to stay at T'Ash Residence, or the Clovers."

"No." He turned his head, and his hazel eyes had shifted more into the brown range. "Is it true, what T'Blackthorn said about being better for you to live at his Residence?"

She recalled how she struggled to hear Straif's house. "I think so."

Antenn withdrew subtly. Mitchella hurried on, "But those aren't all our options!" She waved expansively. "There's space over The Four Leaf Clover," three tiny rooms. "We could look for an apartment in MidClass Lodge—"

"Let's go to T'Blackthorn's. I can keep an eye on him so he doesn't hurt you."

She was flabbergasted. "Hurt me!"

Antenn's mouth set. "He wants you on a bedsponge."

A flush started around her breasts and slipped up her skin. The room was dim, and Mitchella hoped Antenn wouldn't notice. "That doesn't mean we'll end up lovers. I can be completely professional."

"Yes, but like Aunt Pratty says, he's a FirstFamily Lord, and they've had centuries of getting what they want."

"Circumstances have changed with T'Blackthorn." Mitchella wondered how public his situation would become, and when. "There's another claimant to his title."

Eyes gleaming, Antenn said, "Really? Zow, that's interesting. T'Blackthorn screwed up, didn't he? We'd be in the middle of that? High politics."

Antenn was reviving too quickly. "I believe so," she said.

He straightened, setting Pinky back on his lap. "Living there, in a FirstFamily Residence, will really impress the Cang Zhus." The Cang Zhus were the architectural Family Antenn apprenticed with three days a week.

Mitchella caught the edge in his voice. "Have the Cang Zhus been a problem? I thought SupremeJudge Ailim Elder's staff checked on them and you. If you have concerns, tell me. I'll speak with them, and Elder, too."

Antenn hunched a shoulder. "They're not too bad. Just snobs, and I won't find better architects to apprentice with. Seems like a long time before I'll be a Master, though."

Mitchella patted his knee. "Time goes faster than you think."

Antenn snorted, then smiled. "But GrandLord Cang Zhu *will* envy me if we live at T'Blackthorn's. The CZs are strong in Flair, but their Family wasn't founded until three generations after Landing. I hear that often enough. The Mosses—"

"Your family is as Common as dirt, like the Clovers," Mitchella said.

"Yeah, but the Clovers have the honor of being the most prolific Family on Celta. So you have status. People envy you. Even FirstFamilies."

"There is that," Mitchella said evenly.

Lifting Pinky gently, Antenn stood and began to pace. After

one short back-and-forth he nodded. "Yeah, I think we should move in with T'Blackthorn."

"Hmm," Mitchella said. "You're sensitive to homes like I am, and you have more Flair. You might be able to learn to speak to the Residence."

His eyes lit, and he skipped. "Really? Really! Zow."

"In fact," Mitchella rose and shook out her full trous and overtunic, "you can help me." She searched his face. "T'Blackthorn has trouble with some of his Family rooms. If I gave you the Heir'sSuite, you might—no, that won't work."

"Why not? Live in T'Blackthorn's old rooms? Zow! I can help redesign them for a modern boy."

She raised her eyebrows. "There is no Oracle or Seer yet to say the heir will be a boy."

Antenn rolled his eyes. "Yeah, yeah. Well, I can help make it good for a girl, too."

She grinned. "Exactly, but we have a problem. The heir's playroom belongs to Drina."

Antenn frowned. "Drina?"

"T'Blackthorn's Fam, a cat."

Cuddling Pinky close, Antenn asked, "What kind of Fam?"

"A half-Siamese, snotty Fam."

"Is she bigger than Pinky?"

"A little, but she's prissy, and not nearly as muscular."

"Then she won't bother us. We can live at T'Blackthorns and make a bunch of gilt and fame and even help," he ended.

Mitchella figured Drina would be a pain, but let the topic go. She gnawed her lower lip. "I'll put you in T'Blackthorn's sister's old suite. Give the rooms a different resonance with your energy, and T'Blackthorn new memories of the place."

"A *girl's* room?"

"I believe she was a very active girl, and it's a suite."

Antenn scratched Pinky's head, the cat's whiskers twitched. Antenn nodded, standing taller. "If that's what I can do to help, it will be good." He grinned.

Mitchella smiled back. She might get a suite, too. The guest suite. Being from Families as Common as dirt, they'd never had suites of their own.

Beyond the door, the level of noise rose—disturbed people

talking loudly. Mitchella gave Antenn a hard one-armed hug, Pinky one long stroke. "We'd better go back in."

"Yes, we've made our decision, and it's a good one." Antenn nodded again.

Setting her shoulders, Mitchella said, "It sounds as if they are discussing the fire." At the recollection of her loss, tears hovered in her throat. She sniffed, swallowed, then opened the door and walked through it, back to the elegant sitting room and the others.

Eleven

♥

Winterberry, the guardsman, had arrived. He eyed everyone in the Noble Sitting room of Primary Healing Hall, then said, "Yes, the fire was started by a delayed firebombspell."

Blood drained from Mitchella. How could that be? "A firebombspell? I don't have any enemies."

"Firebombspell!" T'Ash's tones were vicious. His lip curled, making him appear infinitely dangerous. She'd seen that look directed at her, once, so she shuddered and stepped back.

Back into Straif's solid, supporting form. He was bigger than she, taller, wider, very comforting despite his own tension. She liked the comfort of him too much, so stepped forward.

His hands curved over her shoulders.

Winterberry raised both his hands toward T'Ash and said, "Calm. You frighten the ladies." Though he spoke in the plural, he stared at Trif who leaned against her mother, face averted. Antenn went to sit with Pratty and Trif.

Danith moved to her husband and pulled his arms around her.

Mitchella envied her easiness with her man. Envied her HeartMate status.

"Mitchella wouldn't know anyone who has the Flair or

malice to set such a spell, especially since a delayed-action spell demands so much Flair," Straif said.

She was learning more about firebombspells than she ever wanted to know. She shook her head in disbelief. "The only one I know who has such Flair is T'Ash." When that man's eyes glittered, she rushed on, "He wouldn't *ever* have done such a thing since his home and Family were destroyed by the first ever firebombspell." What was she saying? Getting deeper and deeper in trouble. Good thing she'd decided not to stay with Danith.

Straif's calm voice came from behind her. "Winterberry, could you tell when the spell was set to detonate?"

Winterberry dipped his head at Straif. "I think the spell was cast sometime in the late afternoon, perhaps WorkEnd bell."

"I was consulting with T'Ash and D'Ash at that time," Straif said.

Mitchella said, "I was visiting shops on Gentian Row. Antenn was at grove-study with the Clover children. We have no enemies."

Frowning, Winterberry turned. When he faced her, Mitchella felt the cool pressure of his Flair fluttering against her like a breeze. Straif stepped from behind her to move in front of her.

The guardsman said, "There was only a slight trace of Flair on the firebombspell, but no one in this room matches that aura."

Mitchella walked from the shield of Straif's body in time to see Winterberry's face go expressionless. "You are all weary. I'll contact you later for more in-depth interviews." He bowed in the direction of Aunt Pratty and headed for the door.

"One moment." Straif curved his palm around Mitchella's shoulder again. "Mitchella and Antenn may be staying with me."

"No!" Aunt Pratty said, flushing when they stared at her.

Straif went to her and sat on his heels, meeting her eyes. "It's Mitchella's and Antenn's decision, but I can protect them. If anyone *is* after Mitchella, she wouldn't want to put the rest of her Family in danger, as she would if she lived in the Clover Compound. I promise you, she will be safe with me."

Pratty seemed mesmerized by Straif. Trif shifted against

her mother, revealing a bright and avid eye and a half smile. The girl's curiosity had been piqued, and she was forgetting her trauma. All to the good, but Mitchella felt a sinking sensation that she and T'Blackthorn would be the subject of great discussion and wild rumor among the Clovers.

Though Antenn glared at Straif, Antenn nodded. He still wanted to stay at T'Blackthorn Residence. His thin shoulders braced, and pride welled in her. He was such a strong person already, he'd grow into a excellent man. "Antenn and I have decided to accept T'Blackthorn's offer."

Aunt Pratty's expression was troubled. "Are you sure?"

Not at all, but Straif had spoken truly of her main reasons. Further, she still needed the job to save her business and didn't want to lost Straif as a client. Mitchella nodded. "Yes, I'm sure of our decision."

"I promise I will protect them," Straif said again.

" 'Say it three and the word will be,' " T'Ash said dryly.

Straif stood. "Then I'll repeat it a third time, I will protect Mitchella and Antenn. Winterberry, you can find them at my Residence for interviews."

"Very good. I will examine the house ruins once more. May you all bide well." With a last sweeping gaze, he left.

Aunt Pratty stood and said, "It's time we left you Nobles to your sche—plans." She kept her arm around Trif. Nodding with great dignity, she finished, "Good night to you all."

Danith hugged them. "Well done, Trif and Pratty. I called T'Ash's driver and glider to take you home. He's outside waiting. Blessed be."

Pratty's face softened. "Blessed be, Danith." Pratty shot a look at Mitchella, then Antenn. "Your family loves you. You'll always be welcome at home."

"Thanks," Antenn whispered, hiding his face.

A rush of tears stung Mitchella's eyes. She went to Pratty and brushed her lips across her face. "We know, Aunt Pratty. I love you. You, too, Trif. I'm so sorry this happened."

Trif kissed Mitchella. "I'm sorry your house is gone. But we're fine, and that's what matters." Her voice was rough from smoke.

Hugging Trif tight, Mitchella managed a weak smile. "Yes. You and Antenn safe is all that matters. Blessings."

Pratty and Trif moved slowly to the door, then out of it.

The realization that she'd lost everything struck Mitchella like a blow. Her sketchbooks. All her pretty clothes. All the furniture she'd spent septhours refinishing. She tottered to the couch, putting an arm around Antenn. She *would not* weep in front of the men.

Danith hurried to sit beside her. "You'll be fine."

"I know." Mitchella forced words around a lump in her throat, tried another smile; it was even weaker. "I didn't lose everything. I have some old things at the Clover Compound. So does Antenn." She'd only lost everything she'd made and purchased as an adult. Her childhood belongings were at the compound—most of the things she'd passed on to others. She cleared her throat. "I have plenty of time to find another place, and the family will furnish it for me." With secondhands or defects from their furniture factory. "And I have a good job, with room and board, such as it is." She looked for Straif and found him studying her with dark eyes.

"We still should have the new twinmoons Ritual in three days," he said.

"Of course," Mitchella croaked.

The door opened, and Drina walked in, tail high. *You left Me. I had to come here all by Myself. All alone.* She sniffed.

"Lady and Lord," Mitchella muttered, and wondered how she could make the Residence look decent in three days.

S*traif woke the next morning, instantly alert. Staring at* the molded and gilded ceiling of the purple parlor, he wished he was still wrapped up in sleep. Contrary to all fears, he'd slept long and dreamlessly. Now that he was awake, all his troubles slithered back into his brain.

His jaw clenched with determination. He'd fight, and fight hard for his estate. Perhaps he *had* run away at seventeen, hadn't done right by his Residence or lands, but he was home now and by the Cave of the Dark Goddess, he'd set his home in order. He'd show the upstart claimant that Straif Blackthorn could not be beaten. He already had the best designer in Druida on-site and ready to help. The Residence would soon be beautiful again.

He'd faithfully attend all the upcoming FirstFamily and Noble Rituals; he grimaced at that thought, but duty was duty. If he was lucky, he'd even find a cure for his faulty gene. Time to have a Healer examine him again. He should also consult the premiere prophet of Celta, young Vinni T'Vine.

With luck and Mitchella's aid, he could groom the Grove of the Dark Goddess for a GreatRitual. He'd never fashioned a GreatRitual, but the Family annals must detail some. He'd brave the ResidenceDen and read them. His lip curled. He had no time to be sensitive about the Residence or his memories. Avoiding the pain of certain rooms was a luxury he could no longer afford.

"Say it three and the spell will be," T'Ash had said. Whispering, Straif vowed, "I will fight for and hold my estate," and repeated it two more times. When the final word faded, a potent mantle of power enveloped him, from the T'Blackthorn land itself, strengthening him.

Mitchella and Antenn had rooms on the second floor, Mitchella in the guest suite, Antenn in Straif's sister's room. That idea had bothered him just about as long as the glider ride from Primary Healing Hall to the Residence.

A smile tugged at Straif's lips. At least one aspect of his life proceeded well. He had the woman he wanted under his roof.

Drina pushed open the door and stalked in. *You did not tell Me that that little, miserable tomCat was staying here, in My Residence.*

"You are much superior to him," Straif soothed. "Consider living with him in peace a challenge."

Lashing her tail, Drina stared at him with narrowed blue eyes. Would she be convinced?

She sniffed.

Probably not.

I will make sure he knows who is Fam and who is only a Cat. The Residence is Mine.

"Right." He foresaw cat fights and frowned.

She yowled in his face. He jumped from his bedroll. *The Cat and his human boy are in My kitchen, eating My food!*

"We can't have that. Where is Mitchella?"

Drina sniffed. *She is there, too. She tried to feed Me, but you are My FamMan.*

He sighed. He'd have been happy to delegate fulfilling Drina's every whim to Mitchella. "I thought you liked Mitchella." Straif dressed.

I like her, but do not want her here except to fix the Residence.

"She and Antenn and Pinky will be staying until the project is done."

Drina whipped her tail. *Then you must work fast.*

"Working fast isn't as important as doing good work, and I'll need your help readying the Grove of the Dark Goddess for a GreatRitual."

"Ggrrrrrr." *Dirty paws work.*

"Right. But as my Fam, I expect you to help. You didn't think you'd do nothing for that blue diamond collar, did you?"

Drina cast a big-eyed gaze at him. *I still get the blue diamond collar?*

"That should wait until I am reconfirmed as T'Blackthorn." She whined.

"Or do you plan on deserting me?"

We had a probation period, she said.

"That was my request, I never heard you agree."

I am your Fam.

"You might want to consider the new claimant."

Drina said, *The land and the Residence support you.*

"How do you know?"

The Residence says so. It says the other Blackthorn was here.

"What!" But it made sense that the other had visited, even entered the Residence. A sour taste coated Straif's mouth, but he was thinking hard. He could walk the estate, looking for his distant relative's tracks, discover who the other claimant was.

The thought of the many tasks he must accomplish gave some satisfaction. He was settling into his new life. He'd review his personal accounts to ensure he could afford the renovations—and hoped he didn't have to trade many favors with other Lords and Ladies. He'd continue on his quest—in Druida—for a fix for his defective gene by consulting the great Healer, GrandLord T'Heather. Straif would set an appointment with the new GreatLord T'Vine—the prophet with the greatest Flair.

Without another word to Drina, he headed for the kitchen. Mitchella wasn't there. The only sign of her was a sheaf of papyrus. A glance at them froze him. All were inscribed with the Blackthorn coat of arms. As he reached for them, he knew that he'd face more memories every day. Probably a good thing. The time for running had long passed. Escape from guilt and pain and loneliness was acceptable in a seventeen-year-old boy, not in a thirty-two-year-old man.

He sat at a table and flipped through the papyrus, scrutinizing Mitchella's plans for renovating the kitchen. A couple of the sheets had finger-imprints. When he touched them, holomodels sprang into being. His suspicions of the day before were right. The Flair appliances were far out of date. At the end were two budgets—one titled "Good" and one titled "No Expense Spared." Straif winced. He could no longer restore the Residence in the manner he'd anticipated—or was that true?

He crossed the room, took the scrybowl from a shelf, and carried it to the table. "Scry T'Reed," he said.

A moment passed. "Here," said T'Reed as the scrybowl showed his old, wrinkled face.

"Greetyou, T'Reed," Straif said.

The man hesitated. "Straif," he said, in an informality that Straif had never heard from him. "I trust you received my updated accounting in your collection box."

Straif smiled coolly. "Probably. I'm sure you were meticulous in separating my personal funds from the T'Blackthorn gilt." He paused to adjust his attitude. He wanted this man as an ally. "I assure you that since I have known you all my life I will *of course* leave all Blackthorn funds with your financial establishment." That should get the man thinking of what another claimant might do—where the other Blackthorn might bank.

T'Reed blinked, then frowned. "Of course the FirstFamilies tend to do business with each other. We prefer our affairs in the hands of those greatly Flaired." He paused. The other Blackthorn *wasn't* as Flaired as Straif.

"I'd like to ask your advice. Do you think the Councils might allow me to use the T'Blackthorn fortune to restore the Residence? After all, the Residence is an extremely valuable asset to the Family, and it does need some renovation."

T'Reed looked thoughtful. "You would have to keep detailed and accurate accounts."

"Of course." Mitchella must always do so.

The older GreatLord mulled over the problem. Straif knew T'Reed's younger son belonged to the Noble Council. As did the new claimant. Perhaps the other Blackthorn already banked with T'Reed. Would that one have tried to influence the FirstFamily Lords and Ladies by doing business with them?

Finally, T'Reed said, "The Councils might allow you to use T'Blackthorn gilt for the refurbishment of the Residence." His gaze sharpened. "I'm sure they would put a limit on spending."

Straif nodded. "Reasonable." He didn't want to be reasonable in restoring the Residence. He wanted it to be perfect. If he had to, he'd use his own gilt.

"I'll speak to members of the Councils, their decision may take a couple of days." T'Reed made a note on a piece of papyrus in front of him. "Straif . . ."

"Yes?"

T'Reed leaned forward. "I am acquainted with the claimant. I'll tell you that that—the claimant—is genuinely concerned about how you let the estate deteriorate and ignored your duties. H—the claimant's sincerity is not in question. This is not a frivolous claim by a fortune hunter."

Straif swallowed hard, inclined his head. "I understand. Is this person the type to use a firebombspell to eliminate someone who'll help me prove my claim?"

"No!" T'Reed spit the word out in shock, then his face changed from horror to rapid calculation. "I don't think so. I would say h—the Blackthorn is honorable."

"Do you know for sure?"

"I had heard of a firebombspell detonating. You think this is connected to your situation?"

"It destroyed Mitchella Clover's house. She is in charge of renovating the Residence."

T'Reed shook his head. "I can't think it of the other Blackthorn."

"Make sure the Noble Council is alerted to the incident and how it relates to T'Blackthorn."

"I will." T'Reed tapped his writestick. "T'Holly sent a message this morning that you will have an open house for representatives of the Councils on summer solstice and the restoration of the Residence could be proof of your dedication to your name and title. The Councils agreed."

"Right," Straif said.

"I think we all understand each other. At the moment. Merry meet," said T'Reed.

"And merry part,"

"And merry meet again," ended T'Reed, then he splashed his scrybowl, cutting the call.

Relief eased a constriction in his chest at T'Reed's use of the ancient words. It was a subtle indication that the man approved of Straif's claim. Sweat prickled at the small of his back.

He recalled he hadn't bathed under a waterfall yet. Glancing around the kitchen, he realized he hadn't eaten either. Still no breakfasts in the no-time, and he didn't want to eat in the GardenShed. He rasped a hand over his beard. Yes, he should clean up before he met Mitchella.

Little slurping noises impinged on his hearing. He circled the counter to see that Drina had been single-minded in getting and eating her breakfast. It looked like shredded furrabeast. Even though he didn't want such a meal, his mouth watered.

"A cook arrived this morning. He said T'Holly sent him," the Residence said.

"Yes?" The day looked better.

"The cook has been cleaning and settling into his apartments. I will tell him you wish to see him."

"Right." Straif had wanted to use those rooms. Too bad.

He looked around, wondering if he should stand or sit. He didn't have experience in being an employer, none in working with household staff. Anything he might have remembered from his boyhood would play him false because then everyone had been Blackthorns. He shrugged renewed pain aside.

The door at the far end of the kitchen opened, and a gangly young man entered. Straif stared. "You're my new cook? How old are you?"

"Twenty," the youngster flushed. "I'm Gwine Honey, and I'm good. I'm the Holly cook's nephew. He's been adopted into the Holly Family."

"I don't do adoptions." Bloodline was paramount to Straif.

Gwine reddened more, jerked his head up. "That's fine. But I cook well, and I want to learn and practice fancy dishes. This would be a good place for that. And I work cheap."

Straif ground his teeth. "I don't think—"

"Pride!" Mitchella scolded from the door behind him. "I think you have a bit too much pride right now, *T'Blackthorn.*" She passed him, and her fragrance set him to thinking of other pleasures than food. She held out a hand to Gwine. "I'm Mitchella Clover, overseeing the Residence restoration. Since T'Holly sent you, you must be qualified. Lady and Lord knows, we need all the staff we can get." She smiled at the young man.

He lifted her hand to his lips and kissed it.

Twelve

❦

Straif smiled—with teeth—at his new cook, Gwine Honey.
The young man hastily dropped Mitchella's hand.

Straif said, "I'm particularly fond of breakfast. Why don't we start with that meal?"

Without a word, Gwine disappeared into the cook's apartments. Straif scowled, feeling rumpled, and glanced down. He *was* rumpled. His clothes looked as if he'd slept in them. He hadn't, but he hadn't put them in the cleanser either. They were a good sturdy shirt and trous, bespelled for toughness as opposed to cleanliness or to be wrinkle-free.

Mitchella watched him with raised eyebrows. "I think the Residence has enough energy to cleanse our garments." Her chin wobbled. "Several of my cuzes will be sending me clothes. There are plenty of Clover boys who can outfit Antenn. My family will be delivering things for us"—she shot Straif a look—"along with some top-of-their-line furniture." Her spine straightened. "The Clovers don't often furnish FirstFamily Residences, but I promise you, the pieces I have chosen will be exactly what is needed for the Heir'sSuite and guest rooms."

"Of course," Straif said softly. She wore the same elegant evening tunic and trous that she'd worn the night before and looked as fresh as she had then. But there was a shadow in her eyes—the shadow of loss.

He wanted to see her smile. More, make her smile. He said, "I suppose that sexy green onesuit you wore when we met is gone?"

Her lips tipped up a little, sending a spurt of satisfaction through him.

"Yes."

"I'll pay for a replacement. I'd like to see you in a tight onesuit again." He'd like to see her happy. Oddly enough, his own grief seemed much less this morning.

Mitchella stepped toward him.

The cook hurried into the room, carrying a large basket. "My tools," he said. He set the basket on the floor next to the hot-square, pulled out some long-handled items that Straif vaguely recognized. "What do you want for breakfast?"

"Eggs. I always like eggs, at least three. Some porcine strips—crispy," Straif said.

"There are eggs and porcine strips in the supply no-time," the Residence said.

Honey jumped.

Straif smiled. "Residence, I make you known to Gwine Honey, currently our cook."

"Greetyou," said the Residence politely.

Still looking unnerved, Honey stared around, headed to the no-time cabinets.

Drina hissed.

Honey jumped again, looked down. "A cat, a cat in the kitchen."

"She says you nearly stepped on her tail. And she's a Fam-Cat. My FamCat," Straif said, beginning to enjoy himself.

"I can do this," Honey muttered. "Uncle Holly said there might be a cat. I can do this. Talking houses. I can do this. A talking house could be a benefit. If Uncle Holly can do this, *I* can do this. No-time storage present three eggs, ten porcine strips, and best oil." The cabinet door opened.

Straif leaned against the large counter in the middle of the room. "Feel free to make several breakfasts and stock the prepared meals no-time. We are woefully short of breakfasts."

Scooping up the food and closing the no-time door, Honey

muttered, "Eggs the proper temperature, good." At the hot-square, he glanced at Straif. "How do you like your eggs?"

"Just soft-flip them." Straif grinned.

Mitchella hooked her arm in his. "The Residence has cleaned the small dining parlor, let's leave GentleSir Honey to his work." She beamed a smile at him. "The Residence will tell you the way."

He flinched, flicked his fingers over the hot-square. "High heat," he ordered, then bent, took a pan from his basket, set it on the hot-square. "Breakfast will be ready in ten minutes."

Letting Mitchella lead him into the open-doored small dining parlor, Straif decided the young Honey could stay. There was a sizzle, and the aroma of frying porcine ladened the air. A wonderful odor. Food.

"He's hired. For the moment," Straif said.

As Straif ate the tasty meal, he listened to Mitchella's initial plans for the Residence. They impressed him. He relayed his conversation with T'Reed, and a shadow seemed to lift from her when she heard of a larger budget.

After Honey cleared his plate, Straif complimented the young man. "Please have dinner ready at Sunset bell. Also, I'll be hosting a Ritual here in three days with many of the First-Families and their dependents." Straif's brows knit. "Give ideas for food to Mitchella. You both can decide what to serve."

"Me?" said Mitchella.

He smiled reassuringly. "Just serve what you would to your Family at a GreatRitual." He waved a hand.

"We do potluck," Mitchella muttered. "Residence, provide the menus for the last major spring Ritual, or any GreatRitual where the current T'Blackthorn was absent." She glanced at Straif. "So scents and tastes won't trigger memories."

"I will recite the menus to Honey when he returns to the kitchen," said the Residence.

"Good idea, Mitchella," Straif said, pleased she was conscious of his comfort. "GentleSir Honey, you are hired through summer solstice. At that time we will be having a large open house and most of the Noble Council will attend. The food must be the best, and, uh, well presented."

The young cook swallowed. "Yes, through summer solstice."

His grip went white on the china. The job was more important to the cook than he'd indicated. Interesting.

Just as Straif reached for Mitchella's hand with the intent of changing the topic from business to pleasure, a boy strode into the breakfast parlor. Since he wore a metallic-cloth cape that glistened with rainbows, he was hard to ignore. He marched up to Mitchella and executed a flawless bow.

"Vinni T'Vine," he said.

The boy prophet. Mitchella uttered a polite, "Greetyou, GreatLord. Pardon me, I must oversee the tinters in the MasterSuite." She curved her lips in a strained smile and slid from the room.

Vinni gazed after her. "I often have that effect on people." He whirled off his cape, tossed it over a chair, then sat next to Straif. "I heard you wanted a consult."

"News travels fast in FirstFamily circles, but I didn't think anyone at T'Ash's would have told you," Straif said.

Drina pranced in, a fleck of porcine on her whiskers. With a delicate tongue, she found it, then gave a refined burp. *T'Vine, good. You came.* She sat down by Straif's foot and curled her tail around her paws. *He has come to tell Us how We will remain T'Blackthorns.*

Straif stared at his Fam. "I'm reconsidering our provisional agreement *and* your diamond collar."

Drina hissed.

Vinni cocked his head. "You *do* want a consultation, don't you? I heard you often conferred with D'Lobelia."

Though the boy had eyes older than his ten years, Straif wouldn't admit that his conferences with Kalmi were more often conducted rolling around a bedsponge than in her ResidenceDen. But T'Vine was right. Straif wanted to ask the GreatLord of prophecy one significant question. He just hadn't expected the Lord to come to him, or so soon. His throat suddenly dry, Straif picked up his glass of water and sipped.

He met the boy's gray gaze. He could have sworn when Vinni walked in his eyes had been blue gray, but they had looked green when watching Mitchella. An eerie feeling feathered along Straif's spine. He quashed incipient nerves. "With the recent change in my circumstances, I don't know if

I could pay your fee." He set his glass down. "I have to watch my gilt."

Smiling, Vinni said, "An invitation to your party could be my fee. Aren't you going to invite me to your party?"

"What party?" Straif asked.

Vinni gestured expansively. "Your new twinmoons party, your summer solstice party, your celebration of . . ." He stopped. Straif was sure he'd been about to reveal a slice of the future and let out a held breath. Vinni raised his eyebrows. The young prophet had learned a little discretion, then. Straif's cuz Holm had told him the boy had made prophecies to Lark and Holm that they hadn't wanted to hear. Vinni's eyes flickered colors.

"Yes?" Straif asked softly.

The boy's mouth turned sulky. "I think we should discuss this in your ResidenceDen. Do a Full Future Reading."

Straif was glad he was sitting, the young Lord's Flair pulsed so strongly it made Straif wary. "Shouldn't I fast or meditate?"

"That's best, but we could do it anyway," Vinni said.

Straif didn't think so. "Your fee, besides a party invitation?"

"Alliance with you during your lifetime."

Straif wondered if that meant he'd live long. He noticed that the boy said nothing about T'Blackthorn heirs, and an eerie chill touched his spine again.

"I don't ally with just *anyone,* you know."

Drina mewed encouragement, then a moth distracted her and she followed it to the windowseat where she caught and ate it.

Vinni stared at her. "I don't have a Fam." Straif didn't know if the boy's statement was gratitude or envy.

Loud, pounding footsteps approached, then another boy shot into the chamber. Straif decided the room needed a door. Antenn skidded to a stop, taking in Straif and Vinni.

Standing, Straif said, "Greetyou, Antenn." The boy was about twelve, but he was not much larger than Vinni—his early childhood years in the slum Downwind had taken a toll. Straif frowned. There was something familiar about Antenn's face.

After a glance around, Antenn said, "Mitchella isn't here."

"She left to supervise the tinters in the MasterSuite."

"Huh," said Antenn. He stared at Vinni. "Who are you?"

Vinni rose and made his perfect bow. "Vinni T'Vine."

Antenn scowled. "I heard about you from Lark Collinson Apple."

Vinni looked intrigued. "How?"

"Lark is a good friend of Trif Clover, my guardian's cuz."

"Ah," Vinni said.

"I don't want you upsetting Mitchella like you upset Lark." Antenn stuck out his chin.

Shrugging, Vinni said, "I'll do what I please."

Straif sat and leaned back, prepared to be diverted by the boys. Antenn had unobtrusively settled into a fighting stance. Straif would put his gilt on the older boy in a fight.

"Spoilt," Antenn said.

"Oh?" Vinni sneered.

"You wouldn't last a minute in a scrim with the Clover boys." Antenn's lip curled.

"You don't think so?"

Since Vinni's Flair sparked, Straif prepared to intervene.

Antenn's eyes widened, but he hunkered down. "No, I don't think so, not without your Flair. But we're all just Commoners, you probably don't know how to fight without Flair."

"Name the time and place," Vinni said.

"Clover Compound, tomorrow afternoon, after grove-study. Even *you* have grove-study, don't you?"

Vinni flushed. "Yes, but I have meetings tomorrow morning. You're a Moss, not a Clover. Can you speak for them?"

"Yes."

With a grand gesture, Vinni pulled on his cape, nodded to Straif. "We should consult before your new twinmoons Ritual, like tomorrow morning. Go ahead and fast before the session, and align your energies with your HouseHeart." Vinni lingered at the open door, smiling faintly. *I knew I was supposed to come to you this morning, but I thought it had to do with your future, not mine,* he sent mentally. With a dip of his head, he left.

"What did he say to you?" demanded Antenn.

"He's a prophet. Do you really want to know?"

Antenn faded a step back, frowning, and Straif knew why he looked familiar. "Antenn Moss, brother to a murderer,"

Straif said softly. "I was there. I witnessed what happened."

The boy seemed to shrink. He looked confused, vulnerable.

"Do you judge him by what his brother did?" asked Mitchella, striding into the room, her expression furious. Straif wouldn't have been surprised if her red hair burst into flames.

He made his voice even. "Antenn would know what a fire-bombspell looked like."

"And explode it on himself! Besides, he wouldn't." She put an arm around her ward. "His brother was one of a Triad, mentally bound to two other boys, unbalanced when they died. That one's Flair was for fire, and he used it destructively. Antenn's Flair is for architecture, for *construction*. He could help us with the Residence, but you only see the past. For him and for yourself. Thinking like this you can't move from the past to the present, let alone plan for the future."

Her words lashed at him, hit wounds. Pain blinded him, all the worse for previously having been soothed by her. Straif couldn't speak. He'd insulted the boy, and Mitchella.

"We'll go now. No charge for my time. I suggest you let the tinters finish coloring the MasterSuite walls. They'll be done by this evening."

"Don't go," he forced the words beyond pain. Looking directly at Antenn, Straif bowed elegantly and as deep as if Antenn had been a FirstFamily GreatLord, noblest of the Noble. "Forgive me. Mitchella is right, I live too much in the past. I would appreciate it if you gave me another chance. The Residence needs Mitchella, and so do I. That is the simple truth. I'm sorry I hurt you. I apologize." It had been contemptible to be so rude to a boy under his protection. "I would be honored if you worked with us in restoring the Residence."

Antenn stared at him with eyes darkened into brown, a hurt, burning gaze.

"It is Antenn's decision," Mitchella said.

A small cream-colored tomcat trotted into the room. Drina bolted from the windowseat to attack. The cats fought and rolled in a yowling battle.

"Drina!" shouted Mitchella.

Straif took his glass of water and tossed the liquid on the cats. They broke apart, Pinky growling and Drina screeching.

Snatching Pinky, Antenn held the small tomcat to his chest and crooned, but his eyes blazed.

"I apologize for Drina, too," Straif said.

I can apologize for Myself. If I care to, Drina said. She had bloody dents in her right ear from Pinky's teeth.

Antenn's eyes narrowed. "I bet *she* won't apologize."

Straif put a fist on his hip and stared at Drina. "You advised me to ask Mitchella to assist us with this project. She's the best person to restore the Residence."

I will not apologize, Drina lifted her nose.

"I apologize for Drina," Straif repeated, glancing at Antenn and Pinky. Pinky looked smug.

Drina sniffed.

"If you decide to remain here, I assure you that Drina will not attack Pinky again."

I will do what I please!

If you attack Pinky, you will forfeit your collar. He meant it, and she knew it. She licked a patch of hair on her shoulder.

"We will stay. You will give all three of us room and board and pay Mitchella's salary like you agreed to, even if you aren't confirmed as T'Blackthorn," Antenn said.

"Mitchella and I signed a contract. I'll honor it." Straif reached out and touched the chair he'd been sitting in—the Lord's chair—and sent the energy of his anger through the wood and into the floor, where the Residence could gather and use it for housekeeping spells. When he met Antenn's gaze again, he knew that the boy would not forgive or forget his words. Antenn would be a big obstacle in Straif's wooing of Mitchella.

"I'm going back to work on the girl's suite," Antenn said. "Mitchella, the Uncles have arrived with our things. Didn't you want them to move some furniture? Since Uncle Mel 'ports well, he can send some items into the attic storerooms. With our help, you should meet your daily goal." He smiled at Mitchella with an expression excluding Straif.

"Daily goals?" murmured Straif.

Mitchella strolled over to Antenn, scratched Pinky behind the ears, and put her arm around Antenn's shoulders again.

When she gazed at Straif, her expression was one of cool professionalism. "Since we have a summer solstice deadline, we need daily goals. I'm working on the MasterSuite. It should be ready this evening. Under the circumstances, I think you should take possession of the suite, just as you should keep possession of the Residence."

He didn't want her cool. He liked her hot, even with anger at him, but now was not the time for conflict. "Right."

She nodded and they left, Pinky purring loudly.

Drina came over and smiled up at Straif, ingratiatingly. *If you work fast and hard, We can send them away soon.*

Straif laughed.

*T*he rest of the morning he scried the First Family Lords and Ladies he thought would support him, or would like to have him indebted, and invited them to the new twinmoons Ritual. He invited twenty-three Lords and Ladies of the First-Families. Nineteen had agreed to come and bring their spouses and heirs.

He noted the proposed allies in the T'Blackthorn History, his first entry as T'Blackthorn. When he'd said the opening spell, he'd sealed the pages of his FatherSire and father. The spell would diminish each day. By the time it wore off Straif hoped he could face reading his father's writing—learning as a man of his father's disappointments and triumphs.

That afternoon he meditated in the Grove of the Dark Goddess, and cleaned out the fountain. T'Ash had told Straif that replacement stones were ready to be fitted into the basins.

Straif raised his Flair and quartered the estate, checking every life-trace. Just walking the land eased his spirit, as it had the day before. It would be good for himself and the estate if he made surveying the grounds a daily goal.

Today he banished the lingering emotional vestiges of the Downwind gangs, T'Ash and Danith D'Ash. Zanth, T'Ash's Fam, had newer, brighter tracks everywhere. As arrogant as his daughter Drina. The thought of the cats lightened Straif's mood. Finally, near the main entrance, he found the other Blackthorn's track.

He stared at it, heart thumping hard at the telltale familial color of silver, the core of a cord-track of blue green gray. He'd never thought to see that bright silver again until he had children. Why couldn't the other have contacted Straif? He'd have welcomed the man into the Family. But now they were adversaries and his relative was hiding.

And it was a man.

Straif settled into his balance, connected with T'Black-thorn land, increased his Flair until the air resting on his skin was almost painful. He drew all he could of the other into himself to analyze. It was more difficult than he imagined. The energy did not combine well with his. It was sluggish, not as pure a bloodline, not as Flaired. As he pulled the energy from the track upward into his body, he knew he could not let the other's essence near his heart, soul, or balls. He pinched off a bit and shot it to the seat of his Flair, examined it in a burst of his own psi power that destroyed the morsel.

A man, nearly as old as Straif. Not as Flaired, more staid. HeartBonded.

That was a shock. The other Blackthorn was already Heart-Bonded, and Straif wasn't ready to search for his HeartMate.

The other Blackthorn was a father. Two children.

Straif fell to his knees at the insight.

Should he yield to the other claimant? Perhaps.

Could he yield?

No!

His Family had died, and he was flawed, but with that defective gene Straif had the pure traits of the Blackthorns, the great Flair for tracking and hunting. He had the heart, blood, bone tie with the lands and Residence.

He wasn't happy that he had to fight a relative for the T'Blackthorn title, but he'd do it.

The sky around him dimmed as Bel set. The evening turned humid, indicating more rain. His bond with the land, and his appointment with T'Vine in the morning spurred Straif to visit the HouseHeart. He'd do it after dinner. Much as he wanted to spend that time with Mitchella, his duty lay elsewhere.

Thirteen

♥

Mitchella and Antenn ate dinner by themselves in the small dining parlor, then went upstairs to finish the suite Straif's sister, Fasha, had lived in and Antenn now occupied.

"We did really well," Antenn said, examining the bedroom. "I like it." The rooms had been cleaned by simple spells and physical labor, the walls tinted white with a tinge of cream. The color was the best for full-room holos. Antenn was in a phase where the Great Platte Ocean fascinated him, so the entire suite was set at Maroon Beach. The inexpensive carpet was the same dark red color of the sand that edged the bottom of the holos. Walls showed ever-changing surf. The ceiling was dark now, as if fading with the day, stars coming out. Tomorrow it would show a lovely summer sky. One of Mitchella's specialties was holo walls. This was her best yet. A new bedsponge with linens lay in the corner where Pinky snoozed.

Dismantling the rooms had been heartbreaking. She'd known at once that the girl—Fasha—and her mother had decorated it. The suite had been perfect for an active girl—causing Mitchella a twinge of envy at the luxury. But the rooms also reflected that Fasha had been well loved.

Mitchella had taken great care with the holos and portraits, the small prized treasures, packing them carefully. Someday Straif might want to tell his daughter of her Aunt Fasha.

The bathroom was spare, suiting the boy, and the playroom would soon hold boy things. "So there are rooms the guy won't go into, huh?" His voice held a sneer.

"If you lived in the house where your dead brother's room was, would you visit it? Or would you want to change it?"

"I'm not like Shade! And Shade was trying to reform."

"I know you aren't like Shade, no more than I'm like my brothers, and in the end Shade became unbalanced. He killed people, hideously."

"You think I don't know that? You think I don't hear about it all the time?"

"What? Tell me!"

Antenn flopped down onto his new bedsponge. "The Clovers don't care if I'm a murderer's brother, especially the adults. They don't talk about it at all. The Cang Zhus do talk."

"We'll find you a better apprenticeship. You don't have to live with that."

He stared at her with dark eyes. "Yes, I do. Every day. You know all about living with nasty facts every day." Antenn looked away. "I know that it will affect my future—my career and any family I might want."

Pinky awoke and curled up on Antenn's stomach.

Mitchella sighed and dropped down beside him, took his hand. "You've been doing so well since you went to the mind-Healer."

"So have you," Antenn said.

She winced. He'd insisted that if a mind-Healer treated him, she should go, too. Mitchella stroked his head. "We're looking forward instead of past, which is healthy. But you don't need to stay with people who believe you're flawed because of your brother's crimes."

He lifted a shoulder. "I usually ignore the CZs' attitude. They aren't so bad, and they're excellent architects. That's what matters—learning from them. They won't ever offer me a position with their firm, and I don't want one."

"All right."

"T'Blackthorn will always think of me as Shade's brother." Antenn slanted her a look. "He's stuck in the past."

"In a way, Straif had a worse experience. He was older than we were when we lost our family—my future family, your brother. He'd had everything, then everything destroyed."

"Yes, Fasha's stuff was unbelievable. Everything top-of-the-pyramid."

"We don't need to stay here, if you don't want to."

"What, give up my ocean suite?" He smiled. "No."

Glancing around the room, he said, "Well, we've done the heir's playroom for the snotty cat, Fasha's suite is now mine, and you worked hard on the MasterSuite. It's so different, Blackthorn shouldn't have problems living there."

Mitchella wasn't so sure—but she'd changed everything she could—walls, floors, ceilings, window treatments, and most of the furnishings. The bed had presented a problem.

Antenn brushed his hands together. "So we've redesigned several of the rooms Blackthorn didn't like."

"The MistrysSuite has been cleaned, D'Blackthorn's furniture placed in storage." Straif's mother's rooms had been emptied of her clothes and small personal items. Mitchella deduced the Hollys had done that. "Straif's HeartMate can decorate the MistrysSuite in her own style." If Mitchella kept repeating the word *HeartMate,* perhaps it would penetrate more than her brain—slip into her own heart like a throbbing sliver to prevent a worse wound. She lightened her tone. "The next difficult task is the ResidenceDen. Straif has many memories of that room, and must use it."

"You told me he hates the ballroom. That's a pretty big space, tough to renovate. I've only seen it from the outside terrace. Have you been in it yet?"

"No, the other rooms demanded all my attention."

With a satisfied look at their surroundings, Antenn stood. "Let's go see." He grinned. "A FirstFamily Residence Ballroom, the height of luxury. What an opportunity for you. I don't remember T'Ash Residence having a ballroom, but it's new." He went into the corridor.

Mitchella followed. "T'Ash has three rooms that can be combined for a ballroom. Danith D'Ash and I haven't decorated them yet." Mitchella's steps lagged. She'd accomplished a great deal today, but much of the time had been emotionally draining as well as physically tiring. She didn't know if she could face another sad chamber. But Antenn's eyes gleamed with curiosity, and she set her misgivings aside. "I want to check Drina's room first." So they went to the heir's playroom.

The FamCat lay smugly in the center of the bedsponge surrounded by beautiful, iridescent gauze.

"Sure looks like a snotty cat," Antenn said.

Drina sat up, stared haughtily at them, flicked the tip of her brown tail, mewed. *Everyone adores Me.* She sent the words so loud Mitchella heard them."

Antenn snorted. "I don't."

The small cat sniffed. *Everyone who is Anyone adores Me.* She turned her back on them and settled into a soft pillow.

"I guess we've been dismissed," Mitchella said. The room was lovely, perfect.

A few minutes later they hovered outside the ballroom. Unlike this morning, she wasn't concentrating on the building or Straif. She felt the sheer dread around the threshold.

"This is bad. There's something really bad about the atmosphere in that room," Antenn said.

"I'm afraid so."

"I can feel it from here," he muttered.

With a big breath, she set her hand on the latch, pushed. It was locked. "Residence," she said, voice not quite steady, "can you unlock?"

The air hummed beneath her hearing. Antenn looked at her wide-eyed.

"T'Blackthorn has given no orders barring you from this room," the Residence said.

She hesitated. "Is there any threat to us?"

"No," said the Residence. "The Hollys cleaned the room molecularly twice. As ordered I have cleaned every season."

"No big swooping cobwebs, then," Antenn said.

Mitchella opened the door. The windows and doors along the terrace wall opposite were swathed in curtains, so the chamber was dim. No fetid air enveloped them, but strong emotional echoes lingered. Sickness, death, grief. Most of all, despair.

"Curtains up," snapped Mitchella. "Open windows." The pale spun-silver curtains shuddered, rolled up to reveal lovely glass. With protesting creaks, the windows opened.

"Doors open, too."

More groans of wood on wood as the glass-paned doors swung open onto the terrace. Cool air and the soft scent of rain swept into the room.

The ballroom was beautiful. The walls were tinted pink with silver flourishes. The square windows and doors were tall and elegant, the hardwood floor shone.

It was empty of everything except oppressive emotion.

"Why is it so scary?" asked Antenn in a tight voice.

Mitchella had decided to ask the Hollys, but the Residence seemed cooperative. Clearing her throat, she said, "Residence, this room needs a Ritual spiritual cleansing. Old feelings still linger too heavily. What happened here?"

"Everyone died," Straif said from the doorway. He glanced in, then averted his gaze.

She jumped. He moved so quietly, with tracker's Flair.

"When the household became ill, this room was used as a sick ward," the Residence said.

"There were more than thirty beds in here at one time," Straif said. "Mine was just a little right of the center, near the windows, where Antenn is standing."

Mitchella flinched. Antenn made a strangled sound.

"You didn't know I caught the sickness and was near death?" Straif's silhouette shrugged. "Father was in the center of the room, easiest to reach. Mother next to him. Then me. Then Fasha." His hand swooped. "Then all the rest of my Family who lived and worked here.

"They all died. I lived. One by one, they died. I'll never forget that last night. All noise stopped. Except my coughing. When I woke up the next day, I was the only one alive. I screamed for my Family, and Holm and T'Holly came." Straif's face was white and strained, his expression terrible. "Now you know. Change this place, but don't ever expect me to enter it." He turned on his heel and walked away.

Antenn looked at her and swallowed.

Mitchella set aside the need to run after Straif and comfort him. He wouldn't welcome her. Better to concentrate on the room, make it bearable for him.

"Those pink walls gotta go," Antenn said, voice high.

"I'll make it an oval, with an illusion of a domed ceiling," Mitchella said. She could see it.

Antenn nodded, studying the dimensions. "Curved walls at the corners, used as closets. The walls are plain, add pilasters, moldings, fancy bits that can be easily removed after a few generations." He shook his head. "Talk about a curse."

"A beautiful holo for the ceiling. Holo spells weren't as fashionable, or as well developed as now. A light, Earth-blue sky with clouds would be good. Cream-colored walls would work well." She hardly knew what she was saying.

Thunder boomed, and Antenn shuddered, paled. "I'm tired. I want to go to bed. Stand under the waterfall, then watch and listen to the waves until I fall asleep." He ran out.

A shiver rippled through Mitchella. "Secure the ballroom."

Gusts of wind carrying large raindrops banged the windows and doors shut as the spell took effect. When the fresh rain met floor or wall, it vanished as if sucked up by the intensity of negative emotions. She hurried from the chamber and made a note to use minimally Flaired workers to reconstruct the room.

She climbed the main stairs to the second story. She'd changed the hall lamps from flickering silver torches to glowing bronze globes that illuminated the corridor with a warmer light.

When she reached Antenn's suite he was already in bed. She kissed his forehead and listened to his sleepy "good night," but paused by the door to watch the mesmerizing waves. Live audio of the surf from the nearest beach matched the holoscene on the wall. It should have soothed her, but the pull of the tide matched the pulse of her need to be with Straif.

She left Antenn's suite with the rhythm of the waves surging through her blood. When she thought of Straif, heat flooded her.

Her emotions were more than simple physical attraction, though every moment she spent with him increased her awareness of his virility, reminded her how long it had been since she'd made love with a sexy, demanding man.

Mixed with her desire was empathy, tenderness at his vulnerability, admiration for the strength of him—his body, his mind, his spirit.

"T'Blackthorn hurts," whispered the Residence into her mind. Mitchella flinched. "The Residence hurts when T'Blackthorn aches."

She wanted to deny the Residence's plea, but she heard it easily, her mind had become attuned to it.

What of Drina? she projected to the house.

"She sleeps in her own room on the fancy bedsponge. She does not help her FamMan."

Rest, T'Blackthorn Residence, Mitchella sent.

The atmosphere around her changed as the Residence powered down. Throughout the day she'd felt its weariness as it struggled to keep up with her cleaning requests—and it told her when it siphoned energy from Straif.

The tide of her heart pulled her toward him. The last two days had been full of shocks for him as well as for her. She longed to be with him, comforted by his presence as she could comfort him with hers. She could not stop the tenderness for him that welled through her. He'd been so strong against the emotions that buffeted him.

She had to pass his door before she reached her own rooms—and the furnishings provided by her family. She didn't want to think of the Clovers either. She wished her new suite was as devoid of reminders as Antenn's or Straif's.

She was at the MasterSuite. She'd rearranged silver door panels and tinted them bronze. The door was cracked open.

She hesitated, and Straif's aura flowed out and enveloped her. Did he do that on purpose? She didn't know. His essence brushed over her, bringing with it the scent of sage, the pressure of gentle hands on her arms, drawing her to him. Underlying everything was deep melancholy. She hesitated, but could not pass by.

Pushing the door open, she found him in the sitting room, staring out night-black windows. "It's raining hard."

"Is the suite to your liking?" she asked softly.

He shrugged. "It's fine."

A rush of irritation dissolved her previous mood.

Straif turned—his eyes cast in shadow, his expression stern. He forced a smile. "I seem to be apologizing today. Forgive my lack of enthusiasm. You did very well." He waved at the room around him, painstakingly layered in shades of green, giving the atmosphere of dappled light of a forest. She'd thought it would remind him of his travels instead of his childhood. "You have a wonderful talent. This place is a sanctuary now."

He looked at her for a long moment, and the fascination that spun between them spiraled until she thought it held the force of the tide, sweeping them together. "A wonderful talent," he repeated. "A very womanly talent."

Mitchella could *feel* the roundness of her breasts, her hips, her thighs, was utterly aware of her femininity. Her body longed to press against his hardness.

"Beautiful." He took a step toward her, gazed locked on hers, smiling slightly as she stared at his mouth. "The rooms are as lovely, as complex as yourself."

"Thank you," she said.

His lips formed a true smile. "I'm thanking you. The bed . . . " He waved to the open door of the bedroom, but didn't take his eyes from hers. Mitchella fought to keep her breath and words steady. She wished he hadn't mentioned the bed.

"You like the bed?" Now *she'd* mentioned the bed, what was wrong with her? They should not be thinking of the bed. She should not be thinking of the bed and his lean form naked and over her, of night pleasures that would involve more than her body, of loving that would not survive the light of day.

"You did an incredible job on the bed."

Mitchella flushed, tried to recall how she'd changed the huge, immovable four-poster Earth bed made of dark wood.

Straif took another step toward her. The force of attraction doubled. "I think the vines have already grown up the lattices and are spreading over the top grid. Shall we check?"

Ah. She'd surrounded the posts and headboard in removable cubes of thin wood strips. "No," she croaked. She'd never made love in an old-fashioned Earth bed instead of a bed-sponge. She didn't know what would happen if she did, what effect it might have on her. Straightening her spine, she said, "No bedroom."

His glance fell to her breasts. "So beautiful, so lush."

One more step brought him to within a finger's breadth of her. She tilted her head back to match her gaze with his. His eyes were a deep, fiery blue. She inhaled and smelled sage and Straif, and her mind whirled. Blood pounded in her temples so she couldn't hear his next quiet comment.

His hands reached for hers. He lifted one hand and brushed

a kiss on the back, then his lips kissed her other hand. His mouth was hot. Heat flashed straight to her core.

"Thank you," he said. Since he spoke a little louder and close to her ear, she heard him.

He took a step back, keeping a firm grip on her hands, and she followed.

"Thank you for making the suite homey," he murmured.

Her breath caught at his simple words and the feeling behind them. She shook her head in mute acceptance of his gratitude.

A few more steps and he backed against a forest green wingchair of furrabeast suede. "Thank you for coming to me tonight. You are generous in all ways." He placed her hands over his heart, and her own heart thudded hard as something snapped together. For an instant she thought she saw a bright silver chain, thick as her wrist, linking them. Again she shook her head, overwhelmed by the haze of desire, to collect her wits.

Her vision was clear enough to see his surprise. He blinked, then sat on the chair behind him and drew her between his thighs. Suddenly his mouth was on the level of her breasts. Her whole body went liquid with heat and longing.

"We are right for each other," he whispered. She sensed it was directed more to himself than her. "This time, this place, is for us."

A warning rang in her mind, but he took her hands and kissed the palms, laving the hollow of each and all thought fled. She made a small sound of arousal, and a tremor rippled through him.

"Soft, beautiful woman," he whispered.

She stood swaying with want, with weakness, with passion. The silence thickened, and she thought she felt the hot, wild beat of his own desire. She looked down, only to be trapped by his eyes—dark blue, intent, focused on her. His face was set in lines of need. She slipped her hands from his, and his callouses along her skin made every nerve thrill.

That face, that man's rugged face, called to her. His features showed the stamp of generations of resolve to survive and triumph. His Flair engulfed her, and she glimpsed the bright traces of all the people who'd worked in the room and was awed at his talent. But his own sparkling aura drew her like a lodestone—a silver pool of deep, liquid mercury. She wanted to immerse herself in it, steep herself in him. Know him.

In the stillness of the night, her heartbeat matched his, the ebb and flow of her blood moved with his. The meshing was an exquisite pleasure flooding her, penetrating every cell. Her breath came harsh now. She braced her hands on his shoulders, and they were wide and solid under her touch, thick with sinew and muscle. Her head fell back as she surrendered to the passion spinning between them. Her body arched to him.

Straif groaned.

Fourteen

"*This is too much*," *Straif rasped. His breath came hot* against her breasts. "Stay or go."

She couldn't go. It wasn't possible. The simple magnetism between them was too much for her to break.

She didn't want to go. Desire rose within her, warming her, tempting her with the knowledge that if she stayed she'd enjoy the best loving she'd had in a long, long while.

Looking up at her, he said nothing, but a flush painted his cheekbones, his eyelids lowered, and the pulse in his neck throbbed. She couldn't tear her gaze away from that vein. The thought of tasting the saltiness of his skin right there made her lips tingle, made her nipples tighten.

"I vowed not to touch you, Mitchella." His voice was strained.

Then he tilted his head back against the chair, and his gaze locked on hers. "Mitchella," he said as if savoring the syllables of her name, like he'd savor other parts of her. "Mitshell-ah." Her name was soft, exotic on his lips. She focused on his mouth, and a low ache began between her thighs.

His hands clenched over the arms of the chair. "I want to touch you, Mitchella, so much." Husky, wooing, tender . . . layer upon layer of temptation formed the timbre of his voice.

"Your softness. Your femininity. Your beauty. I need you. Mitchella." His words were the rhythm of the sea, of her heartbeat, of his.

She couldn't go.

She had to stay.

Her fingers touched the backs of his hands, and he turned them over. She brought his palms to her breasts and shuddered when his fingers curved over her, shaped her. She moaned.

One last desperate thought swam through her mind. "You have a HeartMate," she choked out.

He stared up at her with deep, intense eyes. "I know nothing of her. I can see only you."

Mitchella caught her breath. "This is a mistake."

His eyes flamed, the muscle in his jaw flexed. "Just a little touching, then. Here in the chair."

With a smooth move that showed his strength, he set his hands on her waist, lifted her, and brought her close. Mitchella put her hands on his shoulders, opened her legs and folded them on either side of his thighs, then sank down, kneeling in the chair. When her sex settled on his rigid length, the erotic touch seared her so she moaned and closed her eyes. She dared not move, to do so would start the ultimate climb to ecstasy.

"I could remove our clothes with a Word." His voice was so low that it might have come in her mind rather than to her ears.

She shuddered at the idea. She'd never had a lover so Flaired. The thought tempted her. She panted, but shook her head, then swallowed hard. When she'd controlled the rising tide of desire, she opened her eyes. His were the dark blue of a turbulent sea, full of so much naked passion she drew back, and rubbed sex against sex. They both groaned.

He closed his eyes. A bead of sweat appeared at his hairline.

She wanted to bend forward and taste that droplet of sweat, wanted to let her tongue linger on his tense face, trace down to press against his lips, feel the bunched muscle at the corner of his jaw. So she closed her eyes, too.

Behind her eyelids, swirls of colors danced, infused with the tinge of desire. A mist of bright, sparkling orange and silver engulfed her. She was afire. Straif. His passion mixed with hers, she was swept away in an undertow of sensual emotion.

He needed her. To him, she was everything soft and beautiful, the essence of woman. His desire held a wild force that sank into her, raged through her until her blood was as hot and racing as his. A thousand strokes against her skin, arousing every nerve ending, flicks of flame against her nipples and the sweet nub between her legs ignited her passion until she was throbbing, aching, desperate. Nothing mattered except embracing the firestorm, melding with him, merging with him.

Mitchella. His mind whisper was another strong, pure caress rippling through her, throwing her to new heights of sexuality. She wanted to run her hands all over him, but wasn't aware of her physical body. All was heat, all passion. She thought she groaned and sent the fire licking at her loins out to him.

It whipped back to her, lashes of sensation that stroked her core, then burst into sweet release.

Her body fell against his, limp. His heart thundered under her ear. His chest rose and fell in ragged breaths.

She felt as if she glowed with a sheen of fulfillment. No physical climax had shattered her so. She was sated, yet it had been a mental orgasm. His sex was soft, as if all the passionate energy he'd experienced had also been released mentally.

Not just mental fulfillment, but emotional. His arms cradled her with the gentleness of a true lover, and he was utterly open. He hid nothing from her, and his need for her was still there, twining them together. It wrapped around her heart.

His hands stroked her back, and the feel of their width, their power, flashed another surge of pleasure through her. She didn't have the strength to groan, so she lay against him—smelling the clean, crispness of sage, the wild male of Straif. She flushed. She'd matched him in that wildness. Those dancing flames of desire that merged and exploded.

Her breasts were flattened against his chest, and suddenly her tunic was too thin. If she stayed, the sex between them wouldn't be mental. Her hands itched to touch his body.

Summoning the tatters of her control, she pushed herself away, used a little Flair to reach her feet. She'd never had the power to move so easily, floating-flying, but being around him and the Residence had increased her Flair, for now.

"Stay." Straif's fingers opened to grasp, then lay flat.

She looked down on him, knowing that she was far too close to falling in love with the man. "I don't want to discuss this."

"It's only a matter of time—"

"I'm gone."

His hand swept out to grip her wrist. "Gone? No, I won't let you leave the Residence." And he spoke those words that arrowed straight to her heart. "I need you, Mitchella."

She freed her hands, pushed her fingers through her hair, lifting it to cool her thoughts.

His body stiffened. "Your hair is beautiful—the color, the texture, I want it to brush my skin. My naked skin. *All* of my skin."

Images leapt before her eyes, the tough length of his tanned body on cream-colored sheets, the contrast of her red hair against his skin. She couldn't move. Deliberately looking to the black windows where a stream of raindrops spattered, she said, "I'm leaving your suite, not your home."

"It *is* becoming a home for me, Mitchella. I can't thank you enough for that."

She rubbed her temples. "We both have much to deal with. You must defend yourself to keep your title and estate."

He moved abruptly. "I need to find the cure for my flawed gene."

That had been in his mind—all the time before desire had banished it for a while. His other, longer, passion.

It hurt.

This was where their paths separated completely. She could never have him as more than a temporary lover. Better accept they'd be lovers, shield her heart for the inevitable break, try to keep the affair light. Difficult with the emotional connection they'd made but she'd do it.

When she knew she could smile with true sincerity, she looked at him. "I'll see you in the morning. What's your schedule?"

He scowled, turned his head to stare at the windows. "I have an appointment with T'Heather, the Healer, then will be back here to consult with T'Vine."

Both actions were part of his quest, his other passion. His

first passion. The passion that would last longer than the one they shared.

She nodded. "Tomorrow I will work on the Residence-Den." She ignored his stiffening. "If you keep having appointments with FirstFamily Heads of Households, you will have to use the ResidenceDen as a statement of your faith that you are the proper T'Blackthorn."

He growled.

"Then I'll do preliminary work on the Great Hall, my rooms."

"Is your suite all right?" He frowned. "I'm sorry, I'd forgotten your loss. Only last night. Tell me if I can make your stay here easier."

He could keep his hands off her, his mouth, his desire from overwhelming her. That wouldn't happen.

The reminder of her homeless state, of her loss, had tears stinging. She'd thrown herself into her work to keep from thinking too much—feeling too much. She should retire to the guest suite for a good cry. Weep and grieve for what was gone, then accept she'd have to rebuild her life, get a good night's sleep, and move forward. She'd done it before, she'd do it now.

She glanced up to find him gazing at her, his expression softer than she'd seen. "You've done an incredible amount today," he said, then looked to the bedroom's open door, back to her. "You won't stay?"

"No." Not tonight. She turned and walked to the hall door.

"Mitchella?"

Stopping, she looked back at him. "Yes?"

"Merry meet," he said the ritual words, lacing them with so much passion she visualized her sex meeting his.

Incredible. She flushed. "Merry part," she said, opening the door and stepping into the cool corridor.

"And merry meet again!" his voice lilted, but the amusement didn't hide the determination.

Mitchella closed the door with a snap.

The Healer, GrandLord T'Heather, gazed steadily at Straif. Straif's stomach tightened. He stared back at the

GrandLord and composed his face into impassivity. The Healer looked more like a farmer, broad with rough features. They sat in T'Heather's ResidenceDen, furnished for the complete comfort of a man who often worked long hours and came to the place exhausted. After only a couple of days, Straif was learning the concepts of interior design. Scrutinizing the room kept him from anticipating bad news.

GrandLord T'Heather flung a brawny arm along the back of the long sofa they shared. "I am sorry to inform you that nothing has changed. The problem with your genetic code is still there and still incurable by the Healers."

It was a harder blow than it should have been. "Thank you for your expertise." Straif nearly strangled on the words, glad they came out gruff and not ungracious.

Eyes softening, T'Heather said, "I'm sorry my news isn't better. I know you've searched Celta for a remedy. I must warn you that since your gene is flawed, you are still susceptible to the Angh virus, and it could be fatal." He turned away. "Indeed, I don't know how you survived the first time."

Straif did, but it was something he tried never to think of.

Speaking more briskly, T'Heather said, "I will send your updated information to the botanist, Culpeper, who continues to work on the problem. If he'd found any mitigating herbs, he would have told me. I understand that you often checked with him on the occasions you returned to Druida."

Straif heard the disapproving note. Another Lord who thought he should have stayed and minded his home. He stiffened. He *wouldn't* ask T'Heather about the other Blackthorn claimant who had seen Heather's heir.

"Do you still come to my new twinmoons Ritual tonight and offer your Flair in reestablishing my home?"

T'Heather winced. "You're blunt."

"I prefer to know my allies and enemies."

With a short nod, T'Heather replied, "I understand Ailim Elder is officiating with you. She is close to her time, I request that I be next to her in the Circle."

"Done."

"My lady is coming also." He smiled. "We heard Holm and Lark Apple will be arriving from Gael City. We like to see our Daughter'sDaughter as often as possible."

"My cuz Holm supports me on this."

"Holm's father, T'Holly, will be there?"

"I'm allies with T'Holly, many Hollys will participate."

"Should be an interesting evening."

"A lot of energy will be raised."

T'Heather nodded again. "Sufficient for all your needs."

Straif rose. "I'll ensure your standard fee is transferred to your account."

Standing, T'Heather shook his head. "No. You may recall a couple of years ago the Councils sent you to find a man called Stringer in unexplored Brittany."

"Yes." It had been a challenge. He'd found the man barely alive and brought him back to Druida, a long, grueling trip.

"Culpeper made the request for your services to the Councils. Stringer was his younger partner. Like Culpeper, we expect Stringer to marry into the Family. Very good work on your part." T'Heather offered his hand.

Straif shook it.

T'Heather clapped Straif on the shoulder as they walked to the door. "I support your claim as T'Blackthorn, but not this continued quest to find a cure for your genetic heritage—an unhealthy obsession." His mouth thinned. "Trying to Heal you and your Family was the most devastating time of my life, memories I will never forget. Consider letting your line die."

Straif flinched.

"Putting your Family at risk with every generation—you could watch your children die. They could fail to save you. Sooner or later your Family will perish. You have the opportunity to stop this heart-wrenching situation."

Spoken as a man who had four grandchildren and the knowledge his line—his special Flair—was safe.

"I will find a cure," Straif gritted out.

Now T'Heather's eyes held the grief he'd felt at failing to save the Blackthorns, held hard choices, held denial. "I don't think so, you have tried for fifteen years. There is no solution. Give up this quest. It is a fixation."

Heat came to Straif's cheeks. "No."

Scrutinizing him again, T'Heather said slowly. "Since Ruis Elder has recommissioned the Ship, *Nuada's Sword,* it could provide you with answers we Healers can't."

The suggestion stunned Straif. The colonist Ship, *Nuada's Sword*. His pulse beat hard in his ears as excitement raced through him. He couldn't find words.

*S*traif *bumped into Mitchella as she hurried from his* ResidenceDen. He'd known she was there, of course, but having a woman who'd soon be his lover off-balance in his arms was the best thing that had happened to him all morning. Since Vinni T'Vine would soon appear and prophesy about Straif's future, he didn't anticipate his day getting appreciably better.

"Oh, you're here," she said with a bright smile that made him suspicious, though she made no effort to escape his embrace.

He lowered his head to kiss her soundly, liking the slow burn firing his loins. She pressed against him, and he enjoyed that, too. Then she broke the kiss and smiled. This time her eyes were misty with emotion, her lips curved sensually. Good.

"I take it Antenn is at grove-study."

"Yes." Her expression clouded, and she stepped away from him. "I'm sorry you don't get along. It complicates matters."

"Don't suggest that you leave."

She chuckled. "No chance of that once he informs the Cang Zhus that he's staying here." A crash came from the ResidenceDen, and Mitchella scowled. "Drina. There was a vase she didn't care for. We agreed that it didn't match the ResidenceDen, but I was going to put it in storage or—"

"If it's that huge china urn thing—"

"Rrrrr," Drina said, trotting into the hall with a satisfied smirk. Mitchella frowned and disappeared into the Residence-Den.

The Residence said, "I told the FamCat that the vase she just destroyed was one the late T'Blackthorn received as a wedding present and which your parents didn't care for."

It made a nice bang. Drina licked her paw. *Mitchella can clean up the mess.*

Straif said, "So far I haven't seen much Flair from my FamCat. Perhaps I'll decide the amount of jewels on her collar by how much Flair she shows, such as cleaning up her own messes."

I am a very clean Cat. I 'port outside when necessary. During good weather.

He sighed. "Residence, do we have a litter box?"

Mitchella called from the ResidenceDen. "I had a self-cleaning, scented litter box taken from one of the attic store-rooms." She appeared, holding a shard of china, scowling at Drina. "I hope you enjoyed destroying that vase."

It was UGLY.

Mitchella winced. "I heard that 'ugly.' True, but it was valuable. I think Straif could have paid for your collar with the price he would have received from it."

Drina separated her toes to clean between them. *Since the woman doesn't appreciate My assistance, I will take a nap on My new bedsponge, under the veiled canopy.* Her mouth curled.

"Drina's going to her room," Straif said. Seeing Mitchella's set mouth, he took her elbow. "Show me the ResidenceDen." He didn't want to enter the room, but harmony demanded it. Only five beings living in the Residence and the relationships were complicated enough to demand compromises.

At the sight of the room he stopped in amazed horror.

Fifteen

"It's . . . round," Straif said, stunned. Full-length windows circled the room. All had a high view of the ocean. "Illusion." How could he infuse his words with anything but dismay?

"Yes, illusion. I'm one of the best at holospells," Mitchella said proudly, brushing against him as she entered.

Straif took a grip on the doorjamb. He supposed he should have told Mitchella that he had a problem with heights, but why? His home was a solid four stories. A very solid four stories. The ResidenceDen had been on the ground floor. Once.

"It's a very good illusion." His voice cracked. "I recognize the lighthouse on Meindwyr Island." He'd planned to never, ever visit again.

Even cliff edges were better than being in the middle of a small, tall structure that trembled in fierce winds and where you couldn't see any land at all. His sister, Fasha, had danced straight up to one of the windows and looked down and said you could see nasty, pointed rocks, but he hadn't moved from the doorway, and his mother had 'ported them right back to the boat. Straif had no problems with boats. He swallowed.

"You don't like it. Sorry, Antenn is going through an ocean

phase, and I got the idea from him. It *is* completely different," she said.

"Completely," Straif agreed from a dry mouth. *What was an ocean phase?*

"There's always something the client dislikes," Mitchella said philosophically, turning in place and studying the room.

She made him dizzy. He watched as she strolled around the windows. She could fall out of one of those windows, maybe one that was a real wall, and hurt herself, and Straif couldn't move a muscle to save her.

His mind scrambled. Take big, deep, breaths. That's how to handle heights, take big, deep, breaths.

Mitchella shrugged, and his gaze locked on her breasts. Much better thinking of those breasts than taking big, deep, breaths. In fact, he'd like *her* to take big, deep, breaths.

"Ah, well," she sighed, and it had more than a hint of weariness in it. He wondered if she'd slept as poorly as he had the night before, anticipating when they'd truly be lovers.

"If this is my worst misjudgment, we're lucky," she said.

Straif got the impression that it had taken a lot of energy and Flair to make the room. Pity.

Mitchella snapped her fingers, and the illusion disappeared. Straif reeled against the doorjamb as reality shifted. And formed into something wonderful. The room was empty, and he saw the elegant shape of it for the first time. The walls had been newly tinted a dull, metallic gold that held a bit of a shine, the floor was a mellow golden marble with flecks of the real precious metal. The ResidenceDen looked nothing like it had been in his childhood, reminded him of no other room.

His parents had decorated with silver. Straif entered the room to judge its atmosphere.

"This was my first concept," Mitchella said, frowning at the window that overlooked the tangled, riotous plantlife of what had been the front grass gliderdrive. "When I removed the rugs, I found this marvelous floor, so I tinted the walls to match." She bent down to fiddle with something beneath the low window sash of gleaming reddwood, and Straif decided her bottom was the most marvelous thing in the room. Lush, ready for his hands.

"What's that?" he asked, trying to keep his libido in check.

She looked over her shoulder. "It's a viz button, to help anchor the illusions." Her face flushed. "I don't have a great amount of Flair."

"You have other great assets," Straif assured her.

She narrowed her eyes. "What's your favorite view?"

He didn't think she meant her bottom. "My favorite *scenic* view"—he smiled wolfishly—"is the Great Labyrinth. My cuz Holm wed his HeartMate, Lark, in the center of the Great Labyrinth north of Druida. I attended. I hadn't been there for a long time. It's beautiful." The thought crossed his mind that this had been another Ritual he hadn't missed. T'Hawthorn, a FirstFamily GreatLord had officiated, so that event could definitely be counted as a GreatRitual.

"It's in a huge crater, right?" Mitchella asked. "My cuz Trif went to the wedding."

"Yes, the path spirals from the center of the crater to the rim." As a panorama, it was about as far from the top of a lighthouse imaginable. The descent was gentle, so standing on the rim didn't affect his fear of heights. It would be a steep roll down, but definitely a roll. Children loved it. "The Noble Families all have small shrines as decoration."

"Give me an image," Mitchella said, meeting his eyes.

The link between them widened, and he marveled that she was so open to him. Much of it was her weaker Flair, but she was also an open and optimistic woman. He saw to the depths of her and found a dark shadow on her heart. He frowned.

"An image, Blackthorn, I'm waiting." She'd straightened, and that was too bad. If he'd been more interested in watching her derriere than caught by that heart-shadow, he could still be appreciating her figure.

She made a disgusted sound, diminished the link between them—did she know what she was doing?—and flipped him the button.

He caught it and felt the lighthouse ready to materialize. With a thought he wiped that illusion clean, then with surprising ease, he formed one of the Great Labyrinth and imprinted it.

The labyrinth sprang up around them, the huge ash tree in the center towered over them. The rim of the crater, the horizon, was about eye level. All along the visible labyrinth path were symbols of the Nobles . . . a blooming hawthorn hedge, the Vine's blackberry bushes around a grape arbor.

"What time is it?" Straif asked. Vinni T'Vine should arrive for their appointment any moment.

She glanced at her wrist timer. "Nearly Midmorning bell."

"Ah, then we have a septhour or so to make this room ready," Straif said. He didn't think it would take that long. He looked around with a frown. "Much as I like the Great Labyrinth, I don't want to live in it."

Smiling, Mitchella crossed the room and took the viz button. Their fingers touched, and a surge of desire flashed between them. The illusion around them wavered.

"Oops," Mitchella said with the bright smile he didn't trust, the one she wore when she thought of their mutual attraction, he realized. A bright smile and a shadowed heart. He'd find out the emotions that engendered both.

But she walked to the window, and the illusion of the labyrinth diminished. When she reached the window, she set the viz back into place and gestured Straif over. "You imprinted many view segments. Tell me which you want the window to show."

He joined her, stood a few centimeters from her, within her natural energy aura—it sizzled against the length of him and kept him pleasantly, achingly hard. He enjoyed her floral scent.

She'd sized the illusion to the window, and scenes flickered for a minute before Straif spoke. "How many views are there?"

She didn't move, and when she spoke, her voice held the husky note that stoked his desire. "The Great Labyrinth's a big place."

He tilted his head so his lips were near her ear. "Why don't we do a scene from the center."

The images whirled to those near the center. "What . . . what view?" she asked.

"The one with the stand of birches."

With a tap of her fingernail, the illusion spread to the window, shifted, steadied. Straif glanced up from studying the slope of Mitchella's breasts to see the new panorama outside the window and caught his breath. Leaves from the ash tree edged the top of the window, the start of the winding exit path was to the far left, before him was a grove of birches, reflecting the pink of dawn on their white trunks; their green leaves fluttered.

Straif looked to another window, bare of illusion. The day was gray and wet. Rain pattered against the pane.

He glanced at Mitchella. She'd stepped away from the window where Bel had cleared the crater's rim. Golden sunlight danced in the birches, spilled into the room. He looked around again—even bare, the room was warm and welcoming.

"Very nice." He smiled.

"You prefer it to the lighthouse." She chuckled.

"Much. Let's keep holos for windows, not whole rooms." He stared at the illusion window again and made a decision. "Why don't you put an automatic fade to diminish each day on the windows? The grounds must be perfect by the open house on summer solstice. By then I'll be accustomed to living here."

"I have plans to change the landscaping that can be seen from the Residence."

He stared at her in admiration. "You do?"

"Yes, I often work with a landscape designer. The immediate outside space around a home, a grassyard or garden is considered an extension of the home."

"Good." He walked to the windows but saw nothing but sheets of gray rain. "I hope the weather clears before the Ritual. I could weathershield the Grove of the Dark Goddess until the ceremony, but it would cost me Flair I can't afford." Mitchella joined him, and he put a hand on her shoulder, testing their connection and his own control. The bond cycled sweet energy and attraction. His control was threadbare. He dragged his mind back to the Ritual. "Since you are the most informed person about the needs of the Residence you will be helping me shape and direct the spells and energy we raise tonight."

Her eyes widened until her black pupils dominated the deep green of her irises. A very beautiful green, the prettiest shade of green he'd ever seen, true emerald.

Through their link, he felt her anxiety. "You're the expert."

"You'll do fine," said Vinni T'Vine from the doorway.

Mitchella turned to him, slightly pale. "You're the prophet, you should know." She put her hand over her mouth.

Vinni beamed and pushed out his chest. "That's me, Great-Lord T'Vine." He glanced around the empty room, and his eyes changed from pale brown to green. He nodded. "This is correct."

Straif thought Mitchella gulped as he did. Suddenly, he didn't want Vinni commenting about any other rooms. The Lord had already been in the small dining parlor and hadn't said a word, but Straif couldn't depend on the boy's erratic discretion.

There was only one way to keep Vinni in this room and away from others—make the ResidenceDen livable.

Straif strode to Vinni. "Why don't you link with Mitchella and me, and we can 'port a couple of chairs to use in our consultation." Seeing Vinni as disconcerted as he often made others pleased Straif. He held out his hand. "We'll use common, household Flair, nothing that will tire us or won't be replaced in good time for the GreatRitual tonight."

"All right," Vinni said.

"Mitchella, you know the pieces and where they're stored. Will you join with us?" asked Straif.

She straightened her spine and smiled. "I've never linked with two FirstFamily Lords, a new experience and preparation for tonight."

Vinni eyed her. "You've already got a bond with T'Blackthorn."

Mitchella looked surprised. Hadn't she known? Then she said easily, "I occasionally bond with my clients . . ."

Fierce jealousy whipped through Straif.

". . . especially when the project is complex." She shook her head. "This is probably the most demanding project I'll ever have in my life."

Vinni opened his mouth, and she raised a hand. "Please don't speculate. I'd rather not know," Mitchella said.

"I don't speculate," Vinni huffed. "My predictions are correct over ninety-seven percent of the time."

"Very impressive," Mitchella's smile broadened, and a softness came to her eyes. "Antenn's Flair is superior, too."

A blaze of white light flickered in Vinni's gaze. "Antenn Moss," he said in a guttural voice, a voice of prophecy.

Mitchella grabbed Straif's biceps with clutching fingers.

"Blackthorn. Winterberry. Mine."

"Vinni T'Vine, stop!" Straif snapped Flair at the boy.

"Antenn Moss, he'll create a great and unusual building for us," Vinni said mildly, his eyes becoming blue gray.

Straif scowled, Mitchella's fingers had vised around his arm. "Vinni, can we trust you in a common link to 'port furniture? More, can I trust you not to scare my guests tonight before, during, and after my GreatRitual?"

The boy dropped his gaze and scuffed his foot on the polished marble floor. Flecks of mud fell from his boot. "Pardon me," he whispered. "My Flair is usually under excellent control."

"About ninety-seven percent of the time?" teased Mitchella, dropping her hand from Straif's arm. He linked fingers with her.

"Yes," said Vinni, lifting his head to show pinkened cheeks. "Antenn's name caught me by surprise. I'll concentrate on the Ritual tonight, I promise. Most of the FirstFamily Lords and Ladies have their mindshields up when I'm around, anyway."

"And now?" asked Mitchella.

Vinni blushed more. "I'm in full control."

"Good," Straif said coolly. "You'll help us with the furniture, and I won't tell your Family of this unfortunate lapse in the command of your Flair. You worried Mitchella. That isn't the act of an honorable man."

Vinni stiffened, then bowed to Mitchella. "My apologies."

"Granted," Mitchella said, but Straif knew enough of her— and of prophecies—that Vinni's words about Antenn would haunt her.

"Let's form a small circle," Straif said.

Mitchella hesitantly offered the boy her hand. He took it gently, and her tense expression relaxed. Straif stroked her palm with his thumb, and her attention switched to him. Good.

He held out a hand to Vinni. "GreatLord T'Vine, want to practice some household Flair?"

Vinni glanced up at him with bright blue eyes. "They don't

let me do anything like that at home." Straif wasn't surprised.

"This will be interesting," Vinni said. Straif hoped not. He hoped it would be commonplace.

Mitchella scanned the room, and a line formed between her brows. "We'll need a sofa and at least two chairs. I found some beautiful old tapestry chairs in a style popular a century ago that I had in mind when I tinted the walls."

"The FirstFamilies always keep everything they ever had," Vinni said cheerfully. "The T'Vine Residence storerooms are packed. I go hid—um—*meditate* in them now and then."

"We'll need a large desk," Straif said. The step he was about to take was a big one, but it felt right. "I want my father's desk back in the room. It matches the window trim."

"I've already changed the color and texture of the inlaid blotter," Mitchella said.

Vinni grinned. "This sounds fun, let's try." He grasped Straif's hand and closed the circle.

Fog filled Straif's brain, punctuated by bright colors. He struggled to keep reality before his eyes, his mind primed for the use of Flair. *Vinni, you need to rein in your Flair. Also, focus!* The mist withdrew to behind Vinni's mindshield, but Straif could still feel the boy's powerful Flair.

Mitchella, visualize the storeroom, please, Straif asked.

A sofa and chairs are in storeroom five, as is an old comfortchair that can be used as a desk chair, she said, and projected a detailed graph of the storeroom in relation to the rest of the Residence, then zoomed into the room to show the position of the pieces and their appearance.

Straif was sure he'd never have remembered the intricate pattern of the tapestry, or the varying subtle shades. There were colors that he didn't have specific names for. Mitchella probably knew what they were called. He said, "On three we'll bring them down. Mitchella will show us the position she wants them in. One, two, *three.*"

It was as easy as pushing open a door. He and Vinni picked up the pieces, shoved them sideways into a no-time dimension. Mitchella showed them the ResidenceDen grid, Vinni and he pulled the furniture from the no-time and into the room. The chairs and sofa landed with barely a whisper.

"The desk and chair are in storeroom one." Mitchella

sounded breathless. Delight and triumph pulsed through their bond from her.

Straif knew where storeroom one was, and showed Vinni. Mitchella visualized the position of the desk and its detail down to some nicks in the wood he'd never noticed. The blotter was a deep redgold now, not black surrounded by silver. Again Straif counted to three, again they 'ported the items.

Mitchella had moved the desk to face a different wall, changing the focal point and layout of the room. It looked good.

She was the first to break the circle and move away to position the comfortchair. "Since this is an older chair, it needs a Flair couplet spell to adjust instead of three words." She snapped her fingers and a small piece of papyrus appeared in her hand. "Here's the couplet." She put it on the blotter, then crossed to the chairs and sofa grouped near a window on the short end of the rectangular room and fussed with their positions.

Vinni met Straif's eyes, his own gaze sharp. The boy spoke in a whisper. "Has she been able to 'port small objects long?"

Straif gazed at Mitchella, glanced back to Vinni, and murmured, "I've never seen her 'port a small item before."

Nodding, Vinni said, "She doesn't realize her Flair is refining?"

Straif shrugged. "I don't think so."

"It's only been a few days, I wonder—"

"There," Mitchella said, "it's done." Examining the room, she frowned at the windows showing rain. "I'll do the window holos this afternoon—more of the Great Labyrinth. The room needs tables and art. Later we'll discuss other furnishings you might want." She looked at her wrist timer, then the fireplace mantel. "We need a timer, too. I'll check my list of items in storage. Antenn's grove-study was cut short today. Residence, is Antenn near the estate?"

"He is walking to the front greeniron gates," the Residence replied.

"It's muddy and raining out there. He'll need to dry off and have a snack before he takes T'Vine to the Clovers. I'll want to talk to him about his morning lessons. Will a septhour be enough for your consultation?"

"I don't—" started Vinni.

"Yes," Straif said.

Mitchella nodded. She looked at the desk, then at Straif and smiled. "You've taken another step in accepting your past. That's very good. I am proud of you," she said, the warmth in her voice transferred to him, spread throughout his chest.

"You both come to the dining parlor when you're done. I'll have some stew for you. The cook is preparing the food for the Nobles after the Ritual and has requested we leave him alone in the kitchen so he can concentrate on his work."

As she left the room, Straif narrowed his eyes to see her trail and wasn't surprised to also see a silver thread between himself and her.

But when he glanced down at Vinni, who'd also watched her leave, the boy prophet's eyes glowed amber, and he trembled.

Bracing himself, Straif put a hand on Vinni's shoulder. The boy flinched, his Flair spiked and the world spun away from Straif into distorted flashes.

Sixteen

❦

Straif was bombarded by images: of the Residence; Mitchella-child tear-streaked and distraught; Straif himself an older man with a hard, bitter countenance; Mitchella and himself rolling across his bed in sexual abandon; Drina dead on a black altar; the Ship, *Nuada's Sword,* blocking out the sun; Straif playing with a toddler; a dark, square hole emanating death. Straif jerked his hand from Vinni and stumbled, vision grayed, to the sofa where he collapsed.

"Dim lights," ordered Vinni. The spellight in the room faded, leaving only the windows to provide illumination. Vinni's quick footsteps approached.

As mist cleared from his eyes, Straif saw the boy choose the chair closest to where Straif sprawled. He stared at the young GreatLord, whose smile held irony. "Now you understand why people shy away from me."

"Explain what just happened, please," Straif croaked.

"When you touched me unexpectedly our Flair mingled and triggered my psi. You saw flashes of time—some options. Do you want to discuss what you saw or do a formal reading?"

Straif steadied his breath, sat up on the couch, and moved nearer to Vinni. "What does the formal reading consist of? The late GreatLady D'Vine refused to consult for me."

"Options," Vinni said quietly. "Like I said. Time is in flux—some experiences are set and cannot be avoided, but there are always options to diminish or expand the effects of those destined events."

"I only want to know one thing, and I want to know the accuracy of your answer. Will I find a remedy for my flawed genetic heritage?"

*B*undled *in a hooded rainsuit, Mitchella trudged down* the long, unkempt drive of the T'Blackthorn estate to the greeniron gates where she'd meet Antenn. The fizz of satisfaction at pleasing Straif and seeing his rare smile had dissipated. Now she was only conscious of the heavy mud sticking to her boots, making her trek to the estate entrance interminable. The grassdrive dipped, and her foot slid down and hit a large rock. A gust of wind slanted a heavy sheet of rain against her. She smacked against a large tree that lined the drive.

Short, flexible branches whipped around her, caging her, trapping her.

Her throat closed in fear.

She tried to move, but only her fingers twitched. She tried to shout, but no sound came from her mouth. She tried to send a telepathic cry to Straif, but her mind couldn't form the Flair.

Blinking, staring out at the landscape between the trickling streams of rain from her hood and the leafy twigs, she found the world had faded. The green of the leaves was no longer *as* green, the mud was an uninspired brown, not rich with shades. The raindrops held no slight sparkle of silver.

She struggled again and felt malicious Flair press against her. Flair, beyond her poor powers.

She was trapped! For an instant Mitchella panicked, throwing her whole weight and will against her bonds. Though she broke a few twigs, the branches didn't release her. Rough bark scraped her back through the rainsuit. Gasping in deep breaths, she pushed the panic aside and *thought*.

This was an inconvenience, that was all. Antenn might find her as he walked up the drive. She would be missed by Straif and Vinni T'Vine—quite soon if Antenn told them he hadn't seen her—Antenn! What if he fell into the trap, too! Would it be harder on a boy? Could it seriously injure him? She couldn't take the chance, she had to warn him.

So she studied her situation and realized she *was* caged, but some branches weren't pressing against her as they had before. They seemed more like living bars than restraining manacles. The thickest limbs had wrapped around her shoulders and upper arms, and just below her breasts, and again around her arms. She had a little wiggle room there, but not enough to raise her hands for good leverage. Her feet were barely constrained.

She flung herself against the branches, kicked, and angled her wrists to tear at them from the outside, then subsided and took stock again. The branches had receded a few centimeters. Grimly, she stared at them. She might be at this all night, but eventually she'd free herself.

All night! This was the night of the new twinmoons Ritual— a lot of people with great Flair would be attending. They'd find her for sure. What a reputation she'd have then! Mitchella Clover, the woman bound to a tree . . . mortifying.

Beyond the drip of the lessening rain, she heard something. Antenn! She thought she saw a smudgy shadow cutting across the overgrown grassyard to the Residence.

"Antenn!" she cried. It echoed back at her in a din that hurt her ears. The moving object didn't hesitate.

Vinni looked down, smoothed the fabric of his trous. "Some think that even asking questions changes the outcome."

Straif grunted.

"If you want such a limited reading, I can give it to you, but the answer may not please you."

"I know, from the moment your predecessor refused me a consultation before I left."

"In our GreatHouse History she stated matters were in great flux around you at that time. The winds of destiny still howled. No knowledge could have come of a consultation." Vinni met his eyes. "I will not speak of her or our histories further. If you want your consult now, give me your hand and send yourself into a meditative trance."

Straif offered his hand. Vinni took it, and Straif felt nothing from the boy but Flair waiting for direction. Breathing deeply, Straif set aside past angers and regrets and expectations and cleared his mind.

Vinni's Flair built a many-faceted crystal between them, but this time Straif couldn't see images in any of the sides, as he'd glimpsed before.

"The question?" a voice asked, sounding too deep and resonant for a boy.

"Will I find a remedy for my flawed genetic heritage?"

The crystal spun, flashing diamond-bright light into Straif's eyes, blinding spears that he *felt* sink into every vein of him, every cell.

Distantly he heard, "The question has been answered."

*D*esperate, *Mitchella* watched the small blurred figure move away. There was some sort of shield between her and the world. *Antenn!* she shrieked mentally. Her head banged hard against the tree trunk. When the pain receded, she realized the shield had used her own Flair against her. No doubt the more Flair, the more a person tried to use it, the more trapped they would be. Perhaps it was lucky that she had just common Flair.

She slumped against the tree trunk and found she had a good ten centimeters between her and the strongest branches, even around the largest part of her—her hips. She still couldn't move her arms upward, the cage was too high for her elbows to angle out. Her thrashing had freed her legs up to her knees. She might be able to slither down and out.

But she had to overcome the Flair shield as well as the strong basket of branches around her, and she didn't know its properties.

She eyed the cage near her knees, much narrower than her hips. Bracing herself, she jumped and plunged forward, jumped and plunged forward. Five times. Ten. Rested.

*S*lowly *Straif* exhaled and rose from the depth of his meditation. Fully awake, he found young Vinni examining him with hazel eyes glinting with silver. Straif froze as if being stalked by something bigger and nastier than himself. "Was the answer to my question revealed to you?" His voice was hoarse.

Vinni blinked, and his eyes changed color back to blue gray. Straif set his jaw.

"The answer to your question has always been clear," the boy said gently, not sounding at all like a boy.

"And that is?"

"You will find an immunization against the Angh virus."

Total relief washed through Straif, leaving him weak. He thought his blood had drained to his feet. He leaned back against fat cushions. "Thank the Lord and Lady."

Vinni performed a little half-bow and crossed the room to pick up his iridescent raincape. "Perhaps," he said.

"Perhaps? *Perhaps* I should thank the Lord and Lady for a fix for my heritage?" Straif jumped up. "What do you mean?"

"I thought you only wanted the answer to one question," Vinni smirked.

Straif growled. Before he could grab the boy, the Residence spoke. "T'Vine notified me that the Prophetic Session is finished, so I wish to inform you that the Seer, GrandLady Lobelia, has left an urgent scry message for you."

$\mathcal{M}$*itchella jumped and kicked out, jumped and kicked* out. Jumped and kicked out and hit the mud and slipped and fell downward until branches dug into her hips and stomach, her legs slanting out, heels jammed against wet clods of soil.

She panted. Sweat dribbled down her. Nasty. She leaned against the tree and tried not to think of all her body's scrapes, scratches, and aches. She'd never been beaten, but thought she knew what it felt like. When she got her breath back, she looked out of the cage . . . and couldn't see her feet.

Cold grue shivered up her spine. Her feet were there, she could *feel* them. She wiggled her toes, and her heels slid a little, and bark dug into her butt.

$\mathcal{S}$*traif stared at the* Residence *Den desk.* There *was no* scrybowl.

"A forecast from another Seer. Fascinating," Vinni murmured. He took a seat, eyes bright, curious youngster again.

"My ancestress knew you often consulted with GrandLady Lobelia."

"Can you play the message from the cache and amplify it to us here?" Straif asked the Residence.

"Only audio. There is not enough humidity in the ResidenceDen to gather and project—"

"Yes, yes," Straif said. "Do it."

Lobelia's vibrant voice said, "Straif. You should reconsider staying with me during the renovation of your Residence." Her voice quickened a little from her usual languid tones. "I see danger on and surrounding your estate. Beware—"

There was a crash. "What's that?" asked Straif.

The Residence sighed. "I'm afraid the message startled our new cook, and he broke the scrybowl."

"The message is gone?"

"Regrettably," said the Residence.

"Right. Thank you."

"My pleasure," said the Residence.

Straif shot a look at Vinni who appeared troubled. "Danger?"

Vinni bit his lip. "Yes."

"Here on the estate?"

Mouth compressed, Vinni nodded.

The door to the ResidenceDen banged open, and Antenn ran into the room, coat dripping. "Where's Mitchella? Residence said she went to meet me, but she *didn't*."

Straif jumped to his feet, everything inside him went cold. "Residence?" he demanded.

"The Lady left by the front door, walking on the grassdrive."

"And then?" Straif waved a hand, and his rain gear appeared. He pulled it on.

"Most of my outside scrystones are not working," the Residence said mournfully.

Drina pranced in. *I have had a nice nap.* She purred at Straif, batted her eyes at Vinni. *The consult is done, did T'Vine confirm that We will continue to be THE T'Blackthorns?*

"We'll search together, Antenn," Straif said. "Drina, we'll discuss your concerns later."

Antenn's mouth went white. He pulled a lump from under his coat and set Pinky on his paws. "Pinky will look, too. He can find her."

"I'm a tracker, Antenn, and we're on my estate. There is no way we can fail to find her," Straif said softly.

The boy scrutinized Straif, then leaned against a chair. His eyes closed. He jolted upward. "I felt her. She's hurt."

"Hurt?" Straif passed the boy and ran down the hallway.

"Hurt but not badly!" Antenn shouted.

Just as Straif yanked the huge front door open, he heard Vinni T'Vine in his mind. *One last thing, T'Blackthorn. Ask yourself this, what price will you pay for that remedy?* The pop of his teleporting away echoed.

A shudder wracked Straif at the statement, then he filed it away to think about later. He had to find Mitchella.

"*Mitchella." It was the faintest whisper, so soft she* nearly missed hearing it from her heavy breathing. She couldn't tell if it was a boy or man.

She writhed, she wriggled, she fought, and slipped centimeter by centimeter downward until her weight broke the knee-hole open to slightly larger than her hips. With one last hard effort she pushed down, slithered under the cage and out! Her head thumped against the soggy ground. She moaned and shut her eyes a moment.

When she opened them, a pristine Drina encased in a weathershield was sniffing at her knee. The cat yowled, lifted her upper lip in the smell-taste extra sense that cats had, and sashayed away.

Mitchella attempted to sit, but her muscles rebelled, still trembling with strain.

She couldn't see past her waist and wondered how much of her was still in the shield. She'd lifted her head just as Pinky appeared, hopped over her elbow, and licked her on the nose. "Urrgh."

Large hands curled around her feet and hauled her a couple of meters, scraping her body over every rock in the estate.

Pop! Suddenly she stared upward into the faces of Straif and Antenn, Drina and Pinky.

"Thank the Lady and Lord!" Straif said, swooping down and lifting her into his arms.

His warmth was incredible, heating her even through her clothes and the rainsuit. He cradled her gently. Wetness trickled down her scratched face. Since the rain had stopped she knew it was tears. She wanted to be cowardly and hide her head against his chest, but saw Pinky trotting over to a suspicious-looking rock.

"No, Pinky!" she screamed, hoping the cat would hesitate. Straif winced.

She clutched his upper arm. "I think the rock is bespelled with a trap."

He muttered a Word, and Pinky stilled, slitted his eyes, and growled over his shoulder at Straif. With two strides Straif was over by the rock. He looked down. "Oh, yes," he said quietly. "I can see the aura of Flair—the trace of the person who did this, but I don't know the trail. It is not—"

"Not what?"

"Not someone I invited tonight, I don't think."

Mitchella knew that wasn't what he was about to say, but she was too tired and aching to protest.

Antenn went and picked up Pinky, petting him, soothing, and watching Mitchella from dark eyes that held a fear she never wanted to see again.

She struggled against Straif's grasp, and he slowly slid her down his hard body and set her feet on the ground. She winced. She hurt, was sweaty, filthy, humiliated. She wanted to get away from this ordeal, fast. She checked her timer. "I must ensure the Residence is as prepared as possible for tonight. I must—"

"Greetyou!" a man called. They all turned to see a smiling Holm Apple and his wife, Lark. Both had orange tabby tomcats trotting beside them. Neither of the cats wore a weathershield.

The sun appeared from behind the last of the clouds and beamed bright rays around them. Mist rose from the ground.

Holm stopped by Straif and Mitchella and studied the rock. "I think I'd like you to invite your distant relative the guardsman Winterberry to the Ritual tonight," Straif said. "We can turn the matter of the trap over to him."

Holm's eyebrows shot up, but he nodded. "I'll scry him from inside. We're staying with the Ashes, and we had a visit from young T'Vine. He strongly suggested that we come over here. I don't know why that boy has to plague us with prophecies."

Mitchella started toward the Residence, Lark kept up, but stared at Mitchella with a Healer's probing gaze. "You're hurt."

"It's nothing much."

"Hmm," said Lark. She scooped up her cat. "Take Phyll, he's very good at Healing minor injuries."

Just lifting her arms to accept the cat made Mitchella grit her teeth in pain. "Very well."

"You should soak in a hot mineral pool," Lark said.

"There's one in my guest suite," Mitchella said. Phyll's purring seemed to sink under her skin to soothe her muscles.

"Very good," Lark said to Mitchella. "Is your cuz Trif coming to the Ritual tonight?"

With a shrug that didn't hurt as much as she expected, Mitchella said, "I don't know. T'Blackthorn issued the invitations."

Lark nodded and returned to the men and all the cats near the rock. Phyll twisted in Mitchella's arms to see what was going on. His purring paused, and a rush of aching pain flooded Mitchella. "Please, Phyll, can you concentrate on me? I hurt." She added a whimper for good effect. Phyll cuddled in her arms and revved up his purr.

Straif watched as Mitchella slowly walked up the drive to the Residence. Holm continued talking about the trap, but Straif didn't listen. Mitchella had been so brave, so smart. A survivor, like him, but he must make the estate safe for her.

The sway of her hips was different than usual. She walked with pain. Straif swore, then felt the soft warmth of Lark's fingers on his arm. "She'll be fine. Phyll is an excellent Healer Cat."

"She's only been here a couple of days, but she's worked so hard that the Residence is already shaping up. She works *too* hard."

"Yes," piped up Antenn. "She's thrown herself into this project. It's a beautiful house. I think her heart aches to see it in such poor condition." He slid his gaze to Straif, then flushed. "GentleSir Holl—Apple, did you say you met Vinni

T'Vine at T'Ash's? He was supposed to meet me here. Huh."

Holm sighed. "Yes." He patted a pocket, drew out a twist of papyrus. "This is for you."

Antenn shook his head at the note. "That boy Vinni is more than a little strange." Antenn's eyes gleamed. "But I bet the Clovers and I can teach him a thing or two." He read the note. "He put off the scrim with the Clovers until tomorrow, after my WorkEnd bell." Antenn's lip curled.

Clapping a hand on the boy's shoulder, Holm said, "In my opinion, he's more concerned about the Ritual here tonight than he is about the Clovers."

"Huh!" said Antenn.

Lark turned to Straif, her lavender eyes meeting his. "The Clovers are a very interesting Family. Did you invite Trif Clover to the Ritual?"

"No." He barely knew Trif Clover.

"With Winterberry as an extra man, you'll need another woman to even out the circle."

"You're right," Straif said. He wanted to go up to the Residence and check on Mitchella. Tell her how much he admired her, appreciated her.

But he had to examine the nasty trap. Her safety came first.

Seventeen

*S*traif *studied the large rock, half embedded in mud, a* pyramid-like point sticking up. He said to Holm, "What do you think of this?"

"A reflective Flair trap. The more you use Flair to escape, the more your Flair is turned against you and you're hurt. Old-fashioned, but not difficult to set, and very effective."

Straif focused his eyes until he could see the trail from the rock that had been the trigger to the nearby tree. "The rock has an attraction field around it, and a dip has been hollowed out before it. If a person wasn't paying too much attention to where they were going, if one wasn't looking for trouble, one would be drawn to it." He *hated* the fact that Mitchella had been hurt on his grounds. His hands fisted. When he found out who'd done this, he'd make them pay.

"When the spell was tripped, the person would be propelled to the tree and into a living cage." Holm whistled.

They stared at the broken, twisted, and frayed branchlets that had encased Mitchella.

Antenn said, "It's a series of nature spells, isn't it?" He scowled, jutted his chin defiantly at Straif. "I don't work with such spells. I'm an apprentice architect. I work with human-made materials to *build*." Pinky sniffed as if punctuating

Antenn's words. "Someone who spent a lot of time outside Druida in the wilds of Celta might know a lot of nature spells."

"Antenn." Lark's voice held a note of reprimand.

"Well, he would," Antenn said. "I've never been outside of the city."

Self-recrimination bit Straif. He'd hurt the feelings of the boy the day before. It would take time before Antenn would trust him. "I didn't set the spell," Straif said quietly. "I have stronger Flair at my command." He frowned. "Mitchella thought it was a threat. The other Blackthorn, perhaps," he slanted a look at his cuz. "You've heard of that?"

Holm nodded. "We seem to be living exciting lives. I don't have the contacts in the Councils to help you there, anymore."

"We can't stay in Druida long, just for the Ritual," Lark said.

"Thank you for coming. The Ritual means a great deal to me. I believe most of the Hollys living at T'Holly Residence will be here tonight," Straif said, tidying up the torn branches. They pulsed with Mitchella's energy.

Holm stiffened, and Lark embraced him. "Your mamá will be glad to see you," she said.

Straif met his cuz's hard gray eyes. "T'Holly is coming to realize his mistake—his many mistakes—with regard to you and your HeartMate."

"He won't admit to the world that he errored very soon," Holm said, his expression resigned. He held his HeartMate tightly.

Straif felt the emptiness of his own arms, his own heart, and yearned for another—a woman. Mitchella.

"Better take care of the trap," Antenn said. He tilted his head to look at the rock. "Do you think the rock should be destroyed?"

"It holds malice," Straif said. The Flair trace surrounding it was a nasty yellow green. Not a sane color. "Even if ground to dust, the fragments would carry the malice. It will have to be cleansed."

"You should let T'Ash do that," Holm said. "He's the best with stones."

"Right. He might be able to tell us more about it. But I'm giving it to Winterberry."

"Hard to understand who the spell was aimed at—you, Mitchella, Antenn, or someone coming tonight." Holm shook his head.

Fury flashed through Straif. "My estate has been defiled too often."

Lark touched his arm. "The Ritual will secure it tonight."

He rolled his shoulders to ease tense muscles. "Yes. You remind me that I should be preparing myself for the Ritual."

"No sex," Holm said cheerfully.

Straif glanced at Antenn, but he was watching Pinky stalk Holm's cat, the lazy Meserv. "Is my attraction that obvious?"

Holm grinned and took his HeartMate's hand from Straif's sleeve. "Quite. The Clovers are a remarkable Family."

*T'*Holly arrived in the evening, about a septhour before the Ritual. Straif was proud to lead the Captain of the Council into his newly refurbished ResidenceDen.

The GreatLord looked around with approval. "Very nice. In fact, I like it better than the way it was in your father's time." His face tensed. "Your request for the use of the T'Blackthorn funds to restore the house has been denied. Whatever monies you have spent will be taken from your own account."

Straif kept his expression blank, but couldn't prevent the heat of humiliation from warming his face. Even as he strove to total what he'd spent, he nodded. "Thank you for telling me."

"Are you sure everyone coming tonight is a good ally?" T'Holly asked.

Acid roiled in the pit of Straif's stomach. "As sure as I can be." He glanced at the timer. He'd cleansed himself, dressed in his finest ritual robe woven of bright metallic threads, and meditated. He was due at the sacred grove for the preliminary steps of the Ritual. He couldn't brief T'Holly on the trap.

"Be careful." T'Holly squeezed Straif's shoulder. "There are whispers going around the Councils that your obsession with remedying your genetic flaw is unhealthy, that you picked up odd notions traveling in the wilds of Celta, that you will not be able emotionally to face your past and restore your estate. It's said that you will continue to neglect your home, your land, and your duties by wandering Celta. I've heard gossip that your great Flair is unstable, which makes a lesser Flaired Blackthorn with no health problems more attractive to the Councils. I haven't been able to track down who started the rumors. Everyone will be watching you tonight."

Straif swore.

"I can't lend you gilt openly, but if you need help . . ." T'Holly shook his head. "We'll figure out something."

"T'Blackthorn and I have discussed finances," Mitchella said from the doorway. She wore a long, purplish gown shot with golden threads that clung to her incredible figure. No scratches or bruises marred her pale skin. "With what we can accomplish tonight, my contacts, and the Residence stores, we should be fine. We'll scale back on expenditures and outside work, unless T'Blackthorn trades in favors with his allies."

Straif said, "I will be more careful as I pursue my quest here in Druida."

The sympathy and vitality flowing to him from Mitchella withdrew, and Straif ached with the loss.

She said, "Ailim Elder awaits you in the Grove of the Dark Goddess." A sad smile passed over her face. "She is very pregnant. T'Heather, the Healer, is with her. The grove and the fountain are secure." She curtseyed, Commoner to FirstFamily Lord, and Straif didn't like it. "You should go."

Straif walked up to her, took her hands, and kissed them in turn. "I'll go. You'll join us shortly?"

She pinkened and withdrew her hands, gave her deepest curtsey to T'Holly, and left.

"A very beautiful and talented woman," T'Holly said. Still something in his manner made Straif uncomfortable— did T'Holly approve or disapprove of his relationship with Mitchella, and why? Straif didn't want to know. He bowed, equally as formal as Mitchella. "I'll see you later, Uncle."

T'Holly hesitated. "Is Holm here?"

"Of course. He and his HeartMate arrived earlier."

Now T'Holly seemed to want to avoid impossible questions and impossible answers. "I'll see you later," he grated.

_M_itchella knocked on Antenn's suite door. When he didn't call out, she glanced at her timer, then opened the door a crack. "Antenn? It's time we go down to the Grove of the Dark Goddess."

He walked out of his bedroom, wearing a long bloused-sleeved tunic with small stand-up collar that fell to his knees, and bloused trous that fit at the ankles. Both were black shot with gold thread and dressier than anything she'd ever seen him in. He fussed with a black furrabeast leather belt.

"Isn't that Cago's Nameday Ritual outfit?" she asked.

Antenn flinched. "He outgrew it. He didn't like it anyway. I *asked* if I could have it. I knew we were participating in a Ritual where a lot of FirstFamilies will come, and I wanted to look right. They're your clients. I hope they'll be my clients, too. Cago said I could have it."

He sounded so defensive that she hugged him and stroked his hair, but only once because of his pride. Then she stepped away. "You're very dashing." She curtseyed to him. "Gentle-Sir Moss."

Eyeing her, he said, "Yeah?"

"Yes. Now you're making me nervous."

"You always look beautiful," he said, and gave her a sweet smile that touched her, since he used it so infrequently. She did love him, this child of her heart.

"You're wearing your old third Passage celebration gown."

She laughed. "I thought I'd better wear my fanciest dress, too. And though it's not black for the Dark Goddess and the new twinmoons, it's purple for this month—Hawthorn. I'm not sure if GreatLord T'Hawthorn is coming, but if he is, he should be pleased that I'm wearing his color."

"Everyone will be pleased just seeing you." He scowled. "T'Blackthorn will like that gown. You'll be next to him at the Ritual. He'll probably look down the neckline."

The neckline was of soft folds, but could definitely shift.

Hands on hips, Antenn stared at her, still frowning. "Are you going to have sex with him?"

Her stomach squeezed. "The attraction is there, and I'm thinking of it." She'd never lied to Antenn and wouldn't start now, though she'd been much more discreet in her affairs since he'd become her ward.

"It can't last. It can't ever lead to anything serious."

"Of course not." In her early years, more than one man

ended a relationship because she was sterile. Now she preferred very light and surface affairs. Except with Straif Blackthorn. "I'd like to have an affectionate and passionate affair."

"He's a client."

She grit her teeth. He wasn't saying anything that hadn't circled round and round in her mind, but it was tough hearing it. "I'm well aware of all the disadvantages of an affair with Straif Blackthorn."

Antenn's gaze searched her face. "Does he know you're sterile?"

Mitchella shrugged. "It's old Commoner news that likely wouldn't reach Noble ears, but he's friends with T'Ash and D'Ash, who know I'm sterile. Probably."

Lip curling, Antenn said, "I don't like him using you."

"I plan on using *him* for"—*good, hot, sex*—"pleasure."

"You won't get hurt?"

Mitchella put her hand on his shoulder. "Antenn, I try to make sure that no one ever gets hurt in my affairs, including me."

"Huh. That doesn't mean it won't happen." He slanted her a dark look.

"No, but I weigh the pleasure versus the pain factor. Sometimes the pleasure is worth any pain. Like having you. We've had our arguments, some resentments, but we worked through them and we're together. I can't think of a time when you won't be in my life, as my—friend."

He flung himself at her, squeezed her tight, and strode from the room, moving rapidly from the suite and through the Residence. Mitchella followed. Finally he said, "Yes. We'll be together until I'm grown." His voice sounded choked, and as they left the house, he lifted eyes that could have shone from tears. "You and the Clovers have taken care of me. I'll always take care of you, especially when you're old."

"Thanks a lot," Mitchella said, but the spring night touched her with soft air, with incredible streams of starlight and quickened her blood. She was on her way to see Straif, to link with him in a power circle, to be part of a FirstFamilies Ritual. She, *she,* Mitchella Clover, would be directing the energy to restore the Residence. She'd never felt so vital.

When they reached the narrow path to the Grove of the

Dark Goddess, Antenn slipped his left hand into Mitchella's right. She had no doubt that it was to claim her for the Ritual. Straif would officiate as the Lord, pregnant Ailim Elder as the Lady, but Mitchella would be on Straif's right. Since the circle would alternate male-female, Antenn had made sure he'd be connected with Mitchella.

She looked down at him and said, "You have more Flair than I. I'll be providing the detailed direction of the energy we raise to restore the Residence, so I'll be depending on you."

Antenn nodded soberly. "I won't let you down."

"Of course you won't. You never could." When she saw him smile, anxiety that had lodged in her vanished. They'd face what would come as a familial unit. Two Commoners amongst the greatest Flaired of Celta.

The path spilled out from between towering trees to a grassy glen inside the grove. Only the very tips of the budding trees met, showing the black swath of sky and brilliant starshine. At the far end of the grove was the Fountain of the Black Goddess. She stood in the top, smallest bowl of five basins, her hands palms out, away from her sides. Water would stream from her hands when they repaired the pipes.

With one glance, Mitchella saw that Straif had been busy, grooming the glen, the bushes and trees surrounding them, cleaning out, preparing and polishing the fountain. The white marble gleamed in the starlight.

No twinmoons. This was the night Cymru and Eire were dark. The time of the new twinmoons. Another little shiver tingled down her spine. A time of great power, and she felt it around her.

In the center of the clearing was an altar Mitchella had never seen before, of black marble that seemed to absorb the night dark, trapping starlight. The altar scarf was a filmy black, shot with silver, the tools atop the altar glowed with the Flair that came from much use. Sweet, heady incense rose in a plume from the miniature cauldron.

Many people already stood in the RitualCircle. Mitchella noticed they were mostly of Straif's generation or younger. T'Ash and D'Ash, Holm and Lark Apple, young Vinni T'Vine paired with Mitchella's cuz, Trif Clover. But the elders of the Circle were awesome, T'Holly, the Captain of all the Councils, and his HeartMate, D'Holly, with most of their Family who resided in T'Holly Residence.

Mitchella saw D'Holly, Holm Apple's mother, catch his hand and pull her disowned son firmly to her side. Tears glittered in her eyes. T'Apple, D'Holly's father, had given Holm his new surname.

T'Heather, the premier Healer of Celta, stood frowning down on the pregnant Ailim Elder's left. Other major Great-Lords were T'Hawthorn and T'Reed; the GreatLadies included D'Rowan and D'Alder. Mitchella gulped. Antenn squeezed her hand. He said nothing, but she sensed he was as overawed as she.

In a brief count, she figured there were at least sixty people ready to ally with Straif. She wondered what it would cost him.

Then Ailim Elder glided to them. Mitchella didn't know how she did it, she was so hugely pregnant. It was a tremendous mark of support and distinction that Ailim graced the Ritual. Ailim placed her hands on Mitchella and Antenn, and a blessing moved from Ailim to them. In her well-modulated SupremeJudge's voice, she said, "Welcome to the New Twin-moons Ritual. I'm very pleased to see both of you together." Ailim had been the judge who had placed Antenn with Mitchella.

Antenn shuffled his feet. He'd never gotten over his awe of the SupremeJudge. Mitchella brushed a kiss on Ailim's cheek. "Thank you for the welcome, and the blessing, and most of all, Antenn. You're beautiful, the embodiment of the Lady as Matron."

"You look like you're gonna pop any minute," Antenn blurted, then stepped closer to Mitchella. She felt the heat of his flush.

Ailim threw back her head and laughed. Her blond hair seemed spun starlight. "Come, friends, it is time we started."

So Mitchella and Antenn took their places in the Circle.

Straif looked cool and calm, but when he linked hands with her, excitement surged through their link and to Antenn. He jumped and stared at Straif.

The man's lips twitched up, but his eyes looked a little wild. Mitchella dredged up calm and sent him a measure. He exhaled slowly, nodded thanks.

When Ailim Elder placed her hand in his, he inhaled deeply and dropped Mitchella's fingers, going with Ailim to the center of the Circle to begin the ceremony. The opening of the Ritual was like many others Mitchella had attended, except for the sheer Flair being generated, and that helped her settle.

With each moment that passed, Mitchella became more aware of her surroundings, and the people linked with her. Wispy clouds veiled the bright Celtan night, and only starshine provided illumination. They stood hand-in-hand in a large Circle, more Nobles than Mitchella had ever seen together at once in person, and she was part of it! So was Antenn, and to the surprise and amusement of many, so were the FamCats Drina, Zanth, Samba, the FamDog Primrose, and even Pinky. The Fam animals sat or lay on their person's foot, connected with the circle of humans and providing a hint of wildness in the cycling link. From the auras she could see clearly, she understood that she was one of the weakest in Flair.

The FirstFamily Lords and Ladies shone as bright as stars, surrounded by white energy, until she could only see their outlines, not their features, a mixed blessing. Families gathered together as their energies often complemented and magnified power. The most unexpected grouping was the Hollys, with Lark Hawthorn Apple and her disowned Holly husband, Holm, linked to the rest through his brother Tinne and then to D'Holly.

Ailim Elder shifted from foot to foot as if trying to stay comfortable. Her Flair was rich with burgeoning creation. Mitchella wasn't talented enough to tell whether her unborn babe contributed a hint of energy, too.

As the Ritual proceeded, Mitchella's mind hazed at the sheer power of it all—power that came to her to direct, since she had the clearest vision of a restored Residence. Flair ran up her hands, encasing her, whirling around her so potently that she felt like a galaxy wheeling in the heavens. She couldn't have contained it, couldn't have guided it, except for Straif. He was there next to her, rock solid, connected to the land itself, to steady and help her.

An energy sphere formed, grew massive and a thousand times more powerful than what she'd seen the AirMages control when they'd smothered the fire at her home.

The sphere was a golden bubble, unhampered by air or ground. She saw it in her mind's eye, and Straif moved it from the grove to the Residence until the energy enveloped the house. Sweat trickled down his arm to dampen his palm; his scent drifted to her.

Mitchella blinked, but her mind's eye remained clear. She saw the *entire* Residence, including the hidden HouseHeart that only Family should know. She wanted to ask Straif about that, but Flair held her in its grip and she couldn't move, could barely breathe. She sensed that Straif understood she saw the HouseHeart, but shielded that knowledge from everyone else. An honor, she supposed. Better if she could breathe easily.

We will bless and renovate the Residence first, then restore the shieldspells of the walls around the land, said Straif.

Focusing on the house, Mitchella saw it as if it were a viz. *Yes, blessing, first,* she managed to project.

Ailim Elder, as the Lady, began the blessing chant, others joined, and Mitchella gasped at the beauty of the song. Everyone raised their linked arms overhead; the cats purred. A stream of pure, potent Flair—*positive* Flair, with no ill-wishes, no negative thoughts toward Straif or T'Blackthorns—surged from the Circle to the sphere surrounding the Residence, and the house glowed golden, starting with a burst of light from the HouseHeart and spreading like benevolent fire throughout the home.

The energy circled like a whirlwind in the ballroom, eliminating layers of despair. Yet the place contained so much negativity, it might take all—

Straif sent the blessing to cleanse other rooms, faster, completely. His gratitude at the gathering spilled from him to warm Mitchella, and she sent the feeling back to him, adding the affection and a blessing. She caught a glimpse of a hard, crusted wound in his spirit breaking open, being soothed. Swallowing hard, she fixed her gaze on the glow beyond the trees. She saw the blessing sift through the Residence. Something more was needed. "Peace," whispered Mitchella.

A quarter-way around the Circle from Straif, T'Hawthorn changed the beat of the chorus of the blessing song to a rhythmic poem of Peace. One by one, clockwise, each person picked up the verse. This spell, too, Mitchella knew. She had celebrated the spell with her own family, only its sheer power differed.

Finally, the last one added her voice to the rest. The circling energy calmed. Ailim Elder rested a little and smiled beautifully up at Straif. He looked down at her with tenderness, then turned to Mitchella. For the first time, his gaze was free of torment. They all repeated the verse three times.

Then Straif shouted, "Security!"

Eighteen

With Straif's yell of "Security," T'Oak, at the bottom of the Circle, raised his voice and sent his Flair cycling, raising the energy again. The Circle shuddered, and that force was added to the bubble of gold. An image of ice came to Mitchella's mind, coating the outside walls, doors, and windows in thick layers. Straif smiled in satisfaction. His shoulders straightened in relief that his home was safe again.

But the Residence needed more. "Beauty!" Mitchella cried. T'Apple, a few people to her right started another song, a lilting lyrical song. D'Spindle joined her lovely voice to his, then her HeartMate picked up the tune. Alternating male/female, each sang. Mitchella heard Antenn, and pride filled her at his competence.

When her turn came, she'd learned the words from the minds of those around her and she sang with all her spirit. Straif jerked a little, and the rest of the Circle raised their voices to overcome her screechy tones. She laughed inside. Again they sang the spell thrice, then Ailim Elder started a pattern of Words that raised the power even more. The final, most important spell neared.

"FLAIR!" shouted Straif, and the energy sent to the

Residence sank into every wall, deepened into a large pool in the HouseHeart, stored, available for use for years to come.

With a rolling, rushing sound, water shot from the pipes in the palms of the Dark Goddess and filled the first small basin in which she stood. Instants later, it cascaded into the next larger bowl. In a moment, it had filled the last basin and misting droplets dewed the celebratants. Mitchella felt her hair dampen, saw the gleam of a drop on her eyelashes.

Triumph zipped around the circle, and Mitchella cried out with joy, her shout joining others.

In gentle steps, Straif modulated their energy, sent the remnants back to them, calmed them. Ailim Elder's quiet voice joined with his as they ended the Ritual and finally broke the Circle, unlinked hands.

Mitchella forcibly locked her knees to keep from swaying, weak from all the Flair that had sizzled through her at her command. Her brain and ears buzzed. Licking dry lips, she announced, "The west terrace has tents of food and drink for your refreshment. Please follow Antenn."

Most of the others strolled, laughing and gesturing, from the grove to the west terrace. The air hummed with good cheer and their speculation on the state of the Residence and grounds.

GreatLady D'Heather whispered in her HeartMate's ear. In the bright starlight his flush was obvious. "Will you need me, SupremeJudge Elder?" he asked Ailim, eyeing her belly.

"MotherSire, I'm a FirstLevel Healer and still here," Lark Apple said.

The Heathers said their good-byes and left.

Mitchella smiled from her heart. If she squinted, she could see tiny motes of Flair—silver, gold—glistening in the air. She felt surrounded by champagne, breathing it in, letting it settle on her skin, slip along her nerves and into her blood.

Ailim Elder swayed, paled. "The baby's coming!"

Lark Apple ran to support her. Straif followed.

Taking both of Ailim's hands, Lark frowned, then glanced at Straif. "I think it best that she isn't moved. We can bring the babe into the world here, and shortly."

Straif gulped. "This will be a great blessing on my House." The bond between him and Mitchella pulsed with a shade of fear. It would be disaster if something went wrong.

"Hold her while I arrange a bedsponge from the heavy moss here," Lark said, and efficiently formed a birthing bed. "Let's make her comfortable."

Straif gently lowered Ailim to the soft moss. She gripped his hand, wet her lips. "Send to the Ship, *Nuada's Sword*, for my husband, Ruis. I want him here."

Mitchella felt Straif hesitate. Having the Null on the estate could be harmful. It could cancel some of the newly made spells, blunt the pretty atmosphere around them.

"Of course," Straif said. "I don't have a functioning glider—"

"No Flair technology will work around Captain Elder," Vinni T'Vine said. He'd been standing on the other side of the fountain, and Mitchella hadn't noticed him. "I'm staying. I'll be the Oracle for the babe—to tell the strength and perhaps the bent of its Flair."

Ailim panted as a labor pain rippled through her body, then said, "T'Blackthorn Residence might be linked in communication with the Ship—"

Residence! Straif sent mentally, and Mitchella heard him, easily. She shivered.

T'Blackthorn? answered the Residence.

Send word to Captain Ruis Elder of Nuada's Sword *that his Lady is giving birth to their child here in the Grove of the Dark Goddess.*

A swirl of bright colors hitting her mind—emotions from Ailim—made Mitchella gasp. She tottered, fell against a huge tree. As she set her hands against the bark to push away in reactive fear, she sensed the deep hum of the tree's lifeforce, its pleasure in connecting with her—the one who had helped revitalize the land. She leaned back against the tree, blinking in surprise at this new connection and missed the rest of Straif's words until he smiled down at Ailim Elder.

Cradling her hand between both of his, he said, "T'Blackthorn Residence told me that your man is running for his horse and will be here in a few moments."

"Horse?" Mitchella asked.

"My . . . husband . . . keeps . . . several . . . horses . . . and stridebeasts—" Ailim bit her lip.

"There is no reason for you to hurt," Lark said. "Holm and

I will administer pain relief until your husband comes to Nullify our Flair." The Healer held out her hand for her HeartMate.

Holm swallowed, then joined Lark sitting on the ground and gingerly took her hand. He inhaled sharply, his color paled, then steadied. "Done," he said tightly.

Lark said, "Your baby is fine. Strong and healthy, ready to be born. We will move her along a little, perhaps have her arrive soon after her father is here. Straif, notify us as soon as Captain Elder rides onto the estate."

"I'm opening the gates now," Straif said calmly, belying the spiking emotions shooting through his and Mitchella's link. "Many people came through the front gates and straight to the grove. I can light their broad path with my Flair. Captain Elder will see the way. Riding fast, he won't have time to Nullify the path."

Straif gestured with a hand, and a dazzling swath of silver shone from the edge of the grove toward the front of the estate. Mitchella heard the distant appreciation of those who stood on the west terrace as they saw the trail light up.

"The baby is well positioned. Your body is ready, Ailim. Time to *push*. We can help a very little, with Flair," Lark said.

Mitchella set her jaw. She'd always celebrated every Clover birth with her family, but had never been with the mother and babe at the time. Memories marched before her of the new mothers' glowing faces, the new fathers' satisfied grins. The babies themselves, tiny and beautiful.

Residence! she sent strongly.

I hear you well, Mitchella Clover, the Residence said.

The newborn Elder girl will need washcloths, swaddling clothes, a blanket . . . She waved her hands even though she knew it couldn't see her.

I will warm the water of the fountain of the Dark Goddess, she can be bathed in the basin there. I will retrieve from storage newborn garments and accoutrements.

Not Fasha's, Mitchella said.

No. We have others. I have called Antenn to take them from the ResidenceDen and bring them to you.

Wait! Ruis Elder comes, he will want to hold his child. Any clothing made with Flair will fall apart. Mitchella was pleased with herself that she'd thought of this.

One moment. I am sorting. I have found some blankets and other clothes, but no baby clothes that are not Flaired. Antenn is laughing at us. The Residence sounded stiff.

Mitchella was smiling herself.

Chuckling, Mitchella refocused on the scene in front of her to discover Straif staring, the bond between them pulsing with a mixture of emotions—excitement, tenderness, pleasure in sharing all they had this night.

She couldn't look away from him. Everything around her sharpened preternaturally. She heard Ailim's soft pants and Lark's murmurs, saw the dark tracing of new leaves against the starry sky, smelled *him,* Straif—who had the fragrance of his land, and sage, and the hot tang of his Flair.

"Bring Ailim a stronger connection with this land, Straif," Lark requested.

Straif turned to murmur something to Ailim, then he slowly drew some Earth-energy into himself, some running to Mitchella, the rest to Ailim to help her.

Mitchella found enough wits to say, "The Residence has prepared some un-Flaired swaddling clothes for the baby."

Ailim's gaze turned from inward concentration to meet Mitchella's, and she smiled. "Our thanks." A pang crossed her face, and her eyes unfocused.

Holm withdrew his hand from Lark's and jumped to his feet, appearing pale. "I still don't do well in Healing situations." He shrugged. "I'll go pick up the clothes." He ignored his HeartMate's frown and smiled charmingly at Mitchella.

She smiled back. "Antenn has stacked them on a small table in the Great Hall."

Holm nodded and loped off.

"Mitchella, I need you," Lark said.

"I don't have much more than common Flair."

"But tonight you are linked with the land, and there's a bond between you and T'Blackthorn. If you switch places with him and link with him, you can filter his strong Flair to me through a woman's psi-pattern. I want more pain relief here."

Ailim looked up at them again, hurt glazing her eyes. "Mitchella . . . should . . . not . . . feel . . . obliged."

And Mitchella knew then that Ailim, the telempathic

judge, was feeling Mitchella's own ache and renewed grief at being sterile. But she couldn't refuse a woman in need. With more courage than she felt, she left the sweet calmness of the tree and sat near Ailim.

"Take Ailim's hand, now," Lark said.

Mitchella slid her left hand under Straif's, and he grasped her right hand with his left.

Lark tensed and she settled the fluctuating Flair. As their connection steadied, Mitchella became part of another powerful ritual. From Straif, she received a deep sense of the T'Blackthorn land, integral to him. *How could anyone believe someone else would be better for the estate?*

"They won't," Ailim whispered, answering Mitchella's mental question. Ailim stared at Straif and Mitchella. "This birth will be the talk of Druida for a few eightdays, and I'll be sure the Councils know of T'Blackthorn's honor and bond with his land." She spoke easily now, and Mitchella knew with wonder that she helped ease Ailim's labor.

For herself, Mitchella felt the gravid body of a woman carrying a baby ready to be born. The deep heaviness in her womb, the lushness of a body prepared to nurture a child, and she cherished the feeling—something that would never happen to her. Macha's disease had destroyed her eggs, ruined the lining of her uterus. She could never carry a child.

She sank into the physicality of Ailim's condition, and Lark let her—the Healer knowing as well as Ailim that Mitchella was sterile. The three women shared the knowledge in glances, in the flow of their Flair. Straif didn't seem to notice.

Tears trickled down Mitchella's cheeks.

"We will have to name the child after you, too, Mitchella," Ailim said.

Lark snorted. "I can tell you that a woman can have too many names."

Ailim smiled serenely. "Many of our FirstFamily names are used by both male and female, but I want my little girl to have a feminine name."

Mitchella dug deep to keep her voice steady. "Then you shouldn't name her Mitchella."

"What's your middle . . . name?" Ailim asked after a contraction had passed.

"Eve," Mitchella said.

"Beautiful," Ailim said, and closed her eyes.

Within the cycling Flair, Mitchella realized that the birth would soon be over. With Ailim's pain controlled, and others to help her push, the babe could be born shortly. Lark monitored both mother and baby, using her Healing Flair to ease the birth.

Straif, Ailim, and Lark all had great Flair. The sensation was incredible, as if it opened new doors in her mind, in her own Flair, speeding down unused pathways of her mind and body. She didn't deceive herself—the boost in her Flair wouldn't last, and she didn't care that it wouldn't. Great Flair made great demands upon the user. She'd seen others lose weight in a few days from the extensive use of Flair.

Lark, the Healer, shot her a glance, and Mitchella realized that the woman noted everyone's health. Mitchella realized more than one FirstFamily Lady or Lord died from too much stress on the organs when using great Flair.

"I'm back," Holm Apple said. He clutched the swaddling blankets tightly, as if to protect them with his life. "I'll stand over by the fountain, with T'Vine. How's it going?" he asked heartily.

His HeartMate sent him a cool glance. "Very well, all is ready for the babe to enter the world. We only wait for the father."

A few moments later, the sound of thundering hooves echoed, the ground vibrated, an instant before a man bent low over the neck of a horse burst into the grove clearing. The rider stopped the horse near Mitchella, flung himself off the animal, and strode to the little group.

The fountain stopped bubbling. The remaining Flair floating in the grove dimmed, flickered out.

"Ailim, beloved!"

"Don't hold her yet, Ruis. One last push, Ailim!"

Ailim and Mitchella pushed.

The babe slid into Lark's waiting hands—screaming.

"This isn't right!" Lark muttered, placing the baby on Ailim's stomach, waving hands over the child and chanting a spell. Futilely.

T'Vine stepped forward with a wet cloth and washed the

baby, making her scream louder. He cradled her head in his hands. "As the formal Oracle attending this birth, I state that this baby is a Null like her father. Able to negate Flair and Flair technology." He caressed the little one's head. "May she have a long and happy life."

"I wondered," murmured Ailim. "My cuz told me I should hear the babe, connect with it if it had Flair." She seemed supremely unconcerned that her girl child was lacking in what most people would consider a sense as important as any of the others. Mitchella gritted her teeth against a wash of envy. She wouldn't care if her baby was a Null, either, not if she could hold it in her arms, parent it, not even if she had to fight the entire world for it.

Not to be.

With Flair, Lark drew out the afterbirth and sent it into the land. "A blessing for the estate."

"Yes," whispered Straif. He didn't move his awed stare from the infant.

"She's beautiful," Ruis said, then frowned, stroking his daughter with one hand and holding his mate's fingers with the other. "We won't let anyone sneer at her."

"Of course not." Ailim smiled at him with love and tears in her eyes. "No one will ever believe Nulls are not essential to Celta ever again. Not after you." She kissed his fingers. "And the Ship is prepared to teach her to be another captain." She smiled. "The Ship is avid to raise a child within it again."

"When can I take them home?" Captain Elder demanded.

Lark set her hands on the child, shook her head, then physically examined her. "I have to use old ways without Flair on her. Frustrating. But I know she's healthy."

"Ship will examine her, too. It made a special cradle."

Switching her attention to Ailim, Lark said, "She is Healed with the remnants of the birthing spell."

"I'm not taking any chances," Captain Elder said. "I've ordered an automatic speeder to follow me. It should be here in a moment."

"The gates are still open," Straif said. "Many of my guests have been leaving—no doubt to spread the news."

Shouts erupted, then a steady humming sounded, and a sleek silver vehicle appeared.

The men stared at it. Even Mitchella noticed that the speeder was much smaller and prettier than any glider.

"How does it work?" asked Holm.

"Antigravity," said Captain Elder.

As the men gathered around the vehicle, Ruis lifted his wife and child inside to the thick sponge enveloping the floor, then entered himself. He bowed to them. "Thank you all for your gracious generosity. Merry meet."

"Very merrily met." Straif smiled. "And merry part."

"And merry meet again. Door down," Ruis said and the capsule closed. The others stepped back and the thing flew away.

"Interesting conveyance," Straif said. "I have an appointment with the Ship tomorrow morning and will be sure to ask the captain about that transport."

Water poured into the fountain of the Dark Goddess as Flair spells resumed. Mitchella sensed all they had done was still in place.

T'Vine stared after the vehicle a while, small face knit in concentration.

"So, Vinni," said Holm, "Can you read the fates of the Nulls?"

"Now father and daughter are gone, I can extrapolate paths in their lives as well as anyone else's." He looked back, and his eyes glittered with a shard of darkness. "You don't always take me seriously, Lords and Ladies, but I could tell you which of this little group will live the longest. That is nearly immutable, stamped on the visage for me to *see,* it's—"

"No!" Lark had finished tidying the area where the birth had taken place. "Sometimes *you* misread us, Vinni. None of us here underestimate you."

Mitchella laughed nervously. "I certainly don't."

Vinni stared at her, and she shifted her feet, then he smiled—a pure, boy's smile. "I don't know *everything*." A dimple flashed. "I don't know who will win in my scuffle with the Clover boys later today."

Time had escaped Mitchella. "It's after midnight?"

"Indeed it is," Straif said. He cocked his head. "The Ritual was wearing on most of my guests, and those up at the Residence have left."

"Sounds like we should go, too." Holm stretched, yawned,

and curved his arm around Lark. "A very good evening. Lark got to talk to her father and her MotherSire and MotherDam, and Trif Clover. We blessed and amassed Flair for the T'Blackthorn Residence for years to come. We participated in a birth—and my father addressed a civil greeting to me. A memorable night."

"Blessings abound," Straif said. "I'm glad that there is a break in T'Holly's attitude against you."

Holm flicked some dirt off his sleeve. "I spoke to him first, of course. They don't look good, T'Holly and D'Holly."

"Living under broken vows of honor is not easy," Lark said. "T'Heather and other Healers are doing their best to remediate the health aspects."

"Anyone with sense would use bad health as a reason to heal the breach with me and my HeartMate, but not the fighter T'Holly. He thinks he'd be seen as weak, cowardly. His damned pride. He's the captain of the FirstFamilies Council, he has nothing to prove to anyone."

"Wrong," Mitchella said, and realized she'd said it aloud when they all looked at her, so she chose her words carefully, "From what I understand, T'Holly has to admit he was wrong in disowning you, and that is something he doesn't often do."

Holm snorted. "Never. He has never admitted he was wrong."

"So that's an aspect of himself he has to confront and accept and modify if the situation is to change and be mended. It's not easy facing that something basic in yourself is deficient." How well she knew that.

"You put it very well, GentleLady Clover," Vinni bowed to her. "Sometimes we must understand that past dreams must be put aside in order to live a full life."

"Well, the boy's not talking about me," Holm said. "I've given up my past and live for present and future."

Mitchella didn't dare look at Straif.

Holm kissed his HeartMate, Lark. "We have a long trip back to Gael City, so let's say farewell and go to our soft bed-sponge at T'Ash's."

Ignoring Vinni, Straif embraced Holm and Lark and wished them well. Mitchella said her good-byes, too, and the couple teleported away.

Face stubborn in the starlight, Vinni stared with compressed lips at Straif, and Mitchella suddenly understood that the young prophet wanted Straif to give up his quest.

For a moment hope sputtered through her. But even if he gave up his first passion, Straif would never turn to her. She didn't know what he would do if he couldn't find a cure, probably decide to have children anyway. The FirstFamilies were much different from the Clovers.

Straif would never take her as more than a temporary lover. *Never.* The word Holm used regarding T'Holly. It still sounded hopeless.

"Time for me to go, too," Vinni said. "Farewell, Gentle-Lady, you have found your way."

Had she? Dared she let Straif blind her to her path, even for a short time? But she felt his heat beside her, the emotions flowing between them, kindling desire within her to know him better. Physically.

Time for another decision.

As she stared at Vinni, he nodded to Straif. "I will remind you that the price for my services is an invitation to *all* your parties." Then he disappeared with a pop.

Strain left Straif's muscles. He turned in a circle, and Mitchella felt him sending his senses into the night, searching for threats. The quiet pulse of night wafted to him, to her. No one other than those living at the Residence was within the estate walls. A slight breeze brought the scent of spring blossoms with it.

Straif turned to her. "Can you feel it? The new energy of the estate." And with his words, she could, some of the effervescence that she'd felt before tingled through her soles from the ground and spread through her, sparkling along her nerves, reviving her spirits.

Thickening the bond she had with Straif, calling her to him.

This man was special. Not because of his title or his name or his Flair, but because of what he'd survived, what he'd striven for. And like redecorating a FirstFamily Residence, the opportunity to love a man like this would come to her only once. Did she dare *not* grasp the pleasure? If she didn't take this chance, how often in the future would bitter regret gnaw at her? And how long had it been since she allowed herself to connect with a man more than superficially? Years. She wanted to drink deep of such powerful pleasure.

Whatever he saw in her eyes made his own go dark, potent. He bent down and brushed her lips with his, and Mitchella's insides clenched. Her body wanted his. Fire whispered through her veins, burst over their connection to hit him. He groaned, pulled her close. His mouth ravaged her own, opened her lips. His tongue swept in to learn every cranny of her mouth as his arms caged her so his hard body could learn every curve of hers—and tempt her with ravishing pleasure.

Nineteen

♥

"*Will you let me touch you, lovely Mitchella?*" *Straif* asked.

The desire throbbing between them made thinking hard, but Mitchella knew what she wanted—the feel of his calloused palms against her face. She took his hands and curved them over her cheeks, closing her eyes at the delicious texture.

When he exhaled, his breath tickled her temple, which stirred something so deep inside her that she craved fulfillment.

"Will you let me kiss you, beautiful Mitchella?"

She didn't know if she heard his words in her ear or in her mind, but her lips pulsated with the need to have them covered. Her head dropped back on her neck, and she said, "Yes," and left her mouth open for him to claim it.

He did. Lips firm, then nibbling, each press, each touch of the edge of his teeth increased the ache within her. Her lips needed his touch, as did her breasts, her core.

She didn't know if she trembled or he shuddered. Probably both. They swayed like trees in a high wind, but the air was still, only pulsating with heady passion. The rushing of the fountain matched the blood in her ears.

He lifted his head, and Mitchella stared up at his face, skin taut over muscle and bone. Noble features.

"I can't offer you everything you want," he said hoarsely. "Everything you deserve."

It hurt, a jolt of flaming lightning, and his body jerked as he felt it, too, so linked were they. His eyes went darker, more needy than she'd ever seen.

"I can only offer you all I have at this moment," he ground out.

"Yes," she said, and with her decision, all her doubts faded like mist in the hot sun. They might return, but now she'd seize the moment, seize the awful pleasure he could give her, seize *him*. She held on to him tight and threw her head back at the wondrous, sparkling desire and laughed up to the bright stars.

He held her so close she could feel the long cords of his muscles, the sinews of his tendons. The iron of his arousal nestling in the softness of her belly.

She laughed again and discovered it was he who shook.

"Here, now. In the soft moss of the grove. Under the eyes of the Dark Goddess," he said.

Her heart tripped, and she shook her head at the sweet madness engulfing them. "Yes!"

With a Word, he had them naked. Then her back sank into the cool, springy moss, and each tiny sprig rippled against her skin, and fire bloomed inside her. He watched her, sex jutting. And his body was everything she'd ever wanted, long, lean, hard.

She arched against the ground, repeating the sensation of the caressing moss, reveling in it. Holding up her arms to encourage him. Or perhaps it was to embrace the moment, or the sky, or the universe. Her nipples peaked with anticipation and fine droplets from the fountain.

Standing, his body angled to hers. His hands fisted at his sides, and she knew he wanted to take her hard and fast, but her softness, her femininity, the pure delight he took in observing her lush body against the rich black of the moss made him pause.

His nostrils flared. Images more than thought sped into her mind. *Woman. Goddess.*

She opened her thighs.

Mine.

He came down on her, and their spiraling passion merged, and he was between her legs, and his heart pounded against hers, and his hands, those tough, fabulous hands, sped over her, and his need was deep and dangerous and drew her into a firestorm of blinding craving, and he was inside her and plunging, and she was riding the whirlwind of glittering ecstasy and feeling all of him against her and inside her and merged with her, and they were screaming and shattering into a million stars flung across the sky.

Sensation returned first, the weight and heat of him atop her, the warm moss beneath her. He panted raggedly, chest caressing her breasts, causing her body to clench in orgasm one more time. He groaned.

I can't let you go, he said mentally.

But he would, she knew. As soon as cool thought and generations of tradition and duty replaced the need of his emotions, the greed of lust, he'd let her leave. After the job was done.

She wouldn't let it matter. She'd survived a devastating emotional blow before, could do so again. Right now she would take everything to keep in her memory forever. And she'd stop anticipating the worst. She'd live in the moment, celebrate this love.

She stroked his back, fingers gliding through the sheen of sweat, and was suddenly aware of his scent. The scent of sage, of the moss of the land, of the water of the fountain, of man.

"I had forgotten how wonderful sex with a soft, passionate woman was."

He had never known. Because he had never known her, or her love for him. She chuckled at his obtuseness.

He rolled until they lay on their sides, concerned about his weight on hers. He was all solid muscle. His breathing hadn't steadied, and wicked glee tripped through her.

The energy from the land, from the Residence, from the night of the new twinmoons—energy of birthing and growing and becoming—was back. She bounced to her feet, grinned down at him, and tossed her head, feeling the loose flow of her hair.

His stare had fastened on her breasts, and his eyes glazed. His manhood twitched. He groaned.

She shook her head and held out a hand to him.

"Wha—?" he asked.

Bending, she grasped his hand and pulled him up, Flair bringing him to his feet. He swayed.

"Let's play in the fountain."

Complete disbelief radiated from him.

She tugged, and he stumbled the few paces to the fountain. She climbed into the large, lowest bowl of the five. Let him go to bend under the water and circle the fountain, feeling the fresh water sluicing over her back, sliding into her hair, down her butt and her legs. Wet hair tangled in front of her eyes, she rounded the basin and bumped into him. He reached and grabbed the lip of the fourth bowl to steady himself.

"It's cold," he gasped.

She laughed.

"How can you do that?" he asked. "How can you move? How can you *see* to move?"

She stepped around him, brushing against him with her full body, and his grip on the stone basin showed white knuckles. Filling her cupped hands with water, she flung it against his chest.

He inhaled on a rush of air. She giggled and admired the pattern of droplets caught on his chest hair.

Blinking down at her, his eyes widened as she plopped into the basin. The coldness of the water only refreshed her. She washed the sex from her, eyed him from behind a swath of hair.

He stepped back. "I'll do it." Planting his feet, he curved his hands, dipped up water and said "warm," then let the water trickle down around his groin.

"Sissy," Mitchella said between giggles as he repeated the process.

"I've lived in untamed Celta too long to like cold water when it can be warm. I *appreciate* the niceties of civilization." He slapped the rim of the stone bowl. "Like running fountains." Watching her with gleaming eyes, he finally smiled— lustily. "Like the curves of a city woman." He bent down, both hands reaching.

Mitchella scooted back over the smooth marble, then glanced at the sky, searching for the dark shadows of the twinmoons that must be setting—a few septhours before the dawn. "It's very late."

"Very early," corrected Straif, then scanned the sky himself. He pointed out the round blackness of the moons that blocked the starlight. When she followed his finger, she saw them herself, slight curves of obscurity above the grove.

Straif stepped from the fountain, dried himself with a Word, and plucked her from the basin to do the same. A moment later they were clothed. He sighed, twined his fingers into hers. "Let's pursue this activity, longer and on a proper bedsponge."

She didn't think she could face making love on the Blackthorn generational bed, so she smiled slowly, putting every iota of sex and charm into the curve of her lips, the lowering of her lashes. She licked her lips. "My room."

He shuddered. Nodded. "Right. Let's 'port."

With a throaty chuckle, she shook her head. "Let's walk." And started through the grove to the path toward the Residence. He curled an arm around her waist, and their height was so even they walked in stride. She sensed him fumbling for words.

"Don't," she said, not looking at him. "There's no need for any explanations between us."

He hesitated, then picked up the pace. They walked to the great lawn, then up to the west terrace. There was no sign of detritus of a gathering.

"All my housekeeping spells are at full strength and work as designed," the Residence said proudly, booming through the night.

"Very good," Mitchella said, and they entered the quiet house. It gleamed around them, clean and energized.

Drina and Antenn, Pinky asleep in his arms, awaited them, sitting on the bottom stair. Both boy and Fam looked disgruntled.

The moment Drina saw them, she launched into complaining mews. Pinky woke and hissed, but that didn't stop the little cat.

Where have you been? You left Me to be hostess to everyone. The thought chilled Mitchella. That was exactly what had happened.

Drina preened. *Though I handled it well, and everyone admired Me, it was much work.* She lifted a paw and licked it—with no hint of any exhaustion. *You should have been here to admire Me, too, as was your duty.*

Mitchella's eyebrows raised. She heard the little cat, probably because they'd been linked in the Circle. Mitchella hoped her connection with Drina would go away. Fast.

Antenn stood stiffly, looking angry, and Mitchella realized that he knew she and Straif had had sex. Mitchella had been very discreet about her lovers, never taking them to her bed at home—and the thought crashed down on her that she had no home. All her previous exuberance vanished. "The birthing went very well. Captain Elder and SupremeJudge Elder have a lovely baby girl. She's a Null."

That caught Antenn's curiosity. "Really?"

"Yes," Mitchella said.

"Then she might be captain of *Nuada's Sword* someday," Antenn said. His eyes gleamed with possibilities, with speculation as to what his generation might do, looking toward the future. Good. Mitchella smiled. "You can talk it over with the Clovers later today, at Trif's nameday party."

"That will be great," he said, rubbing his hands. "That Vinni Lord didn't come up after the Ritual."

"He stayed to be the Oracle at the new baby's birth," Straif said. "Thank you for taking part in the Ritual. Your Flair and bond with Mitchella helped her. Your energy and knowledge of the Residence, as well as architecture, was also an asset."

Antenn eyed him warily, hunched a shoulder. "You're welcome." His expression went distant, he shook his head. "Incredible experience. So much Flair. Really sizzling event. Those FirstFamilies . . ." He shook his head. "Zow."

"We try to please," Straif said. Drina walked up to him, muttering cat sounds, then leapt onto his right shoulder. Straif winced, but didn't answer her, keeping his gaze on Antenn. "I appreciate you working with the Residence in my absence."

"Not much to organize, just oversaw the cook, followed the Residence's advice." Antenn sneered at Drina. "T'Holly and D'Holly acted as host and hostess. Nobody came inside, like you ordered. I told everyone that T'Blackthorn Residence was a work in progress and invited them to your summer solstice open house."

"Again, my thanks," Straif said.

Yawning, Antenn stared at Mitchella. "Will you see me to my bedsponge?" He looked more worried than angry now. Straif treating him as an adult had soothed the boy's pride.

"Of course," Mitchella said, walking up to him and putting an arm around his shoulders. She looked down at Pinky, who grinned back at her. The small tom had flecks of food on his whiskers, and something that looked like cream. "As Straif said, you did very well. You have much more Flair than I, and you and Trif stabilized me so I could direct the energy to rehabilitate the Residence." She and Antenn climbed the stairs.

He grinned up at her. "Yeah?"

"Yes," she gave his shoulders another squeeze. "I couldn't have done it without you."

"Yes, you could have." He stopped at the top of the flight, looked down. Mitchella followed his gaze. Straif and Drina were gone. Still, Antenn kept his voice low. "You and T'Blackthorn have a strong link, and that was even *before*."

As they walked along the corridor, Mitchella sighed. "True, not as strong as yours and mine, though, and my connection with Straif Blackthorn is strictly temporary. You know nothing can come of it."

His mouth set. He didn't look at her. "I don't want you getting hurt."

"Living full-heartedly can hurt," she said. "I'm not going to step back from pleasure, from life, because later circumstances may bring me pain."

Antenn snorted. "You Clovers." But he was reassured. She kissed the top of his head and opened his door.

He looked back down the corridor, at the door to the MasterSuite and beyond to the door to her guest suite on the opposite side of the hallway. "Are you going to sleep in that T'Blackthorn bed?"

"Not tonight," she said.

He nodded, lifted to his toes to kiss her cheek. "Night blessings."

Bending, she returned the kiss to his cheek. "Night blessings."

With a half-sigh, half-yawn, Antenn stepped into the sitting room, and Mitchella heard the muffled roar of surf. The door closed.

Mitchella bit her lip and marched back the way she'd come to her own door. She'd spoken lightly to Antenn, and he'd believed her surface emotions. Mitchella was all too aware that she was deep over her head in every way with Straif, GrandLord T'Blackthorn. The only thing she could do was not to show it. To keep the affair light between them, too, despite the fact that she was rapidly falling in love with the man. When this ended, she was going to hurt badly. She straightened her spine. She was a survivor.

Straif came to her. They gave and took. And shared. Their loving was beyond anything Mitchella had known.

S*traif awoke in the soft white sunlight*, sated and with a lightness of spirit he hadn't felt in many years—after the first terrible grief of loss had faded and when he'd been certain he'd find a remedy for his heritage.

He stretched languidly, enjoying the scent of sex around him, the easy play of his muscles, the smooth, luxurious silkeen sheets under his body.

Mitchella gasped, and a quiver of terror sped to him through their link. He was out of bed with a long knife in his hand before she had time to turn her head.

She stood at the window, hand at her throat, eyes so wide only an edge of green showed around the pupils. Blood fled her face, making it nearly as pale as the white gown she wore, highlighting the fire of her hair. When her stare fixed on the knife he held, met his own gaze, she flinched. He hated that.

He was with her in three strides, forcing her away from the window, stretching his Flair as he'd stretched his body. Nothing threatened.

Until he looked out the window, down onto the grounds and saw the black furrows of torn earth spelling "MitchBitch Will Die."

Rage flashed through him. The estate was secure, had been

secure since they'd raised the shieldspells during the Ritual last night. How could this happen?

"Well, now we know who the trap was set for. Who the target is," Mitchella said, her voice shaky. She let out a ragged breath. "Me."

Straif sent the knife back under the bed, hauled her into his arms, felt her yield to his embrace, her face turn into his shoulder, her arms circle him. She was afraid, and that sent his anger spiraling once more, but he held her gently. He comforted her with stroking hands, distracted himself from his fury with the fragrance of her—full-bodied summer flowers. He tunneled his fingers into her hair. Strands clung to his fingers, and he wanted to hold on to them forever. They stood there as one moment passed into two, three, six. Their breaths sighed together, their heartbeats matched.

Finally she lifted her head, and the sweetness in her gaze caught at his heart. She was so open to him. Then she stepped away, not looking at the window, but gesturing to it. "You're the tracker, you can figure out who did that." Her brows dipped in question. "Could it be done with Flair?"

Since she sounded interested, not frightened, Straif answered her honestly. "Flair would have been more illusory. Those ruts are real."

She nodded, went to the wardrobe, drew out clothes, and dressed. Straif couldn't watch. If he did, he'd lose control and they'd be back in bed. There was too much to accomplish.

As if answering his thoughts, she said, "Your Residence-Den still needs work if we want it perfect by summer solstice, to keep your estate and title. I have several ideas for furnishing it with items in storage since our budget is cut to the bone. I'll have three holomodels ready for you by noon." She glanced at the clock. "When is your appointment with *Nuada's Sword*?"

An undertone in her voice alerted him that she was withdrawing from him. He couldn't have that. Not now, this moment. He glanced at her. She was dressed in work tunic and trous of a soft gray emphasizing her vivid coloring. So he went and took her in his arms. She didn't lean on him this time, just stood quietly.

"I've cancelled the appointment with *Nuada's Sword* for the time being." He kissed her temple, lingering until sweet warmth flowed between them. When she stepped away, she was smiling.

"Would you care to see Vinni T'Vine confront the Clover boys? This is the nameday of my cuz, Trif. Her nineteenth, which means the storms of her second Passage to free her Flair are officially over. We're having a big party."

Straif froze. "I have nothing to gift her with."

Mitchella rolled her eyes, opened her arms wide. "She was here last night, invited at the last minute, if you recall. Celebrating a powerful New Twinmoons Ritual with the crème de la crème of Celtan society on the eve of her nameday thrilled her. She socialized with them later. That's gift enough."

Lifting her chin, Mitchella continued, "If that isn't sufficient for your notions, this is the month of Hawthorn, and she'd *love* a bush from your estate. Lady and Lord know that you have plenty of excess brush—find one and pot it to provide greenery for her MidClass Lodge apartment."

Heat crawled up his neck, and he shifted his feet. He hadn't thought a *prized* gift could be so inexpensive.

Mitchella nodded. "That's settled, then. The party is this evening, but we should go a little early to see what happens between the Clover boys and GreatLord T'Vine." Her lips parted over white teeth. "I wonder if Vinni is judging them by Antenn. Antenn is small for his age"—her eyes danced—"but the Clovers are tall, healthy boys. Every one of them." She set her hands on her hips, drawing his gaze. "And the Clover women are sturdy, too."

Her hips were wide and curvy, made to carry babes. His mind dizzied.

She kissed him briefly but hard on the mouth and walked out of the room. As he gazed after her, he recalled the globes of her bottom in his hands and gulped.

His thoughts focused when Drina appeared before him. She gazed up at him, wrinkling her small pink nose, slashing her brown tail. *What are you doing here? You missed breakfast with Me. The cook did not let Me eat in the small dining room. You must inform him that I get what I want. I had to eat in the kitchen with that other Cat. He slurps.* She shuddered delicately.

"Sorry," Straif said, keeping his expression solemn.

Drina sniffed. *You are forgiven.* She smiled, and it didn't look half as sweet as Mitchella's. Rising to her paws, she rubbed against his legs, front and back, purred loudly. *When will My collar be done?*

Straif choked. He'd have thought that Mitchella would be the expensive female in his life, and he figured that if he had pockets full of gilt, she wouldn't hesitate in spending every silver sliver redoing his Residence. Instead she was incredible in making one coin do the work of three, but his little Fam . . . He picked her up, petted her head. She increased her purr.

"I'll see what sort of bargain we can make with T'Ash." Glancing around the room, he said, "Standard housekeeping spell." To his immense satisfaction, the covers on the bed-sponge folded themselves, the rug rippled clean of dirt and lint, and the faintest film of dust disappeared.

A cloud passed over the sun and dimmed the light streaming into the window. Straif's jaw hardened. Mitchella's feelings were important to him, but more important was her safety, and the security of his estate. Setting Drina aside on a table, he opened the window and leaned out into the brisk spring air and scrutinized the black furrows in the ground with his Flair.

What are you looking at? She came to peer out the window. *Someone tore up the lawn. Looks nasty.* She shivered. *It is too cold in here.* She cocked her head. *Mitchella is going shopping! Or at least to The Four Leaf Clover, I must . . .*

"Of course you must."

She lit on the rug with barely a sound and rushed from the room.

Straif manipulated his Flair, enhancing all his senses . . . there was something . . . Narrowing his eyes, he knew the trail he saw lining the words was a color he'd recognize, but . . . smudged. Then he refocused on the large panorama. The words were carved just beyond the drive in the front, obvious from most of the Residence.

He stalked from the guest suite down the hall into the MasterSuite, cleansed himself under the waterfall, and dressed in a set of his tracking leathers. Then he strode through the Grand Entry Hall, down the stairs, and into the front.

The knowledge hit him then. This was the portion of the

estate where most of the fighting had occurred, and though the whole estate had been blessed the night before, this portion would have been most resistant to the overall spell. The area would definitely have to be cleansed by a dedicated priestess or priest. Grumbling, he walked to the dug-in words and squatted. The lines were a faded, ugly green to his Flair vision. Touching a tip of his finger to the first rut, he *knew*.

"Zanth!"

It had been T'Ash's FamCat who'd done this.

Twenty

With an oath at the horrible rutted words dug by T'Ash's FamCat, Straif was back inside and in his Residence-Den. Mitchella had already placed a large copper scrybowl on his desk, full of water. As soon as he had initiated the preparation spell, before he could scry himself, the water whirled and the copper pinged.

"Here," he said.

"T'Ash," said the other. His angry visage formed in the misty droplets above the bowl. He held a limp Zanth in his arms.

"I want to speak to you," Straif said.

"Mutual. Zanth told me what happened. He was hunting on your land near dawn. He says *someone Nasty* overcame his will and forced him to dig *bad holes.*"

"He spelled 'MitchBitch Must Die,'" Sraif said, adding a visual of the letters for T'Ash.

The GreatLord's lip curled at one end. "Like all Fams, Zanth has no spelling skills." He glanced down at the scruffy animal in his arms and a hint of vulnerability showed in his eyes. "His energy and Flair have been drained. His paws were raw. Danith fixed them up some, but the fliggering bastard that forced his will on Zanth nearly killed him. He. Will. Pay."

"One of the worst crimes of Celta is to use Flair to compel

another," Straif said. Cold trickled up his spine, pooling and resting at the back of his neck. He rubbed it. "A person who would do that would stop at nothing."

"Like using a firebombspell or a reflective Flair trap." T'Ash's smile was dagger-sharp. "The trap problem came to light this morning. The FirstFamily Heads of Households were all called and told that you were having security problems at your estate." He shrugged. "Someone is really pushing to show you in a bad light, diminish your status so he can take over."

"Perhaps the same one who sets the spells. T'Blackthorn estate would be easier to penetrate for one with Family blood."

"I think T'Holly pointed that out," T'Ash said. "You have me as a lifetime ally, T'Blackthorn."

"The reflective Flair trap was attached to a rock. I've dismantled the spell, but you're the stone specialist. Winterberry took the rock last night. He will be consulting you."

T'Ash nodded. "One more thing, Zanth doesn't remember much of his ordeal . . ." He cuddled the cat close, and Straif figured that if Zanth hadn't been a tough Downwind tom, he might not have survived—his paws and nose were pallid, his fur rough. The hair on the back of Straif's neck prickled. He'd have to safeguard Drina, too.

". . . but Zanth said the one who did this to him is *Not Right.*"

"Not right?"

Zanth shifted and moaned in T'Ash's arms. "Mad," T'Ash rumbled.

Straif went cold. "I'd appreciate it if you hurried on that Fam collar, set it with a diamond, and sent it over. Please imbue it with strong protection spells. I'll report this to Winterberry."

T'Ash nodded. "I'll do that, but know this. Zanth wears a fortune around his neck and likes to hunt at night. His collar holds the strongest spell I have. Blessed be." He blew on the water in his scrybowl and ended the call.

Straif stood frozen for a moment, then headed out the front door. Time to track his enemy in earnest.

*B*ut the day proved one of the most frustrating Straif ever experienced. He hadn't been able to get a good read on the trail of the other Blackthorn, couldn't track him one more step than before.

All around the estate walls were footprint smears so overlaid that Straif couldn't separate them—all pulsing with excitement. Ex-gang members, thrill seekers, others interested in Straif or the restoration of the Residence. To Straif's surprise, the strongest track of all wasn't human, but fox. He had a small den of the creatures nestled in a corner of the estate—far from where Zanth liked to hunt and the Residence. Foxes were even scarcer than cats, though not as rare as dogs.

The greeniron gate area and the drive all held powerful lines of the greatly Flaired FirstFamilies Lords and Ladies who'd attended the Ritual the night before. Their Flair overwhelmed the trails of everything else.

Straif went to T'Ash's to consult with him and Winterberry about the rock that had held the capture spell. Winterberry questioned T'Ash and Straif, keeping a good stride from the snoring Zanth. Winterberry watched Straif with narrowed eyes. Neither T'Ash nor Winterberry discovered anything new about the rock.

Finally, irritated at the lack of any real progress, Straif returned to his estate only to realize that Mitchella was avoiding him. That was the worst frustration of all.

So he immersed himself in hard labor. With his own hands and shovel, backed with Flair, he turned over the disturbed dirt of the rutted words and dug a rectangular flower bed. He hunted through his verdant, overgrown grounds for bushes. Around the edges he planted elder and the native Celtan plants of glanhawr and purdeb, which would purify the ground until he had a priest and priestess bless it during the next full twinmoons. Then he brought in healthy sage bushes and took seeds of the best Blackthorn-Sloe bushes from the botanical no-time and planted them.

Since the day became fine and clear with Bel white in the deep blue sky, Straif's gardening relaxed and refreshed him. Antenn and the cook were avoiding him, too, but Straif didn't care about them. Drina kept him company. She watched him lay out the flower bed, made comments, chased and ate moths, and napped in the sunshine. She was happy until her collar arrived with "one *puny* diamond and heavy spells," then went to her room to sulk.

When he finished, he grunted. He didn't have Mitchella's artistic eye, but the garden looked good to him. He could live with it, and that was the important thing. He examined his estate. He could live with everything. His land, his glowing Residence, his place. He could rebuild his life and his line and be happy here. If he could conclude his elusive quest.

It was a matter of moments to find a pretty pot and transplant a hawthorn bush that he'd had blessed by GreatLord Hawthorn himself. Straif smiled. His gift was good.

After standing under the waterfall and dressing in casual clothes, he went to the ResidenceDen. The other windows now held illusions of the Great Labyrinth instead of unkempt grounds. It would take many people to clear the grounds, though with Mitchella's help he'd arranged a trade in services for the best landscape design available.

"The glider you requested from T'Holly has arrived," the Residence said. "It is yours for as long as you wish and bespelled to accept your Flair. Mitchella and Antenn wait in the front. The FamCat refuses to visit Commoners in an ugly collar."

Straif picked up his hawthorn bush in the Grand Hall and did a little, excited 'port to the front gliderway. Antenn wore a moss green tunic-trous suit, and Mitchella a gown of nearly the same color that accented her eyes. Something in the cut, workmanship, or material of their clothes proclaimed them unashamedly middle class. Straif himself wore a tunic-trous suit he'd kept at T'Holly's that was several years out of style. He grimaced. He appeared a shabby, down-on-his-luck Lord. Just what he was. "Where's Pinky?" asked Straif.

"Trif wanted to play with him today, he's already there." Antenn frowned at the glider. "It's very old and big."

"Antenn," Mitchella chided.

"Sorry," Antenn said, not looking at Straif. The boy shifted a large, gaily wrapped present.

"True, it's old, but it's big and comfortable. Open windows and doors," Straif ordered. The windows faded to nothing, then the doors rose open. "There's plenty of room for us and our gifts. What do you have there, Antenn?"

The boy climbed into the glider and slid over on the bench,

keeping his package close. After Mitchella and Straif had entered and the doors were sealed, Antenn looked at Straif and said hesitantly, "T'Vine asked if we could pick him up, and I said yes, but I didn't know he lived outside Druida."

"That's fine." Straif ordered the glider to T'Vine Residence. The glider was fast, and they were soon outside the southgate of Druida and climbing the hill where GreatHouse T'Vine's Residence stood.

Antenn shifted in his seat. "Trif studies old Earth stuff to help understand her Flair."

Straif glanced at Mitchella. "What's her Flair?"

"She *sees* past events, even as far back as ancient Earth," Mitchella said.

"Unusual," Straif said.

"Yeah," Antenn said. "Well she likes old stuff, but she thinks about the future, too, and what sort of front she wants on her house."

"Front?" Straif said.

Mitchella said, "A few generations ago our family heads of households got together and purchased the whole square. We've been building around the block. We call it the Clover Compound, and the playspace is the center courtyard. Antenn and I didn't want a house of our own—there are several new and empty ones at the moment, and some being built— so we lived in the rented cottage. Trif is living in MidClass Lodge now, but has chosen one of the new places that isn't quite finished."

"I've made a solid three-dimensional model of her house for her. The front and windows: trim, architectural details. I'm pretty sure she'll like it. It can be a working model for when the rest of the family finishes her house," Antenn said.

"It's wonderful." Mitchella beamed. "Trif will love it. Like a dollhouse, but her own."

"I look forward to seeing it," Straif said. He'd spent more time thinking about homes and houses—architectural, interior, and landscape design—in the last few days than he'd ever done in all his thirty-two years. And as the glider slid through the lower shieldspelled gates of the T'Vine estate and up to the first walled gate of the T'Vine Residence, Mitchella's eyes widened and Antenn's mouth dropped open. The huge redstone fortress towered in walled levels above them, and Straif realized another discussion about Residences was upon them.

"I didn't know it was so huge," Mitchella breathed.

"Has to be modeled after one of those old Earth castles," Antenn said. They both looked at Straif.

"It's outside Druida because of the sensitive nature of the Vines' Flair." Straif cudgeled his memory.

"Like SilverFir is on a little island." Antenn nodded. "'Cause they are sometimes empaths."

"Right," Straif said. "I don't know of anyone who has been inside the Vine inner keep—the last D'Vine was so old, and the present T'Vine is so young . . . if anyone was there, it might have been the Hollys. They never mentioned it to me, though."

Mitchella nibbled at her lip. "I'm thinking. I know the name of the Earth castle. Funny name, long—Hohozinger, no, um, Hohenzollern. That's it." She smiled. "I read up on the FirstFamily Residences when you hired me." She glanced up the layered hillside. "I didn't pay much attention to this one. It's so unlike T'Blackthorn Residence." The way she said it, Straif knew that she preferred his home. He smiled at her.

"Greetyou," said Vinni T'Vine, near the window beside Straif. The young Lord was surrounded by huge men who eyed Straif suspiciously.

Straif opened the door and stepped out, blocking access to Mitchella and Antenn.

One of the men scrutinized him up and down and grunted. "T'Blackthorn?"

"That's right."

Another of the men offered his hand. "We're Vines, Muin's . . . tutors."

"GreatLord Muin T'Vine, Vinni will be safe with me." Narrowing his eyes, Straif looked down at the man's hand. Obviously the guy had Flair that entailed touch—telepathy or empathy, or danger-sense or truth-detector. He grasped the man's hand and sent his own Flair zinging through the contact, keeping all his shields up.

The man jumped back, shook his fingers.

"Can I go now?" Vinni sounded furious.

"Of course," the first man said smoothly. They all took a

couple of paces back from the glider. Straif stood aside so Vinni could enter the glider, but kept a wary eye on the bodyguards. When the young Lord was inside, Straif nodded to the men, slid in himself, said the Word to shield the vehicle, then took off.

He watched the men until they faded in the distance.

"Huh," said Antenn.

"What do you mean by that?" Vinni asked.

Antenn shrugged. "Nuthin'." He turned to look out the window as they neared Druida's eastgate. "Seems like whether you stand up to the Clover boys or not, you might like folks your own age. Lots of Clovers in our generation."

"Huh," said Vinni.

When they neared the gate, the guards stepped aside and the glider moved smoothly into the city. "Can you open the windows again, please, Straif?" Mitchella asked.

"Of course."

Vinni eyed the gaily wrapped packages. "You have gifts."

"It's my cuz Trif's nameday," Mitchella explained.

"I met her at the New Twinmoons Ritual," Vinni said. His eyebrows dipped. "She has much Flair and will be starting her quest soon."

"Quest, what quest?" asked Antenn.

"That is for her to tell you if she so pleases," Vinni said.

Antenn made a disgusted sound.

With a tinkling pop, a small crystal ball set on a pretty silver stand appeared in Vinni's hands.

Antenn goggled. "You can't do that. Not supposed to be able to 'port things into a moving vehicle."

Straif gave a short laugh. "My father said once that it was disconcerting to see someone of a younger generation do a trick that demonstrated their better Flair. Excellent, T'Vine."

The young Lord glanced up, a flash of vulnerability in his eyes. "Call me Vinni." He gazed down at his gift. "It's a multicrys. To focus her Flair, or form holos to keep, or a calendar globe . . ."

"Good choice," Mitchella said. "If you'll give it to me, I'll wrap it."

Vinni blinked at her, but handed over the crystal. Mitchella pulled out some iridescent netting and a ribbon from her purseal, set the stand on the netting, and said, "Nameday wrap." In an instant the netting covered the gift and shimmered so that only tantalizing hints of the present could be seen. The ribbon curled around the gift in an explosion of frills. Vinni stared at it, studied it when Mitchella gave it back to him.

A kilometer inside the walls, solidly in the middle-class district, the glider began to slow.

"We're near the Clover compound!" Antenn leaned so he could stick his head out the window. Straif could hear the Family from a block away, a muted bubble of happy voices.

Antenn smirked at Vinni. "We'll give our nameday gifts to Trif, then we'll see who's tougher."

"Antenn," Mitchella reprimanded, but her smile blossomed as she looked to the square with buildings on three sides. "Two of the green parks around the compound are ours, and we just purchased the parcel of land to the north to make our own grove," she said.

It was mind-boggling. "If you want any trees or brush from my estate, take them. You know I'll be thinning growth."

Her eyes widened. "We could even take some large trees— with your help." She grinned at him. "An even trade."

From her words, he sensed her Family had been less than pleased to help Straif and she'd convinced them. Humiliation kindled in his gut.

Silence draped the glider, and more sounds of jollity came as the vehicle settled at the entrance to the Clover Compound. Antenn hopped out, then held a hand out for Mitchella. She slid over and out of the glider. Straif curled his fingers around Vinni's wrist. "Don't open the far door." He smiled grimly. "Security. Follow me out."

Vinni snorted but obeyed.

Straif touched the planter containing his bush, and it rose to bob behind him. Since there were no other vehicles on the street, Straif left the glider where it was.

The door to the compound was partially open. Straif and Vinni shared a disbelieving glance. Vinni straightened his shoulders. "Better get the trouncing over with."

Straif put a hand on his shoulder, squeezed. "Remember this, duck and roll."

Vinni stopped and glanced at him. "That's all the advice you have? Duck and roll?"

"If you've been training—"

Vinni nodded.

"—with your *tutors*, you might be able to read the boys a little, evade faster, take glancing blows."

Wincing, Vinni nodded. "Duck and roll," he said gloomily and marched through the door that led to a corridor to the courtyard.

A piercing, girlish shriek met them as they stepped into the inner rectangle. A young woman was bouncing with excitement as she tore open Antenn's gift. When the model appeared she squealed again. "Come look!" A small crowd gathered.

"Very good work, son," said one of the beefy Clover men.

"See the detail!" Trif said, pointing out tiny glass lanterns that held equally tiny lightspells. Antenn stood tall. He smirked at Straif and Vinni.

"I'm bigger than he is," Vinni muttered. "I have more Flair."

"He's in the midst of Family, and he's older," Straif said.

Vinni sighed. "I am an only child. My cuzes are a lot older than me, too. And they're *girls*."

Straif patted his shoulder again. "Then your sight told you true. These boys can be very good for you." A bunch of them stood a couple of meters away, studying Straif and Vinni. Their clothes looked dusty as if they'd already had a tussle or two.

"Fresh meat," Vinni muttered, shifted his shoulders again. "Duck and roll." Then he glanced up at Straif. "These Clovers could be very good for *you*, too. The difference between us is that I'll let them be my friends. Will you?" He shrugged out from under Straif's hand and went to meet his fate.

Mitchella separated herself from those around Trif and walked back to Straif, hooking her arm in his. He thought he'd met his fate, too.

"Don't be concerned." Mitchella leaned against him, and thoughts of Vinni's plight would have faded from his mind if he hadn't been watching the boy. Mitchella nearby was always a distraction.

She nibbled at his earlobe, and his blood heated to racing

speed. "We Clovers aren't mean, and the battle won't be all against one, see?"

Sure enough, the boys had split into two teams and walked to a corner of the yard where a large patch of dirt showed a gamefield. Though small and of different coloring, Antenn looked like he belonged. Vinni was dressed casually—for a GreatLord—but his tunic and trous didn't look anything like the other boys' tough play clothes.

The mock battle began. Straif tensed with every blow Vinni took, flinched when the whole bunch of boys piled on each other, with him near the bottom. Straif and Mitchella were the only adults truly watching the engagement; the others concentrated on their own concerns.

Slowly the boys untangled. Vinni's team had obviously lost. Antenn grinned and shrieked in glee, hopping up and down.

"Nothing like a gracious winner," Straif muttered.

Mitchella chuckled.

Vinni lay on the ground, bleeding from a cut lip. The biggest Clover boy, who'd been on the opposite team, held out a hand. Vinni clasped it and was hauled to his feet. The Clover wiped blood from his nose with his palm, spit on it, and said, "Friends." Vinni stared at the boy's palm, swiped his hand across his lip, spit in it, and grabbed the boy's hand. "Friends," he said.

"That is so disgusting," Mitchella said, then turned to Straif and said, "Let's go converse, have fun. We'll eat and drink, and later we will be very, very merry." She towed him off to a crowd of relatives.

Once word spread that Straif was donating trees "from an ancient FirstFamily estate" for the Clover's grove, any wariness the Clovers had vanished. He was thanked more than once, with sincere gratitude. The Clover Family observed him and Mitchella, but no one seemed to warn her against him. Even her parents were warm and welcoming.

As the party wound down, Antenn decided to stay overnight. The Clovers invited Vinni to stay, too. A glider from the T'Vines arrived with two bodyguards who were made welcome.

Straif stared at the Clovers disappearing into different houses. They obviously enjoyed life—and each other. The number of people who had filled the courtyard was incredible. Straif had never seen so many people all belonging to one Family. True, other Family reunions would be large, but they would consist of nine or ten branches that had grown incrementally over four centuries. To his knowledge, this was only four lines, others were flourishing in Wales and Brittany.

He caught his breath. Mitchella came from this Family. Mitchella, the woman he cared for deeply.

A wonderful, warm feeling started at his center and moved outward—hope, something he hadn't felt in a long, long time. Maybe he'd found his cure in this woman, this wonderful Commoner who came from such substantial genes. If any group of genes could dominate his own, could fight the virus, he'd bet it would be the Clovers'. Children with Mitchella's blood might be safe.

He was nearly giddy with the thought. Then she walked to him, smiling, hips swaying, invitation in her eyes and body, and all he could think about was the woman herself.

Twenty-one

During the next week, Mitchella had never been happier in her life. Refurbishing the Residence continued to be a dream come true.

Every day the Residence's mental voice came clearer. To her amazement she found that restoring the house on a tiny budget was more fun as well as more of a challenge than if she'd had unlimited funds. Any designer could have returned the Residence to uncommon beauty with no expense spared, but she didn't think that anyone could have done better than she with such budget constraints. Further, it was her best project. Straif's obvious comfort and pleasure in his home touched her heart.

Then there were the gifts from Straif's allies that trickled in—usually exquisite pieces from the FirstFamilies, many new, some antique. From these, she got the idea that most of the highest Nobles in the land were supporting him—or at least keeping the appearance of doing so. Danith informed Mitchella that many of the snobbish were appalled at the thought of a lower-class man trying to take Straif's title away.

Antenn seemed happy. He helped her with the Residence, and she made sure the Cang Zhus counted it as part of his apprenticeship hours. Every morning that he went to the CZs she sent a holo of the work he'd done. She believed the architectural firm was getting vicarious pleasure looking at the Residence, and knew gossip was spreading that they had holos . . . excellent for everyone's business.

Even Drina was easier to work with. The little cat made her preferences known in no uncertain terms, but Mitchella managed to eke out a compromise or two. The Fam spent most of her time with Straif, demanding petting, curling to nap on his lap when he worked in his ResidenceDen, sometimes sneaking into the bed during the middle of the night and sleeping next to Straif. He relaxed under her and Drina's affection.

Her love affair with Straif kept her dizzy with delight—her body in a state of aching awareness or well-pleasured vitality. Their loving ran the gamut of slow and tender hours on her bedsponge to fast and hard in a large closet. She knew she was far too in love with him to keep her heart safe and unbroken, so she concentrated on wringing the pleasure out of every moment she spent with him, whether it was in breakfast conversation or running her hands over his long, lean body. He acted differently—bringing her flowers, taking her on an impromptu picnic, and to her knowledge he hadn't pursued any other avenues to find a remedy for his flawed gene. She didn't know what to think of that, but was grateful his quest wasn't a difficulty between them.

One morning she was working in the parlor she used as her office, inventorying art pieces Straif could sell if necessary. Straif had spent a lot of gilt lately. He walked in, eyes narrowed and stride as wary as if he were treading a forest path of untamed Celta. Drina was hunkered down on his shoulder, hissing lowly.

"Bad news," he said as he sat in a chair opposite her desk.

Mitchella glanced at the wall timer. "I deduce that your morning talk with T'Reed didn't go well. I *know* the budgets and progress reports we've been sending to the man have been excellent."

Straif grunted. "Too excellent, I'm afraid. We've made incredible progress, kept within my budget. They've moved the date for the open house up on us."

Her fingers clutching the writestick began to shake, and she hid her hands under the desk. "When?"

"Spring equinox."

"That's in two weeks!" Her voice was so shrill it hurt her own ears.

Drina yowled.

Nodding grimly, Straif said, "Right. The grounds are still a mess. All the structural problems of the estate have been addressed, but—"

"—we still have a lot of cosmetic work to do. Not to mention the ballroom."

"No, we won't mention it."

"I'd planned on using that room for the refreshments, a buffet and tables. We've started remodeling, but there's still a lot of negativity there, we need a priest and priestess . . ." She'd lost him. He was staring out the window behind her. She'd given Antenn the ballroom project. He seemed less affected by the chamber and knew exactly what she planned.

Drina walked down Straif's chest to his lap then back and forth across his thighs, rubbing against him. Absently he lifted his hand to stroke her. The cat purred loudly, and Straif's expression became less strained.

Mitchella nibbled on her bottom lip and began listing things that would have to be done, numbering them by priority. "T'Ash planned a Ritual for spring equinox."

"I contacted him. He graciously conceded the date to us."

"Oh."

Straif glanced around the room. "We'll have to concentrate more on the public rooms." His smile was wintry. "The Family Suites—Master, Mistrys and Heir—will be off-limits. The library can be a gathering place for the more introverted. A couple of the parlors for smaller groups."

They hadn't touched the library. It was a large room, full of books, holos, art, and artifacts. Mitchella moved it to the top of her list.

"Can the Great Hall be done in two weeks?"

She smiled with more assurance than she felt in the chill pit of her stomach. "I'll do it myself. Have you told the cook?"

Straif laughed, and his expression lightened even more. "He went pale. I think he wanted to pass out, but he said he could make a tasty spread and started muttering to himself. He'll be fine. I'm going to walk the estate again, see what can be done in the time allowed. The gliderdrive must be trimmed. I know we planned gardens in the large area behind the Residence, but we'll only have time enough to develop a grassyard."

"That can be beautiful, and well decorated. It's large enough to hold everyone you'd care to invite. If the day is good."

"I'll have to institute a weathershield if it's cold or rainy. That expanse, and the view of the Residence from there, is the most well-known part of the estate. It must be as perfect as possible. The wall supporting the terrace and the terrace itself must look to be completely restored as well as the steps down to the river."

Mitchella rose and walked behind Straif. She kissed the top of his head, set her hands on his shoulders, and worked at his knotted muscles.

There was a moment of humming silence, then Straif said, "Thank you. You've already made the Residence so much more a home, as well as a show place. We'll win my title back."

Drina meowed.

"Drina will help."

"Of course," Mitchella choked at the thought of the Fam's "help." "I'd like to use Antenn more, if that's all right."

"Fine."

The scrybowl on Mitchella's desk played a melodious tune. She brushed another kiss against Straif's temple, then went to the bowl and circled her finger around the rim, accepting the call. "Here," she said.

T'Reed's sour face projected above the bowl. He blinked, then focused on Straif, who sat slightly behind and to one side of Mitchella.

"Greetyou, GentleLady. Blackthorn, there's a new condition that just came up."

"What now? I *know* the other claimant is behind this, what more of a burden does he place on my back?"

T'Reed's lips thinned, his eyes flickered, his nostrils pinched. "Think of this from another perspective, if you manage to address every concern AllClass Council has—and I agree they are more than many Lords and Ladies anticipated—you will be completely validated."

"Right. What next?"

The sound of shuffling papyrus came over the scrybowl. "It has been brought to the Councils' attention that the first structure ever erected on the Blackthorn estate was the little Summer Folly, halfway down the path to the river. AllClass Council is most particular that this structure be available for inspection during the open house."

Straif's face set in granite. "I hear you."

Drina leapt from his lap to land on Mitchella's desk. She slapped the surface of the water in the scrybowl with her paw, breaking the call, then stalked the desk, hissing.

"I don't recall a folly," Mitchella said. She'd seen no small decorative building in the grounds.

Smiling bleakly, Straif said, "It fell to ruin in my Father-Sire's time." He stood. "I'll go look at it now. My father once said it would need specialists to restore." He jerked a nod to Mitchella. "I'd be grateful if you mapped a strategy to address the additional demands upon us, please."

His body was stiff, he didn't want to be touched. Best for him was sheer professionalism. "I'll do that."

He gave a little half bow. "My thanks."

Mitchella worked through the morning, making lists, examining the library. With a molecular cleaning, a little rearranging, and a bit of a glisten-glamour spell, it could look comfortably shabby—a style she could make seem deliberate—as if it had been in use and loved for its ambience for centuries. That could definitely save time.

When Straif arrived for midday meal, his demeanor wasn't nearly as somber as Mitchella expected, and the very steadiness of the man quieted her own frantic nerves. She explained her idea about the library to Straif and received a penetrating gaze and a quiet smile.

"I have an idea about the folly," he said. "But I want to do some research with the ResidenceLibrary and the city GreatLibrary before I—ah—present it to you."

Intrigued, Mitchella raised her brows.

Straif shrugged, but his complexion turned ruddy. "I'll be back in two hours. Can you be here?"

"Yes, I haven't finished organizing and inventorying the storerooms. The Residence and I have lists of what is in the first couple of rooms, and anything in the last two centuries, but not what is contained inside the fields of the oldest preservation spells. I'll be in the attic."

"It's not too hot up there?"

"No, not yet."

He nodded, then excused himself.

*M*idafternoon, *Mitchella was back at her desk. She'd* stood under the waterfall and changed her heavy working clothes for a soft short-tunic and trous in teal. She *felt* the heat of Straif's gaze and looked up to see him standing at the threshold of the room. He, too, had changed. He wore a robe of bronze that made his tanned skin golden. He looked like a god.

Her heart thudded hard in her chest. How easily he stirred her. A glance, a thought.

Instinctively she smiled, believed all her love showed in her face and hoped he would not understand how much she cared. When she met his eyes, they held a banked wildness that ignited a flash of desire.

He wet his lips, and she clenched inside; her breasts grew heavy.

When he spoke, his voice was rough. "I found a ritual that will restore the Summer Folly. I need you to perform it with me as Lady to my Lord."

She swallowed. "Just the two of us?"

"Yes," he whispered. His gaze dropped to her breasts.

"I don't have great Flair."

Color tinged his cheeks. "It's a sex Ritual."

Heat infused her. She'd never done anything like that. She didn't think anyone in her family had ever done such a Ritual, though Danith and T'Ash . . .

"Please." His voice was even huskier. He held out a hand not quite steady.

She burned, touched her fingers to her throat, and thought she could feel hot blood racing beneath her tunic collar.

"You're dressed fine. Lovely. Beautiful. Woman." His eyes were bright blue as if he burned, too.

"I don't know how—"

He smiled. "I've drawn most of the circle around the pavilion, charged it with spells. We need only to complete the circle together, say words as Lady and Lord. Mate to infuse the spells with energy and initiate them."

A hot, red cord of desire, pulsing with golden sparks, snaked between them, easy to see.

"I don't think I've ever felt so aroused in my life as thinking about performing a sex Ritual with my lovely Mitchella."

She couldn't help standing, going to him, placing her fingers in his and feeling a jolt of passion between them. He grasped her other hand, and she swayed from the sexual punch. Her sex dampened. She yearned for him. For Straif.

He teleported them to a level place halfway down the river stairs, and it didn't seem instantaneous, but flying through bands of colors, of heat, of need, to a place that would be only their own.

Tangles of brush lay outside a small circle of short grass that surrounded the remnants of a small circular temple. The marble flooring was no more than twelve feet across. A meditation place, then, or a site for intimate Rituals.

Fluted Greek columns lay broken. The dome was in three pieces. A tiny part of Mitchella's mind wondered how they could repair such damage, but there was no doubt. She thought the sexual energy sizzling between her and Straif rivaled that of the sun. She wondered if ecstasy's fire would consume her and shuddered in delight.

Straif had arranged an altar, only large enough to hold the minimum amount of instruments. He led her through the small opening of the circle he'd drawn in the ground, set her hand around the athame knife that still had clods of earth on its shining blade. Her fingers curled around the knife, and her breath caught in her throat. It was like a living thing, powerful with Flair. She trembled, wanted to fall to the soft bedsponge Straif had set just beyond the altar.

His hand closed over hers that gripped the knife, his body brushing her back, and he was a seething, dark pillar of energy in her mind, one ready to take her to the limits of desire. He urged her to the unfinished circle, curved her under his body, directed her on what words to say with him as they completed the circle. Golden flames of Flair danced high above them.

They straightened, and Mitchella moaned at the feel of his hard body behind her, male primed to take. His breath came ragged in her ear.

"Please," she whispered, dampening her lips.

His chest vibrated with a low groan. Waves of passion radiated from him, sensitizing her skin. Her lips were swollen, her breasts full, her core empty. She craved him.

But he led her back to the altar, and they plunged the athame into a deep goblet full of golden wine. His hips arched into her buttocks, and she thought she'd go mad with aching, unrealized passion.

She passed through the ceremony in a sensual haze. He murmured the Lord's words. She didn't know scripted responses, but replied from her heart, her soul, her aching womanhood wanting to be filled. They fed each other honey cake, his fingers traced her bottom lip, his tongue flitted out to taste her fingers. They twined their hands around a goblet of crisp wine and took turns drinking. She thought she'd give him anything in that moment, and his eyes held promises she dared not believe.

Slowly, every touch a caress, they undressed each other and stood in white-golden pillars of sunlight. Straif picked her up, took her to the bed, and placed her on it. He stared at her as if she were a treasure. Again he looked like a god.

He fell upon her, making a place for himself between her thighs.

His fingers twined with hers. "Join with me. Now!" He plunged into her. She rose to meet him. His tongue took her mouth. And a white hot force melded them together, pulsing between them.

They began to move . . . slow, steady, carefully stoking the mounting passion. Just at the moment before all thought fled, Straif flung back his head—neck sinews straining, he shouted, "Build!"

The world became vibration: the mattress beneath her, the thrumming air, the beating sunlight. Mitchella knew this was how the little temple had been built.

Then Straif let his head fall to her, bit her on the neck.

They went wild. Her fingernails sank into his back. He pounded into her. She moaned in response.

Finally, she shrieked her ecstasy, splintering brilliantly.

Straif shouted with her, pumping into her. The heat of the sun vanished, replaced by cool shade. Straif's trembling body kept her warm.

A few moments later she opened her eyes to see a dome overhead, tinted the light blue of the ancient Earth sky. Turning her head, she saw the fluted columns, glowing white gold where the sunlight caught them. There were no dirt-encrusted cracks in the smooth, white marble floor.

"We did it," she whispered.

Straif moaned, shifted, and all her nerve endings clenched in a tiny climax. She forgot everything except him.

The sun dipped lower than the dome and streaked into the folly. The atmosphere changed from wild passion to deep contentment.

His lips feathered over the curve of her cheek. "Marry me. We can make a life together with strong children. The Clover genes will augment the Blackthorn."

She recoiled. All the heated pleasure drained from her. All the joy. Into the cool marble pavement beneath her. "I deluded myself into thinking you knew," she whispered. She'd ignored the signs of his ignorance, wanting to prolong the easy loving between them—not only the sex, but the tender companionship. Now she'd hurt them both.

His head jerked up until his deep blue eyes met hers. A frown knit between his brows. "What?" he said harshly, as if prepared for a blow.

Cowardly, she couldn't watch him as she told him, couldn't see the change in his now wary eyes. It would be enough that she'd have to feel his body. She closed her eyes. "I had Macha's disease as a child. I'm sterile."

He flinched, then a deep shudder racked his body.

Heavy silence weighed between them until he finally said, "I'm sorry." And the words echoed through him, through her, through the folly. She opened her eyes, and a mask had fallen over his features. Through their bond she felt anguish. Pain for them both. His smile was empty as he held out a hand.

She put hers in his. He was so strong, to live with what he had—the deaths of all he loved. She was strong, too, to live with the knowledge that men wouldn't want her since she could not give them children. She smiled wistfully. "So," she said.

"We have this in common. We cannot or should not have children."

"I'll find a cure for my flaw." The statement was steel.

Mitchella dipped her head, summoned control when she wanted to scream with pain and grief, squelched bitterness.

With a gesture, he clothed them both. He circled her with his arms. His body was stiff as they 'ported to the Grand Hall.

"I must work," Straif said.

"Of course," she said.

Before she reached the top of the stairs, her eyes were blurred with tears, and as she turned down the hallway, she heard Antenn's startled voice.

"Mitchella? What's wrong?"

"Let's go into your suite," she said, her voice thick. It was the closest.

Her chin quivered. She hated that.

When they were alone, Antenn's words were savage as he paced his sitting room. "He hurt you. I knew he would." Fists balled, he looked up at her for confirmation.

"We hurt each other. He didn't know I was sterile."

Antenn snarled.

"Apparently he thought the Clover genes might mend his own."

"Fligger."

She didn't correct his language. Managed not to agree. "Every person has points in their life when they're a fligger."

The boy vibrated. "What are you going to do to him?"

"That's how a gang member would talk," she snapped.

Antenn paled.

She crossed to a chair and let her weak knees fail, fell into the cushioned depths. "I'm going to love him."

"How could you—"

"He's hurting, too. I believe he loves me, too. I'm going to love him." She smiled, and tears began to trickle down her face. "I'm going to love him for the duration of this project, then I'm going to put him away in my memory and live my life. But I still want him now."

"How could you?"

Mitchella shook her head. "I don't know. I never thought love could be this deep, this painful. This wonderful. I want it for the little time we have." Since her time with Straif was so short, so doomed, she wanted all the glorious, agonizing moments she could greedily gather.

"Some man will marry you, someone who doesn't care if you can't have kids," Antenn said.

"I *can* have children. I have one now," she said, opening her eyes wide. "I know you're too big to be held, but I need to hold you, need you to hold me."

Antenn was on her lap in a flash. Pinky trotted into the room and jumped onto Antenn, draping himself over them both. For several moments the only sound was the cat's purring and Mitchella's weeping. She held Antenn tight.

Finally, when her tears were all gone, she kissed Antenn on the top of his head. Scowling, he went to his desk and his grove-study assignments, but she thought she'd distracted him from his learning and sighed.

After her emotional storm, Mitchella gathered herself together and for the third time that day, washed and changed clothes. She shoved away her pain and let a little natural optimism seep through. She'd get through this time, meantime she'd win back the man. Could she act breezy, casual? Yes. Just the way to keep him off balance.

But she didn't see Straif or Drina as evening fell into darkness, as Antenn and she ate dinner, as she kissed him before he slept, and she walked to her own suite.

A glint caught her eye from one of the corridor's end windows, light she'd never seen. She drifted to it, realizing what it was just as she neared the window. A glow came from the vicinity of the small pavilion. She didn't know how long the effect would last. Until Straif found his HeartMate? What would that woman think of the Summer Folly?

Fierce possessiveness rushed through Mitchella. She'd left her mark all over the Residence, and for this short while Straif was *hers*.

She wanted him still. Despite all the pain, she wished to continue the affair until the very last moment when she had to walk away.

Or he left to track his HeartMate.

Twenty-two

❦

Straif went to the HouseHeart to recover from the blow Mitchella had dealt him. Somehow he survived the agony. Perhaps he should have known she was sterile, but he'd been away from Druida a long time, and most gossip he heard was about the First Families. He meditated deep in the Residence and recalled Vinni T'Vine's words about the price for his cure. Drina kept close to him, now and then licking his face, and she was a comfort. But he wanted Mitchella's arms around him, Mitchella to hold him while he hurt.

He didn't sleep with her that night or invite her to his bed. In the weeks they'd been lovers, they'd missed an occasional night of loving, because one or both of them had been exhausted, or they'd indulged in passionate sex during the day.

When he awoke, he reached for her and she wasn't there, wasn't close and warm and soft in the huge generational bed. He was alone. In the bed. In the room. In the suite.

The last Blackthorn. His throat ached. His heart was torn——he could have his woman and turn his back on his duty to his line. Or he could follow ingrained responsibilities to his Family, to those who'd come before, those who'd sacrificed for him, and reject the woman he loved. Almost inconceivable. His Family line would die, the great Flair of the Black-thorns would die.

The faces of his lost parents haunted him. He'd already failed—in his quest, in abandoning his home, in nearly losing his estate. How could he selfishly turn his back on his heritage again? He couldn't. Not now.

Scowling, he corrected himself. He was the last Blackthorn with great Flair, the true blessing of tracking talent. That qualification didn't lift his spirits, but darkened his mood. He was still alone, craving the sweet loving he'd become accustomed to, the woman's inventive hands, her soft body, which he could sink into and forget all his problems. More, her cheerful optimism, her laughter, her gentleness. He'd been starved for affection and connection, and she'd given it to him, withholding nothing. So he'd filled himself with her, ignoring the quest that had kept him sane and purposeful for all the years of his adult life. It had felt as if she could cure his genetic flaw with her loving, just as she had made his emotions, his heart, whole.

But she couldn't.

And she'd known all along that she couldn't, but loved him anyway. He was sure of that. She loved him. He thought he might love her, but that notion opened a dark chasm of pain, so he set it aside. Recalling the night before, he realized that she had never taken their sleeping together for granted. He had always asked her to come to his bed, or had followed her to the guest suite—something that hadn't registered. But he hadn't asked her last night.

How strong she must be to love a man who couldn't take her as his wife.

He rubbed his face. He didn't know if he had her strength.

The afternoon before, in the stunned grief of realization that Mitchella couldn't give him what he most longed for, a healthy child from his loins, he'd rescheduled his appointment with the colonist Ship, *Nuada's Sword*. Perhaps now the Ship was running, his ancestors' technology could mend what Celtan Flair could not. Captain Ruis Elder had done what Straif himself was attempting, had found and restored a home for himself—but rehabilitating an ancient Ship must have been much more difficult than bringing a GreatHouse back from more than a decade's neglect.

A prickle of hair rose on the back of his neck, then Straif heard the running footsteps of the boy, Antenn. Straif hadn't made much progress in making friends with the boy. Had that meant Straif hadn't accepted Mitchella completely in his life? He was confused, and thinking about it hurt, so no more pondering. He headed for the waterfall. He'd skip breakfast.

Straif reached his ResidenceDen without meeting Mitchella or Antenn. As usual, Mitchella's updated models were on his desk. He glanced out the window and the view of the Great Labyrinth annoyed him. Yesterday he'd hired a mass of low-paid workers to clear the land, had marked bushes and trees that would stay, or be donated to the Clovers for their Family grove. He wanted to see the progress.

Knowing more about decorating and holowindows than he had before, he strode over to the sill and plucked two imaging buttons from under the slight ledge and deactivated them. The shortened grass of the gliderdrive and the emerging grassyard and gardens beyond sprang into view. The sheer green startled him. It was the green of upcoming summer.

With the Ritual, he'd strengthened and protected the Residence, set shieldspells. But to restore—or relandscape—the grounds would take much more Flair-energy than he had, than he could spare. Or he could become indebted to FirstFamilies who he didn't count as allies.

A holocalendar ball appeared and said, "Time to leave for your appointment with *Nuada's Sword*," then vanished. Straif grimaced. Time to prepare himself for hours without Flair. Drina decided to accompany him to play with her sister, Samba. Straif sensed his Fam wanted to boast. If Samba was anything like Drina and every other FamCat, Samba would turn the tables on Drina, and Straif would leave with a Fam with wounded pride.

A couple of septhours later, Straif lay naked on a medical bed and listened to the Ship.

"We will work on the problem of your genetic code," Ship said cheerfully. Straif ached all over after the intense examination. Ship had taken "samples."

Ship continued, "If you allow us to keep the samples, we can store them in our banks with all the other code."

The idea was too intriguing to disregard. "Other code?"

"There are *many* animals and plants from Earth that aren't currently alive on Celta. Many that didn't survive during the generations that we Ships were in space. Many that the colonists didn't revive. Many that didn't flourish on Celta.

"As the planet becomes more civilized and the Healers and scientists such as the Heathers and Culpeper grow more knowledgeable, as well as Ourselves, it might be possible to grow and release more adaptable Earth species."

Straif grasped the kernal of information. "You could keep my DNA and, uh, other samples—"

"Your sperm," Ship said helpfully.

Straif shuddered again at the unpleasant way that had been obtained. "—and store my code until a complete cure could be found, until your, um, nanobots could fix it."

"True."

"Does the code contain the information for great Flair and the Blackthorn hereditary tracking ability?"

"Of course."

"So even if you can't find a cure at this time—"

"We are sure we will be successful. We anticipate having a positive answer for you within two weeks."

That news should have been thrilling. Instead he calculated that the date would be when his relationship with Mitchella would end. The open house was in two weeks, the main restoration of the Residence would be done, Mitchella might be gone. Though they hadn't talked about it, Straif knew she would not stay with him when the project ended.

After the Ship found a cure, there would be no reason for him to delay finding his HeartMate, a woman he should go to with a free heart, ready to start a new life. He couldn't imagine loving another woman.

Taking his silence for interest, Ship began lecturing, "The fact that hybrids can occur between Celtan and Earth species is fascinating. It extrapolates that the ancient idea of a 'seeding of life' throughout several galaxies actually occurred."

Straif's ears hurt, and his head began to ache.

"Stop, Ship," Captain Ruis Elder said. He lounged against the metallic doorjamb. Straif hadn't heard the doors open.

"Am I done?" Straif asked, sliding to the floor and dressing.

"Yes."

For some reason, perhaps because the man had faced incredible challenges, triumphed, and now had a lady and a baby, Straif didn't want to talk to Elder. He nodded to the man, feeling white around the lips. He didn't like Ship's Healing. "Sorry, Captain, but I must leave. I didn't realize the tests would take so long." Straif inclined his head. "Merry meet,"

Elder smiled and moved from the doorway. "And merry part."

"And merry meet again," Straif ended and hurried from the Ship. Drina waited for him in Landing Park, teleported herself around his shoulders and purred all the way home, telling him how she'd bested her sister in boasting.

When they entered the estate, the cat spied a flurry of moths and hopped down to pursue. Straif watched her a moment, saw her snatch a moth out of the air and munch it, and winced. He left her to her hunting.

Mitchella met him at the door with a genuine smile. Though a shadow lurked behind her eyes, and she didn't greet him with a lover's kiss, she said, "Welcome. I have another attic storeroom finished, why don't you come look?" In her voice was pride for herself and affection for him. She reached out for his hand, stopped, and her smile brightened. She tossed her loose mane of red hair over her shoulder as she turned to cross the Great Hall and climb the grand staircase. "You should take stock," she said.

"I'll be with you in a minute," he choked out, and went to the ResidenceDen, sealed the door, primed the scrybowl and said, "Connect me with *Nuada's Sword*."

A moment later the Ship's voice, sounding tinny and distant, answered. "*Nuada's Sword* acknowledges communication from T'Blackthorn Residence and T'Blackthorn."

"I forgot to ask today—what of a woman who experienced Macha's disease as a child and is sterile; can you fix her?"

There came a faint whoosh from the Ship, like a sigh. "If the disease has passed, then her eggs would have been destroyed. She will have no children from her individual genetic code. As for carrying another's fertilized egg becoming a fetus and a child, of course we can mitigate that. We understand her uterine lining is damaged, but with monthly invasive surgical procedures of minimal pain—"

"Stop," Straif said. The metallic, alien Ship had just unnerved him. He could not imagine subjecting Mitchella to its procedures. "Thank you for your time," he said and disconnected. He stuffed the knowledge and everything he'd experienced to the back of his mind. Mitchella was waiting for him.

She stood on the steps of the grand staircase, and he thought the beautiful sweep must have been made as a backdrop for her—the hard, white, square marble steps contrasting with the vibrant, lush woman. She wore an emerald onesuit, cut a little tight, and he swallowed. He didn't know what to do.

Mitchella tilted her head at him, then her smile faded. She descended the staircase, but didn't speak until she was close to him, intimately close. He could hardly breathe.

"Why are you so disturbed, Straif? We both knew our association was only professional"—she gestured widely—"and any affair between us could only be temporary."

"You're in love with me!"

Her eyebrows raised. "Am I?"

He didn't like her response, but he didn't want to argue. "You aren't angry with me?"

"Any affair between us can only be temporary," she repeated.

"Then we're still lovers?" He was confused.

She smiled that sexy smile that sent blood pounding from his brain to his loins. She lowered her eyelids. "If we want to be."

"I want," he said. "I want now. You're a fascinating woman, Mitchella." He didn't know how he'd do without her, but that was weeks away. He needed her this very moment. "Let's go to bed."

She touched her fingertips to his chest, and his breath caught, went ragged. "There's more than one bedsponge in the attic storerooms." Her hand slid down and cupped him, and his cock strained against his trous, his hips thrust instinctively. Bedsponge. Attic. Sex. Now. "Give me a viz," he said. He might be able to 'port them in this condition.

An image formed in his mind, straight from hers—of them naked and rolling around on a stack of huge carpets. Mating. He groaned, dragged one tiny thought after another through the haze of passion back into his brain, ordered his thick tongue—which yearned to taste her—to form words. "Viz locale."

The illusion of the two of them vanished, the pile of rugs remained, a grid glowed on the room. He grabbed her. 'Ported them to the rug pile. The moments without her touch since the afternoon before had stretched into an eternity. His need was too great for him to be gentle. He needed the feel of her under his palms, the smooth pliancy of her skin against his callouses, to send the zing of raw sexuality through him so he'd *feel. Live.* He let sensation rule, ravishing them both.

Later, when he had time to look around the room, he found that she'd tinted the walls a creamy yellow. Crowded with colorful rugs, a jumble of polished furniture, it still seemed utterly comfortable, welcoming. Like the woman. Like his Residence.

For only this moment.

*A*ntenn *joined them for lunch in the small dining room.*

"How is your quest coming?" Mitchella asked.

Straif didn't like the shaky undertone of her voice, so he followed her cue.

"The Healers and scholars of Celta hold no hope." He kept his tones even. He cut the marinated furrabeast and ate. It seemed to melt in his mouth. The fresh vegetables were sprinkled with tasty spices. He'd definitely have to keep the cook.

"And?" Mitchella prodded.

Antenn watched him with a narrowed gaze.

"The Ship, *Nuada's Sword,* is working on a remedy. The more I've thought about it, the more I want to send a man to the mines T'Ash spoke of, get some scrapings or cultures or whatever. T'Ash sent me a map." He waved his fork. "Residence and I researched. The problem with the Blackthorns definitely dates around the time we took the lambenthysts from the mines to install in the Fountain of the Dark Goddess."

"That's interesting," Mitchella said, but she didn't sound as if she meant it. Antenn didn't speak at all until he excused himself from the table and stomped away.

"I take it that Antenn is upset with me," Straif said.

Mitchella raised her eyebrows. "I was slightly upset yesterday afternoon. He is very protective."

"Right. He's resentful of me, too."

She shrugged. "We'll manage for the little while we're here."

Anxiety arrowed through Straif. "When I'm confirmed as GrandLord T'Blackthorn, I'll want to do a few," he hunted for a word that wouldn't insult what she'd already done on such a limited amount of gilt. *"Upgrades,"* he finally said.

With an exasperated huff, Mitchella said, "Straif, you're a man. So far you're perfectly happy with all the changes we've made. Live with the Residence as it is for a while. Concentrate on the landscaping and your other duties." Her voice lowered. "Let your HeartMate upgrade when you find her. She'll want to make changes to suit herself."

"No." He didn't want Mitchella putting an unknown, uncared-for woman between them as a barrier. He reached across the table and grabbed her hand, held on to it hard as she tried to slide her fingers away.

The scrybowl on the sideboard trilled. Straif glanced at the grass green color pulsing from the water. "It's GreatLord T'Reed."

Mitchella looked up. "Oh?"

Straif grimaced. "I was gone this morning at the time of his usual call." He flicked his thumbnail against the bowl. "Here," he said.

"Greetyou." T'Reed's sour countenance appeared in the water droplets hovering over the bowl.

Smiling thinly, Straif said, "What can I do for you?"

"He—the Councils are concerned at the amount of remodeling going on with the Residence. It is one of the most beautiful FirstFamilies homes, modeled after one of the great houses of Ancient Earth."

Mitchella jumped to her feet. Straif waved for her to stay silent.

"Who's there with you?" demanded T'Reed.

"My interior designer, Mitchella Clover, of The Four Leaf Clover."

"Ah," T'Reed said.

Silence lengthened as Straif waited for T'Reed to speak first. Strategy.

T'Reed cleared his throat again and said, "The Councils

want to know if there have been any structural changes to the building during the restoration."

"Let me handle this," Mitchella said, swinging around the desk to face T'Reed. She placed a hand on Straif's shoulder and licks of fiery irritation radiated from her to him.

"Greetyou, GreatLord." Mitchella ducked her head in courtesy.

"Greetyou, GentleLady," T'Reed said.

"The Councils want to know if there have been any structural changes to T'Blackthorn Residence?" she asked.

"Yes."

"No," Mitchella said and touched the water of the bowl, ending the spell.

Straif turned his comfortchair and pulled her into his lap, nuzzling her ear. "That's my domestic Goddess. Tell them all off." He laughed.

"How dare they believe that I would harm this Residence! That I have no sense or taste. Make structural changes to the Residence, indeed."

She was a warm, vibrant armful, and her wiggling aroused him. "How dare they," Straif whispered, turning her in his arms. He did like sitting with Mitchella in chairs. His mouth found hers, and his tongue plunged in, savoring the taste he couldn't get enough of.

Her arms twined around his neck, and her tongue forayed into his mouth. His body heated, thought vanishing.

"Mitchella!" Antenn banged through the door, then gasped.

She broke the kiss and pushed against Straif. He let her go. A moment later she was standing beside Straif and smiling at Antenn.

"What can I do for you?" she asked, her voice low and husky and full of affection.

Antenn flushed, looked aside. "I need to talk to you."

"I care for Mitchella, Antenn. I won't hurt her." Straif had no idea why he said the words.

Eyes blazing, Antenn's mouth worked, then he said, "You already have. You don't think of her *first*. You don't really want her. You want your curse broken, that's all you want." He turned back and strode through the door.

"I'll go see what he needs," Mitchella said, gliding away from Straif.

"I won't hurt you," Straif said.

"Antenn was rude, but he is right," she said softly, smiling gently in a way that pierced Straif but left his mind scrambling. Words jammed in his throat, and he could only watch as she sauntered away and followed her ward.

He stood, only knowing that he must go after them.

*M*itchella *saw Antenn pause by the ballroom door, scrub* his sleeve across his face, stiffen his spine, and stride across the threshold.

A booming voice said, "Are you back, little boy?"

The sneer quickened her pace, until she nearly ran to catch up. As soon as she entered the room, she saw him, chin jutting, glaring up at a tall man with a mean expression. She stopped her rushing steps to stroll to them at the end of the room. The man was the supervisor of a crew she hadn't worked with before—because they all had little Flair. The New Twinmoons Ritual had done a lot to cleanse the ballroom of despair, but the chamber's vibrations were still slightly negative. This confrontation would only reinforce the undertone of dark emotions.

Three of the room's corners had been hidden by inserts of curved paneling, turning the area into an oval. They stood at the fourth, with the paneling half up.

When Mitchella joined them, the man switched his contempt to her. She blinked at his inimical stare. She'd never encountered anything quite like it before. Her heart thumped faster at the threat. She wanted to put her arm around Antenn's shoulders, but he was in charge of this project and that would be unprofessional. "What's the problem, foreman?"

The man stuck his thumbs in his pockets and rocked back on his heels. He was taller than she, and since he looked down his nose as well as curling his lip, she didn't think the conversation would go smoothly.

"I don't got no problem," the foreman said. He jerked his unshaven chin at Antenn. "He's the one that gots the problem."

"Antenn?" she asked.

The tops of his ears were red. "They're using different wood for this corner. Less expensive, not what we ordered."

The man shrugged. "I thought that in spite a' the fact this here's a Residence, you wanted to keep the costs down. So I did. No one's gonna notice."

Antenn said, "The width of the panels are different, it will unbalance the symmetry of the room."

The rest of the crew watched with interest.

Mitchella studied the half-built circular insert. "Antenn's right. It's absolutely necessary that this corner is like the others. Take down what you've built here and replace it with matching paneling."

Someone shuffled behind her. "Don't got enough wood."

Every instinct in Mitchella sharpened. "I'd like to see the receipts for the materials . . . both types."

The foreman grinned, showing crooked, stained teeth from tobacchew. "Now I don' seem to have them receipts."

"What happened to them?"

He shrugged.

"You're fired. I'll file a complaint against you at the Guild-Hall, and since I contract out a lot of remodeling work, I'll make sure that your company, and you yourself, will have a black mark against you. Leave, now."

He slapped her. Pain shot along her cheekbone, fired in her face. She staggered back.

Antenn jumped on the man, shrieking.

The man yelled, wrenched the boy's arms from him, and flung him away.

Twenty-three

❦

$\mathcal{F}$lair sizzled. Invisible force slammed the foreman into the half-built wall; it fell on him. He and the splintered wood crashed to the floor.

Straif strode into the room. He swept the rest of the workers with a look, and they stood as if petrified.

Twisting a hand in the foreman's shirt, Straif dragged him to his feet. "I don't tolerate abuse of my dependents. I don't care to be cheated, and I don't like your face," he said softly. Danger whisked around the room.

With his free hand, he snapped his fingers, then curled his palm upward. A tiny scrybowl appeared. Straif blew on it. "Guardsman Winterberry," he ordered.

A few seconds later the deep voice of the guard answered. "Winterberry here."

"T'Blackthorn. I think we have a suspect in the firebombing, the reflective Flair trap, and other threats."

"No, no!" howled the foreman.

"Quiet!" Straif ordered, and though the man's mouth continued to work, dribbling spittle that mixed with blood from a cut on his forehead, no words were heard. To Winterberry, Straif said, "We certainly have a case of assault and fraud. The fligger hit Mitchella."

"I'll be right there," said Winterberry.

"I'll wait for you in the workroom in the east wing."

"Let me handle this, GrandLord," Winterberry said.

Straif swore. Staring at the foreman in front of him, Straif said, "Workroom," and snapped his fingers. The man vanished.

"FirstFamily Lords," muttered Winterberry, "Always difficult. *I will handle this*. Done." He ended the scryspell.

Glancing at the rest of the crew, Straif said, "I want you all to wait in the workroom in the east wing. Winterberry and I will discover everything you know."

A rapping came on the doorjamb.

Everyone turned to see the cook. "An early dinner will be served in a septhour," he said, and hastened away. The others scurried out of the room.

Finally able to tear her attention from Straif, Mitchella ignored her throbbing face to pat Antenn all over. "Are you all right? Are you hurt anywhere?" Her lip was cut and swollen, and her words were a little garbled.

Antenn shook himself, glared furiously at Straif. Mitchella could sense the boy's anger that he couldn't protect her, his humiliation, his resentment that Straif had handled the situation so quickly and easily. Antenn's emotions seethed, nearly explosive. He shrugged her hands away. "I'm all right."

"I can see that," Straif said. "You did well, defended her, kept him from striking her again." He swept Mitchella up in his arms. "I'm taking Mitchella to her suite. I'll have T'Heather come and Heal her face."

Mitchella held out a hand to her ward. "Antenn? Come with us."

He turned away from her and huddled into himself.

Worried, she nibbled her lower lip, then gasped at the pain.

"There, there," crooned Straif in a voice that didn't match his grim face or dangerous eyes.

Since Antenn was beyond her reach as Straif's strides ate up the ground, Mitchella switched her attention to him, trailed her fingertips along his clenched jaw. His steps hesitated.

"There, there, yourself," she said.

He held her close as he climbed the staircase. "I did not kill the man. I didn't even beat him to a pulp."

"Very restrained of you."

When he reached the top of the stairs, he leaned a moment against the wall next to Mitchella's door, rested his forehead on hers. "I can't believe a beast like that was allowed in my home."

"My fault," Mitchella whispered, stroking his face. "I wanted workers who weren't disturbed by the ballroom."

Straif shuddered out a breath. A corner of his mouth lifted ironically. "Just added more rough energies to the place. We definitely need to get a priest and priestess for a Ritual cleansing." He pushed away from the wall. "Open," he ordered the door. The knob turned, and the door swung open. Straif crossed to an overstuffed chair and sank into it, still holding Mitchella. She knew she should move, but the rush of danger had faded, languor replacing it. Straif was being so tender, so gentle with her.

"Let's see that cheek of yours," he said, urging her to turn her head with his fingertip against her chin. He swore when he saw it. "That fliggering bastard left his handprint on you!" His eyes took on the wild tint of blue.

Mitchella slid her hands into his silky hair on each side of his face, her eyes fixed on his. "Kiss it and make it better?"

His muscles eased from battle-tension, his gaze softened. "Yes." With no more pressure than a butterfly's wing, his lips brushed against her stinging cheek, once, twice, again, and again. Then his tongue wetted her lips. His mouth touched hers. Warmth unfurled inside her, she surrendered to him, to anything he wanted. The bond between them opened wide.

Straif's outer hand slid from her hip to her butt and squeezed.

"Ahem!"

Straif's head jerked up. Mitchella blinked and turned to see a flushed T'Heather at the open door, holding a Healer's bag.

"Winterberry vized me. Said there was an assault on a lady." T'Heather stumped in. "The guard is downstairs in the workroom. The Residence informed me you were here. Now, let's see that face of yours, GentleLady Clover."

Mitchella stood, her knees wobbly. She tilted her head toward T'Heather. He swore worse than Straif. "The injury itself is not that bad," T'Heather said. He set his hand against her face exactly as the foreman's hand had struck her. With a flash of warmth and a Word, the pain was gone. T'Heather moved his palm all over her face, jaw, and neck, and the swelling subsided. He grunted. "Minimal skin and muscle trauma; you won't even have a bruise."

"You do good work." Mitchella smiled tentatively, and when nothing hurt, grinned.

But the Healer was looking at Straif. "It's a bad day when a man can assault a woman in a FirstFamily Residence."

Straif growled.

T'Heather continued, "Too many nasty surprises going on here, Blackthorn. Stop them."

"Right." Straif stood. He wrapped an arm around Mitchella's waist. "I don't know how many of those actions the other Blackthorn is behind. I would guess the workman who did this to Mitchella was his spy."

T'Heather jerked a nod. "Winterberry will figure it out. He doesn't fail. The Councils will listen to his report."

"They'd damn well better. Keeping me in the dark doesn't help me in stopping those 'nasty surprises.' What do I owe you?"

Eyes narrowed, T'Heather's lips curled in an edgy smile. "I will bill the Councils. Let them see the consequences of their actions."

Straif's smile matched the Healer's. "Good idea."

"Blessed be," T'Heather said.

"Blessed be," Mitchella and Straif said.

With a wave, T'Heather 'ported from the room.

When he was gone, Mitchella saw another person standing at the open door, the cook, Gwine Honey, eyes bulging.

"Yes?" asked Straif.

Honey squared his shoulders. "The guardsman sent the workers home and the foreman to jail."

"Yes?"

"Dinner's ready. I can't find the boy."

Mitchella sighed. "He was very irritated with us."

"He came up a few minutes ago," Honey said.

Had Antenn seen them kissing? That would have hurt him more. She must talk with him.

"Thank you, Honey," said Straif. "We'll be right down to dinner."

"You look a whole lot better," Honey said, staring at Mitchella. He nodded. "Good." He clumped down the west stairs.

"I'll get Antenn," Mitchella said.

"Kiss me, first." Straif tapped his lips. "A good one. Just to make sure everything is working properly." He grinned and Mitchella couldn't help smiling back.

"Oh, very well." She pressed herself against him, centimeter by centimeter until their bodies were flush. To her dazzled mind the bond between them pulsed a throbbing rainbow of colors. She reveled in holding him until their scents mingled—sage and summer flowers. She looked at him, a chuckle in her throat at the sheer delight of the anticipatory heat running through her body. "Mmm, good," she said.

He appeared dazed, and that was even better. Flexing her knees to make sure they'd hold, she walked away with an extra roll in her hips. He moaned behind her.

All her pleasure fled when she discovered Antenn wasn't in his rooms. "Antenn!" A tiny blue white holosphere bobbed to her from the mantle of the bedroom.

"Mitchella, I want to spend tonight with the Clovers. I'll see you after my apprenticeship tomorrow." His words were stiff, and in the holo his eyes shifted.

Desperate panic speared her. She hurried to the scrybowl and called the Clover Compound. He was probably with Mel and Pratty.

"Here," answered Pratty.

"Aunt Pratty, is Antenn there?"

Pratty's kindly face folded into resignation. "Yes, he's here, and angry. He won't tell us what is wrong, and he won't talk about you."

"I'll be right there."

Pratty looked troubled. "I don't think you should come, dear, give him time to cool off. I don't know what happened, but all his boy's pride is raw. Leave him be."

"I'd like to speak to him, please."

Sighing, Pratty called, "Tell Antenn that Mitchella wants to talk to him."

Mitchella heard his dragging steps even through the scrybowl. When he appeared, his expression was closed, and when he saw her, his shoulders hunched. Not good signs.

"I was worried about you. Are you all right?"

"Yes," he replied, and she knew he was physically fine, but emotionally hurt.

She kept her tone even. "Thank you for letting me know where you were." She searched for words. "I know you're upset."

He stood still, mutinous.

Mitchella sighed. "We don't have to talk about this now, but I think we should discuss this tomorrow."

Antenn shrugged.

His eyes showed hurt and anger. Was this the boy who'd let her hold him just the night before? There had been such tenderness between them, yet now he seemed on the other side of a chasm. "I love you, Antenn," Mitchella said quietly.

His lip thrust out like the little boy he'd never been allowed to be. Perhaps he finally believed he could act nastily and still be loved. Mitchella had thought they'd conquered that mountain long ago. "Do you?" he asked.

"Yes," she put all the warmth and love she felt into her words. "I love you."

He seemed to relax. Then a shadow passed behind his eyes and he inhaled deeply and said, "I want—"

"An-tennn!" called one of the Clover boys, "Dinnnerrr!"

"I want—" Antenn started again, then his gaze went past her and he looked angry again. "I want to stay here tonight, in a big place full of people. I don't want to live in an empty formal Residence anymore. I want us to look for our own place."

Straif's hand curled over Mitchella's shoulder, his fingers warm, his thumb stroking her shoulder blade.

"We'll talk about that tomorrow afternoon. Sleep well and blessed be."

"Blessed be," Antenn choked and cut the scryspell.

"I'm sorry I've made your lives difficult," Straif said, then added, "Dinner is served. Since it's one of the entrees Gwine is practicing, he's almost hopping up and down for us to sample it." Straif turned her and kissed her brow. He took her hand in his, and they went to the dining parlor.

"What of Winterberry?"

"Winterberry cleverly left me a report. The work crew noticed a change in the foreman's habits when he took this job. Though they aren't saying anything against him, it's evident that he's been defrauding us."

"I should have kept a better eye on him."

"You gave the job to Antenn, and the boy is not as experienced as you are."

"I'll reimburse—" Mitchella started stiffly.

"That wasn't a complaint. It was well done of you. From the models I've now reviewed of the ballroom, which don't look like your style, I'd say that Antenn made the samples and that he has a good amount of talent and Flair. I like the new look." He kissed her fingers before releasing them to seat her. He took a chair next to her.

Glancing at the open door to make sure the cook wasn't near, he said lowly, "Mitchella, I'm sorry I hurt you."

Equally quiet, she said, "I'm sorry you hurt both of us." She shrugged. "We let our emotions deepen when we shouldn't—"

"Don't tell me you're reconsidering me as a lover! I won't let you go." He gripped her hand.

She smiled sadly. "This intensity of yours isn't helping. No, I haven't reconsidered. I want you. I intend to live my life to the fullest. If that means the hurt of living without you comes after the joy of being with you, I accept that. I—" She broke off as the cook cut and served a delicate puff pastry of fancy mushrooms embedded in melted cheese. Mitchella savored the combination of tastes and textures and swallowed and sighed with pleasure. "I'll miss the food when this project ends, too."

"Don't—"

"Don't what? Talk about the end? We *must* accept that this will end, Straif. You are a FirstFamily GrandLord, nothing permanent can come of a liaison with a sterile woman. Especially since you have a HeartMate."

His expression looked as if he were eating ashes instead of a delectable dish. "I don't want to discuss this topic further."

Probably didn't want to think about it—feel the pain of inevitable loss. Neither did she. She willed her damp eyes to dry, managed a smile. "Eat, Straif. And follow my lead—keep the rest of the time we have together light and happy."

He scowled. "I'm not a very lighthearted man."

"Try."

She went with him to his bed that night. After a bout of in-credible sex where Mitchella had ravished him, Straif held her while she slid into sleep. He knew she worried about Antenn and tried to soothe her. But she'd wanted sex, and Straif had wanted more . . . but he also knew that since that time when he'd turned away, she wouldn't trust him with her soul-deep feelings. Like she trusted Antenn.

Straif was a temporary item in her life. A temporary prior-ity. And that bit sharp. It was the way it should be—the way he'd intended, but somehow his emotions had gotten entan-gled around her, had started building more than his mind had deemed wise. She'd done the same thing, opening herself so much to him. Encouraging the bond between them. It would be hard to let go.

Sleep wouldn't come. Beyond the matter of his relation-ship with Mitchella was the simple fact that he had been in the ballroom that evening. He'd heard the angry voices, felt the throb of anxiety and fear from Mitchella and Antenn—but most of all had been a darkening of the atmosphere, like a plume of soot issuing from the room.

He hadn't hesitated to intervene, and it had been the right action, but he *had* been in the ballroom, the setting of his worst memories, most hideous nightmares. If he could stand to be there once, he could do so again. Time to confront the ghost of his lost and grief-stricken self that still lingered in the room.

So he got up slowly, put on soft trous, and padded down to the room. Lights brightened at his approach, but with the re-newed energy of the Residence, they were now automatic. The Residence didn't speak.

Without hesitation, he opened the door to the ballroom and walked inside. Six small nightglobes lit the room. The rectan-gular chamber had been shaped into an oval, with curving wooden panels masking the corners. Of course, his brain prodded. That had been the basis of the argument, one of the panels was of cheaper wood than the rest.

"Maximum lights." The five chandeliers, dripping with crystal, shone, dazzling. His gut tightened. He remembered those chandeliers all too well. Not much for a dying boy flat on his back to look at except the chandeliers and the ceiling. He would have to look up at the ceiling. Acid pitched in his stomach, bringing rising nausea. He glanced up. And didn't see the colorful mural he'd expected. No colonists descending the ramp of the Ship, *Arianrhod's Wheel*, at the east end of the room, no building of Druida at the west end of the ceiling. No solemn GreatRitual Circle in the middle.

How he'd hated that Circle. It had blurred in his sick eyes, but he'd known it was there. He'd prayed with every breath of his cracked lips that he would live, his mother, father, Fasha. In the delirium of his second Passage, he'd cried out to those painted people to help him, them. Nothing had happened.

Hands fisted at his side, he groaned, and it was almost loud enough to cover the moans of the dying that always sounded in his memory of this place, and the time. The time of his second Passage and the perishing of his Family.

He sucked in a breath, and the fragrance of newly cut and shaped wood came with it. His vision of the past cleared, and he saw the new ceiling again, a sunrise, radiating pastel color in all directions. It had to be a sunrise, Mitchella wasn't one to ever tint a room with a sunset. And below the ceiling, faint clouds formed, wisped across the room, dispersed.

He choked on a sob or a laugh, cleared his throat. "I'd have hated that when I was sick. It was hard enough to see clearly, to try and see the ceiling through clouds would have been maddening."

"But you can live with it now?" Mitchella asked softly.

He pivoted to see her hovering near the door. His heart pounded hard and fast. She was so lovely in the white lace nightgown, fiery hair tumbled over her shoulders. He didn't want her touched by this place, the old, horrible emotions it held. Himself.

But he wanted her in his arms, close, where he could warm himself in her unstinting comfort. He was always torn between emotions with her.

She took a hesitant step in, another, scanned the room, and Straif noted with surprise that her look was all professional, weighing the work that had been done, that which would be done, comparing the room to the finished mental image in her head. She wasn't being bombarded by negative vibrations.

So he examined the place. The curved panels were fine, the ceiling with its misty clouds, the French doors that led out to the terrace were covered with long swathes of material he thought was temporary. The floor had been restored and polished and whitewashed and—

A shudder took him. Step-by-step he crossed to the windows, drawn by the dark marks incised in the wooden ballroom floor. He stopped where he'd lain as a youngster, gaze fixed on the wood. Horror thundered through him. He'd forgotten. Had never recalled that he'd done this.

Close to the wall, next to the molding, he'd carved "Straif." His name. To the left of where he stood, he read the small, dark letters. "T'Blackthorn died here." To the left of that was the name, Leea Holly Blackthorn, his mother. To the right of his name was Fasha Blackthorn.

All along the border of the room, he'd incised names. A cry ripped from his throat.

Mitchella grabbed his hand, and the warmth of her flooded through his fingers, but was not enough to banish the icy revulsion. "Come away," she ordered.

He shook, but he didn't move. "No," he said. "No." He had to finally accept their deaths, move through the horror and grief, move on. Or die himself.

"I did that. I couldn't believe they were all gone, not even when I carved their names in the floor. Not everyone. And I lived. Then ran away." His voice was hoarse.

"You were seventeen!"

"Yes, I was seventeen, and dying of the virus. And experiencing my second Passage."

"No!" She lifted teary eyes to him; wet tracks rippled down her face.

"Yes."

She wrapped herself around him, comforting him. For the first time in this room, his emotions calmed. Perhaps now he could admit what he'd hidden from himself, from everyone.

"We were all dying. Fasha went first that night. I was eaten by my Flair, terrible dreams, illusions. My father and mother tried to help, but they were dying, too. It was only a matter of time. Father was the weakest. He'd spent huge amounts of

Flair trying to keep everyone strong for the Healers to do their work. But the Healers couldn't save us."

He licked his lips that were dry as they'd been that night. "So Father and Mother agreed. They would guide me through Passage, send me all their strength. They died. I lived."

"They wanted to save their son."

"And they did, but for what?"

She shook him. "Life! For life! To live! They loved you."

"Yes. And I loved them, but I didn't want their sacrifice."

Her soft hands stroked his face. "No one would. No one."

He looked down at all the names. "In the morning everyone was dead. But not me. Because my parents sent me all their energy."

He couldn't bear to walk down the wall, looking at familiar names that would conjure up the image of the person. So he put his arms around Mitchella, rested his head on hers. "I carved every name I could, crawling along with my whittling knife. Perhaps it was still the fever, maybe it was grief. I collapsed, then my cuz Holm Holly was there, more people, and I was gone from here, and it was all over."

Mitchella trembled in his arms. "A terrible story."

"Yes, one I've done my best to forget. But a sacrifice like that—how can a boy or a man live up to it?"

Silence shrouded the room.

"If they were HeartMates and your father was dying . . ."

"Yes, Mother would have followed, probably that night. Instead they went together. They were cradled in each other's arms when I last saw them."

Mitchella cried, and a hideous weight in his chest began to break, like a chunk of ice cracking.

Straif looked around the chamber. "It's a pretty room. Perhaps it can be a good place, now."

She sobbed, quivering in his arms.

"Come away," he said. "Come away. This was a dancing room, Mother's favorite. It's not a place to be sad."

But Mitchella didn't move. So he picked her up. Small dots of wetness showed on the floor, her tears. They glowed, gathering bits of dark smoke—the negativity in this room, his guilt he'd never acknowledged—and vanquished it.

Twenty-four

❤

*W*ork bell woke *Mitchella* and as she stretched, the recollection of the whole dreadful night rushed through her mind. Straif looked pale beside her, but peaceful. She stroked back a lock of his light brown hair with tenderness.

Then she thought of Antenn and fear punched. She slipped from bed, put on a green silkeen robe, and padded to the other side of the huge bed to the nightstand where an elegant china scrybowl sat. She eyed it uneasily. She didn't want to leave Straif, didn't want to wake him, but needed to check on Antenn.

Straif reached out a long, tanned arm. His strong fingers wrapped her wrist. "I'm awake."

She met his eyes, and they were blue, blue. Her heart turned over with love.

He shut his eyes, then sent her a stream of feeling that stopped her breath—affection, passion, love? Most of all, gratitude. When he spoke again, his voice was rough. "Last night—my wounds ripped open and let the poison out." He went white around the lips. "Now I can heal."

His fingers tightened around her wrist, wave after wave of immense emotions, too tangled for her to sort out, radiated from him. He took a deep breath, opened his eyes, and said,

"Thank you." Letting her wrist go, he stretched to flick the scrybowl with a fingernail. "Clover Compound—"

"Mel and Pratty," Mitchella said. She'd have had to circle the bowl with her finger and say a couple of spellwords to connect it. She sighed. Straif and she were so far apart in Flair.

He tilted his head, and she knew he'd heard her thought. "We may be 'far apart' in Flair, but your emotional strength— it awes me. Antenn is lucky to have you as a guardian."

"He's more than a ward to me. He's the child of my heart," she said.

At that moment, Pratty Clover answered the scry. When she saw Mitchella, her face crumpled. "Oh, Mitchella! Antenn's gone!"

A huge fist squeezed Mitchella's chest. "What do you mean he's gone?" She tried to sound cool, calm, reasonable, but was suddenly cold, and her teeth wanted to chatter.

Aunt Pratty flushed, fluttered her hands. "You know how many boys there are in the family, Mitchella. We aren't used to keeping an eye on him and all the others were covering for him, and—" She broke out in noisy tears. "We've lost him. We've lost a child!"

Uncle Mel gently moved her away from the scrybowl. "The last time we saw him was at dinner last night. My boys," he scowled and gazed to his left, "said he left at dawn." He breathed deeply. "By the way, Pinky is with him. I think you'd better ask T'Blackthorn to help us out on this. We'll work a trade."

"Done!" said Straif. He was already dressed in the same worn leathers Mitchella had first seen him in. He inclined his head to Mel. "We've had a very good balance of value between us, this will just continue the business relationship. I'll check the Residence for his traces; he may have left some clues as to where he intended to go. Then I'll be by your compound to pick up his trail from there."

"Yes," Mel said, looking relieved. Pratty had stopped sobbing and stared at Straif with desperate hope. "I'm sure you'll find him, T'Blackthorn. Our thanks."

"My pleasure," Straif said, and ended the call.

Mitchella flung herself into Straif's arms. Now *she* needed reassurance.

He held her tightly, stroked her back, and murmured, "I've never failed to find any youngster."

She clutched at him, but the rock-steadiness of his body, his complete certainty, helped. "Thank you."

With a last hug, he stepped away, a slight smile on his lips. "We seem to be saying that to each other a great deal this morning."

Before he could speak again, the scrybowl sounded a deep chord.

"Here," said Straif stepping in front of it, blocking Mitchella from whoever gazed out from the other end.

"Caprea Sallow," said a deep voice. Mitchella knew the man to be an animal trainer and owner of the best stable in Druida.

She drew on a heavier robe and moved to where she could see him. He was a man of Straif's age with tanned skin and dark eyes. "One of my travel horses is missing," he said calmly. "I have a note from one Antenn Moss that he will pay for its use. I believe that person has been living under your roof."

"Yes. I'll stand as surety for any charges," Straif said.

Caprea nodded, hesitated. "I trust you, *T'Blackthorn*. I'll collect when the beast is returned. The horse has the best travel-shieldspell available cast upon him and his rider."

Mitchella shuddered in relief.

"Good to know," Straif said.

Caprea said, "I hope to see you and your Residence at your open house."

"I'll be honored if you, and anyone you wish to invite, will come," Straif said.

"Merry meet," Caprea said.

"And merry part."

"And merry meet again." Caprea ended the scryspell.

When Straif turned to Mitchella, she had gone white and was sitting on the bed. "He stole a horse."

"Borrowed without paying in advance. Not quite the same thing."

"He's not an expert horseman."

"Since horses are rare, not many people are."

She lifted wide eyes to him. "You are?"

He smiled. "I track all over Celta. Yes." He caught her hands, found her fingers trembling, and gave her strength.

Drina mewed. She was sitting near the bedroom door, dark brown tail curled around her paws. *I saw the boy in that-special-Blackthorn-room yesterday evening.*

Straif stared at her. "The Blackthorn Travel-Prep room?"

"Yessssssss," the cat vocalized.

"And you didn't stop him."

Good riddance.

"Not if he left Druida by horse."

Drina's next mew was plaintive. *Young ones outside the city is not good.*

"No, not good," Straif repeated for Mitchella. "Pinky is with him. I'm going to follow. I may be gone a couple of hours or days. Mitchella will be in charge of the Residence."

Drina hissed, lashed her tail.

"Amazing Fam that you are, you still can't talk to many people." Straif tugged on Mitchella's hand, and they left the MasterSuite. Drina followed, walking haughtily.

Everyone who is Anyone can talk to Me. She mewed.

"Let's get to work." He looked down at Drina. "Do you want to help or not?"

You are as good as I am.

He was better.

I will help in Druida, but not outside. I am a City Cat. That other Cat, Pinky, is sensible. He will help his person.

"Drina is of the opinion that Pinky will help Antenn," he relayed.

Mitchella rolled her eyes. Straif stopped at the door of the suite Antenn had used. Straif narrowed his eyes, changing his vision to see Antenn's track—vibrant with youth. The bright thread was a mixture of greens since the boy hadn't experienced his second Passage to master his Flair. It also looked as if he was uncertain of his identity.

"This way." Straif looked at Mitchella and found her eyes gleaming with tenderness. For him? For Antenn? He yearned to ask, but also feared to.

Drina sniffed. *He went to the kitchen. Time for breakfast. I will eat now.* She trotted to the stairs and down to the kitchen.

Straif brought Mitchella's hand to his lips. "I've never failed to find a youngster," he repeated.

She smiled with such confidence in him that his very bones warmed. He would not fail her.

The cook was busy and frowned when they intruded. "What?"

"Are any of the travel food supplies gone?" Straif asked.

The cook glanced at the bank of no-times. "Huh. Someone messed with my no-times." He touched a small door, and it rose open. "Three are gone."

Drina worked her food no-time and the chef jumped. "Cats in the kitchen," he muttered.

"Three? Good, the boy is well provisioned." Hardly glancing at Antenn's line, he and Mitchella went to the Travel-Prep room. Full of maps and equipment, like the HouseHeart, it rarely changed over the centuries. So many T'Blackthorns, D'Blackthorns, Heirs, and Family had used the place that the emotional layers were nearly impersonal. He hadn't spent much time in the room, but it hadn't ever bothered him. Now that he'd faced the ballroom, Straif didn't think any of the rooms of his Residence would ever cause him discomfort again.

One glance told him that Antenn was more than well provisioned, he was well equipped. "Not as bad as it could be, he took a good deal of my wilderness gear."

"I'm sorry," Mitchella whispered.

Again Straif kissed her fingers that were tightly curled around his own. "We were both blind. He was more upset than we thought. I should have remembered how intensely boys feel."

None of the older maps or the holospheres in the wall of cubbyholes were touched. Antenn had gone straight to the huge old table that held information about current projects.

"The map T'Ash sent me of the lambenthyst mine is gone," Straif said. "It makes sense." He chuckled without humor. "I haven't visited the mine. It's dangerous to me, so he'll show himself to be stronger, braver than I am." He met Mitchella's eyes, now dark green. "He'll show *you* that he is the better of the two of us."

She shook her head as if confused. "There's no comparison.

He's the child of my heart, and you're my lover. Two different relationships."

Hurt stabbed Straif. Another difference was that Antenn would always be close to Mitchella, and she could very well be done with Straif in a couple of eightdays.

At that moment the scrybowl on the table chirruped. Loosening his tense shoulders, Straif answered, "Here."

The image of his uncle T'Holly formed in the droplets above the wide, shallow pan.

"Good, you haven't left yet," T'Holly said. "I must warn you, boy. You know what this will look like to the Councils, don't you? As if you're running away again."

Straif flinched.

"That isn't true!" Mitchella cried, flinging her arms wide. "Look at all we've done with the Residence. He's restored it!"

T'Holly spoke softly. "Think how a prosecutor will present the facts. Straif's done his duty and is now back on his benighted, futile quest." T'Holly shrugged. "Straif has the wanderlust and will only be in Druida now and then. He's not a civilized man anymore. He tried, but when the going got tough, he left."

Fury burned through Straif. "That isn't the situation. I'm going to find and restore a runaway to his Family."

"The Councils—"

"Let the Councils believe what they want, but you can record this and play the scry back to them." Straif leaned forward to the scrybowl, every muscle in his body set. "I'm going to rescue a boy, and I'll be back, and I'll fight forever for what is mine. Every minute, every septhour, every day. If they thought my fifteen years on a quest was obsessive, let them contemplate living the rest of their lives fighting me, especially those who are against me. They will never have rest."

To his surprise, Mitchella pushed him aside to talk to T'Holly. "And tell them that Antenn isn't the first child to run away to the wilds and won't be the last. T'Blackthorn is the *best* in tracking. Those who alienate him—"

Straif cut in. "—will have to pay very, very well, or appeal to the Councils to pay my fee. If they show so little respect for me and my skills now, they'd better not complain about huge fees later when they need me. Keeping note of allies and enemies has been a generational business for every FirstFamily. I'll know who supported me and who didn't."

T'Holly raised his eyebrows. "You have a good point about the runaways, GentleLady." He paused. "I have a runaway of my own."

Standing close to Mitchella, Straif said, "Your son didn't run away, he was cast out."

Now T'Holly flinched.

"Get that through your thick head. Your son accompanied his wife to build a new life when his old one fell into a shambles.

"Look at me, Holm senior. *Look at me.* I'm the sole Blackthorn. I'd give my Flair to have my sister back, or my parents. I lost my Family to a ravaging disease. You lost yours through hurt pride. Don't you *ever* hint to me that you were the wronged one in this matter. You and your Lady broke your vows of honor. You suffer under it. She suffers under it. The whole T'Holly household is affected, which is one of the reasons I moved out. Scry ended." His lungs pumped raggedly.

Mitchella put her arms around him. When she whispered, her breath caressed his neck. It should have tickled or aroused. It consoled. "Family problems are very difficult." Her laugh was a little watery. "No matter the circumstances, Family troubles are the worst."

They stood that way, holding each other for a long moment. "I'll return your son to you."

Clearing her throat, Mitchella said, "Yes, I know." She busied herself aligning the contents of the cubbyholes.

As Straif packed, from the corner of his eye he saw Mitchella open her mouth. "You aren't going," he said harshly, stowing the last of his gear and turning to her. "You're a city woman." She stood there, looking lush, looking like the most expensive luxury he'd ever had. He wondered if this stunt by Antenn had destroyed his relationship with Mitchella. Straif sent determination—and tenderness—down the strong bond between himself and his lady. The connection was there, he wouldn't let her cut it before their time was done.

Worry lived in her eyes. Her hands twined in a completely un-Mitchella like gesture.

"You'd slow me down," he said gently. The heavy forests

of the northeastern Hard Rock Mountains were too dangerous for her.

Her shoulders slumped. "I know." Tears filled her eyes, trickled down her cheeks. "You'll find him, won't you?"

"I'll bring him back to you." He'd lost his own Family, his beloved young sister. He wouldn't let Mitchella lose Antenn.

She flung herself into his arms, feeling soft and solid and vital, like no one else he'd ever known. He held her tight, as if he'd be allowed to hold her forever. Or as if he'd lose her in the next moment.

"Find my boy, Straif. Take care of him." She lifted a tear-stained face and kissed him hard on the lips, sending an arc of lightning through every vein. "Take care of yourself."

The scrybowl pinged. Straif sighed. "I can tell I'm a GrandLord again, never a dull moment. Here."

T'Ash's serious face formed. "Is Mitchella there?"

"Here." Mitchella stepped into view.

"Danith heard that Antenn is missing. How, I don't know, because she's in the fishing town of Anglesey. There's a beached whale. She wanted me to call, let you know that if you need anything, you're supposed to come over, do you hear?"

"I hear."

He shifted his gaze to Straif. "And I heard you're leaving to track down Antenn. Those allies of our generation will fight for you while you're gone. I've arranged for a traveling companion for you, to keep the Councils rational."

"What?"

"Accept him. He'll be a great help. The Councils approve."

"Not Zanth, I hope."

"Zanth is still feeling 'puny,' and being pampered by Danith for all he's worth. He's sulking this morning while she's freeing the fliggering whale. Probably riding it out to sea. *Not* what a newly pregnant woman should be doing. She wouldn't let me come, said I'd intimidate the fisherfolk." The GreatLord appeared to be sulking himself. There was a mournful cat moan beyond the scrybowl. T'Ash grimaced. "Winterberry's coming. He should be there shortly with stridebeasts."

"Antenn stol—took a horse."

T'Ash grinned. "Enterprising boy. They're faster, but not as tough. Expensive, too."

"I'll pay any penalties," Mitchella said.

They all knew that if the horse died she could work all her life and never pay the bill.

T'Ash nodded. "We stand behind you, too, Mitchella. Feel free to come and stay here while Straif is gone."

Mitchella didn't look at Straif. "Thanks, but T'Blackthorn Residence and I understand each other. I can get a lot done if I stay." She'd need the work to keep her mind occupied.

Grunting agreement, T'Ash said, "Ask for what you need and it will be provided. Straif, you're lucky to have Mitchella there to continue the work."

Mitchella's mouth hung open. She snapped it shut. "Thank you for the compliment, T'Ash."

"Only the truth," the man said, turned his gaze to Straif. "Anything else I can do for you?"

"Yes, can you test my defenses?"

T'Ash frowned, a moment later thunder rumbled overhead. A bead of sweat trickled from his temple. "Your shields are strong, they'll hold."

"My thanks," Straif said. "I also need another copy of that map to the mines. I believe Antenn took my map. It's missing, and his trace is all over my desk."

"One moment." T'Ash frowned in concentration. "'Port grid, please," he said.

"I'll do it," Mitchella said, and laid a glowing grid on the room, as well as showing a small three-dimensional model of it before them.

"It comes," said T'Ash.

There was a slight "pop" and a many-folded large square of papyrus appeared at their feet. Straif stooped to pick it up. When he rose, T'Ash said, "Merry meet,"

"And merry part," Straif said.

"You, too, Mitchella," T'Ash chided.

"And merry part," Mitchella said.

"And merry meet again," T'Ash said and ended the call.

"Well," Mitchella whooshed out a breath, still looking at the place where T'Ash's image had formed. "I suppose he's finally forgiven me for telling him that Danith was sterile."

"You did that! Cruel."

She whipped around to face him, poked a finger in his chest. "You FirstFamily Lords are complex men, hard work. He was exhausting Danith with his moods. He made her *cry*." She set her shoulders back. "No one makes my best friend cry without answering to *me*." She shook her head. "And I've forgiven him for flinging me across town to Danith's house in a rage."

"I had no idea you had this interesting past," Straif said, and kissed her briefly on her mouth, sweeping his tongue over her lips, and she tasted the essence of him, sage.

Mitchella found a smile on her face. "You and Winterberry. With all that help, Antenn is sure to be found."

"Right."

Closing her eyes, she tested the bond she had with the child of her heart. "He's resentful, and proud, and feeling snotty, but he's fine. Pinky is with him, excited at the adventure. Glad he's away from Drina." The horse trotted and Mitchella winced. "Though according to what Danith's told me about riding horses, he's going to be very sore this evening." She opened her eyes.

Straif held out his hand, and a tube of Flaired liniment smacked into it. "I'd better pack this, then."

He slanted her a look. "Since you have bonds with Antenn and me, bonds that should stay strong over a long distance, you'll be able to send to me immediately if he's in danger."

"I'll do that." She placed her hands on his chest, liking the solidity of him, his steady heartbeat. "You're a good man, Straif T'Blackthorn." They stood like that for a moment until he pulled away, folded over the saddlebag flap, buckled it shut, and said a Word to keep it fastened and safe.

Mitchella saw a worn roll of celtaroon about the length of her hand still on his desk. "Wait, you've forgotten this." She picked it up and heard metal clinking, and knew it was his whittling tools. They stared at each other, remembering the names incised in the ballroom floor. Hurt throbbed from him to her.

She took his hand and put the roll in it. "Why don't you carve something for me while you're on the trail? Something you see along the way that will show a city girl like me a little of the wild."

He turned the roll over in his hands, straightened the tie that circled it, must have felt her question at the lack of Flair spells. "If I can't untie the cord with my fingers, they're no good for carving. If I can't protect and take care of my whittling knives, I'm not much of a man." He smiled wryly. "My G'Uncle Prunus told me that when he gave me these. They were my first set."

Antenn had had Mitchella work personally on the edge of the floor that contained the names, so she knew Prunus was a name that had been cut deeply into the wood.

"A wonderful gift for a boy. One that would continue to give him pleasure."

Straif's eyes went dark blue. "Yes." He opened the saddle-bag and placed the celtaroon roll on the top. "Would you like an animal or plant?" he asked briskly, slipping the saddlebag over his shoulder, picking up an extra survivalsleeper, and setting a wide-brimmed hat on his head.

"Surprise me." She kissed him, curved her hands around his face, and sought the most sacred feeling she had within her, the speck of herself that connected to the Lady during rituals. Then she stepped back. "Blessings on you, Straif T'Blackthorn."

He ducked his head, accepting the sparkling white light that accompanied her words.

Then he hauled her into his arms again and took her mouth, opening her lips, darting his tongue past her teeth, exploring her entirely. She yielded to his need.

"Promise me you'll stay inside the estate's shields."

Finally he broke the kiss. "I promise."

"Good." He strode from the room. She followed him to the Grand Hall and out the door. There, waiting patiently on the grassdrive at the bottom of the steps, was Winterberry, mounted on the most beautiful stridebeast Mitchella had ever seen, hardly shaggy at all, and it appeared fast. Winterberry's traveling leathers were immaculate.

Straif eyed Winterberry and grunted, then studied the stridebeasts and whistled. "Someone has influence with Caprea Sallow."

"Danith D'Ash," Winterberry grinned, as if very pleased to be so well mounted himself.

"No one involved with animals refuses Danith anything." Mitchella smiled, pleased and comforted at the thought of her friend providing for her and Antenn.

"Greetyou, GentleLady Clover," Winterberry said.

"Blessings to you, Winterberry. My deepest thanks for your help."

Winterberry shook his head. "The Councils want me to keep an eye on him." He jerked his head toward Straif, who was introducing himself to the stridebeasts.

"You'll be handy to have around," Straif said. "If you don't mind getting those leathers dirty."

"They're bespelled," Winterberry said calmly.

Straif settled the saddlebags and survivalsleeper on his stridebeast, and mounted. "We'll bring Antenn back safe and sound." It rang like a vow of honor.

He waved, circled his mount, and took off, racing down the grassdrive.

Winterberry looked pained, dipped his head to Mitchella, then tore off after Straif.

A few instants later, the T'Blackthorn gates clanged open. Then shut.

The males she loved most in her life, Straif and Antenn, were gone.

She turned and saw the cook staring after the men, frowning deeply.

Twenty-five

❦

$\mathcal{A}$s they rode along the wall of his estate, Straif became aware of a young dog fox keeping pace.

Greet-you males of the hu-man, it said. *You fol-low the scent of the kit-male of the hu-man and the kit-male of the fe-line.*

Winterberry threw it a startled look. Straif slowed his stridebeast to a walk. *That is so,* he replied to the fox, and knew the guardsman heard the mental conversation.

I want an ad-ven-ture. I would like to go with you. The fox's eyes held humor. He looked as if he smiled.

I would be honored, Straif said. *But we go to the rocky and wooded mountains with much danger.*

I will go, too. The fox barked. He looked at Winterberry. *And you, male-hu-man-who-pro-tects?*

I, too, would be honored, male of the vulpes, said Winterberry.

You may call me Vertic, said the fox, serenely.

Winterberry stared. *Vertic is a Winterberry name.*

The fox shot ahead of them, running. Straif clucked at his stridebeast to keep up. "Well, well, well," Straif said. "This will be interesting."

Winterberry swallowed. "Looks like the fox—Vertic—knows where he's going."

"You and I have similar Flair," Straif said.

Shrugging, Winterberry said, "You have the greater—you can 'see' trails, right? I can only sense them—and I have to use all my senses." He smiled lopsidedly. "On the other hand, I don't think I rely as much on my Flair as you do."

Straif stared at the man. "You can't travel Celta and not use all the skills you have."

"Good point, my apology."

But however differently they used their Flair, it was obvious to Straif that Winterberry tracked almost as well as he did himself.

They were riding within the foothills when the talk turned to women. By this time, to Straif's amusement, the fox was sitting on a makeshift pad behind Winterberry. Straif would have bet his estate that the guardsman would bond with the animal and have a Familiar before the trip was done.

"You're in a mess with GentleLady Clover," Winterberry said.

"What made you decide that my love life is a good topic to discuss?"

The guardsman raised an eyebrow. "Trying to untangle the knot your love life is in will probably last us to the mine."

Straif winced. "What makes you think I'd like your advice?"

"Couldn't get any worse."

"Worse advice?"

Winterberry chuckled. "No, your situation. You should use this trip as the time to break off the affair."

"No."

"You have a HeartMate, and Mitchella is sterile—and a Commoner. Put her out of your life and search for your mate."

Straif's jaw hurt from teeth clamped tight. "You seem to know all the facts."

"I try to know everything relevant to the FirstFamilies. I'm assigned to you lot. I know you've set *Nuada's Sword* on track of a remedy for your heritage. Put Mitchella out of your life and search for your mate."

"I'm not ready."

"Not ready to break with Mitchella or search for your HeartMate?"

"Neither."

"Then let's look at this from a cold and practical point of view," Winterberry said in a conversational tone, yet something warned Straif that the words to come would be hard to hear. "Accept that the line from your flesh must die. Accept Mitchella and the love she can give you."

Straif sent a questioning glance to the guard. "Are her feelings that obvious?" The thought of Mitchella's love lightened his spirit.

"Yes. You can hurt her deeply."

That disturbed Straif. He'd hurt her before, and if he kept on with the affair, the ending would be painful for both of them. Yet he thought he didn't have the strength to step away from her loving.

Winterberry met Straif's eyes. "And she isn't the only one who could love you. There is the boy."

Straif snorted. "He resents and dislikes me."

"I have a small gift of foresight," Winterberry said. "And I think that by the time we return to Druida, the boy will respect and admire you."

"Unlikely."

"Perhaps. This is the perfect time to consider your circumstances, to straighten out your life, and since you have no intention of having a permanent connection with Mitchella, you should let her go."

"I want her," Straif said starkly.

"Ah, there's the core of the matter. You want your woman. I understand the feeling exactly." Winterberry's smile was ironic. "But it's not always best for you or her or you both to be mated. Of course the Clovers are survivors, and Mitchella in particular. She can weather an affair with you and then find a man who will marry and cherish her."

Straif *hated* that thought. He didn't want to think about Mitchella in another man's arms, didn't want to talk anymore. He clucked his tongue to his stridebeast and set the pace too fast for discussion. He did know one thing. He wasn't going to give her up yet. Straif sent a pulse of affection to her along their emotional link and it was instantly returned. He wanted that. He wanted her. He wanted it all.

$\mathcal{D}$rina *stayed near* Mitchella *the whole day, and* Mitchella found the little cat unexpectedly good company. She worked until she was exhausted, testing her bond with Antenn and Straif every few minutes.

In the evening she ate what Gwine fed her, took a long, hot bath in the mineral spring, and went to bed. But Mitchella tossed and turned. She was all too aware that Antenn was alone with only a delicate creature of a horse, that Straif was hurrying after the boy. She could only pray that neither of them were taking risks, but to her, any expedition outside the city walls was fraught with danger. It didn't matter that Antenn was tough from his Downwind years, a survivor. It didn't matter that Straif had spent more time in untamed Celta than in the city of Druida. She feared for them both.

The first night she slept on Antenn's bedsponge, surrounded by his treasures, the drawings and models of his vocation, the rush of water from the sea, and the scent of boy.

The next day she labored like a fiend, personally restoring every marble square in the Great Hall floor. She hadn't planned on doing that, since it was a delicate, concentration-demanding, time-consuming job—examining the marble, bringing the underlying essence of beauty once more to the surface, shining each vein of silver or gold from the inside with her Flair, then polishing the black or white square. But it was just the labor she needed to keep herself from going mad with worry.

The second night she hauled her exhausted self into the MasterSuite and the ancient T'Blackthorn generational bed. The bed had probably been the place of conception for many a Blackthorn, perhaps even Straif himself, and she had no right sleeping in it when she was sterile, when she was not the man's HeartMate, never could even be his wife. But beaten down by anxiety, she crawled into its soft comfort anyway.

And dreamed.

A deep chasm opened between herself and Straif. She stood on the edge, behind her lay well-kept verdant gardens.

She held out her arms and shrieked for him, gulping with tears, and he donned his most expressionless face, picked up his travel pack, and walked away across a dry and barren plain.

She called out, "Straif, Straif, my love!" and woke with tears on her face. She couldn't bear being in the T'Blackthorn bed. She shot out from under the covers, hopped to the floor. She was a Common Celtan woman, she should stick to bed-sponges. With a few muttered Words, she cleansed the sheets, made the bed, initiated a housekeeping spell for the room, and took herself off to her own suite. But she was all too aware that it wasn't *her* suite. It was the guest suite in the T'Blackthorn estate that she'd made minimal changes to. The suite was lovely as it was, though a little outdated. She could, of course, make it unique if she moved antique Blackthorn objects d'art into the rooms, changed the holos and paintings.

Sleep eluded her, so she decided to go to the attic store-rooms. She hadn't finished her inventory of everything. Sighing, she stretched and donned brown work tunic and trous.

"Residence," she said, "please provide soft lighting for me to attic room five."

"Yes, Mitchella," it said. "I will also heat attic room five. Are you going to inventory the room now?"

"Yes." She picked up her note flexistrip.

"Attic room five contains many pieces of the Head of Household two and a half centuries ago, GrandLady T'Black-thorn. As was the style of the times, her taste ran to the florid. She was a Lady of great intensity and Flair."

The Residence's voice comforted Mitchella. She'd miss the sentient house when she left. Right now it calmed her to know she wasn't entirely alone. Of course, Gwine Honey was in the cook's apartments, but she couldn't imagine engaging the young, nervous man in any conversation that didn't focus on food.

She'd reached the stairs to the attic, mounted them, and passed down the narrow hall to the last storeroom. "What was the name of the GrandLady?"

"Straif, of course," the Residence answered.

"Of course." The brass handle gleamed in the dim light, pleasing Mitchella. Everything in the hallway looked in good order. She entered the room and closed the door after her. The room was crowded with furniture under preservative-spell sheets of a pristine white. The air smelled of lavender—the type of molecular cleaning that Mitchella favored always left that scent. She smiled in satisfaction.

"Bright light," she ordered, and the room lit up like a summer's day.

"You usually like music," the Residence said.

Mitchella chuckled. "That would be great. Some dance music, please, to keep my mind off—"

The dance music started low, and the Residence spoke over it, "I have a copy of the map in my ResidenceLibrary memory, and by my calculations, if the boy gets all the way to the mine and T'Blackthorn finds him there, and they return, they should be back in two more days."

"Thank you," Mitchella said and went to work.

A septhour later, she'd noted all the large pieces of furniture and marked a large mirror to be sent to the guest suite, as well as a series of colorful china vases. She could tint one wall of the sitting room a dark, brick red. With the vases on a low table and the gilded mirror on the opposite wall, the room would be dramatic and give the feel of rich elegance.

She took a little break and sat on a soft twoseat, letting her head fall back on the wing. Though the piece was delightfully cushy, the fabric was too shabby to use.

The room was warm, the twoseat comfortable, and Mitchella was worn out from worry and work. She drew a stained, exquisitely soft llamawoolweave cover over herself and dozed. A little later she bent her legs and scooted down to snuggle into the welcoming cushions.

As she rested in the pleasant state of half-sleep, half-wakefulness, she became aware of a deep hum that later separated into a pattern of long, slow, rhythmic beats. Just listening to it caused a mixture of yearning and delight to twist inside her.

It *pulled* at her.

First a little tug, every twenty beats or so. She shifted, but felt too comfy to stir. She wanted to sink deeper into sleep.

But color was added to the sound, a fascinating rainbow wash, fluctuating with the rhythm. And the sound became *beyond* sound, something more or less, something that began to prickle Mitchella's nerves, even under the soft cover.

She shifted, but was no longer dozing, more aware than ever of the sound, the colors. Opening her eyes, she found that the colors pulsed through the room, tinting the white walls, spreading like circles from one far corner of the room. She watched, enchanted, admiring the slight variations of colors—not only the primary colors of a prism, but shade upon shade of green slightly changing into shade upon shade of yellow until it reached the bright white of Bel's sunlight. Then it darkened to black, pulsed into indigo.

The beat was louder, like a drum reverberating inside her, compelling her. She almost thought she could hear syllables, but couldn't understand the words.

Drawn by the colors and the pulse, she wove her way through the crammed space to the corner of the room and the object that hummed.

The chest in the corner was was intricately carved redd-wood and about two-thirds of a meter long by half a meter wide, with a rounded top. As soon as she touched it, her pulse picked up pace and anticipation thrilled through her. She felt as if she was going to discover her heart's desire, and she laughed at the absurdity.

She sat down and raised the lid. The strong scent of sage set her mind spinning, and a few even more exotic fragrances issued from the chest—musky amber, jasmine, wild nicotine. The headiness of the odors filled her nostrils, sifted inside her to curl like smoke, caressing her lungs, making her feel as if this was *the* scent. The most perfect smell she'd ever know.

The contents were hidden by a dark blue, coarsely woven blanket. Atop the blanket, affixed by a small sticky-spell, was a piece of rich papyrus with elegant writing. "Chest of Straif Blackthorn, T'Blackthorn, left with the Hollys after his third Passage, deliver to T'Blackthorn Residence. Passiflora D'Holly."

Mitchella stilled. She should not lift the blanket. She should leave the chest in peace. She should not—

A wave of fierce desire inundated her, rolling over her like a riptide.

She couldn't stop her hands from untucking the blanket,

even as her dull mind thought that it was good Straif had sought out his relatives to experience his third Passage. Passages that freed the Flair were nothing to take lightly. Psychic storms could kill a person.

Mitchella lifted the blanket, fingers running over it to stroke the rough texture, as rough as Straif's manners could be. She smoothed its folds and set it aside to see old travel garments. Her throat closed as she noted the nasty rips and tears in the almost indestructible celtaroon. Straif didn't have that many scars on himself, so he'd been lucky, the garments had saved his hide.

Mitchella lifted out the shirt and held it to her nose, inhaling the scent of untamed Celta and a younger Straif, then set the shirt aside, the trous, several pair of tattered gloves. Beneath the clothes was an old knapsack, and when Mitchella touched it, pure emotion flooded her—raw grief at the loss of his Family, the need to leave Druida, the obsession to make sure he'd never be left alone again—to find a cure for his flawed heritage. Later came wonder at the beauty to be found outside the city, excitement as he overcame his own death time and again.

She jerked her fingers away. She didn't want to think of Straif fighting for his life against nature, or wild animals, or other men. Especially when he was outside Druida. Since the pack was Straif's first, the one he'd carried at seventeen, it underscored the danger her own Antenn was in. She shivered, but could not turn away. The power of the thing would not free her.

Trembling, she took out the pack and put it aside. D'Holly had saved it for him, but Mitchella didn't think he'd care to see it again, or the garments. But it wasn't her decision to make.

More clothes, cotton and silkeen, a hat, scarf, cloak were placed on the stack beside her. Faster now, her fingers scrabbled in the chest, stirring the contents, until her hand closed over something in the corner, something hard that her fingers curled partially around, wrapped in silkeen.

Lust flooded her. She fell back, cushioned against the side of an old sofa, and the images came, the remembrance of her last, fast loving with Straif, how his hands had felt on her body, how his sex had filled her. The hard pumping of him, the sweat on his back, the scent of sex, the striving and ultimate release. She gasped as her climax ripped through her. Her fingers loosened and the silkeen stuck to her sweaty palm, but the object unrolled from the cloth to land on the stack of Straif's clothes and sat in the middle of them, glowing like a jewel.

It was a small heart-shaped box intricately carved of dark reddwood. Though she'd never seen a whittling knife in his hand, she knew Straif had carved it. Trying to be objective, she still thought it was one of the most delicate and beautiful things she'd ever seen. The detail was clear—flower blossoms. Tiny vines of An'Alcha, passion flowers, twined around the outside of the box. Carved in three dimensions on the front were interlocking hearts, symbol of the HeartBond.

Heart-shaped boxes had been popular for centuries, though styles changed. Almost everyone wanted to believe they'd have a HeartMate. Mitchella had seen innumerable heart boxes. She'd even purchased one a few months before she'd caught Macha's disease and become sterile. It was packed away with some of her old things in her parents' house, part of her past, just as this one had been hidden away in a chest.

But hers had been an inexpensive red sateen and pink lace, attractive to a young girl.

This one was far too attractive to the woman. Dangerously attractive. Mitchella wondered what visions Straif had seen during his psi Passage that caused him to carve such a delicate piece. She turned it over. Down on the very point of the back was a four leaf clover. She swallowed hard.

She knew what it was.

A HeartGift.

The way it called to her meant only one thing. She was Straif's HeartMate.

And she was sterile.

She didn't want Straif to come to her because of some biological imperative. It was still all very impossible. HeartMate or not, he simply wouldn't marry a sterile woman.

If he ever triumphed in his quest and had the perfect life he wanted, and came looking for his HeartMate, then he would know. But she wasn't going to tell him. It nearly broke her to know that she had a HeartMate but could not bond with him. She could not inflict that pain on him.

She stared at the beautiful, innocuous box. Her own heart thumped hard. She couldn't ignore it, all the laws and mysteries of Celtan culture that focused on it. If she claimed it, it automatically made her Straif's woman. Forever.

If *he* claimed her.

So far he'd shown no interest in the HeartGift; perhaps he'd forgotten it, perhaps he thought it was still at T'Holly Residence.

Her fingers closed fiercely around it, letting passion swamp her. For a moment she teetered between laughing and crying, then a wild sob tore from her. She clenched the little box to her breasts, close to her heart. This HeartGift was *hers*.

Only he who had made it and his HeartMate—her—could sense it, feel the waves of emotion and sensuality from the gift. She'd take it.

It meant nothing to Straif, since he was fixated on his personal quest, but the HeartGift meant everything to her.

She rocked back and forth. She had a HeartMate, and he was wonderful, and exciting and *hers*.

For the moment.

Hers. By all Celtan law, this object was hers. He'd made it for her, then discarded it.

He wouldn't want her any more than he wanted the box— not someone who was sterile.

She wanted it.

Her fingers traced the lovely texture of the carving. What if she showed it to him—proving her status? She shuddered at the revulsion she might see in his eyes. He wasn't interested in finding his HeartMate, all his focus was on his quest.

He wouldn't want her, and if she insisted on binding him to her by law and honor, he'd come to hate her—and she him.

She'd keep it.

When she and Antenn moved into their own place, she'd take it with her.

The thought of Antenn steadied her, as always, and she blessed the boy. He wouldn't be with her forever, either, he'd follow his own path. But he'd be family forever. The child of her heart, her son.

And if Straif ever discovered the HeartGift missing, thought that she might know where it went—she'd deal with that later. Surely their affair would be well over by then and she'd have gotten some perspective on it.

Sniffling, she took a rag from the chest, wiped her eyes and nose. There were mages who made strong spell boxes. She'd need to find one to put the HeartGift in. She couldn't afford to look at it, stroke it, pretend she made love to Straif by yielding to its sexual power. The thought revolted her. Her lip curled. No, *she* wouldn't allow an obsession into her life. It had been too well balanced, would be too balanced, to let something that potent skew it. She would *not* focus on a love she could never have. That way lay madness.

Yes, she'd keep it, but as a lovely treasure, out of sight and in the back of her mind. Blowing her nose one last time, she efficiently straightened the items in the chest, then repacked the ones she'd taken out of the box.

She decided to work and stay awake, then she'd eat breakfast and ask Danith D'Ash to come by. Danith would help her with the HeartGift, shield the little box so it wouldn't affect Mitchella. Just as she'd helped Danith with T'Ash's. Her lips curved. Odd how events circled around.

Twenty-six

On the third morning of the trip, they located the mine. Antenn's track had been clear and easy to follow, the weather had been fine and the previous days uneventful.

It had been the nights that had troubled Straif. He'd ached for Mitchella, and dreamed. Last night was the worst—he awoke from a dream where he'd watched her open a door. Her face showed despair, shock, incredulity, resolution, and again despair. He'd called out to her, but she hadn't heard him.

He prayed he wouldn't return to find she'd decided their affair should end. He yearned to feel her close and soft and warm, didn't know how he'd slept alone so long. His whittling and good conversation with Winterberry kept him sane.

As soon as they saw the mine, Straif stopped. Winterberry continued on, and Vertic the fox disappeared quickly, exploring.

Straif's heart thumped hard as he stared at the black hole in the small hillock. The mine. He shouldn't be so affected—after all, some of the depictions of the traditional Blackthorn symbol—the Dark Goddess—showed the same thing, a black hole in a hill, a dark square between standing stones or pillars.

Had that been why his ancestors had thought that they

could tear the living lambenthysts from the mine without harmful consequences? Or had they just been too insensitive to know the lambenthysts were living? Lord and Lady knew, but if T'Ash said the stones lived, then he'd be right. But Straif wasn't certain that anyone except T'Ash would have known.

He dismounted and tied his stridebeast where it could feed on fresh spring grass, then approached the mine. If he went down into it, would he sense the living stones?

If he apologized, conducted a Ritual Healing for the stones, would his flaw be Healed, too? Why hadn't he considered these questions *before* the trip, when he could ask T'Ash?

But he shuffled the thoughts away as he circled the hill to find Antenn's horse grazing in a grassy meadow.

"He's here," Straif called to Winterberry. "Antenn's definitely here. Probably in the mine."

A stunning blow of Flair hit the back of Straif's head. He crumpled.

When he awoke, he was sitting against a boulder at the top of a sloping incline with his wrists and waist attached to a big rock by Flaired restraints, surrounded by a spherical forcefield.

Winterberry sat on a sunny rock watching him.

Straif found his tongue and said, "Do you always attack men from behind?"

"Always when they're FirstFamily Lords with great Flair." Winterberry showed no remorse. He stood and dusted off his trous, spending Flair on a Word to keep his clothes clean.

Straif snorted. "Always elegant, as usual."

Winterberry tipped his head. "Thank you." He looked at the black opening of the mine and sighed. "I suppose I'll have to go after the boy."

"You could let me loose, and I'd do that for you."

"I promised T'Ash that I wouldn't let you go into the mine, if the boy got that far."

Straif snorted again.

Winterberry lifted his eyebrows. "So, tell me that *you* would cross T'Ash."

They held stares for a moment. Straif shrugged and looked away. "Man's a blacksmith."

"And a GreatLord with great Flair and a Downwind background. Any one of those is a quality to be wary of."

"I'd cross T'Ash if I had to," Straif muttered.

"So would I, but neither of us would go against him lightly. This situation is not so desperate as to thwart T'Ash."

"If the boy isn't in trouble—" Straif said.

"He isn't. I've heard him in the mine, taking samples, I think."

Winterberry rose and walked to his stridebeast, stroked the long-legged animal, then rummaged in his saddlebag and pulled out his own sampling kit.

"Aren't you going to release me?" called Straif.

"Surely, as soon as you give me your word of honor that you won't go into the mine."

Straif was silent.

"I thought so." Winterberry waved and returned to his task. Without another word, he entered the mine.

The acoustics of the mineshafts brought the sound of voices, Antenn truculent, Winterberry mild, as usual. Once again Straif strained against his bonds and failed to free himself. Then he set his teeth and waited impatiently for the two to return. Half a septhour later he heard them approach.

"You said T'Blackthorn was here, too. Where?" Antenn asked. "He afraid that whatever ate at his ancestors gonna get him?"

Anger flashed through Straif, but the boy was just resentful of Mitchella's place in Straif's life. Her affection toward him.

Then the boy, looking dirty and with torn clothes, appeared followed by Pinky, then Winterberrry, who went to his stridebeast and stowed all the samples.

"You've got him bound—to a rock!" Antenn hooted with laughter.

Pinky mewed hello. Straif nodded to the little cat.

"Yes, I do. Because he was going to risk his life for you by going into the mine."

Antenn sobered.

Winterberry continued. "Now the mine might not be lethal to you or me, but if it ruined the Blackthorns in the first place, it could do more damage to Straif. He was willing to risk it for you. Me? I don't know as if I'd done that for you."

"He only wants to look good for my guardian, wants to keep her happy, especially on a bedsponge."

"Boy, you have a serious difficulty with perspective."

"Let him be, Winterberry. I insulted him when we first met. Though I apologized, Antenn hasn't been able to get past the incident. He's young. Let him sort out his own problems."

Winterberry glanced at Straif, then stared hard at Antenn. "So T'Blackthorn said something about your brother being a murderer—probably the truth, and you haven't been able to forgive him." The guard shook his head. "Your brother's actions are always going to define how people look at you. You shouldn't let them define *you*, too." Winterberry jerked his chin at Straif. "He was there. I was, too. Didn't know that, did you?

Antenn took a step away from the guard.

"It was the most horrible thing I've ever seen in my life, and I'm a guardsman. Someday when you're older, you should have someone who was there give you a true-memory ball of the event. Your new friend, Vinni T'Vine came into his title because your brother murdered old D'Vine."

"Winterberry, that's enough," Straif said. He turned to the boy, trying not to feel like a fool bound to a rock. "You are not responsible for your brother's actions."

"He doesn't want to be judged by his brother's actions, wants a little tolerance from others, but he judges others by how they react to him, won't give those who were at the massacre a little tolerance."

"Quiet, guardsman!" Straif roared, struggling against his bonds. Suddenly he was free, and plunging straight for Antenn. Straif dug in his feet, angled his body, but still hit the boy. They went rolling, and Straif did his best to protect the child from the rocks littering the ground. They finally ended up against another boulder.

Winterberry strolled up and lifted a dazed Antenn to his feet, dusted the boy off. "Any hurts, Antenn?"

"Uh." Antenn shook himself like a dog. "No." Pinky sniffed at him, then purred and hopped to the boy's shoulder.

Winterberry offered his hand to Straif, Straif grasped it, and the man hauled Straif to his feet with easy strength. "How about you, T'Blackthorn? Got a cut on your cheek, I see."

Straif rubbed his shoulder. "I'll be fine."

"A bad bruise on your shoulder, too, eh?" Winterberry said. He turned to Antenn. "Did you feel how he protected you? Tried to take any knocks that might have hurt you? That's not the action of a man who is only thinking of pleasing a woman many kilometers away. Those are the actions of a man who cares for a boy. Think about it."

Antenn said, "You don't like me. You don't respect me. You want Mitchella all to yourself and will later cast her aside."

Straif shut his eyes a moment, then met the boy's green gaze. "I do like and respect you. As for Mitchella—I don't know what will happen." It was all he could think to say.

Antenn looked at Straif, then Winterberry, then shook his head and walked away.

"I don't think I like how you teach your lessons, guardsman." Straif limped in the direction of the horse and stridebeasts, his hip had taken a blow from a sharp rock.

Winterberry bowed. "Always my pleasure to expand young minds."

Pulling a cloth from his trous pocket, Straif dabbed at the scratch on his cheek. "Try to keep me out of your lessons in the future."

"Oh, but you complement my instruction process so well. You play to my strengths, as it were."

Straif eyed the man, his snowy hair, tough build, wondered if he could take him in a fight.

"No," said Winterberry. "I may be older, but I am wilier."

Straif grunted. "If we leave now, we can camp in that sweet little valley, the one with the spring. I do best with water Healing spells, they'll take our aches away. I'd like another bath and Lord and Lady knows the boy needs one."

From his trous pocket, Straif took a piece of parchment and a drawstick. Enhancing the map with his Flair, he marked the mine opening, the large meadow, the boulder-strewn incline and everything else he'd observed. Part of his life had always been revising maps—and sending them to the GuildHall for the official cartographers. Yes, he'd earned his noblegilt— every bit. He hadn't been idle or totally self-serving on his quest. He tapped a finger against the map. "Let's take this short-cut I discovered. It will save us a whole day."

Winterberry nodded. "Anything that will get me back into Druida sooner is fine by me."

Antenn shrieked. "A beastie!"

Both men flinched.

And saw the fox staring at Antenn, between the boy and his horse.

"That's my Fam, Vertic," Winterberry said. "He accompanied us from Druida. Surely you've seen foxes before."

Antenn frowned. "I don't think so." He clasped Pinky in his arms and glared at the guard. "You have a fox Fam?"

Winterberry sighed. "It appears so."

Lip stuck out, Antenn looked away and said, "Pinky wants to become a Fam."

Straif and Winterberry exchanged a look.

Can that be done? asked Winterberry.

I don't know. Straif walked over to the boy, put his hand on the thin shoulder, and looked down at the cat, which was smaller than Drina. "I'll talk to Danith D'Ash when we get back. If Pinky can become a Fam, it will be done."

Antenn sniffed. "My thanks."

"If you give him to me, I'll—where does he ride?" Straif looked at the horse; there wasn't a pad as they'd fashioned for Vertic.

"Right here." Antenn pointed proudly at a makeshift bag— it was sturdy enough to hold the cat, but had netting so Pinky could watch the world go by. "Or sometimes he lies on the horse's neck."

"About that horse—"

"It's fine. I didn't hurt it at all. It liked the travel!" Antenn said.

"Then you will get to explain that to Caprea Sallow. I'm sure Mitchella has already made payment arrangements."

"I'll pay for him!"

"Of course you will."

"I have gilt from my job on your ballroom. When you pay Mitchella, she'll pay me."

Straif stared at the boy, his world skewing. He had a young boy depending upon him that he cared for. His chest tightened.

He took Pinky from Antenn and gently placed the cat in his

carrier, then lifted Antenn onto the horse. "Everything has turned out fine."

"You think that you'll be T'Blackthorn?"

"I intend to be," Straif said.

Antenn nodded. "You'll probably stay a GrandLord, then. But don't you hurt Mitchella." He hesitated. "Try not to hurt her anymore, I mean."

Straif winced. Winterberry joined them, Vertic on the pad behind his saddle.

"Sometimes the moth flies into the flame," Winterberry said.

The return trip was going well—too well for travel in the northeastern edge of the Hard Rock Mountains. As the most knowledgeable in camp craft, Straif set the last shieldspell on the outer concentric circle. The fox and the cat were staring at each other. Winterberry had taken Antenn off to bathe and for another "little talk." Straif figured the man was giving the boy a better target to loathe than Straif himself.

Blackthorn. Male grychomp. Two meters from us. Winterberry's mental probe was tense.

Grychomps were Celtan beasts three times the size of a large man, with fur and claws, mean tempers, and very, very large teeth. Straif sent, *Don't move. Don't use Flair. Flair attracts it.* Cold coated Straif's guts. He had to act fast, but carefully if he wanted to save all their lives. He ran for a mechanical gun, praying it would work. He hadn't often used it.

Next to the gun was a Flairstorage he'd carved for himself. He didn't often use that, either; no one on Celta wanted to be without Flair. Pulsing with fear, he sent his Flair shooting into the storage, then whirled and tracked his friends by sight only, remembering the direction of Winterberry's call. Straif was grateful for the trip he'd made to *Nuada's Sword,* the time he'd spent with Ruis Elder. He'd been without Flair recently, so had practice in coping with the odd off-balance sensation.

The metal of the rifle was cold in his hands.

No noise. A good sign that the grychomp wasn't feeding.

He glimpsed the man and boy near a rock wall, they both had their trous down. Straif winced, no running fast for them.

The grychomp was big and ugly and not too hungry since it

sat and watched its prey. Straif was behind it. Its head, which Straif had decided to aim for, was sunk beneath its body. There was a boulder that would give him a better shot, but Straif was sure he couldn't climb up it without making noise.

Winterberry saw him and stiffened. His tension communicated to Antenn. The boy looked petrified. Good.

Straif wondered if he could wound the beast, then run. Not a good plan, but it would distract it from the others. He raised the rifle.

A horrible, ululating shriek came from Antenn, a gang cry. The grychomp's head popped up.

Straif squeezed three exploding bullets into the head. Bright blood spattering, the thing fell, landing with a force that vibrated the ground beneath Straif's feet.

Winterberry and Antenn pulled up their pants, and stumbled around the beast until they joined Straif.

They stared at the hulking body. It didn't twitch.

Winterberry licked his lips. "Good shots. That's a *gun,* isn't it?"

Antenn turned to heave his lunch into a bush. Straif handed the rifle to Winterberry and squatted before Antenn. Taking a clean rag from his pocket, he wiped Antenn's mouth, then lifted the boy into his arms. "I need to hold you, right?" he said, thinking the boy needed to be held. "That's the closest I've ever come to losing a person on any of my treks. I don't like it." The boy smelled like sweat and wild child.

"What do we do with the body?" asked Winterberry as Straif carried Antenn back to the camp.

"Nothing, unless you want souvenirs. Other animals will dispose of it tonight, primarily celtaroons, but grychomp teeth command a nice price." Antenn had curved his arms around Straif, and he felt good through the crashing from the adrenaline rush. Straif was alive. The boy was alive. Even Winterberry was alive.

Winterberry grimaced. "Hack at the thing? I don't believe I will."

"You could use Flair."

"Oh, Flair, right. That quality that almost got us killed," Winterberry said. He squinted at Straif. "You don't have much about you. I'm not picking up a trace." He sounded irritated.

"I put it in a Flairstorage. I'll draw it out shortly."

"You brought a Flairstorage with you. One you probably made yourself?" Winterberry said.

Straif kept patting Antenn on the back, for both of them. "Yes."

"And a gun," Winterberry said.

"It's best to be prepared."

Antenn lifted his head from Straif's shoulder. "You stalked and killed a grychomp *without* any Flair?"

"Yes."

Grunting, Winterberry said, "I can barely walk when I don't have Flair."

Straif strode into camp and set Antenn on his feet by his tent. "Winterberry, you close the shieldspell circles."

Before his sentence was done all three protective circles had been activated. "Good job," Straif said.

A muscle flexed in Winterberry's jaw. "When I'm not caught with my pants down, I can be an asset to the team."

Letting his knees go loose, Straif sank into a cross-legged position and looked up at Antenn. "You did very, very well, Antenn. That shout was just what I needed to distract the grychomp and get a good shot."

Antenn wiped his nose on his arm. "I thought so." He smiled a little. "It was our old gang cry. That, that—"

"Grychomp," Winterberry said, breaking down the gun to examine every piece. Cleaning items had appeared near him, and he went to work.

"—*thing*," Antenn said. "Loomed over us just like T'Ash did, once. It made me think. Enough."

"Good," Straif said, "though I won't tell T'Ash that."

The gun snicked together. Straif looked at Winterberry and shook his head.

"What?" asked the guardsman, then glanced down at himself. His fawn-colored leathers were smeared with dark blood. He sighed. "My travel clothes will never be the same."

"Probably not, but you just used Flair on my non-Flaired weapon that I keep because it doesn't attract such beasts as the grychomp."

"Ah, fligger. Sorry."

"You," Straif aimed a finger at the guard. "I am not taking into the wild again." He pointed at Antenn. "You, I would."

The boy flushed, looked down, scrubbed the stains on his tunic. "Thanks." When he raised his eyes, admiration glinted in them.

Straif decided that was better than resentment or loathing, but wondered if it would cost him as much.

The rest of the trip passed reasonably well. Straif had harvested three grychomp teeth as mementos and given one each to Winterberry and Antenn. Winterberry had just shaken his head, knowing that someday, sometime, the story of being caught with his pants down facing a grychomp would make the rounds of guardhouses in Celta.

Antenn had turned his tooth around in his hands with a thoughtful expression. "Guess this will be a good reminder."

Straif wasn't sure what the boy wanted to be reminded of, and didn't ask.

As the day progressed, Antenn treated Straif like a good friend and talked up a storm on the road back to Druida. The three of them took turns riding the horse. That animal impressed Straif with its intelligence and pace, both of which were far better than a stridebeast's. He wondered if he could get a pair of horses, perhaps breed them like the Sallows. They bred for beauty and speed, but Straif knew of many an explorer who'd like intelligence and toughness. Horses' Flair was minimal, and he wondered how to boost it, a question for Danith D'Ash, but he felt very good thinking of the future, plans for once that didn't focus on finding a cure for his inherited physical flaw.

*T*hey will be back tomorrow, *T'Blackthorn Residence* sent to Mitchella's mind the next afternoon as she was handrefinishing the doors of the first-floor hall. The Residence sounded as if it were reassuring itself, but then Straif had often left it, hadn't returned even to visit. A bit of anger spurted through her.

"Yes, they will. Straif will never desert you again." She was sure. She tried to sound cheerful, the day was gloomy enough with threatening rain, without having to deal with a depressed house. "Soon you'll have a Family again."

A hollow grumbling passed through the hallway.

She was nearly done with the messy job and dressed in her oldest work clothes with her hair caught up in a kerchief when the Residence spoke. "There is a delegation requesting entrance at the greeniron gates."

"What?"

The Residence repeated itself.

"Who?" She dropped her brush in cleansing liquid, swept the cloth off her head, stared at her stained hands.

"A delegation from the Councils: T'Reed, representative of FirstFamilies Council, GraceLord Stachys Betony, representing the Noble Council and GuildCouncil. Finally, Gentle-Lady Kudzu, representing the Commoner Council. They wish a preliminary view of the Residence."

Mitchella swore. "Tell Drina to meet and greet them."

"I am doing so. The Blackthorn Fam agrees."

She wondered what to do. Let them in? Scry someone— who?

"Shall I alert T'Blackthorns's allies?"

Was that appropriate? "Not yet. I'll tell you if and when we might need them."

A couple minutes later, dressed in an elegant trous suit and after a whirlwind spell left her feeling as if her skin had been scoured and hair yanked a dozen ways to fall in pretty curls, she walked down the gliderway. When she came to the gates, she chuckled. Drina sat framed between greeniron bars on this side of the gate and stared at the impatient reps on the other. The cat flicked her tail in arrogance.

Casually, Mitchella set her hand against the scrystone in the brick wall to keep contact with the Residence. All three of the people before her had more Flair than she.

"Greetyou," she said to the delegation. She'd seen T'Reed at the New Twinmoons Ritual, had met Stachys Betony, and knew of the GentleLady.

"Greetyou, GentleLady Clover. Can you admit us, please?" It was more of a demand than a request by T'Reed.

Mitchella smiled. "I'm afraid I don't have that authority. I am a contracted employee of T'Blackthorn. I especially wouldn't go against the Family Familiar, Drina, who is the only member of the Family on site at the moment."

GentleLady Kudzu looked down on the cat. "She won't speak to us. She just sits there, smirking."

"I suggest you return tomorrow, when T'Blackthorn is here. He can give you a tour then."

Stachys stepped forward. "I believe we must insist." He held up a sheaf of papyrus and passed it through the gate for Mitchella to read. She took it and scanned it. Anger simmered through her. "These are charges that T'Blackthorn has damaged the estate with his renovation. It will take me time to read—"

Thunder rolled.

"May we please be allowed to wait inside?" Commoner Representative Kudzu was a plump woman with thick, long hair.

Drina shifted her bottom until she sat on Mitchella's foot. *We can handle them. Residence agrees.*

Mitchella wasn't so sure, but she looked each of the others in the eyes. "I am not authorized to let you in. T'Blackthorn has been very concerned with security. If you all give me your words of honor that you will remain in the library while we sort this out, I will admit you. You can observe what you can of the estate and Residence as we walk to the library."

"I agree," snapped T'Reed. The GentleLady followed. Stachys Betony hesitated until everyone looked at him.

"You're the one pushing for this inspection, Stachys," GentleLady Kudzu said.

"I agree," he ground out.

Mitchella lifted a finger. "I also want your words that should I suffer from this action, the Councils will reimburse me."

"You are trying to deflect us from doing our duty," Stachys said.

Mitchella tossed her head. "I am protecting myself."

"Too late for that, everyone knows you're the alleged T'Blackthorn's lover," Stachys said.

"Rudeness and disrespect will not help our cause, GraceLord," GentleLady Kudzu muttered.

"The Noble Council will recompense you if the current T'Blackthorn finds fault with your actions," T'Reed said impatiently as large raindrops splatted around them.

"Residence, open the gates, please," Mitchella said.

As little as you can, Drina sniffed. *Let that Stachys man squeeze.*

He was the largest of the three.

As the spitting rain increased, Drina shot across the yard to the Residence and inside. The others hurried after the cat, casting glances at the estate and the Residence. Mitchella ensured that the gates were locked before following.

When she reached the library, the reps had chosen to sit in a conversational grouping of several chairs around a table near the huge fireplace that held a crackling fire.

Stachys curled his lip at the comfortably shabby room. "Disgraceful."

"It looks just as it did the last time I was here with the late T'Blackthorn," T'Reed said. "Well done, GentleLady Clover."

"I like the room," GentleLady Kudzu said.

Mitchella dipped her head, "Thank you."

At that moment the door swung open and the cook entered with a tray of beverages and pastries. "The Residence informed me of your tastes." He set the tray on the table and departed quickly. The delegation dug into the food while Mitchella went to a small desk where she scanned the papyrus.

"I have been charged as an accessory in the ruin of this estate." Fury turned her vision red.

Twenty-seven

❤

$\mathcal{M}$itchella jumped to her feet, uncaring that the desk chair toppled to the floor. All the work she'd done on the estate—the aches of her body, the pummeling of her mind to make it warm and welcoming and a *home* again, was being condemned.

She could barely see to stalk over to the delegates.

Straining to keep her temper, she 'ported all her models and notes to stack at her feet. Energy was no problem, rage fueled her Flair.

With a snap of her fingers, she showed a holomodel of the estate as she'd found it, then the progression of the work—a record she always kept.

After that holo faded, she projected models of the chambers she'd finished room by room. This cycle took long enough for her to calm a bit. When it ended, she had her temper under firm control and her hands didn't shake as she poured a cup of hot cocoa. "What is it about these rooms we've refinished and the Residence itself that you find 'ruined'?"

"These are only the things you've shown us, not our own tour," Stachys said.

Mitchella glanced at T'Reed. "T'Blackthorn's reported to

you every day. What in those reports made you doubt so you had to visit?"

"Nothing. The FirstFamily Council was overruled," T'Reed replied stiffly.

"This is only a preliminary walk-through," GentleLady Kudzu said.

That had no effect on Mitchella. "I don't see you defending my work. I see a FirstFamily GreatLord who says nothing about the accusations against me, and a GraceLord representing the Noble and Guild Councils who still doubts my word despite everything I've shown you." With a sweeping gesture she indicated the pile of documents, flexistrips, holos of her work.

"You three have forced this issue, but *I'm* not a FirstFamilies Lord or Lady. *I'm* a Commoner, and it's my understanding that a member of the Noble Council is smearing my reputation, casting doubt on my skills as a designer. Since I am of lower rank, I have the right to know my accuser, see him, put questions to him."

T'Reed looked at her with respect, Stachys with discomfort, and GentleLady Kudzu nodded decisively. "She's right."

"Who filed these papers?"

"We should go," Stachys said.

T'Reed said, "From what I've seen and experienced, I believe the accusations are incorrect. The estate walls, gates, and glideway are in top order. The library provided shelter and comfort. The kitchen is capable of delivering excellent food on a moment's notice. These are not the signs of a ruined First-Family Residence."

"I've seen and heard plenty. These papyrus should be discounted as being proven false," GentleLady Kudzu said.

"That's not acceptable," Mitchella said. "My reputation is at stake, as well as T'Blackthorn's. This mess has just grown. I suggest to *all* the Councils that they make a determination on the T'Blackthorn claims in the next few days, or I assure you, I will file charges against the Councils themselves for acting hastily and falsely and harming my livelihood.

"I know of the accusations against T'Blackthorn, and they are wrong, too. No one can prove that the estate is in ruins."

"It's disgusting—" Stachys said.

"—It *was* neglected. But I've been studying FirstFamily

Residences—and I've worked with houses and homes all my professional life—and nothing about this Residence is in ruin. *By your own laws—Council laws*—a HouseHeart must be gone, the Residence must not be sentient, that is not the case here. Residence, what say you?"

"I support T'Blackthorn," boomed the Residence. "He is a good FirstFamily GrandLord."

Mitchella said, "Furthermore, Straif *has* done his duty. He has officiated or participated in an acceptable number of Rituals. This case has dragged on long enough, especially since it's been shrouded in secrecy to T'Blackthorn. But you can't hide my accuser from me—not if he's higher rank. End it, Councilfolk. You have listened to a false claimant."

Pale, Stachys shot to his feet. "I only want to claim what I have a right to. The T'Blackthorn's estate. I am of the blood, and the current man has let the Residence fall into ruin, neglected the estate and his responsibilities to society."

Mitchella's knees went weak at the revelation. She leaned against the sofa. Her wits scrabbled, but she managed to reply, "Untrue. You were waiting for one more season to pass before pressing your claim, but when Straif came back you had to move quickly and hope you could prove that he'd missed too many GreatRituals. You erred."

Stachys's fingers bunched. "You've just proven that he's seduced you. Since he is a FirstFamilies GrandLord and supposedly an honorable nobleman, it is easy for everyone to close their eyes to his long and many faults. Because honorable *Nobles* don't run away from their duties, don't let their homes fall into ruin. But this one did. And has done so again. For centuries the twenty-five FirstFamiles of Celta have always held GreatRituals to direct energy in bettering our people, but they have also grown arrogant. How long will the *twenty-four* FirstFamiles let the present T'Blackthorn ignore the responsibilities that were his since birth? I contend that this T'Blackthorn isn't honorable, but dishonorable—and cowardly, too!"

"Is that so?" Straif said from the doorway, looking every centimeter a dangerous outlaw, not a noble FirstFamily GrandLord.

Everyone turned to scrutinize him, but his stare focused on

Stachys, and Straif prowled into the room. Even Mitchella saw his aura pulsate with fury.

"Did you just call me a dishonorable coward?" Straif asked softly.

Stachys paled, but drew himself up. Now that the two men were together, there was the hint of a family resemblance. "Yes," he whispered, "I did."

Straif nodded. "Do you care to retract your words?"

Stachys glanced around the room. T'Reed and GentleLady Kudzu sat frozen in their chairs. No question that Straif dominated the scene. Stachys could not back down and save his claim. He coughed. "No, I don't retract my words." His voice cracked, but he plowed on. "I meant what I said."

Silence seethed through the room.

Straif narrowed his eyes, examining Stachys. "Right. I can't allow such insult to pass, not in my own home, not even from a distant cuz." He stripped off a heavily worn celtaroon glove and dropped it at Stachys's feet. "My seconds will contact you. Expect a visit from Tinne Holly." He stared at T'Reed. "Teleport these—people—out of here."

"I don't like 'porting," GentleLady Kudzu said. "I'm leaving on my own two feet." But she lingered near the door to watch the scene.

Stachys swayed. T'Reed steadied him.

Straif raised Mitchella's fingers to his lips and bowed over them. Energy sizzled to her core. Then he tucked her hand into his elbow. "GentleLady Clover, I found your ward hardy and healthy and have returned Antenn to your Family. He is at the Clover Compound."

"Thank you, GrandLord. My heart is eased at the knowledge." She wanted to throw herself in his arms and rain kisses over his face, question him in detail about Antenn, but the situation prevented it.

He glanced at the three. "Again, you remind those of the Councils of my usefulness in retrieving lost ones," he said. "And pray that the great Flair I have for tracking doesn't die with me."

That should certainly give his detractors pause, even when they thought of him pursuing his quest. But it only reminded Mitchella that, HeartMate or not, he would never HeartBond

with her. She didn't know if she could bear the pain. Though
the project of restoring the Residence was almost done, she
had Antenn back. She might be able to squeeze a few more
days and nights with Straif into her life before they both moved
on. After all, she'd never made love to him as a HeartMate.

"Blessings upon you," T'Reed said. He set an arm
around Stachys, and they disappeared. GentleLady Kudzu
slipped away.

Mitchella's mind spun with dizziness, with Straif's familiar scent mixing with the odor of burning logs.

"I'm sorry you had to endure that," Straif waved at the papyrus still on the small desk. "I 'ported as soon as I realized
something was wrong—I was at your Family's place."

She grabbed at him. Found herself trembling in his arms,
holding back sobs.

"Shhhhh." He patted her back. "It's all right. We are all
back safe and sound."

"Antenn is all right?"

"Not a scratch on him. Though you might find him more ma-
ture than he was when he left. We came to an understanding."

"You're all right." Her hands measured the strength of his
back, stroked his sides, went to his butt.

He choked. "Antenn's on his way by glider. He'll be here
in a few minutes, but I want you in my bed, now. We'll 'port.
Hold on tight."

She wanted nothing more to be able to do that forever.
When they came together, she ravished him. And when they
shared the waterfall, she touched him with tenderness. Earlier
she'd thought she'd never made love to him as if he were a
beloved HeartMate, linked with her. But she'd been wrong.
She'd loved him like that since their first kiss.

Hand-in-hand they walked to the front door together, but in
the entry hall, the Residence announced, "An incoming message from *Nuada's Sword* for you, T'Blackthorn, it starts
'Good News'."

Mitchella's stomach clutched. She twisted her fingers from
Straif and pasted on a calm smile. "Sounds like you might finally have succeeded in your quest." She brushed her lips
against his cheek. "Go check on the message, I need to meet
Antenn."

"Mitchella—"

She didn't turn back, just waved a hand and walked forward. When she got outside the Residence, she raced to the gates, wanting the pumping of blood in her head to drown out thought.

Antenn arrived in a hired glider. The rain had stopped, the clouds had blown away, leaving the bright sunlight of a perfect spring day. The warmth of the sun on her face, sinking into her clothes, steadied her. She inhaled, held her breath, and when she exhaled, she sent the negative emotions that had lodged in her—anxiety, fear, despair, anger—away with her breath.

Antenn hadn't fully emerged from the vehicle when she scooped him up in a tight hug, tears running down her face again.

"The Clovers have already set my punishments for running away!" he announced, but clutched at her, too.

She was glad her family had dealt with the disobedience, because she'd be too hard on him for the worry he'd put her through, or too soft because he was back and safe. She set him on his feet and knew that she'd never pick him up like a boy again, he *had* matured.

Sniffling, she patted his shoulder. "Welcome home, child of my heart."

"If I'm the child of your heart, why didn't you adopt me!" he cried, then turned his face, but not before Mitchella saw his own tears.

She was stunned. She'd never known he wanted that. Never known, until now, how much *she* wanted that legal connection between them. Had she been punishing herself for not being fertile?

She pressed some softleaves into Antenn's hand, waited until he discreetly wiped his face, then walked with him up the gliderway. "It's too late to go to the GuildHall today, but first thing tomorrow we'll go to the Clerk of the Councils and start the adoption process."

He lifted his face. "We will?"

Mitchella took his hand and squeezed his fingers. "Yes. I don't know why I didn't adopt you before. I guess I thought you wouldn't want to give up your own name, or put yourself completely under my authority."

Antenn scowled and rubbed his nose. "Nothing special about the Moss name or bloodlines. I don't know if there are any more of us . . . my two uncles went south to the continent of Brittany a long time ago." He sniffed, then blew his nose again. "I don't care if I'm a Moss. I'd rather be a Clover."

"You'd have plenty of family, then. Interfering family."

"I might like that. And as for your authority over me. Huh. Better you than the entire legal system, than SupremeJudge Ailim Elder. The Clovers said they had to do some fast talking to her." He slowed his pace. "You've always been kind—"

"Even before I loved you." She smacked a kiss on his cheek.

He smiled, and it nearly broke her heart, it was so pleased and hopeful. Tears stung behind her eyes. "You are my son." She hugged him tight, released him.

"Right." The word was an admiring echo of Straif. Antenn looked up to T'Blackthorn's Residence. "It's very beautiful. But it's empty. Very sad, too."

She swallowed hard. "Yes." There would be no children from Straif and her. He wanted children of his blood desperately, as desperately as she once longed to carry a child inside herself. But the boy standing before her proved as nothing else that blood didn't matter. She cleared her throat. "Antenn?"

"Yes?" He glanced up at her—goodness, he'd grown and she hadn't noticed. Soon he'd pass his apprenticeship tests and become a journeyman.

"I'm happy with the two of us as a family. But do you think we might consider a younger brother or sister for you?"

His face clouded, and she knew she'd spoken too soon.

"Maybe. Just us, for now, though, right?"

She set a hand on his shoulder. "Yes, my son."

He flushed. "Let's go back to T'Blackthorn's Residence. I think we should look for a place of our own, too."

Straif came out and stood on the front steps, face impassive.

Antenn nodded to him, said under his breath, "I like him. He's a good man, but you are hurting each other too much."

"The project and the affair will be over soon." Again she sucked in a deep breath. "Finding our own rooms is a good idea. Why don't we look in MidClass Lodge where Trif lives?"

"Trif! Oh, sure." He grinned. "Trif is fun to be with."

So she took the hand of the boy who would be in her future, walked up the steps, and lightly kissed the man who would soon be in her past.

*D*inner *that evening was the most pleasant they'd spent* together. Straif said nothing about his news from *Nuada's Sword,* so Mitchella pushed it to the back of her mind and refrained from mentioning that she and Antenn would be looking for lodgings.

She *had* announced with great pride that Antenn and she would be filing formal adoption papers, and Straif seemed genuinely pleased. He called for a small bottle of champagne and toasted them. Even Antenn got a sip of the sparkling wine in celebration.

After dinner, Antenn dragged off to his suite and Mitchella checked on him a little later. Relief tore at her heart. She blinked back tears as he fell asleep before her eyes. Straif put a hand on her shoulder, then stepped even closer, until his body brushed hers. Her eyes dried, and she became exquisitely aware of him. "Antenn is excellent in the wild. I thought you should know."

She turned and buried her face in the crook of his neck, laughed. "As if I ever want him out of the safety of Druida ever again."

Straif patted her, and though his body was reacting to hers, the bond between them pulsed only with slightly sexual feelings. He seemed distracted.

"I see what you mean by an ocean phase."

Emotions under control, Mitchella stepped away, slipping her fingers down to link with his. Straif's gaze was on the rolling surf of Maroon Beach. He cocked his head. "Live audio?"

"Yes."

"The wall is an illusion, though."

"I've set the spell to make the waves correspond with the height and force of the audio."

"Excellent." He strolled into the sitting room, again looking at the beach, then his attention focused on her. She felt it in the sparks shooting through their bond. "But then you do everything most excellently." He took her hand and cupped it behind her, shaping her fingers around his sex. Shuddered. "Lord and Lady, I've missed you. More than I could ever say." He nibbled below her ear.

The waves had entered her blood, become pulsing desire.

"Straif, your cuz, Tinne Holly, has arrived by glider," the Residence said.

Straif exhaled a soft groan by her ear.

"Exactly what I didn't want to do tonight. Talk duels." He took a pace back. "Where shall we have this discussion?" he whispered.

She turned to face him, shooed her hands so that he'd leave the suite, let Antenn sleep. Outside in the corridor, she said, "I'm invited?"

He grasped both of her hands, lifted one, then the other to his lips. "I want you with me all night."

Mitchella cleared her voice to address the Residence. "Please guide Tinne Holly to the Large Sitting Room."

Straif pressed her against the wall and took her mouth. Using lips and tongue, he kissed her until she shuddered, until he trembled, until the Residence announced in a loud voice that Tinne was waiting for them. Mitchella got the impression that Straif, too, felt that these were the last days of their loving. The open house was next week. When they broke the kiss, she trailed her fingers over his cheek before preceding him down the stairs and into the Large Sitting Room.

The Large Sitting Room was the closest thing to a mainspace that Mitchella could fashion in such an elegant Residence. With a glance she made sure the room looked welcoming. Satisfaction unfurled in her. The room was versatile enough to handle rambunctious children as well as an intimate gathering of FirstFamily Lords and Ladies.

And Tinne Holly was the most ornamental thing in the chamber. Tall, with white-blond hair and gray eyes, he was every bit as handsome as his brother, Holm. Now the Holly-Heir, he appeared more serious than he'd been a year ago. He was just a year or two older than Trif, but he'd matured. But then, the broken vow affected everyone in T'Holly Household.

Tinne's marriage wristbands glowed golden, that had probably settled him, too. With a twinge, Mitchella thought that Trif might be considering marriage. As was usual with more than ordinary Flair, she'd connected with her HeartMate during her last Passage.

When Tinne saw Mitchella, he bowed with all the Holly grace and charm, then greeted his cuz, Straif, with a raised eyebrow and the words, "I heard you took my name in vain today when the delegates of the Councils visited here. Always a cause for *strife*, Straif."

Straif winced. "My cuz, here, spares no pitiful attempt to use my name in a pun at every opportunity. All my life."

Mitchella smiled, they weren't too different from her brothers. She nodded to Tinne, then sat on a twoseat.

Straif went to the discreet liquor cabinet at the side of the room and took out warmed brithe brandy for Tinne and chilled wine for her and himself from the small no-time storage.

"It seems to be a Holly quality, making strategic entrances after trips in the wilds," Straif said. "You had a dramatic one yourself. I was there." He sat down next to Mitchella and played with her fingers as he sipped his wine.

Tinne smiled crookedly. "You would turn my words against me." He sipped the brandy. "Good vintage." Pointedly scanning the room, he said, "A lovely, well-cared for room, as is everything I saw inside the Residence. The grounds still need work, but I'd say you're well on the way to proving you're a fine GrandLord. Despite your little trip, and the matter of a duel. I did hear right, I'm to second you in a duel?"

Straif winced again. "I forgot to send you a note, didn't I?"

Sitting down in a wingchair, Tinne crossed his ankles. "There are expected procedures for such matters of honor. One of them is notifying the men who are going to organize the duel."

"Cave of the Dark Goddess." Straif ran a hand through his hair. "I've been too long gone from Druida."

"I think everyone would agree with that," Tinne said. He uncrossed his feet and stretched his legs. "Have you thought who else would be your second? It is customary to have two."

"No."

"My sire offered but I think the Captain of the Council

would be a bit too intimidating for Stachys Betony." Tinne's face hardened. "Besides, T'Holly doesn't deserve any fun."

"Fun!" Mitchella choked on her wine and stared at the men. Suddenly she realized that she was in the company of two FirstFamily Noblemen. She might think of them acting like her brothers, might pretend to understand them, might be able to decorate a room in which they'd be comfortable, but their mind-sets *were* far too different for her to comprehend— their traditions, their status, their Flair.

Tinne sighed. "Just the reason why one doesn't discuss the details of duels before Ladies who are not warrior trained." He looked at Straif with reproof.

"Sorry." Straif partially hid his smile behind his glass. He was enjoying the discussion.

Maybe the reason she didn't understand them wasn't because they were from ancient and noble FirstFamily lines. Maybe it was because they were men. But she'd always had a good handle on men. Then again, no Clover had ever fought a duel.

"How about T'Ash as your other second?" Tinne asked.

Straif grunt. "I don't think so."

"Who, then? It's not as if you have a number of close friends here in Druida." When he spoke next, it was quietly. "Most of those who attended your Ritual wanted alliances and favors. You don't have many close friends at all."

"I'm working on that." Straif finished his wine. "Let's keep it in the Family. The T'Holly Family. Why not G'Uncle Tab?"

"Why not?" Tinne grinned. "He'd be honored. I don't think he's participated in a formal duel in forty years. He'll love this." Throwing back his head, he laughed, and Mitchella saw traces of the careless youth he'd once been. "Lady and Lord, with G'Uncle Tab in charge, this duel will be so proper it will be the talk of Druida for decades. Tab will show *every-one* how a duello of honor is handled. My sire will be so envi-ous that he is not invited."

"You should get over this bitterness, Tinne," Straif said.

"And you should get over your obsession for finding a cure for your line. Don't give advice if you don't want to hear some."

Mitchella decided a friendly comment was called for. "How's your wife?" she asked Tinne.

He smiled and relaxed back into his chair. "Genista is very well. We are doing fine, even with the tension in the Residence." He drank the last of his brandy, stood, gave a half-bow to Mitchella, and clapped Straif on the shoulder. "I'll let Tab contact you about everything if you don't have specific ideas about time and place?"

"No." Straif stood, and Mitchella rose.

"The duel will only be for first blood, I presume. Your honor will be satisfied at that?"

Straif snorted. "Yes."

Tinne nodded. "I heard you called him a distant relative. That will give the man pause."

"It's the truth."

"Then Stachys will really be thinking hard about his place in life. Excellent strategy."

Smiling, Tinne blew a kiss from his fingertips at Mitchella. "And praises to you for flushing the man out so we can deal with him as he deserves."

"Spilling his blood?" Mitchella said faintly.

"Straif will just nick him, you'll see." Tinne smiled.

"*I'm* invited?" She didn't think she wanted to go.

"Of course, always nice to have one's woman around when one is going to show his fighting prowess," Tinne said.

Mitchella rolled her eyes. *Men.*

Tinne grinned. "G'Uncle Tab will contact you tomorrow. Be guided by him. Blessings on you both." Whistling, he left the Residence.

Twenty-eight

♥

Straif teleported to Landing Park, then strolled through the spring-scented trees and fragrant high grass before going to the Ship's eastern entrance.

A ramp extended, the iris-door swiveled open, and Straif braced himself. As soon as he passed through this airlock, he'd start losing Flair. The atmosphere of the Ship was set to olden Earth standards, and it functioned on a different system than the psi-technology the Celtans had developed.

With a brisk step that belied his wish to drag his feet, he entered *Nuada's Sword,* strode through the airlock and into the surrounding, gleaming metal corridors. He hesitated.

"Blackthorn!"

Straif turned to see Ruis Elder, Captain of *Nuada's Sword* and Null, trotting down the hall. He had a small bulging pouch strapped to his chest. When Ruis reached Straif, he realized the pouch held the new Elder baby. He froze. He hadn't been close to an infant for fifteen years. Two Blackthorn babies had been the first to succumb to the horrible virus. Had he remembered to carve their names in the ballroom floor? Yes.

Ruis must have mistaken Straif's horrified stare as deep interest, because he opened the carrier to expose a tiny face and minuscule fingers. "Beautiful, isn't she?"

"Very."

"Ailim is at JudgementGrove, of course, so Ship and I watch Dani Eve until Grove breaks for midday recess, then Ailim will come home to feed the greedy girl."

Straif couldn't believe such a small scrap of humanity contained anything like greed. He touched the tip of his index finger to a rounded baby cheek. So soft. Incredible. "You are very lucky."

"Yes, I am. When you found me here that day three years ago, I thought my life was over."

All of Celta would remember that day when the first firebombspell was set off in the Council Chamber forever.

Ruis said, "But I have a lovely wife, a child. A daughter who is a Null and won't be scorned." He said it like a vow.

"No. She won't. She's lucky in her father, too."

"Thank you." Ruis hesitated, sighed. "Ship wants me to take you to Fern's Garden in the Great Greensward." Ruis squeezed Straif's upper arm. "It prefers to deliver bad news in beautiful surroundings."

"Ship stated that it had found a remedy for the Blackthorn Curse."

Ruis winced, gestured Straif into the omnivator. Straif had only been in the little moving cubicle a few times.

"Greensward," Ruis said.

A moment later they were in the greenspace that comprised a third of the Ship. Every time he saw the Great Greensward it was more beautiful. The garden Ruis led him to was as well kept as any FirstFamily estate, blooming with ancient flowers. In the distance, Straif could see little mechanical beings trundling along, grooming the greensward.

He narrowed his eyes. "Do you hire those out?"

Ruis laughed. "No, I'm unsure how they'd fare outside."

Straif pulled up a chair and sat. The gardens were beautiful, but inside he was wary and bleak. He raised his voice. "What do you need to tell me, Ship? Have you found some way to fix my heritage so the Blackthorns don't perish from the Angh virus, or not?"

A low hum came, then the Ship's male voice. "You spoke about a genetic flaw, but the impairment involves several interconnected systems, your blood, the construction of the cells lining your veins. The matter is trickier than we thought."

Straif stared at the beautiful garden. "Do you have a fix for my problem, or not?"

"Your immune system magnifies the effects of a common Celtan virus until it is fatal."

"Have. You. Found. A. Cure?"

"We have a remedy."

He still felt wary. "But?"

"It is complicated."

"How complicated?"

"There is no permanent fix at this time. We have processed your genetic samples and placed them in storage for future regeneration when our knowledge or Celtan knowledge progresses to a point where your DNA can be altered to produce a child of your line without the current flaw you carry."

"Right. We discussed this before. Get to the point."

"We can provide you and your descendants with a temporary, ongoing immunization to the Angh virus."

"The Healers said it couldn't be done."

"The Healers still do not have complete knowledge of or access to our Earth plants."

Straif licked dry lips. "What do you mean by temporary?"

"You must grow the plant to have it on hand—crush the leaves, distill and drink them within a few moments of the process. The immunization must be imbibed on a daily basis."

"Daily."

"Yes, it must be freshly brewed daily."

"No no-time?"

"I am aware of your no-time spell facilities." *Nuada's Sword* sounded disapproving of Celtan technology. "I do not know the effects it might have on the plant properties, so I would advise an old-fashioned stillroom such as we have here."

For a moment Straif envisioned trekking to the Ship every day for the rest of his life. "You can help me with the—equipment and process?"

"Indeed. I recommend that since you are the person most concerned with the quality and efficacy, you should be the one to prepare it."

"Fresh daily." Now he imagined himself in the Residence's stillroom.

"What efficacy do you project for the immunization, Ship?" asked Ruis.

"Made and taken daily, the beverage should prevent the Angh virus from spreading inside a person of the T'Blackthorn line with an effective rate of 99.97 percent."

That stunned Straif. Time telescoped until he saw the past—before the virus had hit the Family—the last big gathering. All those people, all his loved ones might have been saved. If the Ship had been activated at the time. If it had discovered this cure. If *they* had taken it. If, if, if. Too many ifs to ever know how many might have lived instead of died.

"I have a sample," Ship said. A little mechanical box on spindly legs minced up to Straif carrying a tall glass of gray brown liquid with bits of material floating in it.

Straif picked up the glass and gulped it down, choking. It was the nastiest thing he'd ever tasted.

He stood. "Please have the plants, equipment, and instructions delivered to my Residence as soon as possible."

"The dosage has been calculated for your mass," Ship said. "You will have to drink it on an empty stomach and eat no sooner than a septhour later."

Straif frowned. He glanced at the babe Ruis Elder held and thought of forcing such a vile drink on a tiny child every day of its life. He couldn't imagine doing so. But then, he'd have a long time to accustom himself to the notion. If the potion saved lives, it would have to be done.

Turning to Captain Elder, Straif said, "As for payment—"

"There is no payment due," Ruis said, rocking his baby. "You provided the best Healers on Celta to attend to my wife when she delivered our baby, as well as a traditional Oracle. Though Ship wanted Ailim to have the child here, I know Ailim was anxious. Her time at T'Blackthorn estate was a blessing."

"A blessing for me and my land, too," Straif said.

Ruis nodded. "You also graciously allowed me on your estate, even though you knew I could harm spells. I appreciate that. There will be no payment for these consultations or

anything else we've done so far." He winked. "We'll negoti-
ate other services in the future."

Straif bowed. "My thanks." And with that, he took his
leave, a foul taste still coating his tongue.

He walked home. The incredible surging joy he'd always
thought this moment would bring didn't come. Instead the
dread he'd lived with a long time increased. Didn't he think he
was allowed to feel joy?

Of course he was allowed joy. He'd come to terms with the
guilt of surviving when the rest of his Family died. They'd
want him to have a full, happy life.

But he couldn't envision such a life without Mitchella.

The more he had her, the more he wanted her, and not just
for sex. When he thought of how she'd defended him to the
delegates the day before, his whole being warmed. How could
he have managed without her? He had the lowering feeling
that he could very well have lost his estate—even lost himself
in grief in the echoing empty rooms of his Residence, if she
hadn't helped him.

But he also thought of his line, and that yearning was so
old, so ingrained—healthy children of his own body, carrying
his name and Flair into the future, linked to all their ancestors
of the past—that he couldn't give up his heritage.

The two desires tore at him, mutually exclusive. He could
only follow one path, must discard the other.

He'd keep Mitchella as long as he could. Yet he felt her
slipping away, like water through his fingers—both his withdrawing to shield himself from hurt and her own.

When he arrived home, he found the duel had been set for
the next morning. Mitchella gave him the news, but didn't ask
about his appointment on *Nuada's Sword*. Instead, she made
love to him with a wildness that shattered him.

*T*he next morning dawned clear and bright, and warm
enough that no outer garments were needed on the walk to the
dueling field.

They'd chosen Tureric Square, the most ancient dueling
ground. Both it and the day were dedicated to the Lord instead

of the Lady. Fighting done in a roundpark on a Lady's day tended to have an odd outcome.

No Council or Guild member had objected to the duel. On the surface, the opponents seemed well matched. It was understood that no Flair would be used, and both men had been trained with knife, sword, and blaser since they'd been young adults.

Stachys may have had T'Blackthorn blood, but Straif also had Holly blood, warrior blood, Mitchella assured herself, worried for Straif. Stachys may have trained with a good, middle-class salon, but Straif had been taught by the Hollys in the premiere fighting salon on Celta. While Stachys had been leading a sedentary life, Straif had been trekking through wild Celta, sometimes hiring out his sword. No, Straif would win the fight. She hoped.

Mitchella, Antenn, and Tinne Holly walked with Straif to the square. The duel had elevated Straif even higher in Antenn's eyes. For Mitchella it was a clutch of the heart at the thought of an accidental hurting of her lover, and a resignation.

Tinne, however, grumbled all the way. He'd wanted to hold it privately, in the exercise yard behind The Green Knight Fencing and Fighting salon, but that hadn't suited either G'Uncle Tab or Stachys.

"First blood only," Tinne said. "But you have my permission to beat the snot out of him."

"Is that a special dueling phrase?" asked Mitchella. "Beat the snot out of?"

Tinne laughed, his expression lightening. "The man deserves some hard bruises. He's been nothing but a black thorn in Straif's side."

Looking pained, Straif said, "Another miserable pun on my name."

"Perhaps you should beat the snot out of him," Mitchella suggested.

Straif pretended to look struck with surprise. "An excellent idea." He lifted her hand and covered it with noisy kisses. She laughed.

But as soon as they reached the square, any amusement

faded. It was surrounded by people, and there were even a couple of food and drink vendors.

Tab Holly stood in the middle of the place, tall and impressive, a huge staff in his hand. A shorter, burlier man stood with him, looking nervous. Mitchella noticed the grass had been clipped in a large rectangle.

Straif loosened his sword in his sheath. "Stachys chose swords."

"He'd have been better off with blasers," Tinne said, eyeing the crowd. "Faster, not much as a show."

Snorting, Straif said, "With G'Uncle Tab presiding, it was bound to be a show. Looks like he has Stachys's man cowed."

"We march in there." Tinne waved to a corridor lined with bright spelllights.

Mitchella tried to hang back, but Straif kept a firm grip on her hand. "Please come," he whispered. "I promise it won't be long or messy."

Mouth dry, Mitchella had difficulty in replying. "All these people—they'll think I'm a Commoner seduced by a First-Family Lord."

"They'll think you're my *Lady,* and you have the presence of the highest Noblewoman. Where's that charisma Flair of yours?" Straif teased.

She couldn't believe how lightly he was taking this. *Men.* But she lifted her chin, straightened her spine, and rolled back her shoulders—and added a little glamour spell as they walked through the crowd to a padded bench on the sidelines where Straif seated her. Her stomach jittered with nerves, but he seemed as cool as if he were in the park for a walk.

Tinne said, "Make sure you take care. There was dew on the grass this morning, it may still be damp near the soil, though we've rolled the dueling area to smooth it. Anything can happen in a swordfight, one slip of the boot . . ." He shook his head.

A murmur rose as another lady walked in, Tinne's wife, Genista, escorted by T'Holly.

"I should have known," Tinne murmured. But he hurried up to take his Lady's hand and seat her beside Mitchella.

Genista whispered to Mitchella, "Isn't this exciting?"

A lone woman sat on the opposite side of the square, hands clenched in her lap. Though she was dressed in fine, GraceLady clothes, she looked more uncomfortable than Mitchella—Stachys's wife. The man himself strode to the center of the square.

Watching Stachys, Straif flexed his fingers, then he bent and brushed Mitchella's lips with his own. "That favor you're supposed to give to me?" he asked, prompting her.

She took a length of silver and gold ribbon from her purse-nal. As she opened the small bag wide, Straif reached in and touched the little carving he'd given her two nights before. The two porcupines touching noses nestled in a corner of her bag.

His smile was full and brilliant, and her heart twinged. "I see you carry my favor. Good."

Mitchella tied the ribbon around his hard biceps. The ends fluttered in the small breeze. She frowned. "Won't this be a distraction?"

"For me, no. For Stachys—depends on his experience in swordplay, maybe," Straif said. He kissed her cheek again and walked to the center of the square, his mind focusing on imminent battle. As he passed over a gleaming forcefield denoting the Field of Honor, it sent a tingle through him, priming him to fight.

Straif faced his distant cuz, the man who'd caused him so much trouble, the man who wanted what Straif had for his own. Anger welled, and Straif squelched it. No place for anger in a duel.

Stachys appeared pale but determined.

Straif nodded to him, "GraceLord."

He received the briefest dip of the chin in return. A hint of wildness showed in Stachys's eyes—panic or anger?

"Does either of the duelists wish to apologize to the other?" G'Uncle Tab's voice boomed, startling Straif. He jerked and saw a certain satisfaction enter Stachys's gaze.

He smiled himself, feeling wolfish anticipation, and the man took a step back. "No!" Straif said.

"No," Stachys said.

"I declare this duel has begun," Tab said. When he withdrew his hand from his staff, it stood by itself. Tab unrolled a papyrus scroll. "I will read the controversy between these two."

"Not necessary," Straif said. He didn't want all his troubles detailed by Tab in loud, rolling tones that everyone around the square could hear. "Not necessary, is it, cuz?"

Stachys narrowed his eyes, then shrugged. "No."

Tab huffed, frowned. "Very well." He said a Word, and the scroll disappeared in flame. The crowd oohed.

"Let's inspect your weapons. Broadswords, no longer than a meter and a half."

Straif whipped his out, gave it to Tab. It gleamed in the sunlight. He'd had it made a few years ago by T'Ash while on a trip. T'Ash had renewed the edge the night before.

Tab, Tinne, and Stachys's seconds looked over the blades. Tab grunted. "Good work," he said of Straif's, handing it back to him, then gave Stachys his sword back.

Taking his staff, Tab thumped it three times. "Proceed to the center of the dueling field. When I say 'go,' you may start the fight. Neither of you are to face the sun."

So Straif separated from the men, took his stance in the cleared rectangle of grass, and stamped a couple of times to get the feel of the earth beneath his feet. He felt a slight connection with it—as if Blackthorn blood had been spilled on it before.

Stachys trod heavily to the field, stood beyond sword length from Straif, and shifted his shoulders, looking grim.

"Salute!" Tab said.

Grinning, Straif carved the air in the most intricate pattern he knew. Stachys lifted his blade vertically, dipped it, and held it in first position guard.

"En garde!" Tab shouted.

They settled into their stances. Straif's eyes narrowed.

"Go!" Tab shouted.

Their blades clanged together. A fierce joy at finally fighting his enemy filled Straif as the vibration of the blow shot up his sword arm. For a couple of minutes he rejoiced in the sharpening of all his senses—the touch of the sun, the scent of the cut grass, but then things changed.

As they fought, a thread curled between them. With each sweep of blade against blade, each circling step on the other's previous place, the blood of the Blackthorns rose to weave between them. By ten passes, Straif was grim himself. He knew he couldn't hurt Stachys, not the last member of his Family that shared his blood. Not the father of children who shared the same heritage. Straif couldn't bring himself to even scratch the man. He'd spill no Blackthorn blood.

So the fight went on as Straif figured out a new strategy. He saw Tab and Tinne frown at him, knowing that he failed to press his attack, used all his skills to defend while he was deep in thought. Then he put his plan into effect.

Twenty-nine

♥

A *few sword clashes later, Straif and Stachys were hilt to* hilt, eye to eye. "What do you really want?" panted Straif.

Stachys grunted, "The Blackthorn estate."

"Never!" Straif smiled with all his teeth, but wondered how long he could fight defensively and not lose the duel.

Five minutes later sweat ran down his spine, coated Stachys's face. Through his link with Stachys, Straif knew his cuz was tiring faster than himself, but Stachys's less superficial emotions had peeled away to a deep and burning anger, and the uppermost fury was that Straif had abandoned his estate.

Straif had swallowed the bitter guilt of that often enough—but hadn't acknowledged it publicly. Again, he manuevered until their sword hilts clashed. "I neglected the estate, but it won't happen again. I'll work and fight for my land forever. Let us quit this duel."

Stachys snarled, tilted his blade, aiming for Straif's eye.

Jumping back, Straif let the revitalizing surge of his own anger fill him—but only until he realized that Stachys's core anger was the treatment his mother and MotherDam had received from Straif's FatherSire. Contempt, disregard, neglect, *abandonment.* Exactly how Stachys believed Straif treated the Blackthorn estate, now and in the future.

The murmur of the crowd hummed in Straif's ears. He thought they realized he wasn't pressing the attack. Did they think his hesitation meant he knew he was guilty?

Neglect—yes, but not complete abandonment, and not a disregard of all his responsibilities as a GrandLord, and nothing he would *ever* do again.

Stachys didn't know that, he was wrapped in unseeing rage—fueled by memories of past ills.

Straif pounced and caught Stachys's gaze with his own, tangled Stachys's blade with his own. "You aren't angry at me, not enough for a duel. You are angry at my FatherSire! Think, man!" Straif sent the reflection of Stachys's old anger back at him through the bond. The man reeled back.

They continued to fight, Stachys awkwardly as his mind pondered words and slowed his reflexes. Straif practiced standard thrusts and ripostes. He wanted Stachys as a member of the Blackthorn Family again. Through his *other* familial bond, the Holly connection, Straif felt Tab and Tinne's grumbling at his reluctance to end the duel.

Then Stachys pressed Straif, his foot slipped, he fell, rolled, recovered to find himself gazing over crossed swords into Stachys's serious, clear eyes.

Stachys said, "I want to be acknowledged a Blackthorn."

Straif pushed the man away with all his strength, hopped back himself, lowered his sword. "Done!" he shouted loudly. "I hereby acknowledge this man before me, Stachys Betony and all his Family, to be legitimate Blackthorns."

When the crowd entered into loud speculation, Straif ignored the comments. Stachys goggled at him, let his own sword point drop, and took a couple of steps toward Straif, who kept his sword pointed to the ground.

"It was ill done of my FatherSire not to acknowledge his child, welcome her into the Family. My side of the Family owes you that, and since you have risen so far on your own, you deserve it. I'll file the documents immediately."

Stachys's mouth opened and closed.

Straif smiled. "You think I'm not glad to have more Family, *cuz?*" He offered his hand.

Stachys hesitated, then set his fingers below Straif's elbow. They clasped arms as male relatives. Straif hoped his eyes hadn't sheened like Stachys's, but Straif swallowed and cleared his throat. "I've done some investigating, too. I know that your Lady's health,"—he couldn't say HeartMate— "would improve if you lived in the country. What do you say to owning the T'Blackthorn estate south on the Ruby Ananda River?"

Stachys's jaw dropped. "That's half the T'Blackthorn's holdings."

Straif shrugged. "It's yours, free and clear."

Stachys's brows knit. "Without swearing a loyalty oath of obedience to you?"

Straif's head came up, he broke the arm-clasp. "Only if you want to," he said simply. He wanted Family again, and there were too few Blackthorns for Stachys and he to be estranged.

They stared at each other for a long moment. Stachys inclined his head. "I'll take the estate and cherish it well."

Straif smiled. "I know."

Stachys pursed his lips. "I'll think on the loyalty oath."

Straif nodded.

Tab strode over. "This is my G'Uncle Tab on my mother's side of the Family," Straif said and introduced Stachys to Tab.

Jerking a nod, Tab said, "I take it your quarrel has been settled?"

"Yes," Straif said.

"Yes," Stachys said.

Tab grunted, shook his head. "Very unusual." Then he shrugged. "But a good outcome. I hereby decree this duel is *over!*" Tab announced.

The woman on Stachys's side of the square jumped from her bench and flew past the golden line denoting the Field of Honor and up to Stachys.

"My love," Stachys said, his face softening.

Her color was too high. She coughed, then found her voice. "You stup!" she cried. "You should be ashamed of yourself. And you, too." She shook her finger under Straif's nose.

"GraceLady—" Tab said in a forbidding tone.

She ignored him, put her hands on her ample hips, and glared at Straif and Stachys. "I don't think I want my children associating with either of you! You Blackthorn men are a bad influence."

"Agra, dear!" Stachys half sputtered, half choked. He snicked his sword back into its sheath, grabbed his wife, and kissed her hard.

Tab, Straif, and Tinne raised their eyebrows. A great bubble of happiness grew in Straif. Family.

Stachys broke the kiss, and his wife gasped, firmed her mouth and said, "*My* children—"

"Let's go make another," Stachys said, still hugging his wife. "Can't have too many children in a Family, right . . . cuz?" He looked hesitantly at Straif.

"Right."

"Excellent tactics," Tab murmured.

Stachys started moving away, but said, "I can't stop the Councils's procedures. Several members believe you've been too irresponsible. You will still have to prove yourself at the open house."

"We're ready," Mitchella said, and Straif saw she waited just beyond the boundary of the Field of Honor.

Tab sighed. "Get these women out of here."

Straif sheathed his sword, bowed to Stachys's friends, Tab, and Tinne. "My greatest thanks for ensuring this duel was properly conducted."

The others bowed, then Tinne took a laughing Genista's arm. The crowd was dispersing from the square. Straif slipped his arm around Mitchella's waist. "Let's go back to the Residence," he whispered in her ear. He tried not to think that their lovemaking would produce no children. "I have a surfeit of energy."

She laughed, but before they could leave, T'Ash joined them. "I heard from Ship about its vaccine for you."

Mitchella stiffened beside him, slipped from his arms. He wanted to follow, but a clump of common people gathered around her as she walked away.

T'Ash continued with his story. "Ship consulted with me after it reviewed the mine scrapings Winterberry sent Ship and the scientist Culpeper. It wanted my notes and the scrapings I took on my visit to the mine. At the time, I got a sample from the empty socket where your ancestors tore the living gems from the rock. There were indications of some sort of virulent pest in the rock that was long dead when I got there, but which would have been live and fearsome when your ancestors were there. Very infectious, too." T'Ash shrugged his heavy shoulders. "Ship babbled its scientific language at me, but that was the gist of it. Your ancestors freed something living within the rock or attached to the lambenthysts, were infected, spread the infection to the rest of your Family members who worked in the mine, and that pest killed your immunity to the Angh virus, or something like that." He waved. "You can sort it out."

Straif only wished he could, but it didn't sound as if there was anything he could do about it now. "Thank you," he said in a stilted voice. He'd lost sight of Mitchella.

T'Ash grimaced. "Much good it does you. When I set the gems back into the mine, I did the best I could to Heal them; Danith and I did a Ritual, too. I believe the stones were pleased to be back in their proper place, but crippled for the next few millennia."

Just as he was—Healed but crippled. Truly, fate cycled around.

For Mitchella, the remaining days until the official T'Blackthorn open house passed with unprecedented swiftness. The hours of light were filled with restoring the Residence, particularly the ballroom. In the nights she barely slept, steeping herself in lovemaking with Straif. As often as she reached for him, he took her, until the dark hours became a blur of wondrous sensation.

Finally it was the eve of the open house. The workers had left. Antenn was spending the night at Vinni T'Vine's castle. The cook had everything prepared for the morrow and had retired to his rooms in nervous exhaustion. Drina was upstairs testing Danith D'Ash's new Fam Grooming Cabinet and Spa.

So Mitchella stood in the Grand Hall, ready to review the Residence one last time. Her stay at the house was numbered in septhours, and she seethed with anxiety about the open house and how the great Nobles of the land would judge her work, and dread at the pain that would come when she said good-bye to Straif.

The Hall was gorgeous, the walls a rich, warm cream color

with a mixture of jewel-toned paintings, tapestries, and holos displaying the Blackthorns' collection of art. All the most striking objects were in the Hall to impress the visitor as they stepped through the huge door. The light was soft and focused to show the art at best advantage.

She sighed, shook her head. She didn't see how she could have improved on her job here, and that filled her with a melancholy satisfaction.

There was a quiet "pop," and Straif stood behind her. Every nerve quivered in acknowledgment of his presence. She thought her very skin breathed in the aura of him. He rested his hands on her shoulders and brought his body to touch hers from behind. The feel of him made her knees weak.

"Thank you for giving my home back to me—better than ever before," he said, and his breath brushed her ears. She wanted nothing but to sink back against him. Forever. So she stiffened her knees and locked a door against pain. Pain would be in the future, but she didn't have to suffer it now.

She chuckled. "This will make my reputation, Straif, and Clover Furniture will do well, also. Do you wish to do a last tour with me?"

"No. I've already been through the Residence. It's wonderful. Listen."

Holding still, she strained her ears and heard the Residence murmuring to itself as it checked its rooms and initiated spells. When she inhaled, a mild scent of honeysuckle drifted to her.

"The Residence is happy. Drina is happy. *I* am happy," Straif whispered. "At this moment there is nothing I want more than to make love to you." He turned her around and looked into her eyes, his own dark blue, yearning, shadowed with the knowledge of the end. "Will you come to bed with me?"

One last night in the generational Blackthorn bed, as his HeartMate, but not to HeartBond.

He had restored his home, turned an enemy into welcome Family, bonded with a Fam, and found a potion that granted immunity to the Angh virus. He had broken the Blackthorn Curse and would demonstrate to all tomorrow that he was a FirstFamily GrandLord. No wonder he was happy.

So she said what she'd said so often in the past and would

only say again this one last night. "Of course I'll love you." In bed and forever.

She slid her hands into his thick sandy hair and drew his lips down to hers, opening her mouth wide. His hand covered her bottom and pressed her hard against his aroused body. Their tongues dueled, and she sucked on his and took the taste of him into her, to remember always.

Then his hands were between them, slipping down the grooves of her clothes, opening her tunic, her breastband, cupping her breasts and playing with her nipples until she couldn't breathe, she had to break the kiss, just to groan her delight and desire.

He circled her wrist with his fingers and drew her slowly, as if dancing, across the marble squares of the Hall and to the stairs, leading her up to his bed. Her blood pounded hot. Her core dampened, readying to take him into her.

"Come with me," he said, tempting her. They climbed the staircase, and it seemed like a dream. "Come to me," he said and opened the door to his suite, kicked it shut behind him. "Come *for* me," he said as he put her on the bed and joined her there, side by side.

Matching her gaze with his own, his hand slid beneath the waistband of her trous, under her pantlettes, until his fingers found her swollen flesh begging for his touch.

He stroked her, found the seat of her passion, pressed, and she whimpered and closed her eyelids. He withdrew his hand. "Don't," he said. "Look into my eyes. I want that link, gaze to gaze, body to body, emotion to emotion. Watch me while I watch you."

"Yes," she whispered and lifted her fingers to brush against his cheek.

"Clothes gone," he muttered, and they were naked. His manhood was strong and thick against her thigh.

"Come inside me," she whispered, arching against him, seeing his pupils dilate. She caressed him with her whole body, rubbing, letting the roughness of his chest hair against her breasts push her to a higher level of sensuality. She reached down and found him, brought him to her, over her, in her. And he was *there*. Everywhere. In her body. In her mind. In her heart.

And she was in his eyes.

Her breath clogged in her throat as he filled her, stretched her, caressed her intimately sex to sex. He withdrew, lingered at the entrance of her sheath, slowly penetrated again. The bond between them flowed with nothing but sensation, passion, rising ecstasy.

He rode her, or she rocked under him. His intensity enveloped her, his eyes went unfocused, and all she could see was blue and black and gold-silver-sparkling light of passion. He moved faster, she panted, but kept her eyes on his, open to him in all ways.

He plunged. She cried out. They shattered together, and the pleasure was so sharp that all went starburst-white. He collapsed on her.

A few minutes later, he rolled to his side, tucked her into the curve of his body. They slept together.

When she woke, he was dressing. She glanced at the timer—Work bell, but it wasn't a workday, it was Playday. The open house was set for two septhours after noon.

He watched her with narrow gaze, impassive expression as he closed the tab-groove of his tunic. "Stay with me."

She couldn't discuss this in bed. She got up and dressed in last night's clothes. She'd stand under a waterfall soon. "The project is over."

"There's still a lot to do."

"Not so much, finishing touches that I think your Lady should complete."

"I'm not ready to find my HeartMate."

Mitchella flinched inwardly. "Straif, you weren't ready to stay in Druida, but the Hollys called you back. You weren't ready to rehabilitate your Residence, but living in T'Holly Residence under a broken vow of honor forced you away. Your contract with me and Stachys's claim prodded you to complete this work. The only thing that you've been 'ready' to do is to find the cure for your flawed heritage. I imagine that you'll always search for that. Meantime you have a preventative drink that will shield your children from harm. It's time to move on with your life."

"Are you trying to fight with me?"

"No."

A calendar-globe appeared. "Time to distill and drink the vaccine against the Angh virus," it said.

"I want you to stay with me."

"Antenn and I have our own place."

"Let's talk about this after the open house. Please."

"All right." She hoped she had the willpower to stand against him. An affair, no matter how loving and long term, wasn't an option as long as he wanted children.

Straif nodded. "Right." He smiled the smile that always touched her. "I'm glad you're my hostess today." He looked around the room, "I'm glad that it was you who made my Residence a home for me again."

Mitchella chuckled. "You'll get my bill."

"I'll pay it, and I'll introduce you to *everyone* today." He strode over, pulled her against him, and kissed her. He was aroused. "You can't give this up," he whispered. "I can't give it up. Not yet."

Leaving her breathing hard, he walked away. She sank onto the bed and put her face in her hands. A few more hours—perhaps. Why couldn't she make the break? But it wasn't time to think about it now, even as a thin blade of hurt slipped into her heart as she thought of him in the stillroom, preparing for his future Family. Soon the urge to mate and sire children would override his passion for her. She might be able to hold him if she told him he was her HeartMate—but bitterness would eat at him, ruin their lives together.

Much better to cut their affair clean and quick, especially when she had some tiny hope of being able to build another life for herself—after she survived the pain of losing her love.

*S*traif was fumbling through the distilling process when he heard Mitchella scream. "Residence, report!" he ordered.

"There has been an incident in the Heir's Playroom," the Residence said.

Straif 'ported to the chamber. Drina was on her bedsponge, hissing, the wing of a miller moth drooping from her mouth.

Mitchella trembled in fury as she cursed the cat.

The room was in ruins—the delicate swoops of gauze showed huge holes. The linen covers were ripped. The hoop holding the fragile gathered material over the bedsponge tilted, broken.

"How do you expect me to restore this room before the open house?" Mitchella demanded.

Drina lifted her nose, slurped up the last of the moth, and grinned at Straif. *I got the moths. Three. Tell Mitchella she needs to fix My room.*

"No, Mitchella does not have to fix the room." He took his seething lover's arm and moved her to the door. "We'll just set a spell on the door making it off-limits."

Yowling, Drina said, *But I wanted My room to be admired.*

"Then you shouldn't have ruined it." Mitchella sounded as if she spoke through clenched teeth. "I'm done with you, cat. I won't do one more thing for you." Mitchella turned on her heel and slammed out.

Drina tried to look pitiful. It didn't work. Straif surveyed the room, shrugged. "You're on your own in redecorating this one, Drina. I don't have the time or inclination."

The cat lashed her tail. *You never gave Me more diamonds for My collar. Perhaps I should no longer be your Fam.*

He didn't like the idea, but didn't dare show it to the little cat. Unlike Mitchella, Drina wasn't above manipulation. He shrugged. "Suit yourself. I thought you wanted to be a First-Family Familiar. If you don't, you can leave. I'll forward more diamonds as pay for your work on the Residence. Just let me know where you want them sent."

Perhaps I will go get the diamonds from T'Ash Myself. Perhaps I will stay with Samba or someone who appreciates Me.

"Your decision," Straif said.

The Residence said, "Danith D'Ash is here with Pinky. The young tomcat is now a Fam."

"That must be something to see," Straif said, and left Drina hissing.

He spoke a moment to D'Ash, who studied him and Mitchella intently, then he went back to the stillroom and began the process of making the potion all over again. It was slow going and he could only hope that he'd be faster and better at the process with practice. Lord and Lady knew that he'd be doing it the rest of his life. Every day for the rest of his life. He shuddered but gulped the nasty stuff down.

Residence said, "The cook and Mitchella are arranging the tables for the feast. They say everything is under control and will be ready in a septhour. HouseHeart is expecting you for two septhours of meditation."

Straif sighed. "Tell the others that I'm in the HouseHeart. Invite the Fam."

A moment later the Residence said. "The Fam is not responding."

"Right." Straif went to the secret door, down the passage, then disrobed and entered the HouseHeart.

He'd blessed the HouseHeart and accepted its blessing, had settled into his meditation for a short while before the Residence alarm claxon sounded.

"The scry at the gates has been disabled. The last thing I saw was the Fam leaving. She is missing. I sense violence," the Residence said.

Thirty

Straif was at the greeniron entrance gates, working on the front scrystone when Mitchella ran down the gliderway to join him. He looked grim.

Mitchella panted, "Residence said Drina left. I thought she wanted to sit in the Great Hall and present a portrait of elegance. I was angry with her, but *she* wouldn't run away."

He pointed to clumps of white and brown hair on the other side of the greeniron gate—a gate Drina could slip through, even shieldspelled. Mitchella gasped. "There's blood."

"I see that," Straif said in a hard voice. His whole aspect had changed, refined down to the warrior. Half warrior, half hunter.

He reached for her hand, and she dimly saw what he did, a bright yellow green trail leading away from the gates.

She'd never liked chartreuse. She knew Straif hurt as she had when Antenn had been lost. She lifted his hand to her lips, kissed the warm palm. He drew it away.

"It's been too quiet. I believe my enemy has been waiting for this moment and struck."

"But it wasn't Stachys. He's at the Residence, ready to tell all he confirms you as T'Blackthorn. His Family—the rest of your Family, is with him."

"No, it isn't Stachys. He's sane and solid. The one who left this trail is mad."

"You know who?" Mitchella asked as he paced the Flair trail that she could no longer see.

He hesitated.

"You have an idea."

He nodded shortly. "Perhaps. I was going to deal with this tomorrow, after the party and the formal acknowledgment by all Councils that I am T'Blackthorn. I'll have more credibility, more status tomorrow, enough power for me to do whatever has to be done."

"You mean handle this quietly."

"Yes. T'Ash is involved because of Zanth. I wanted to protect—" He squatted, touched another bit of blood. "Ah, I thought so, *not* Drina's blood. The other's." He brought his fingertip with the dab of red to his mouth, tasted it. Shuddered. Weariness and regret crossed his face. "No time to waste. She is truly mad."

He shifted his stance like he was about to teleport. Mitchella grasped his biceps with both hands. "Take me with you."

Looking down at her, he shook his head. "You could get hurt."

"You can protect me with a shieldspell."

"Yes." He grimaced. "But you'll be going with me to Kalmi Lobelia's home. My old lover."

Her heart jumped, but she nodded and said, "Take me with you. She won't be expecting me. I could provide a distraction."

"I don't know—"

She kissed him hard on the lips, stepped back. "We do this together. A shieldspell, T'Blackthorn!"

He flicked his fingers, and a bubble descended to encase her. It tightened around her body, coating her like a second skin. For an instant she couldn't breathe, then a click sounded inside her head. Moving in the shield was like wearing a heavy onesuit that covered her face and curved around her eyes.

"You're protected," Straif said with satisfaction, took one of her hands in his tight grip. "Let's go."

"Prepare yourself. One and two and *three!*"

There was a whoosh, and the next instant they appeared in the stone courtyard outside a deteriorating house. Scraggly weeds grew between gaps in the paving stones, the plaster on the walls was spiderwebbed with cracks. Mitchella frowned. In itself, the place was beautiful. Surely a Nobleman's home, one of GrandHouse status.

"They definitely need me," she said. "This looks worse than T'Blackthorn Residence did."

Straif winced. "I think it's been like this for years, and I never noticed." A muscle played in his jaw. "I sense great madness. Drina may need us both."

"Yes." It wouldn't be pleasant confronting his old lover, but she'd ignore any proprieties to help Drina. "I should definitely distract the GrandLady." The woman probably had a lot of Flair. Mitchella was glad of the shieldspell.

Straif strode up to the pointed-arched door and shoved it in with his shoulder. It creaked terribly.

"Don't you think we should be quieter?"

"I think she's expecting us . . . at least me."

He left the door open, sagging on its hinges. Bright sunlight from the outside barely penetrated the gloom. Straif strode in silently. Mitchella followed, treading lightly. Something about the place demanded that.

It reeked of madness.

The odor hit her first. Heavy, unfamiliar incense that made her woozy, mixed with mildewed dankness, mice, even spoiled food. At least she hoped it was food. The atmosphere contained an oppression that hinted anything could happen.

The house wept. Mitchella's flesh prickled at the faint sobs. It sounded as if it had been weeping for a long time. She swallowed hard.

She nearly lost Straif as he threaded the shadowed hallways. He was obviously familiar with the house. Mitchella strove to recall anything she'd heard about his affair with Kalmi Lobelia. Nothing. She knew nothing, so she braced herself for a confrontation with a mad stranger.

Abruptly they were in a shrouded room so thick with incense that fumes hung near the ceiling. GrandLady Lobelia sat on a pile of huge pillows made from Chinju rugs, colors faded from too much smoke.

The woman had hair a shade darker than Mitchella's, their coloring was nearly the same, and Mitchella would bet Lobelia had green eyes, too. She was built of rounded curves. Bitterness coated Mitchella's tongue. She froze, wanting nothing more in the world than to be out of the awful crying house with the crazed woman who was Straif's previous lover—and of the same physical type. He didn't even seem to realize that.

The shock that kept Mitchella still served them. Lobelia had focused on Straif, not seeming to notice that he wasn't alone. Mitchella silently sidled back to the deep doorway shadows, ready to spring her appearance on the woman at the right time. She hoped. Surely Straif would give her a cue.

"Kalmi," Straif said in a too quiet voice. "Still using pylor smoke to amplify your powers?"

"I need it to *see,* to retain my Flair and my reputation."

"I'm surprised you have any clients coming to this place." He gestured, but his gaze remained fixed on her.

Kalmi sat up straight. "You've been spending too much time with that Commoner who is working in your house." She spread her arms. "Don't you know *we* are meant to be together? I have *seen* us—and our children." She struggled to rise, but fell back to half-recline against the pillows. "Our children, Straif, strong and healthy, and grown to adulthood. That nasty flaw of yours won't kill them like it did the rest of your Family. You must trust my sight, my love for you. We belong together."

Mitchella saw Straif swallow, but he continued to stand very still. He waved to something to his left, out of her sight. "Harming my Fam won't make me trust you, Kalmi. It will hurt me. Hurt us."

Angling herself, Mitchella strained to see what he was talking about. She stared at the limp Drina on a black altar. She'd been infuriated by the little cat just that morning, but never would have thought to harm an animal.

"This is sick," she whispered. Straif's shoulders tensed, and he pressed her lips together so no more words would escape.

Kalmi smiled with awful delight. "But I've found that a little ceremony to the Dark Goddess and the release of energy at the point of death can boost my Flair. I thought we could use it in our HeartBonding. We *are* HeartMates, Straif. I *saw* it."

The prophetess was so crazy, the atmosphere so gruesome, Mitchella's flesh crept. She fought shudders.

"I must insist on taking my Fam," Straif said, gliding slowly to the altar.

"No. No! She'll bring me power. I'll show you how!" With unexpected speed and agility Kalmi shot to her feet.

To Mitchella's utter amazement, Lobelia jumped Straif. Mitchella ran into the room, scooped up Drina, and ran out, shrieking mentally, *Danith!* Her fear must have made an impression, because her friend appeared—formally dressed for the party—in Lobelia's shabby courtyard.

Mitchella thrust a limp Drina into Danith's arms. "Here, take care of her. I need to help Straif."

Danith looked startled, then turned her attention to the FamCat. "Bad," she said. "Very bad. Bad Flairspells and poison. I'll take her to my home FamClinic." She winked out silently.

Lobelia had definitely been waiting for Straif. He was lying bound by strips of Chinju rug, wrapped around him like the tree branches that had caged Mitchella. Kalmi held a knife, her whole body trembling so much with crazed sobs that Straif was in real danger. Mitchella stormed in, lowered her shoulder in a move she'd learned from her brothers, and ran straight at Kalmi. Mitchella hit the woman in her middle. Her stomach was much larger than Mitchella's. She felt a dull blow on her back, the knife skittered away. Lobelia shrieked, her words garbled. "I've seen in my visions, it's me he's with, *me,* not you, not you, notyou."

Knife gone, Lobelia's clawlike hands grabbed Mitchella, tore at her and slid off the shield. Shrieking, Kalmi pummeled her. The blows didn't hurt much and infuriated Mitchella. She lost all reason, and fought back, striking with fisted hands, kicking.

They rolled over and over, banged into a struggling Straif, then over to the black altar. With a keening triumph, Kalmi reared back, breaking Mitchella's hold, and pulled on the heavy velvet drape. Heavy objects fell on Mitchella, glancing against her head, on her chest, taking her breath.

Kalmi rose above her, with another knife. "He wants me. He needs me. He always came to me before. I *love* him and will take him, curse and all!" She plunged the knife down.

Mitchella curled inward, took the blow on the back again

Pushed against Kalmi, and tangled them both in the cloth. Dust and smoke rose from the fabric, hazing Mitchella's mind, weakening her limbs.

House, help me! I'll help you, I vow! Mitchella cried. The House bordered on sentient, she knew, but could it help? Plaster fell, a beam groaned overhead, and Mitchella fought, kicked, shoved away from the madwoman. Straif tore away his bonds. The end of the beam creaked down, building speed. Mitchella rolled, and Straif yanked her aside, as the rafter fell on Lobelia.

Mitchella staggered to her feet, brushing her hair back, panting.

Straif stood looking at Lobelia, buried in plaster rubble and broken wood. Horror echoed back and forth between them, spiking high in Straif. He'd cared deeply for the woman once.

Mitchella closed her eyes against his hurt and her own.

"Is she . . ."

With careful steps, Straif approached Lobelia's motionless forearm, all that was visible. He bent, felt for a pulse, sent out a flaired probe. Mitchella felt the zip of energy. Lobelia didn't.

"Yes, she's dead. Her soul is gone, circling on the Wheel of Stars, poor thing."

Straif turned and stared at Mitchella, features cast in disbelief. "You talked to the house, and it helped you."

She dusted herself off. The personal shieldspell had attracted the white plaster dust. "You talk to your Residence all the time."

"It's a *Residence*. A . . . a . . . being?"

"Housebeing. Sentient House. Flaired House." Mitchella shrugged. "All you FirstFamilies have sentient houses. That's what makes them Residences. They've been the homes of flaired people so long they're imbued with magic. You store flair within them. You give it to them for scheduled spells. You have Rituals and Ceremonies in them where you all raise energy. Of course they become beings."

Straif still looked shocked. He opened his mouth and closed it, gestured around them. "But this isn't a Residence."

Mitchella sniffed. "It's been the home of Flaired Grandlords and Ladies for many generations, so it's in the act of becoming."

He blinked as if he couldn't get the idea through his head that the house had saved him. "My Residence would never hurt me."

She tilted her head. "Of course not." He was having a hard time comprehending the matter, and she didn't know why. "You know the value of your home. You treat it with respect. It is, after all, another member of your Family. Lobelia never treated the House as a being, never cared for it. Why should a being protect one who never protected it?"

Straif just shook his head, looked at Kalmi, and grimaced. "Um. Can you ask the house to move the debris on Kalmi, so I can teleport her to the Death Grove?"

"The beam and wall fragment are no longer attached to the House, so it has no control over them. Can you take off my shieldspell?"

He looked uneasily around. "What if something else—"

"The House is perfectly in control."

With a Word, the shieldspell was gone. Mitchella checked her own Flair. Sufficient. It wouldn't be the first time she'd cleared rubble from a house, and it wouldn't be the last. It would be the most memorable. With a brief spell, she provided Flair for a debris removal spell and initiated it. The House caught at the magic eagerly, boosting the spell with its own long-stored Flair for housekeeping that hadn't been used for years. The sheer power of the spell spun her and sent her to bump and lean against a wall, facing away from the destruction. She was glad, she hadn't really wanted to watch the revealing of Lobelia.

A few moments later, the room quieted. "Is it done?"

Straif said, "Yes, there's a hole in the ceiling, and the wall is completely gone. Apparently it was a partition that the house didn't like." His voice sounded funny. He'd probably never seen a house remodel itself.

Then he sighed. "I'll 'port Lobelia to the Death Grove," Straif said, then intoned a Word.

A slight sound and a surge of emotion from the house notified Mitchella that Lobelia's body was gone.

She turned back, and the room's appearance had changed dramatically. The smoke stains on the walls had vanished leaving them a nearly blinding white, the pillows gleamed with renewed sateen texture and brilliant, jewel colors. The hole in the ceiling looked square and tidy, waiting for someone to reinsert a beam. As Straif had said, the false wall was gone and the chamber was much larger, with long, clean windows that painted squares of sunlight on the gray stone floor.

Looking around with raised eyebrows, Straif shook his head, stared at her uncomprehendingly. "You are a heroine to a house."

The world whirled around her, and she felt like the set point.

When it settled, she knew it was time.

Time to break off the affair with Straif. It was already far too late for her. She'd hurt for years, part of her heart would be shadowed forever, knowing that she could never have her HeartMate.

She stared around, hardly believing that this was the time and place.

"Mitchella?" Straif touched her cheek, concern in his eyes, and she braced herself for the blow.

"You don't really understand me at all, do you?"

"What?"

"You don't understand what I feel for houses, but more, you don't understand what I feel for Antenn and you." Her voice trailed off to a whisper.

"You love Antenn as your own son."

She began narrowing the bond between them, reeling in the thread as much as she could. It would be bad enough dealing with the devastating blows of her own emotions, she couldn't endure his and not break.

"Yes, I do. He is my son, the child of my heart." She lightly tapped above her left breast. "I love him as much as I'd love any child from my own body."

Straif flinched.

"I know you don't understand that, but it *is* the truth." She inhaled deeply. "And I love you. More than I've ever loved any man before. I'll never love anyone like I love you." *Heart-Mate* echoed in her mind. "But I can't stay with you any longer."

"No!" He reached out, grasped her hands. Energy shot and

pulsed raggedly between them. She shut out all the pain—hers waiting to ambush her in a moment; his, fresh and raw.

"Stay with me," he whispered.

"I can't. Not anymore simply as a lover."

He just stared at her.

She wet her lips. "Will you marry me and have me as the only woman in your life? That's what I want from you, Straif."

His expression was angry, hurting. She steeled her heart.

Straif said, "You know I can't do that. I want children and a Family, more than I want anything else in this life."

"I have a child."

"I must have a child of my own blood to carry on the Family name."

"No. You want children who carry your blood and your great Flair. True Family isn't based on blood, but on love. You haven't figured that out. I have. I'll have more children."

She pulled her hands from him and with strength she didn't know she had, she brushed her lips to Straif's and fixed a smile that was almost genuine on her face. "The time we had together was beautiful. I'll always cherish memories of our affair." He whipped out a hand, but she evaded it—with a little help from the house manipulating the residual Flair.

"You can't leave me!" Torment radiated from him.

She spoke to him, walking fast out of the room, down the hallways. His sharp footsteps followed. "I must leave you, for both our sakes. I love you too much, and you can't give me what I need. To go on would damage us both. Now is the right time. The project of restoring the Residence is done. You'll be confirmed by AllClass Council as T'Blackthorn today. You've found new cuzes. There is no more business between us."

When she reached the door, she found it straight on its hinges and shut. She flung it open easily and without any creaking. A pulse of fear came from the house. She patted the doorjamb. "I'll be back tomorrow."

Outside the sky was blue and the air held the first edge of summer, but Mitchella thought she'd drawn in the atmosphere of the house behind her—hurting with no hope of surcease, only surviving through sheer will. Her eyes burned with the effort to keep tears from falling. Her throat tightened. A horrible hole was inside her that she didn't know how to keep from enveloping her. The blackness of it, of giving in to the urge to scream her hurt, tempted.

Searing agony seeped through the tiny link with Straif. She strove with all her might to ignore his pain, block her heartbreak from flowing back to him. With him, now, she only had her pride.

Her heart contracted with shock, her brain numb, only her body's automatic actions kept her upright, walking. She didn't dare allow herself to think of Straif behind her. She'd fall to the ground and curl up.

And there, outside rusty, hanging gates, was Antenn, Pinky draped around his neck and stretched out on his skinny shoulders. Antenn clutched papyrus in his hands, crumpling them. He looked at her, past her, then back at her face, and gulped. She opened her arms and he ran into them, and she held warm, solid boy. Her son. The reason for her to go on.

Pinky crawled from Antenn to snuggle around her neck, and she welcomed the weight of him and his purring that vibrated against her body.

Antenn rushed into speech. "Danith D'Ash told me you were here. The snotty cat got herself kidnapped. I came by public carrier, and I have the last set of adoption papyrus. I've filled them out. Now you only need to enter your agreement. I thought we could take the papers to the GuildHall and file them and get adopted tomorrow. I mean, *right now*. Then we can go home to the Clovers. Family will be good." He babbled, holding her, until the small displacement of air told her Straif had 'ported away and the bond between them ripped.

Thirty-one

Mitchella cried out as Straif teleported away, tearing their bond. She squeezed Antenn harder.

"Your affair with T'Blackthorn is over?" Antenn asked a moment later.

"Yes."

"I'm sorry." He hesitated. "Can we go to the GuildHall and finish my adoption?" he said.

Tears still threatened. She sniffled, found a softleaf, blew her nose. She could control her emotions, the black emptiness another septhour or two, then when she cried in the dark in her old room in the Clover Compound, she would cry tears of loss mixed with tears of joy. And when she woke up, family would be around her, comforting her, as they always did, as they had when she'd learned she couldn't have children.

But she did. She had a son, right here, and a good son he was. "Yes, let's go to the GuildHall." She checked the horizon for the huge starship to orient herself. From the angle and the distance of the ship, she knew she was in southeast Druida, in an old area populated by lesser nobles.

"Where, exactly, are we?"

"We're near Grain and Palmetto. Danith D'Ash told me where you were. She told all the Clovers. The snotty cat let

herself get kidnapped." He made a disbelieving noise and
looked at Pinky.

Cat was fool-ish. Pinky's telepathy was still shaky. He
raised his nose and sniffed disdainfully. Though his mental
speaking needed work, his attitude was all Fam.

"Anyway, I knew where to come," Antenn said.

"What do you think of the House? It's my next project. It's
becoming sentient. I thought if you liked it, we might . . ."

His eyes widened in horror.

"Look *at* the House. Use your Flair." The House could be a
great distraction. She'd never midwifed one from burgeoning
intelligence to real sentience. This would be challenging. The
House needed her, and its desperate situation overcame any re-
serve she might have at the thought of Kalmi. She could make
a great difference to this House. T'Blackthorn Residence could
help—another flash of pain, another notion to vanquish.

She turned to survey the House herself. Broken, rusty gates
framed a pitifully dead grassyard, the weedy courtyard, the
pathetic House. But it was large and could—possibly, with a
lot of work—be beautiful. As if feeling their gaze, the House
glowed. Turquoise.

Antenn winced, then narrowed his eyes in what she recognized as his Flair sight. Gulped. "I think we could get it
cheap."

A weak chuckle broke from Mitchella.

I like the House, Pinky said.

Frowning, Antenn said, "It's . . . it's . . . it could become a
Residence, couldn't it? We could live in a Residence. The
Mitchella Clover Residence," he whispered.

"Yes."

He straightened his shoulders. "If we all worked hard, you
and me 'n Pinky 'n the Hou–House we could make it a Residence." He nodded. "This could be really good."

"I think so."

"Yes." He looked at Pinky, around Mitchella's shoulders.

Pinky revved his purr. *I will be a Fam with a Res-i-dence.
Good.*

Slipping his hand in hers, Antenn said, "Our Clover family
will help us." He hesitated, said in a little voice, "I suppose
we'll be getting a lot of gilt from—from our last project."

She struggled for even tones. Any swerving of her thoughts to Straif, to the T'Blackthorn Residence, threatened her fraying control. "I haven't calculated our accounts payable yet."

"It will be a lot. Enough." With a last glance at the House, he said, "I don't know why it glows turquoise, but that must go." He stared up at her and frowned. "You look terrible." He led her down the street to the public carrier plinth.

He knew she needed solid contact with him, perhaps he wanted it, too, in this most important septhour of their lives together.

"It's a good thing that I got SupremeJudge Ailim Elder's personal seal on the papyrus." He smoothed the papyrus and pointed to the silver seal of scales against the background of *Nuada's Sword*. Pride filled him and trickled through to her.

Feeling positive emotions, even if they weren't her own, mitigated her pain.

"Ailim Elder filled out some of the dates and info about when you got me and why. She asked me to call her Ailim! Just think, my mo—, my mother is the godmother of Captain's Lady Ailim Elder's baby girl." He grimaced. "I saw the baby, she's really ugly, but Ruis Elder and Ailim like her. Since they look good and are nice people, I guess she'll get better."

"I'm sure she'll always be adorable." There was no tinge of hurt that she'd never hold her own baby . . . because she might. Someday she might be able to adopt a baby.

Antenn glanced at her, studied her face, the state of her dress. "Yeah, it's good that I have her seal, otherwise the GuildHall clerk might not think you wanted me."

"Who wouldn't want you?" she tried a little teasing. Act normal, and the world would soothe her with normality, smooth the edges of her raw pain. Let her accept the deep hurt, and it, too, would become normal.

"Exactly." Antenn attempted to look cherubic, and her breath broke on a shaky laugh.

The public carrier arrived, and they embarked, found a plush bench, and sat. Antenn separated a page of papyrus from the rest and handed her a writestick. "You fill this stuff out." His hands trembled a little, and Mitchella put her arms around him, squeezed, then applied herself to the form, and she found that her eyes and hands worked just fine. She let her world narrow to her child and his needs.

"I bet the Clovers will throw a party to celebrate me becoming one of you." He grinned, and somewhere in the gray cloud that enveloped her, she felt a spark of pleasure at seeing him happy.

Finishing the form, she handed the papyrus and writestick back to him and tousled his hair, boy fine and soft, not as thick as Stra—she ruthlessly squashed the memory. "*Our* family will celebrate with an impromptu party in the compound courtyard. Nothing we like better." Montages of so many past parties flowed before her mind's eye, comforting her. "It will be fun." She could endure it for the amount of time it took for Antenn to gravitate to the Clover boys and start up their own games.

*S*traif *teleported to his ResidenceDen, glanced around with* pain-blinded eyes, and knew he'd have problems living in the Residence again—every room shouted Mitchella. He staggered over to the long, man-sized sofa and fell onto it. Why hadn't he anticipated this pain? This hurt that chilled him to the bone? Why hadn't he realized that he'd have difficult memories again? Because it was supposed to be a sex affair. And though he'd sensed that it had turned into more—that she, at least, had loved him, he had hidden from his own feelings.

Holm opened the door and strolled in, took one glance at Straif, shut the door, and called mentally, *T'Ash get your ass in here.* Aloud, he said, "AllClass Councils' Representatives are here and brought your formal reinstatement as T'Blackthorn. The party's in full swing. The duel, your acknowledgment of Stachys, and the Councils' approval are all old news. Catnapping and the unfortunate death of a madwoman are hot stories."

Straif grunted.

T'Ash walked in. Straif felt him more than anything else. He was having a hard time moving. Maybe it was the debilitating cold encasing him.

"T'Blackthorn looks bad," T'Ash said. He loomed like a dark shadow over the sofa.

"I would guess that my cuz has lost his woman," Holm said.

"Pretty pitiful if a tracker misplaces his own woman," T'Ash said.

A strangled sound escaped Straif.

"Guess he didn't want to marry her," T'Ash said.

Holm said, "He once told me that he wanted Family, yet he's thrown away the love of a good woman, the admiration of a boy. Does that sound reasonable to you, T'Ash?"

Straif didn't like how the two friends ganged up on him, but couldn't muster the effort to defend himself. He was so cold he was sure he was frozen, one movement of a finger could break it off.

T'Ash shrugged. "Probably thinks that since he has a *HeartMate,* he'll find another woman to love him well-enough."

Holm lifted his brows. "Now the Residence is in order again, himself confirmed as T'Blackthorn, he can hunt his HeartMate."

"No!" Straif whispered, but he didn't know if the others heard it, it sounded so raw, like the painful cry of an animal.

"You know Blackthorns always track their HeartMates, don't you, T'Ash?" Holm said.

"Huh. Better wait for a while then. Dead old lover's body in Death Grove, new lover finishes restoring his Residence, and she's gone. Doesn't look good," T'Ash said.

As Straif raised his shoulders to prop them against the arm of the sofa, he watched carefully to make sure his torso didn't break in half, though he didn't know if it mattered.

"I heard the Ship's even given him an immunization for the virus that he can use for his Family. Everything's just rolling along great for Straif, here." Holm tapped Straif on his shoulder, and the heat from just the small contact of his cuz's fingers made Straif whimper.

"Are you two *trying* to kill me?" he asked, then finally managed to look at the men. Holm was stern. He'd make an excellent GreatLord T'Holly when his father reinstated him as Heir. T'Ash appeared impassive as usual, but as he lounged in one of the large chairs, his body language sent out irritation, perhaps even an edge of contempt.

"Don't I hurt enough without you two beating me up?"

"We don't know. Do you hurt?" Holm asked.

Straif closed his eyes. "I don't think I'll ever be warm again." He didn't want to talk. He only wanted to lie still until heat returned to his body—a decade maybe, the way he felt. He was beyond caring if the other two stayed or went.

"You do look real white," T'Ash said. "Might be he's suffering a bit. Losing a woman can do that to you, but it isn't as if it were his *HeartMate*."

Anger moved sluggishly through Straif, he opened his eyes and stared at T'Ash, then heard the clinking of glasses. Surprised at the sound, he saw Holm at a small corner bar that appeared to be stocked with liquor. Something else Mitchella had added to the room. It was beautiful and functional, like all her work.

Holm gave Straif half a glass of whiskey. Wise, since Straif's hand shook so, the liquid almost slopped over the edge. Gritting his teeth in effort, and loathing that the other two watched, he brought the drink to his mouth, then had to force his jaws apart to drink. Whiskey trickled into his mouth, down his throat. Must not be a good brand, he didn't feel the fire.

"We've all known the pain of great loss," Holm said quietly. "The loss of our Family."

T'Ash grunted, accepted the whiskey Holm handed him, and stretched out his legs.

Maybe the liquor was effective after all, Straif felt embers igniting in his gut.

"It's rough," Holm said.

"Rougher if it's done to you instead of doing it yourself," T'Ash said.

That brought Straif's feet down on the floor. "I did not kill my Family." He'd accepted that, finally. He hadn't killed his parents. They'd been dying, just as he had. Both had known that even if one of them had survived, the HeartMate would have perished within the year at the loss of the HeartBond. So they'd given him the strength to live—with love. Even the guilt that he'd survived and everyone else had died had faded—with the work of restoring his Residence, his joy in Mitchella. He tried to recapture those feelings, but they were lost under the frozen tundra of his heart.

"Not one of us was guilty of losing our Family," T'Ash said. "Mine was killed. Straif's died—"

"I chose my HeartMate over my Family," Holm said. "In that way, I'm guilty of losing mine, but we didn't push our women away—"

"Speak for yourself. I did. For her own good," T'Ash muttered, staring out the nearest window.

"Well, *I*—" Holm stopped, coughed.

"So you two made mistakes, too." The smallest tendril of warmth sprouted in Straif.

Holm sank down onto the sofa next to Straif, sipped his own drink, and said, "You could have learned from our experience."

They sat for a moment in silence. Straif downed his whiskey, hoping for more warmth.

"The basic question is whether you want to pay the cost of letting your line die for the love of a woman," Holm said.

Straif's mother and father had cherished each other. Through love they'd died to ensure he lived. Could he, through love, live and let any future progeny die?

"Love is everything." T'Ash turned red and hunched his neck into his shoulders.

"You know very well that if Danith had been sterile, you wouldn't have HeartBonded with her." Straif's voice was harsh, as if all his scorching emotions had scoured his throat.

"It wouldn't have been long before I'd have surrendered," T'Ash mumbled. "I couldn't live without my HeartMate—not even before we HeartBonded." He glared at Straif and Holm. "And I never said that."

"Can you live without the woman?" Holm asked. "I mean *live*, not survive?"

"How do you feel about her marrying another man?" T'Ash asked at the same time.

Two blows, one to the brain, the other, more horrible, to the gut.

When silence stretched, T'Ash rose. "There's a party outside of this room. By the way, the Residence looks great." He tilted his head and his face lit up. "My Lady has arrived. She's putting your sickly FamCat to bed. Thinks Drina will be near full strength after a septhour of rest."

"Thank you, T'Ash, and thank her."

"You'll get a bill," T'Ash said cheerfully. He buffeted Straif on the shoulder. "Now that you're T'Blackthorn again, our fees will be high." He sobered and shook his head. "It's a hard decision you have, but blood isn't as important as we've been taught. I'll be adopting some of the people working for me into my Family. I have Danith, but she always wanted a big Family, so I have connections with the Clovers, too, always will." He spread his large hands. "There's—affection— between all of us. Blessings upon you." He nodded once, then left the room.

"Mitchella's sterile. You won't give up your Family line for her," Holm prodded.

Straif looked at him. Did he see disappointment in Holm's eyes? "You can't—"

"No, I probably can't understand your viewpoint. I gave up everything for my HeartMate. My Family, my future. And I don't regret it." Holm's eyes fired. "I don't regret HeartBonding with her, following her to a new life." Holm poked a finger into Straif's chest. "I'll tell you this. Family is important, but what is more important is love, and I'm not just talking about love between a man and a woman, HeartMate love. True Family isn't based on blood, but on love."

Shock jolted Straif that Holm was repeating words Mitchella had said. "How would you know?"

Now Holm looked aside. "When I was disinherited, I was lost. I thought I'd lost all my Family." His gaze swung back to meet Straif's. "But Tinne stood by me. *You* stood by me. T'Ash and the Apples. Even T'Hawthorn and Lark's Family consider me a part of *their* Family. Would you like me—love me—if I carried no blood linked to yours?"

Holm *did* know. And he'd left himself emotionally open to anything Straif might say. "I told you last year you were my cuz. You're Family."

"Listen to yourself." Holm tapped his finger on Straif's chest. "Listen to your heart."

A rap came on the door, and Holm's eyes lit with pleasure, just as T'Ash's had. "That's Lark." He went and opened the door. "Blessings, cuz," he said, closing the door behind him, leaving Straif alone.

As quiet draped the room, Straif's thoughts roiled. His

emotions tore at him. He wanted Mitchella. He *loved* Mitchella. Deeply, passionately.

But if he chose to marry Mitchella, he'd forsake any children of his blood.

The idea of her wedding another man, loving another man brought a haze of red fury so strong he shuddered with it, yet he knew that was a certainty. She'd survive, she'd look to the future, she'd find and love and *make love with* another man. She'd marry and mother a brood of children.

He'd live in a Residence that she had decorated. The notion of having another woman—even a HeartMate—in the Residence was impossible. He couldn't imagine it.

His Family was long gone. His future of a healthy Family had always been an illusion, something he comforted himself with because of the past. But now it was time to free himself from the past and illusions and move into the bright reality of a solid future. Mitchella.

With the decision, an image of her, vibrant, laughing came to his mind so strongly that he thought he could touch her.

He had to get her back.

He didn't know where she was.

Straif smiled. He'd track his woman, claim her as his own.

Thirty-two

❦

Straif set his glass of whiskey aside, his gut pleasantly warm. He rose from the couch and went to the hidden no-time safe behind a section of the wall. Passing his hand over it, he chanted a couplet, and a drawer extended into the room.

He stared at the treasure, the ancient Blackthorn jewels, then reached for a golden pouch. As he lifted it, metallic clinks sounded, and his hands curved around the Blackthorn marriage bands. He tied the pouch to his belt and banished the drawer, strode to the ResidenceDen door, opened it, and left.

The cook, Gwine Honey, grabbed his arm. "I have a confession to make," he whispered, then swallowed hard.

Straif prayed for patience. He didn't need this now, but the young man panted so rapidly he might faint. "Yes?"

"I am Gwine Honey. My uncle *is* the cook to the Holly's, but T'Holly never recommended me, and neither did my uncle. He just told me of the opening here." Gwine lifted his gaze to Straif. "I came on my own."

Straif didn't have time for this. He clapped a hand on Gwine's shoulder, making him stagger. "You've done a good job. You're hired."

Gwine released his breath in a whistling exhalation of

relief. "Thank you, GrandLord, thank you. You'll never be sorry, I swear." He bobbed bow after bow.

"Why don't you check on the kitchen?" Straif asked.

Gratitude in his eyes, the cook hurried away. Straif, realizing his mistake, stepped back into the ResidenceDen and placed a privacy spell on the door.

D'Holly, he called his uncle's wife with his mind.

Here, she replied in melodious tones.

I go to track my Lady and claim her.

D'Holly laughed. *Mitchella Clover?*

Yes.

I know where she is, D'Holly teased.

Please act as my hostess and give my regrets to the guests.

Blessings upon you, D'Holly said.

Stachys Blackthorn. Straif mentally sent to his new relative along their Familial bond. He sensed anxiety from Stachys, but the man hadn't intruded, and that showed a sensitivity Straif hadn't expected.

Here, Stachys said. *Did you really teleport your old lover to Death Grove? The priestess there says that it was obvious Lobelia was insane from the condition of her body. Is it true—*

Stop! That doesn't matter. What is important is that I am now tracking my Lady. I mean to marry Mitchella Clover.

There was a long pause.

She is sterile, Stachys said hesitantly.

We will be adopting children. You and I will talk about my Heir in the future, but it will be no one who does not swear the Loyalty Oath to me.

I understand, Stachys said.

We will decide which of our children is best suited to be T'Blackthorn or D'Blackthorn, Straif said.

Agreed, said Stachys.

I go, Straif said, but he wanted his Fam. This should be a Family effort. So he 'ported to Drina's bedroom. She lay on her back, paws curled, mouth open and snuffling. Straif fashioned a carrier like he'd seen Ruis Elder carry his baby daughter in, and strapped it on his own chest. He picked up the limp cat, who continued to sleep, and slipped her into the carrier. She was a soft burden against his chest.

Then he teleported to Kalmi Lobelia's house and found it glowing turquoise.

Laughter broke from him, an emotion so opposite the last one he'd experienced here. He bowed to the House. It seemed to pulse with pride. "Greetyou, Residence. I track Mitchella Clover." With one glance, he saw that her trail led away from the place, didn't double back inside.

The House turned gray. Straif sensed fear, so he reassured it. "I know you will be Mitchella's next project."

A tinge of blue green ebbed back to tint the walls. Straif waved a hand and concentrated on Mitchella's trace—mixed with Antenn's, a predictable gray green. Both tracks tangled near a public carrier plinth.

Straif grinned and rubbed his hands. More than one public carrier line served this stop. A real challenge. Mitchella would never be easy. A bubble of excitement lodged in his chest.

He opened the connection between them wide, completely open on his side—as he'd never been since his Family had died. He could find her that way, too, always. But for now he wanted to rely on his Flair. He needed the time to hunt her as a Blackthorn always hunted their mate, conforming to ancient tradition, as he would break with the past and follow her thread into the future.

A septhour later he was in front of the Clover Compound. Noise rose from the inner courtyard, and the door he'd used when he'd visited last was open. So he pushed through and saw another party. Huge glowing, flashing letters circled the compound—common Flair—blinking "Welcome home, Antenn Clover."

Straif swallowed a bitter lump in his throat. He could imagine the pride and love and joy that Mitchella and Antenn had felt when the adoption went through. He had missed being there with them, and that hurt. He'd come to care for the boy.

He looked for Antenn and found him running hard in a game of ball. The boy radiated happiness and didn't notice Straif in the shadows of the short hallway. But another did—Vinni T'Vine.

The boy prophet met Straif's eyes, appearing surprised.

Then a grin broke over his face—right before a group of Clover lads piled on top of him.

Straif took a stride back, patting Drina for comfort. It was obvious T'Vine hadn't expected Straif to marry Mitchella—equally evident that the prophet was pleased. Straif guessed that meant this particular trail into the future was good for him . . . he hoped. He recalled what the boy had said to him weeks before—*Ask yourself this, what price will you pay for that remedy?* Straif shivered in the cool passage—he'd nearly paid the price of a future of love and happiness. Any other way for him now would be nothing but dreadful duty.

From the corner of his eye he caught Mitchella's trail, leading through a door in the short hall he hadn't seen before. He walked up to it, the knob turned under his hand. He shook his head, these Commoners were far too lax in their security. With an inhaled breath and squaring his shoulders he went through and climbed the stairs to the third floor. Anticipation, excitement—a touch of anxiety at Mitchella's reception, she couldn't have fallen out of love with him in a couple of septhours, could she?—trickled through his blood. His pulse and breathing quickened. He couldn't wait to see her, because he'd be seeing her with the knowledge that she would share his life. His loins tightened.

All too soon he was at the corner of the building, in front of a plain wooden door that was no different than any along the corridor. Wouldn't she have decorated it somehow? But he knew the question was minor, he was torn between wanting to see her and knowing that in the next moments his life would change irrevocably. She could refuse him.

He knocked, hard.

She came to the door, her magnificent body draped in an emerald silkeen robe. She was paler than he'd ever seen her, making her green eyes more brilliant and lustrous, her lips redder and more tempting.

His own mouth had gone dry. "May I come in?"

"Why?"

"I've made a mistake. I've come to apologize and—"

"You've made many mistakes."

He winced and said baldly, "I want you."

"You want children," she said.

He paled but met her eyes. "I know now that there are children of the heart as well as children of the body." His smile was weak. "I wanted to be with you and Antenn when you adopted him. I missed that."

She blinked in amazement, then stepped back and held the door wide. The room beyond looked nothing like Mitchella—obviously a temporary abode for her and Antenn.

"Antenn and I have rooms leased in MidClass Lodge, but the current tenants haven't moved out yet."

Straif cared nothing for that. If he had his wish, they'd be at home in T'Blackthorn Residence before the night was over.

Mitchella shut the door, waved to a large, old chair. "Please, sit."

He couldn't, not when she stood and could escape him. "I'm sorry for hurting you."

She shrugged, her face formed into a cool mask that twisted his gut.

"You hurt both of us. Apology accepted. You can go."

He had to touch her. He couldn't find the words without connecting with her, couldn't let her feel what he felt, couldn't convince her. He took her hands. When she didn't pull away, he sent a burst of love to her.

Her eyes widened, and she tugged her fingers. He wouldn't release her. "I can't go. I can't leave you ever again."

"I'm sterile. We can't have children together. You have found a potion so that your future children could be safe from the Blackthorn Curse."

"I don't want it at the cost of you." He kept sending her his feelings—his love, his need, his determination.

Color came to her cheeks, her hands warmed under his, but she didn't open herself or send any emotions back to him.

"What of your HeartMate?" she whispered.

"I couldn't want anyone more than I do you."

She raised her eyebrows, but her gaze was dark and turbulent.

"I *love* you." It was right saying that, telling her that he'd give her everything.

She stared at him. Her slow, sensuous smile bloomed. She tossed her head and slid her hands away. When she turned and walked to a shabby twoseat, her hips swayed, and he muttered a prayer for control.

She sat on the twoseat, feet together, draping her robe primly about her. Now Straif followed more slowly, the knowledge formed in his mind of what she expected.

He grimaced. "You aren't going to let me off easy."

She smiled. "Never," she replied, her charismatic Flair heightening her beauty. "I will never let you off easy. You should know that."

His breath caught in his throat. He shrugged from the sling holding his sleeping Fam, looked around for somewhere to put her.

Mitchella choked with laughter, rose, and took Drina into a room, but left the door open.

His fingers fumbled with the ties to the pouch containing the marriage bands. If he'd been whittling, he'd have cut his fingers. "Come!" he summoned them.

Mitchella's smile broadened as she took her seat again. "Baubles, how nice. You do know how to apologize."

What this woman did to him! The marriage bands slid into his hands. He dropped to his knees before her, grabbed her right arm, and shoved one gold armlet around her wrist, placed the other on the twoseat cushion.

"Please marry me." He hadn't wanted to ask but knew she wouldn't be satisfied with anything less than a begging question.

She looked at him narrowly. His heart thundered. He tried not to think that he was dangling over an abyss suspended by only a strand of hope. With all his strength he poured love from his head and his heart. She sank back against the twoseat.

He laid his head on her lap and nuzzled her knee, the scent of her made him never want to move.

She threaded her hands through his hair and pressed him close for an instant before she stood, but he'd heard the quick beating of her pulse, felt the tremor of her fingers.

"I have something of yours." She opened the door of a nearby cabinet and took out a heart-shaped box encased in a square crystal casket. "The Flaired crystal dampens its effect."

Straif stared at the reddwood box he'd carved during his

third Passage. His HeartGift. The reddwood gleamed from the many hours he'd polished it by hand.

His breathing stopped. "You shouldn't be able to see it or touch it, or take it from—" Where *had* he left it? He couldn't recall.

"No, I wouldn't have been able to unless . . ."

He gulped in a harsh breath. "HeartMate. My own. Oh flig—"

She frowned. "No swearing."

He captured his whirling wits, found his feet, still focused on his HeartGift. A rush of incredible relief—of pure joy, lit him from within until he thought he glowed with sheer happiness. "My HeartMate." He lifted trembling fingers to stroke her cheek. "My *HeartMate*." His throat closed.

"You would have been in a deal of trouble trying to woo another woman without your HeartGift," she whispered.

He'd never wanted to see it again, but he didn't tell her that. For a woman with average Flair, she still managed to be a step or two ahead of him. He delighted in it.

Mitchella gently placed the HeartGift on a table, picked up the remaining gold marriage band, took his right hand, and curved the cuff around his wrist.

Love exploded between them, a burst of cycling heat so huge it overwhelmed. There was only Mitchella, only love. His body quickened.

A yowl came from the other room. *FamMan!*

"I heard her," Mitchella said, but she lifted Straif's fingers to her lips and kissed them. His eyes stung. There was no such pleasure in the world as linking with his HeartMate.

Drina trotted in, saw them embracing, and sniffed. The door swung open, and Antenn, Pinky riding his shoulder, entered.

"Straif and I are HeartMates, and we're marrying!" Mitchella announced.

Drina hissed.

Pinky purred.

"Huh. Good," said Antenn. "Am I going to be a Blackthorn?" He eyed Straif.

Straif opened his arms, and Antenn flung himself into them. Another pleasure. Grinning, Straif rolled to the floor to wrestle with the boy. Mitchella jumped on top of them, and

Straif felt the roundness of her breast, her hip. The cats joined in, and he shouted in happiness. A Family, he had a Family, at last. A few moments later they all lay panting and laughing. Mitchella clasped hands with Antenn and Straif. He took Antenn's hand and completed the circle. The cats lay sprawled atop them.

Mitchella gazed into his eyes, and he found the cure for his tortured heart that he'd always searched for.

"We're a Family. Now and forever," she said.

Turn the page for a special preview of
Robin D. Owens's novel

Heart Quest

Now available from Berkley Sensation!

$\mathcal{B}$lack Ilex Winterberry watched his HeartMate from the shadows. He shouldn't approach her, but knew that he would.

His mouth tightened when Trif Clover performed her little ritual as she hunted for her mate. She held the charmkey she'd fashioned against the door of GrandLord Ginger's mansion and intoned, "HeartMate."

A HeartMate could fashion a key and open their love's door, and Trif was obviously on a quest to find him.

So she truly knew she had a HeartMate. They'd connected emotionally in her last Passage and since her Flair was unstable, a few times since. Each instance left Ilex aroused and wanting, and yearning for more than her body. He hadn't known whether she'd believed the connection was anything other than an erotic dream. He had made it a point to find her—and now she was trying to do the same. But he was an experienced hunter.

He'd kept his distance from her. He was far too old, more than twice her age. Worse, he had a touch of prophetic talent and had experienced a little vision a long time ago that his life would be relatively brief. He might have a few more years left, and he refused to have this lovely, vibrant *young* woman die within a year of his own death, as always occurred with Heart-Mates.

Her face fell when the door refused to open, then she sighed, looked at the key in her hand, shrugged, and straightened her shoulders.

By the time Ilex pushed himself away from the large bole of the tree at the end of the portico, her usual cheerful smile had returned.

"What are you doing, Trif Clover?" he asked.

She jumped and flushed. Her dark green eyes went first to his guardsman's insignia instead of his face, causing a twinge of pain.

"Oh, uh." She whipped her hand holding the key behind her back and increased the charm of her smile.

Ilex shook his head at her.

Her shoulders slumped a little. "You know."

"It is worth our time for me to tell you it can be dangerous wandering the streets of Druida alone?"

She looked startled. "Druida's safe, especially Noble Country."

It didn't help his ego that she hoped her HeartMate was noble. But that wasn't the real problem. The true difficulty was that there had been a string of three murders of young, extremely Flaired people whose psi powers were unstable. Murders that Ilex's superiors wanted kept quiet for the moment.

Indulging his masochistic tendencies, he took her arm and let the touch of her shoot through him, heat his blood. The scent of her came, too, the light fragrance of spring flowers. He'd moved into her apartment building, MidClass Lodge, a couple of months ago, after he'd heard she'd gone door-to-door in the lodge, beginning her search for her HeartMate. And after the first murder.

"Please don't continue to go door-to-door testing your charmkey," he said neutrally, leading her down the drive to the walled entrance of the mansion and the wide-open gates. Ilex frowned. Most of the nobles he knew were paranoid about security, but then, his recent "cases" had included the crème de la crème of Celtan society, the FirstFamilies.

Trif stopped and looked over her shoulder wistfully. "GrandLord Ginger is a widower and he has *three* sons, not to mention all the other unattached male Gingers working in the household."

"Ah, a good source of men."

She shrugged. "I suppose you think my quest is stupid, like everyone else. But it's *my* business."

"Not when you trespass on Noble land."

"Has anyone reported me? Will you?"

"No. Not yet."

"So, are you going to lecture me or not?"

Ilex winced inwardly. That's what she thought of him—an older, neighbor guardsman, ready to lecture.

They had reached the pillar of the entrance when the wind changed—and brought the odor of death.

BERKLEY SENSATION
COMING IN AUGUST 2005

Beyond Control
by Ruth Glick writing as Rebecca York
When journalist Jordan Walker asks Lindsay Fleming for help, it's clear right away that the two have a telepathic bond—and that they are both in great danger.

0-425-20442-1

Gilding the Lady
by Nicole Byrd
Orphan Clarissa Falon has gone from affluent young lady to maid—until her brother rescues her. Now the rakish Earl of Whitby is more than willing to help her re-learn the art of being a lady.

0-425-20443-X

Extreme Exposure
by Pamela Clare
Sparks fly when a hardboiled reporter meets a handsome senator. But political scandal—and threats on her life—may drive them apart forever.

0-425-20633-5

The Last Bride
by Sandra Landry
Haunted in her dreams by a lover from a past life, Claire Pelteir tries to unravel the mystery—and finds herself in the Middle Ages.

0-425-20444-8

Available wherever books are sold or at www.penguin.com

Penguin Group (USA) Inc. Online

What will you be reading tomorrow?

Tom Clancy, Patricia Cornwell, W.E.B. Griffin,
Nora Roberts, William Gibson, Robin Cook,
Brian Jacques, Catherine Coulter, Stephen King,
Dean Koontz, Ken Follett, Clive Cussler,
Eric Jerome Dickey, John Sandford,
Terry McMillan…

You'll find them all at
http://www.penguin.com

*Read excerpts and newsletters, find tour
schedules, and enter contest.*

Subscribe to Penguin Group (USA) Inc. Newsletters
and get an exclusive inside look
at exciting new titles and the authors you love
long before everyone else does.

PENGUIN GROUP (USA) INC. NEWS
http://www.penguin.com/news